William Bentinck Forfar

The Wizard of West Penwith

A Tale of the Land's-End

William Bentinck Forfar

The Wizard of West Penwith
A Tale of the Land's-End

ISBN/EAN: 9783337082314

Printed in Europe, USA, Canada, Australia, Japan

Cover: Foto ©Andreas Hilbeck / pixelio.de

More available books at **www.hansebooks.com**

See Page 49.

THE AWFUL RIDE.

THE

WIZARD OF WEST PENWITH,

A Tale of the Land's-End;

BY

William Bentinck Forfar,

AUTHOR OF "PENTOWAN," "PENGERSICK CASTLE,"

"KYNANCE COVE," &c., &c.

———

PENZANCE:

W. CORNISH, THE LIBRARY,

—

1871.

PREFACE.

_____

In writing my Cornish Tales I have always endeavoured to pourtray the Cornish character in all its native wit and humour, for which the genuine west-country miners are so proverbial. And I have generally taken for the foundation of my Stories incidents which have really happened in the localities wherein the actions of my little dramas have been laid.

The scene of my present story is laid in the neighbourhood of the Land's-End, and most of the characters were well-known there in days gone by;—the names only being fictitious.

The fall of the horse over the cliff is still in the remembrance of some old people in the neighbourhood; and the circumstance is related by the Guides who shew the beauties of the Land's-End scenery to strangers. The marks of the horse's hoofs in the grass at the edge of the cliff are preserved to this day.

The Wizard (or Conjuror as he was called) was a notorious character at St. Just, some fifty years ago;—and the horrid murder related in these pages; and the mistaken identity of the guilty parties are also veritable facts.

Mr. and Mrs. Brown were well-known characters, and are drawn from real life.

This brief sketch of some of the scenes and characters to be found in this little volume may perhaps add an interest to it, and induce a large number of the lovers of Cornish lore to honour it with a perusal.

Plymouth,
    March, 1871.

CONTENTS.

IV.

CONTENTS.

The Wizard of West Penwith.

CHAPTER I.

MR. FREEMAN.

VERY near the most westerly point of Great Britain, and not very far from the promontory called Cape Cornwall, you may see, as you glide along the coast in your pleasure-boat of a calm summer's evening, a pretty little fishing-cove, in shape like a horse-shoe,—the two extreme points being formed by the projecting rocks on either side of the entrance,—the interior, or curved part, immediately under the main land, having a beautiful beach of white sand, on which boats can land with safety, when piloted by those who know the coast outside; for the little cove is guarded by hidden rocks, and is as safe in rough weather against invasion by the uninitiated, as if it had been fortified by a range of well-appointed batteries. Above this beach the cliffs rise gradually, and various zigzag foot-paths are formed by the constant tread of the sailors and others who frequent the cove in going to and coming from the main land.

About a mile inland is a village of some importance, inhabited by sailors of various kinds, and miners and small farmers who occupy a few acres of land, and fill up their spare time by working at the neighbouring mines, either as mine labourers, or as carriers with their horses and carts.

This part of the coast of Cornwall is almost studded with mines, whose lodes, for the most part, run out under the sea; and although they are, consequently, very expensive to work, yet many of them have given large and continuous dividends to the adventurers.

As many of these rich mines were discovered by accident, it may easily be imagined that the smallest indication of a metallic lode in the neighbourhood causes great excitement, and often leads to the expenditure of large sums of money in forming companies and searching for the riches, which in very many instances are never found.

The village of St. Just was not, at the period when our story commences, the important place that it is at present;—it could even then, however, boast of a tolerably comfortable inn in the square, and an inferior public-house in the outskirts of the village.

B

On a dark, tempestuous, winter's night, there sat in the kitchen or public room of the inn, a goodly company, who had assembled to see the old year out and the new year in—and more than this; for they would also on this night witness the termination of one century, and the commencement of another. A huge fire was burning on the hearth, and two or three of the older men had ensconced themselves in the chimney-corner. In those days the fire was made on the flat stones in the chimney in these old houses, with wood and sticks, or peat; and there was room round it, for those who did not mind the smoke, to sit and enjoy a close proximity to the fire, while the others sat round outside the fireplace, having a small table before them, on which was placed the foaming eggy-hot, and the hot beer and sugar, made more potent by the addition of an unlimited quantity of brandy. The wind was howling dismally in the open chimney, and rattling the doors and windows, as if angry at being shut out. As the night advanced the storm seemed to increase; but the comforts of the bright fire and warm room, and the good cheer before them, made the party feel the more happy and exhilarated, from the reflection that they were sheltered from the storm without. The song and jest went round, and many a thrilling story was told by the elders in the chimney-corner, which made some of the younger men draw closer to the fire and take an extra glass of the warm liquor with which the table was supplied; for superstitious fear was indulged in by all, more or less, in those days, and both old and young, rich and poor, loved to hear a tale of horror, although it invariably made them afraid of their own shadows, until daylight appeared again to dispel the vapours of the night, and the toils of the day left no room for idle thoughts or fancies.

In the innermost recess of the chimney-corner, almost hidden by the smoke, sat a sedate looking man, who appeared so absorbed in his own thoughts, that he did not seem to take much interest in the tales that amused and interested his companions so much, except that, when a tale of more than usual horror was told, a slight smile would steal over his countenance, and he would change his pipe from one side of his mouth to the other. In years he might have been about fifty, but in appearance he was ten years older at least; not from any natural defect or want of the usual stamina and vigour generally displayed by men of his age, but from an eccentric habit he had contracted of affecting the old man,—for what reason was best known to himself. His habits and mode of life were very different from those of Cornishmen generally;—he had come into the neighbourhood some years before in a mysterious manner, but how he came, or where he came from, no one seemed to know. He had acquired somehow a good deal of useful knowledge, and therefore he had the power frequently of working upon the superstitious fears of his neighbours; and, although he did not pursue any particular trade or calling, he did not seem to want for money, for he lived comfortably and paid liberally for his supplies; and, although he was reserved and unsociable as a general rule, yet he liked meeting his neighbours in the public room at the inn, where he could sit in the chimney-corner and smoke his pipe, and listen to their conversation, which he seldom joined in; and when he had gathered from them all the information they could impart, he would occasionally gratify them by telling some thrilling story.

It was generally believed that he had something on his mind which troubled him at times, but what it was no one could tell. There he sat, as usual, on this tempestuous night, smoking his pipe and listening to the conversation of his companions.

At length one of the party, addressing him, said,—

"Come, Maister Freeman, we've all had our turn; now you tell es one of your stories,—they be claim off, they be."

"Well," said he, taking his pipe out of his mouth, and knocking out the ashes on his hand, "I'll tell you a tale; but remember, mine are true stories. The one I am about to relate happened in your own neighbourhood. Your superstitious fears will, perhaps, make you afraid to visit the spot again, if I tell it on such a terrible night as this, after the stories you have already heard."

"No! no!" exclaimed his audience, "out weth et, whatever 'tes, Maister."

"Well, then," he began, "you all know the ruins of the old chapel above Cape Cornwall, called Chapel Carn Brea, and the little hillocks that surround it like graves in the churchyard."

A shudder passed round the room at the mention of this well-known spot, for it was believed by most people that those ruins of the old chapel were haunted by evil spirits; so the little circle drew their seats nearer to the chimney, and instinctively looked round, as if they expected to see some sprite or pixey enter through the key-hole at the bare mention of so uncanny a spot at this hour of the night."

"Those little mounds or hillocks," continued Mr. Freeman, "are said to be the graves of the Druid priests and ancient kings of Cornwall, and it is also said that all their riches were buried with them; but it was never known whether this was so or not, for no one had had the courage to disturb the remains of those holy men. I had no such scruples,—so one moonlight night, soon after I came here to reside, I took my pickaxe and shovel, went up to the old ruins, and selected the largest mound and began my work with a hopeful mind, for I believed that I should be rewarded in the end by a rich booty. The earth on the top was soft and easy to work, but as I got down it became harder. I worked with a will for

several hours, and got down several feet before the day began to
dawn. It was a lonely spot, in the dead of the night, to be working
in;—I could hear the waves as they dashed against the high
cliffs under Cape Cornwall, and I sometimes fancied I heard voices
calling to me out of the waves. I must confess, my courage
nearly failed me, more than once; but I took several pulls at
my brandy-bottle, and thought of the treasure underneath, and
worked on.

"When the day began to dawn I left my work, intending to come
the next night and finish it. I knew that no one would venture
there if they could avoid it, even in the daytime, but I did not wish
to be seen working there;—the sight of an open grave in that spot
would, I well knew, scare people away, even if anyone was bold
enough to approach it during the day. A few hours' work more, I
thought, would bring me to the bottom, and then I should reap my
reward. So the next night I took my tools again and repaired to
the spot, when, to my utter astonishment, I found the grave filled in,
and all my labour lost.

"In vain I looked about for some clue to the mystery; I could see
no one; so I set to work again, and soon threw up the loose earth,
and came down to the hard ground. I worked harder than any man
ever worked for his daily bread, and at last my pick touched something hard, which I fancied at first was a rock. I carefully cleared
the earth round it, and found that it was a large stone slab, and, from
the sound, I was convinced it was hollow beneath. The moon was
shining brightly, and threw its light right into the grave, so that I
could see the stone distinctly, and could discern figures cut on it.
Here, then, was the coffin, no doubt; and it doubtless contained the
coveted treasures. I tried to raise the cover, but it baffled all my
skill and strength;—I found that the pit would have to be made
much larger, and even then it might require the united strength of
two or three men to get the cover up. I was then in the grave, which
was deep enough to hide me entirely from the view of anyone on the
surface. While I was thus deliberating what I should do, I heard a
loud shriek just above my head. I got up, with some difficulty,
expecting to see some unfortunate traveller transfixed superstitiously
to the side of the grave, with his hair standing on end, and his knees
knocking together with fear and terror; but there was no one to be
seen. Again I was obliged to abandon my work for the time, and
again I returned the next night and found the grave filled in as before.
They say 'the third time is lucky,' said I to myself,—so, nothing
daunted, I went to work again, for I had now proof positive that there
was a hollow stone coffin underneath, which no doubt contained the
coveted treasure.

"Who the intruder was I neither knew nor cared, except that I did not like the trouble of going over my work so many times, but now I was determined to complete it.

"I got down to the stone slab again, and this time I had lengthened the grave considerably at each end, and I thought I might be able to raise the lid. I drove the point of my pick under the stone, and was about to raise it, when I heard the same shriek I had heard on the previous night,—and I felt at the same time a shower of earth falling all round me.

"'Self-preservation is the first law of nature,' and so, to escape being buried alive, I scrambled out of the grave as fast as I could; and on looking over the heap of earth, thrown up round the sides of the grave, I saw a figure moving swiftly away,—but whether it was a man or a woman, or an imp of darkness, I could not tell, for my toe slipped out of the notch I had made for a footstep, and I fell headlong into the grave again; but, fearing another shower of earth, I scrambled out the best way I could, and went home, determined to give up my search after riches; for I felt sure that, as I had failed the third time, it was useless to attempt again."

"Zackly like that," said the landlord, who had been busily supplying his guests with more liquor at intervals, during the recital of the tale ;—"who wor she, I wondar ?"

"Who should she be but one of the pixies ?" replied a tall, stout, well-built young man, who had been listening with breathless attention to the story.

"Hould thy tongue, 'Siah Trenow," said an elderly man, rising from his seat in the chimney-corner, and taking a long pull at the jug of hot beer and sugar which the landlord had placed on the table ;—"thee'st nevar knaw nothen. I'll tell 'ee, na, tes like as this here. How could a pixie handle a showl for to showley in the stuff again, I should like to knaw ; and where could a pixie get a showl from ?"

"What wor aw like, so fur as you could see, Maister Freeman ?" continued he, turning round to where that gentleman had been sitting a minute ago,—when, to his astonishment, he saw that the seat was vacant.

"Why he's gone like the snoff of a candle, soas !"

"That's zackly like he, na," said the landlord ; "he'll tell a story till he do bring 'ee up to a point, and then lev 'ee to gees the rest; esn't et so, Peggy ?"

"I'll tell 'ee, soas," said the young man who had been addressed as "'Siah Trenow,' but whose proper Christian name was 'Josiah,' "he do knaw bra' things. Why, he ha' got a gashly g'eat room up there that nobody can go in but he, where he do count the stars, so they do say."

"Iss fie," said the landlord, whose name was Brown ; "many people can tell about the conjuring and things, up there."

"Hush, Brown," exclaimed his wife; "you do knaw that when we lost so many pigs you wor glad enough for to go to Maister Freeman for to knaw something about them; and he tould 'ee, so you said, and you b'lieved every word he tould 'ee,—so don't you bark nor growl. His dafter, Miss Reeney, tould me last week that she shud think that Old Nick wor up there sometimes weth her fe-a-thar, they do keep such a caparous,—and I've got my thofts, too, soas!"

"Come! come! Mrs. Brown," exclaimed 'Siah Trenow, rising up in an excited manner; "don't you bring Miss Reeney's name in weth her fe-a-thar's doings, or else I'll ———"

"Arreah! thon," replied Mrs. Brown; that's the way the maggot do jump, es et? Iss sure! Miss Reeney es a bra' tidy maid; an' f'rall she do prink herself up so fine sometimes, and b'en to boarding-school, and all that, and do knaw bra' things, she ha' got nothin' to do weth her fe-a-thar's conjuring-room upstairs, I do believe in my conscience, soas; and ef 'Siah ha' got a mind to her, there's wus than she a bra' deal;—but he do hold his nose brave an' high, soas, don't aw?"

"Miss Reeney esn't the only woman that do live in that house, you knaw," said the old man who had spoken first, with a knowing wink.

"No, sure, there's Miss Freeman herself," said Mrs. Brown, pursing up her lips; "she's a good catch, they do say."

"That's very well," said Mr. Brown, laughing at his wife's wit.

"Brown," said that good lady, "mind your own business;—what have you got to say about Miss Freeman, I shud like to knaw?"

This remark shut up poor Mr. Brown entirely; and whether this discussion of the merits and demerits of Miss Freeman and her niece Alrina (familiarly called Reeney) would have proceeded much further, it is difficult to say; for just at that moment a man, who had evidently been out for a considerable time in the storm, burst into the room, and said there was a vessel wrecked off Pendeen Point.

CHAPTER II.

THE WRECK NEAR THE LAND'S-END.

THE sound of a wreck was sufficient, at any time, to rouse the most lethargic; and old and young rose at once, and left the comfortable fire and warm mixtures, and crowded round the new comer to hear the particulars. All he could tell them, however, was that there was a vessel in distress off the Point; he and several others had heard the gun. She was not a wreck yet, the man said, but it could not be long before she must strike,—for the weather was terrific, and the wind was blowing right in ; so he ran up to the village to give the alarm. There was not a moment's hesitation among the listeners,— everyone prepared to go down to the Point at once.

Some took ropes, and some took baskets, or bags, or whatever came to hand ; and each man got his lantern, and away they started to the scene of distress. The wind was blowing a fearful hurricane, and the rain was falling heavily, beating into the faces of the foremost, and almost taking away the breath of the older and weaker of the party. As they proceeded, others came out of their houses and joined them,—women as well as men. On they went through the storm, with their hats and bonnets tied down with handkerchiefs or pieces of string, to keep them from being blown away. Noble creatures ! thus to brave the storm on such a night as this, for the sake of saving the lives and relieving the sufferings of their fellow-creatures in distress.

To save life, however, was not the only object these poor people had in view ; nor was it, I fear, the principal one with a great many. When a vessel was wrecked on the Cornish coast, in those days, it was believed by most of the lower orders, that all that was washed ashore, became the undoubted property of anyone who was fortunate enough to pick it up ; and so a wreck was looked upon as a God-send, and everyone took care of himself, and sometimes returned with a rich booty.

At length they arrived at the Point, or as near it as it was prudent to approach in this dreadful storm. The night was too dark for them to distinguish the vessel ; but as the gun was fired at intervals, the flash enabled them to see that she was not far from the rocks, on which she might strike at any moment, and all must perish ; for no boat could go out to their rescue, nor could a boat from the vessel live a single moment in such a sea.

Although the watchers remained some hundreds of yards from the Point, the sea dashed up every now and then against the high cliff, and drenched them with its spray ; but still they continued to watch —their lanterns giving out a dim line of light as they stood closely packed together, sheltering one another from the wind and rain. Another gun was fired, and the watchers saw that the vessel was close upon the breakers. A dreadful shriek was now borne towards them by the wind, which was blowing towards the shore, and now they knew that all was over and that the vessel had struck, and was most likely dashed in pieces.

Nothing more could be done till daylight appeared ; so many of the watchers sought the shelter of the rocks to wait for it, in order to begin their work ; for with that wind, and the tide beating in, the contents of the vessel must wash on shore very quickly. The crew must all have perished,—of that there was no doubt. The dreadful shriek they had heard was that of the drowning crew. The only anxiety now was concerning the valuables which might come in with the tide.

As the day dawned, the storm abated a little, and, towards morning, many of the villagers were seen approaching the Point;— among them, Mr. Freeman was conspicuous. He came along feebly, keeping the even tenor of his way,—now speaking to one, and then to another, as he was overtaken and passed on the road by the more energetic and youthful of the wreckers, who were all too intent upon the gains in prospect to pay much attention to an infirm man, although they knew not in their haste and thoughtlessness that their actions were watched and noted down in the memory of one who did not often forget a slight.

Long before it could properly be said to be daylight, the approaches to the little cove were covered with people, watching for the prizes which they expected every wave would wash in. The beautiful white sand was covered with foam, and frequently a huge wave would come dashing in and break beneath the very feet of the most daring and reckless of the watchers, who had approached to the verge of the rocks which bounded the innermost circle of the cove.

No one, as yet, could venture on the sand with safety, and it was yet too dark for the watchers to see far before them, for the daylight on that tempestuous morning was a long time making its appearance. A long and eventful year had just terminated, and the new year seemed very unwilling to take up what the old year had left it to do; but the laws of nature must be obeyed, and so the new year's morning came at last, and, with it, the prizes so much coveted by the wreckers.

Timber, casks, and boxes (some empty and some full) came washed in to the very feet of those who were standing on the lowest rocks; but, before they could reach them, they were carried out again by the receding tide. There were some adventurous enough, however, to make a grasp at the prizes as they came rolling in; but they would have met with a watery grave, had they not been held back by the more prudent. As the tide ebbed, it left the little cove comparatively free from danger, and then many prizes were seized and carried away by the eager finders.

Mr. Freeman having no wish or intention, apparently, to appropriate any of the unfortunate sailors' property to himself, wandered about from one place to the other, watching for the bodies that he knew must be washed on shore soon, in order to ascertain, if possible, by the appearance of the sailors, or from any papers they might have about them, the name of the ship, and her cargo and destination. In the course of the day several bodies were washed ashore; but, even in this short time, they were so disfigured by the sharp-pointed rocks against which they had been dashed by the angry sea, that there were no traces left in any of them of the "human face divine," and even their clothes had been torn off by the merciless rocks and waves.

In the course of his wandering along the coast, Mr. Freeman surprised several parties dividing and disputing about the property which had been washed on shore in different parts. Here would be seen, perhaps, half-a-dozen men quarrelling about the possession of a cask of wine or brandy, and, in the *melée*, the top would be knocked in, whilst, in their eagerness to get at its contents, the cask would be overturned, and the whole contents spilt on the sand. In another place might be seen half-a-score women squabbling about the possession of a cask of fruit or provisions. At length, in turning a sharp point of rock, he came suddenly on a man and two women who were kneeling on the sand between two rocks, intently examining the contents of a large sea-chest which they had broken open. Mr. Freeman stood behind a rock for a few minutes, concealed from their view, and watched their proceedings, as, one by one, they took the things out of the chest, with the evident intention of dividing the spoil. He had not before interfered with any of the wreckers in their unlawful plunder, but he now stepped forward and commanded them to replace all the things in the chest and put on the cover. The two women started to their feet at once (for there was a superstitious dread among the people generally at being "ill-wished" by "The Maister" if they thwarted him); while the man remained kneeling over the chest, holding in his hands the last article which he had taken from it, in seeming doubt as to whether he had better put it back or bid defiance to the apparently feeble form before him, when Josiah Trenow jumped over a rock into the little cranny, and asked what was the matter.

"That chest," said Mr. Freeman, "must be taken care of; I have reasons which I shall not make known at present. If you will get it taken to some safe place, Josiah, I shall feel much obliged to you. In my own house it will be safest, I think."

"By all mains, sar," replied Josiah; "the best place I do knaw es your awn house, Maister. So come, boy," continued he, addressing the man, who was still kneeling by the side of the chest, and looking with longing eyes at its contents, which seemed very valuable, "you and I'll carr'n up."

However reluctant the man was to relinquish the prize, he had not the foolhardiness to oppose two such powerful antagonists. In stature and physical strength and courage, Josiah Trenow was the acknowledged champion of the parish, and very few men liked to be pitted against him, either in the ring or in more serious combat; whilst Mr. Freeman's well-known ability in foretelling the future

and relieving those who were possessed of evil spirits, and even ill-
wishing people himself (as they believed), rendered him an object
of dread to the superstitious and weak-minded, of which there were
not a few in those days. Josiah had not much difficulty, therefore,
in procuring sufficient assistance to carry the chest to Mr. Freeman's
house.

CHAPTER III.

ALRINA.

Mr. Freeman's house seemed, in many respects, as unsociable as
its master; for it was one of those oldfashioned farm-houses one
meets with occasionally in remote, out-of-the-way places, without
having a farm attached to it,—the farm formerly held with the
house having been added to an adjoining farm belonging to the same
proprietor, on which there happened to be a larger and better house.
It was, even then, an oldfashioned house, with an entrance-hall, if
such it might be called, into which you entered from the front door.
On the right was the parlour or best sitting-room, and on the left
the common sitting-room where the family generally sat. Opposite
the front door were the stairs, and on each side of the stairs there
was a door,—the one leading into the kitchen, and the other into the
little back garden. Over the best parlour was Mr. Freeman's private
room, into which no one was permitted to enter except those whose
superstition led them to consult "The Maister," as he was generally
designated, and to seek his aid in extricating them from some dire
misfortune, and then great preparations were made before the visitors
were admitted into this mysterious room.

Mr. Freeman was a widower—so it was said—and his sister kept
his house, and exercised strict dominion over his only daughter, a
young girl of eighteen.

Miss Freeman, the sister, it was generally believed, knew more of
her brother's secrets than she liked to tell; and many a severe
reprimand did Alrina receive from her aunt for her curiosity, in
trying to pry into secrets which the elder lady thought she had no
right to concern herself about. Alice Ann, the servant of all work,
was one of that neighbourhood, and therefore spoke the broad
Cornish dialect; but Alrina, who had received a tolerably good
education, as times went, had not been infected by the dialect, which
is so very contagious when almost everyone speaks it around you.
She had just attained her eighteenth year; but, from her rotundity
of figure, and womanly manners, she might have been taken for a
girl of that age two years before, at least. She had been kept at a

boarding-school in one of our large towns almost from her infancy, and had seen very little either of her father or aunt until recently, and therefore she knew little more of them, or their habits and pursuits, than a stranger, until she left school about twelve months before. In stature she was about the middle height,—very fair, with bright auburn hair, which some were malicious enough to call red, but "golden" would have been the more correct term. Red hair is not generally admired, but there was such a golden hue cast over Alrina's hair, that made her soft blue eyes look softer in the contrast. Hogarth's line of beauty was displayed in the contour of her figure; and such a pretty little foot and ankle might be seen as the rude wind waved the drapery aside, when, like a fairy, she glided over the rocks—so bold and varied on those high cliffs—that, taken *tout ensemble*, she was just the very girl a man would fall in love with at first sight. There were so many beauties visible at once, and such a happy combination of them all; and then the pretty dimples in her cheeks, when she smiled, betokened a temper mild and amiable, and yet with spirit enough to resent a wrong, and assert her own rights against all the world. And thus, although she was obliged to put up with many indignities from her aunt, she managed, by her tact in yielding in minor points, to have her own way in greater, and, to her, more important, ones.

Alrina was in the kitchen assisting Alice Ann on the morning after the wreck, her aunt having gone into the village on some domestic errand, and for a quiet gossip with some of her numerous friends.

"Did my father say he would return to dinner, Alice Ann?" said Alrina, as she prinked the paste round the edge of the pie she had just made.

"No, he dedn't," replied Alice Ann. "When do he say what time he'll be home, or where he's going to?"

"I am tired of all this mystery," said Alrina;—"I wish I knew the meaning of it all. That room upstairs puzzles me very much. I should like to peep into it one day, and see where all the noise comes from, when those 'goostrumnoodles' come here to know who has ill-wished them, and wait in the best parlour while my father goes upstairs to prepare the room for their reception."

"So shud I too, Miss Reeney," replied Alice Ann; "but 'tes no good to try, I b'lieve; for I tried to peep in through the keyhole one day, and a blast of gunpowder came out and nearly blinded me."

"Hush! here he comes," said Alrina, who heard her father's foot-step in the passage.

"Alrina," said he, opening the kitchen-door, "give these men some beer for bringing this chest up from the cove. Take it to the top of the stairs, men, and I shall be able to put it under lock and key myself till the proper owner comes to claim it."

While the other men were taking the chest upstairs, and drinking their beer, Josiah went into the kitchen to speak to Alice Ann, for whom he had a sneaking kindness, as the gossips said, although Mrs. Brown tried to insinuate that it was for the sake of the fair Alrina herself that Josiah so strenuously defended the sayings and doings of the family.

"You've had a bra' night of it, I s'pose," said Alice Ann,—"fust weth your drink up to Maister Brown's, to watch in the new year, and then weth your walk to Pendeen to watch in the wreck. What have 'ee picked up, then, 'Siah?"

"Why nothin' at all, Alice Ann," replied he, "'cept the g'eat chest that's carr'd up in the Maister's room."

"What is that chest brought up here for?" said Alrina, returning from giving the men their beer; "I think we've got lumber enough here already."

"So shud I, Miss Reeney," replied Josiah; "but I'd see the inside of a good many things ef I wor you."

"Come, Josiah," exclaimed Mr. Freeman, "we'll go down to the cove again; there may be more valuables washed in, and more dead bodies perhaps,—living ones I don't expect to see."

Even the bright eyes of Alice Ann were not sufficiently attractive to keep Josiah from trying his luck once more in search of the stray treasures which the sea might yet wash in.

While the men went down into the cove, and over the rocks, in search of treasure, Mr. Freeman took the higher road which led to the Point, and there he stood watching the waves as they dashed against the bold cliffs and fell back again into the white foam beneath, enveloping all the surrounding objects in a hazy mist.

About a quarter of a mile from the promontory on which Mr. Freeman stood, rose a large cluster of high rocks, over which the sea rolled at intervals. As the mist cleared occasionally, Mr. Freeman fancied he could see something move in a crevice of one of the topmost of those rocks; but, after looking again and again, he began at last to think it was nothing but imagination, for it seemed as if it was impossible for any living creature to remain on those rocks so long in safety. He could not rest satisfied, however, so he sought Josiah and brought him to look at the object also.

"'Tes a man or a woman, I do b'lieve!" exclaimed Josiah, after looking on the object for some time through a glass which he had borrowed from one of the wreckers; "but how he got there, or how long he'll stay there, I don't knaw."

It was impossible for any boat to go out, and it seemed almost certain that he must perish, whoever or whatever it was. They made signals by holding up their handkerchiefs tied to a stick, that the poor creature might have the consolation of knowing he was seen, and cared for; and that was all they could do.

Night came on once more, and all hands returned to their homes to rest after the fatigues of the past day and night, and examine the treasures they had picked up.

Josiah had been so much engaged in attending on Mr. Freeman, that he had not succeeded in picking up anything worth carrying home. He thought, therefore, he would remain at the Cove a little longer; so he stole round the Point, and stooped down between two low rocks to conceal himself until the others were gone; and as he stooped, he saw something partially buried in the sand a few yards from him. At first he thought it was a rock; but the waves, as they rolled over it, seemed to move it. He watched for an opportunity when the waves receded, and at last he ran out, at the risk of his life, and seized his prize. It was as much as he could do to pull it up out of the sand, in which it was embedded;—he succeeded, however, and got back to his hiding-place in safety, but not without a good wetting, for a wave washed completely over him while he was getting up the object of his cupidity, and he barely saved himself from being carried out to sea, and that was all. It was a small box, very strongly made, and very heavy. There was something valuable inside it, he had no doubt; so he took off his coat, which was very wet, wrapped it round the box, and made the best of his way home with his treasure.

The next morning Mr. Freeman was early at the Point, but could see nothing of the object which had before attracted his attention, and. he supposed it must have perished;—but he did not like to give it up; and towards the middle of the day, the sea having calmed down a good deal, he induced some stout sailors to go out to those rocks, and see if there was anything there or not.

It was a perilous undertaking; but the boat was got ready and manned, and four brave fellows started amid the shouts of their comrades on the beach. After a severe struggle with the waves, they succeeded in getting near the rocks, but it was impossible yet to land,—so they returned for more help, and to wait till the tide was lower. They saw something lying between two of the rocks, they said, but what it was they couldn't tell.

When the tide was at its lowest, the sea having subsided yet a little more, two boats were manned, and ropes and grappling-irons, and all that was deemed necessary, were put on board; and this time two of the boats' crew succeeded in landing on the rock, where they found a man, apparently lifeless, grasping a sharp rock so firmly, that it was with difficulty they were enabled to extricate him;—it seemed like a death grasp; but, on examination, they found that he still breathed. They brought him on shore and rubbed him, and poured a little brandy down his throat, which revived him; and he was carried at once to the inn, where every attention was paid to him.

It was at first thought he would sink from exhaustion and the want of food for so many hours, but, after a night's sleep, he rallied so as to be able to thank his deliverers, and to give them some information respecting himself, as well as of the vessel which had met with such a melancholy fate.

The ship was an East Indiaman, he said, returning to England with a valuable cargo. The captain died on the voyage, and the mate was too fond of the brandy-bottle, and flirting with the lady-passengers, to attend to his duty, so he missed his reckoning and got on the rocks before he expected, notwithstanding the warnings that were given him by the sailors. The storm arose so suddenly that even the most wary were caught.

The lanterns on the cliffs deceived them too, he said; for they seemed to be close to the edge of the cliff, whereas they were some distance inland. The boats were launched, and filled, but he believed everyone perished. He got hold of some spars that were floating round the wreck when she broke up, and held on as long as he could, but was eventually lifted on to the rocks, where he was so providentially found;—he got jammed between two sharp rocks, and there he held on with all his might; but he could scarcely keep his position, for when the storm was at its height the sea washed over him continually. There were several passengers on board,—some bringing home gold, and others indigo and other kinds of wealth, but all had perished. He was one of the crew, he said, and therefore had not lost much. The ship belonged to the East India Company, and so he supposed they could afford to lose a little; but he believed they had taken care of themselves by insurances.

The poor man was well treated, and when sufficiently recovered a subscription was made for him, and he was sent on to his friends.

CHAPTER IV.

THE UNEXPECTED MEETING.

ALTHOUGH Mr. Freeman was not at all inclined to be sociable or familiar with his neighbours himself, yet he did not object to his sister and daughter being on friendly terms with them;—indeed he rather wished it, and was never more pleased than when they were visiting at the farm-houses in the neighbourhood, or giving entertainments at home—at which he was seldom seen except in some mysterious manner. Strange noises would sometimes be heard in "The Maister's" private room, in the dusk of the evening, before the candles were brought in; and, in the midst of the terror of the visitors, and almost before the noises had subsided, Mr. Freeman would walk quietly into the room, and relate some thrilling story, and disappear again in the same mysterious manner. These scenes would be talked over the next day by the gossips, and after going the round for a few days, the most extraordinary additions would be made and circulated. And so he became a man of great importance, and was looked upon as a superior being, and people feared him and believed that his powers were much greater than they really were.

He was greatly assisted in obtaining information respecting his neighbours, by his sister, who was a shrewd woman, and who by her tact and cunning could lead on her friends imperceptibly to talk of their own and their neighbours' private affairs. She would impart those secrets to "The Maister," who stored them in his memory till opportunities arose for using his information with advantage. And when those ignorant people applied to him to be informed by whom they were ill-wished, or to recover their property, perhaps, which had been stolen, he could guess pretty nearly who the culprits were likely to be, having possession of these little secrets (long since forgotten by them); and he would so work upon their fears, that the property would be restored in some mysterious way, and he then would have the credit for getting it back by some supernatural agency.

Alrina had a good deal of her father's fondness for the mysterious, but in her it took a more romantic turn. She would spend whole days, sometimes, in wandering over the cliffs and examining with curiosity the ruins of chapels and ancient fortifications, of which there were several in that locality; and the tumuli in the neighbourhood of the chapels, supposed to contain the ashes of the Druids and other holy men, afforded great scope to her imagination. Her father, as we have seen, was not very regular in his habits—indeed it would not have suited his purpose to be so—and her aunt was sometimes so intent on sifting out any little secret gossip, and relating it to "The Maister," that Alrina was often left for days without the supervision of either her father or aunt, and so she wandered about alone.

She was sitting, one fine morning after the shipwreck, under the shelter of some high rocks at the Land's-End, watching the vessels as they passed round the point—some inside and some outside the Longships, when she heard herself addressed by some one overhead, and, on looking up, she saw a handsome young man looking down on her from the rocks which overhung her resting-place. It was some stranger, evidently, for he merely said, "You seem fond of seclusion, fair lady;"—but when she looked up, he exclaimed, "Alrina! can it be possible?" and in a moment he was at her side.

A crimson flush overspread her face, extending almost to the roots of her hair, as she jumped up, and extended her hand towards the intruder, who clasped her in his arms, while she exclaimed, without attempting to extricate herself, "Are my dreams and hopes so soon realized? Where have you been? How did you get here?"

"I have surprised you, Alrina," replied he, pressing his lips to her cheek; "and I assure you when I left England, two years ago, so unexpectedly, I thought it would have been a longer separation; but it was cruel of you, Alrina, not to keep your appointment that night, knowing it was the last opportunity I had of seeing you before I quitted England!"

"Indeed, Frederick," replied Alrina, "it was not my fault. You know that one of the servants at the school discovered our secret meetings in the garden, and told Mrs. Horton, who had the window nailed up through which I used to get out, and ———"

"Yes!" said the gentleman, hastily; "but I bribed the other girl, who was not so scrupulous, to manage one more meeting, as it was the last night before my departure, and she faithfully promised to do so."

"Circumstances seemed to thwart us in every way," replied Alrina. "The young lady who slept in my room was suddenly taken ill, just after we went to bed, and the servant who betrayed us before was desired to remain with her all night, so that I was a prisoner."

"I see it all," said he; "and this explanation has relieved my mind from anxious thoughts. But why did you not write me?"

"That was impossible," replied Alrina; "for I was taken from school almost immediately, and didn't know where to address a letter to you. I wrote to your sister, who had been a day-pupil at the same school, and through whom we first became acquainted, but, not having her exact address, I suppose the letter never reached her."

"Never mind, Alrina," said he, as he took a seat by her side in the little sheltered nook she had before occupied; "we have met at last;—and now I will tell you something more about myself and my position than I thought it necessary to tell, or you to ask, in any of our clandestine meetings,—we had other things to think of and talk about then. I have since been knocked about in the world, and the romantic passion of my boyhood has lost, perhaps, much of its romance, but the love I then felt for you still remains in all its purity and devotion."

"I never doubted that," replied Alrina, looking fondly at him, as she used to do;—for her romance had not been rubbed off by contact with the world, but, on the contrary, had increased;—her life had been one of romance and mystery from her childhood, and everything around her seemed veiled in mystery.

"I have never ceased to think of you, and to wonder where you had gone, and whether I should ever see you again," she continued. "These rocks have been my refuge from the monotony and mystery of home ; and here I have ofttimes given vent to my feelings, when I thought and knew I was unobserved. But tell me," she continued, looking up into his fine manly face with love and admiration, "where you have been, and what you have been doing, since we last met."

"I had just obtained my commission in the 63rd Regiment of Light Infantry," he resumed ; "and my fondest hopes, as I thought, were realized when I met you walking in solemn procession with the other young ladies of Mrs. Horton's seminary. I was struck with your appearance, and I asked my sister, who was, as you have said, a day-pupil at the same school, who you were. All she could tell me was that your name was Alrina Freeman ; and, I suppose, that was all I wanted to know just then. She took a note to you from me, and the next time I met the school procession, there was a mutual recognition ; several notes passed between us ; and at last you consented to a clandestine meeting in the garden. Our meetings were discovered. My regiment was ordered abroad suddenly, and, owing to the circumstances already related, we did not meet again before my departure. I returned with my regiment about a month since, and made all the inquiry in my power, but without avail. I went to the school. The mistress was dead, and the school given up. I had a month's furlough ; and, hearing that an old schoolfellow had an appointment at a signal-station near the Land's-End, I packed up my traps in a carpet-bag, and arrived at my friend's station, at Tol-pedn-Penwith about a week since. My friend is a bachelor ;—he is several years my senior, but a right jolly fellow. His name is Fowler. He introduced me to the squire's family at Pendrea-house. The squire has been a queer old chap in his time, I believe ; but his wife seems a good old soul, and the two daughters are charming ;—but the name of Freeman was always in my thoughts. In the course of conversation after dinner at the squire's the other day, some one said that there was a celebrated conjuror residing near the Land's-End, whose name was Freeman. I felt a thrill run through me at the name, and I determined on paying him a visit ; for I thought that if he was so clever as he was reported to be, he might be able to assist me with some information respecting her I so anxiously sought, especially as he bore the same name. You have heard of him, I dare say. I came out to-day alone, determined to see the conjuror, and get all the information I could before I returned ; and seeing a young lady go down over the rocks, I was seized with a little romantic curiosity, and followed, when, as I looked over the rocks above your head, I caught sight of your face, as you turned your head to watch the course of a vessel which was passing. I was not quite sure even then, not expecting to see you here,—so I spoke to you, as to a stranger, and when you looked up at me I saw I was not mistaken: and now," continued he, pressing her hand and laughing, "I need not go to the conjuror."

"I do not know that," said Alrina, in a thoughtful tone; "I think it is most likely you will have to go to 'the conjuror,' after all, if you wish to know anything more of my family, for the person you call 'the conjuror' is my father."

"Your father!" exclaimed Frederick, in great surprise. "No! no! you are joking."

"I am not, indeed," replied Alrina; "there is some mystery hanging over my relatives, that I have never been able to unravel, especially as to my father;—my mother I don't remember; she died when I was very young, I believe. Where we resided before we came here I don't know. My father is very clever,—there is no doubt about that,—and he manages to awe the people here into the belief that he knows more than he really does; and he has a mysterious room which is only entered by himself and those whose fears and superstition he wishes to work upon. My aunt knows something of these mysteries—how much I don't know;—but I know nothing of them; I am kept entirely in ignorance; they don't seem to like to trust me. Oh! how wretched it makes me feel; for I sometimes fancy it may be too dreadful to be told, and then I come out alone, and wander over the rocks, and think of those few happy moments of my life, never to be forgotten. It is very, very hard to feel that no one has confidence in me;" and she burst into tears.

"Don't distress yourself about these things now, dearest Alrina," said her companion, taking her hand. "I will protect you with my life; and I will see the conjuror and his secret chamber before I leave this neighbourhood, and bring him to his bearings, or my name is not Frederick Morley!"

"Oh! but if there should be some dreadful secret," replied Alrina, sobbing, as her lover pressed her to his heart, "we could never be to one another as we have hoped; and now that you know who my father is, I fear you will look cold upon me too, like the rest of the world, and that would kill me. Oh! Frederick, after all my dreams of happiness, if I should lose your love when I feel I want it most, and when the fondest hope of my life seems almost realized by your return so unexpectedly, ———"

"My dearest Alrina," said Morley, "you will find no change in my affections or feelings. I will sift this secret out to the end, cost what it may, and nothing shall separate us now."

Thus did the two youthful lovers talk on, until it was time for them to separate; and so earnest were they in their conversation, and on the renewal of their former loves, that they did not perceive the head that was projecting from the overhanging rocks, nor the eager eyes and ears which had seen and heard all that had passed between them.

"Ho! ho!" exclaimed the individual to whom the head belonged, as it walked quietly away, when the interview between the two lovers was drawing to a close; "secrets worth knowing!"

CHAPTER V.

JOHN BROWN AND HIS FAVOURITE MARE "JESSIE."

Mr. and Mrs. Brown, who now kept the "Commercial" inn at St. Just, had formerly lived, for many years, in the service of one of the ancient aristocratic Cornish families in that neighbourhood,—the one as coachman, the other as cook. Mr. Brown was rather effeminate and methodical in his manners and habits, and particularly neat in his dress. His hair, which he always kept short, was as smooth and sleek as one of his master's coach-horses. He invariably wore a brown coat, always nicely brushed, with light waistcoat and breeches; a white neckerchief enveloped his neck, in which was enclosed a thick pad, and tied in a neat little bow in front. His hat, which he wore continually indoors and out, always looked as if it had just come out of the hatter's shop; and as to his shoes!—if Mr. Brown was more particular in one part of his dress than another, it was in the polish of his shoes, which did credit to "Warren's Jet Blacking" and their master's energy and skill,—for he invariably gave them an extra polish himself before he put them on of a morning, after Bill, the stable-boy, had done his best. If he was not quite the first groom of the chamber indoors, where his wife held rule, he could certainly boast of being first groom of the stall, when he got into the stables, where it was natural to suppose he was in his element, from having been so many years coachman in a gentleman's family.

He was a good judge of horseflesh, and had the sweetest little mare in the stable that you would wish to set your eyes upon—a perfect picture of a horse—a bright bay, with black tail and mane. And, although it was January month, when most horses have their winter coats, yet, what with grooming and clothing, and regular feeding and exercise, Mr. Brown's mare Jessie was as sleek and smooth as if it had been the height of summer, so well was she taken care of and petted by her master. This was his hobby, and in this he spent most of his time, and a good deal of his spare cash.

If Mr. Brown was too effeminate for a man, Mrs. Brown was certainly too masculine for a woman,—at least so Mr. Brown thought sometimes, although he had neither the courage nor the ill manners to say so. She was neat in her dress also, but not quite so particular as her husband. A chintz gown, looped up through the pocket-holes,—a large coloured silk handkerchief thrown over her shoulders, and pinned down in front and confined at the ends by the wide string of her cheque apron, formed the general character of Mrs. Brown's dress; and, like her husband, she invariably wore her bonnet indoors and out.

The general business at "The Commercial" was not very extensive, but as Mr. and Mrs. Brown had no children, and had saved a little money, they kept on the house—which was their own property—more for amusement than profit. They kept one servant indoors (a sort of maid-of-all-work), whose name was Polly, and a boy in the stables to attend to Jessie the mare, and do other little jobs to help the women. Mr. Brown made himself useful in the house if required, when customers came in, by drawing beer and attending to their wants, but he never did a single thing without calling some one to help him; sometimes it was Polly, and sometimes Billy, and sometimes even Peggy his wife; but he generally, poor man, had to do the work alone, whatever it was, although fortunately it was never very laborious.

On the afternoon of the day on which the two lovers met at the Land's-End point, Mr. and Mrs. Brown were sitting in the kitchen alone,—the latter having sent Polly upstairs, to brush up a bit, while she went on with some work she had in hand for her husband. She was knitting him a pair of white lamb's-wool stockings, for general wear, if the truth must be told.

"I wish the boy was come to take the mare out a bit, I think," said Mr. Brown, "this beautiful afternoon. I shall go out a mile or two myself if he don't come soon."

"I tell 'ee what et es, Brown," said his wife; "there's more fuss made about that mare than ef she'd b'en a cheeld. I'd have a glass case made for har ef I wor you!"

"Don't 'ee be vexed, Peggy, 'cause I do take care of the poor thing. There's the boy coming, I do believe," said he, rising from his seat, and going towards the door. "Your sarvant, sar," he continued, as he met a tall handsome young man in the passage; and without waiting for a reply from the stranger, he returned to the kitchen, rubbing his hands, followed by the stranger, and exclaiming, "Bless my life, Peggy! bless my life!—es the best bedroom ready upstairs? here's a gentleman, my dear!"

"Gentleman sure 'nuff!" said his wife, looking unutterable things at her husband, and curtseying at the same time to the stranger;—"gentle or semple is all the same to you, I believe, John Brown."

"Now, don't put yourselves out of the way for me, my good

friends," said the stranger; "all I want is something to eat at once, and a 'shake-down' here for a night or two."

"We've got nothing in the house to eat, I do believe," said Mr. Brown; "have us, Peggy? And as to a 'shake-down!'—why we don't have many visitors here to sleep!"

"Brown!" said his better half, in an authoritative tone, "go and look to the mare!"—and she pointed significantly to the door, through which Mr. Brown made his escape, calling Billy, by way of covering his retreat, without being further exposed to the stranger; for he saw he had gone a little too far, in taking it upon himself to answer for what could or could not be had in the house.

The stranger, in the meantime, had thrown himself carelessly into Mrs. Brown's seat, and extended his legs before him, as if he was quite at home, and was accustomed to make himself comfortable wherever he happened to be.

"Now then, Mrs. Brown," said he, "a glass of your best ale to begin with, and then something to eat, for I'm devilish hungry."

"I can give 'ee some eggs and a rasher at once, sar," replied Mrs. Brown; "but ef you can wait 'bout half-an-hour or so, you shall have a roast fowl and taties."

"I'll have the eggs and bacon by all means," said he; "I couldn't wait half-an-hour for all the fowls in your yard;—and while you are dressing the eggs and bacon, I will try if I can get some one to fetch my carpet-bag." So he sauntered into the stable, where he found Mr. Brown admiring his mare Jessie.

"Isn't she a beauty, sir?" said the landlord, combing his horse's tail with a comb he kept in his pocket for the purpose.

"She is a handsome creature, certainly," said the stranger, looking at the mare with the eye of a connoisseur; "but what can you possibly want with a horse of that kind in this rough country?"

"That's to me, sir—asking your pardon," replied Mr. Brown, touching his hat.

"Oh! of course, of course," said the stranger; "I meant no offence. I came out to know if you could get anyone to go to Tol-pedn-Penwith signal-station, where I have been staying, for my bag."

"Tol-pedn-Penwith signal-station, sir!" replied Mr. Brown; "why that's Lieutenant Foster's 'cabin,' as he calls it, near Lamorna Cove?"

"That's the place," said the stranger;—"could you send anyone?"

"Yes, sir, certainly; when my boy Bill do come in, he shall take the mare and ride down there,—it'll be very good exercise for her this fine a'ternoon. Drat the boy, I wish he was come!"

Bill soon made his appearance, and was despatched on the mare with a note to Lieutenant Fowler, written on a leaf torn from the gentleman's pocket-book, while Mr. Brown walked round the mare twice, and used his comb on her tail and mane.

" Isn't she a beauty, sir ?" said he, as the boy cantered off. " Easy !
easy, now !" exclaimed Mr. Brown, calling after the boy ; " ride her
gently.   Wo ! ho ! Jessie ! gently, lass, gently !"

These remarks might as well have been addressed to the wind as
to the boy or the mare, who seemed both intent on a gallop, and
away they went at full speed.

" Drat the boy," said Mr. Brown; " he'll wind her—that's a sure
thing—one of these days; and then where'll the money come from
to buy another ? But no money could do it ! Why, I wouldn't take
a hundred guineas for that mare, sir, if it was offered to me to-
morrow morning ! she's worth her weight in gold, sir, that mare is !"

" Don't fidget about the mare, Mr. Brown," said the gentleman ;
" she'll be all right; a little gallop will do her good. And now I
shall try Mrs. Brown's cookery,—it smells very good ;" and he
returned into the house to appease his appetite, while the landlord
went into the stable to lament once more over the wilfulness of that
scamp of a boy, as he called him, and to see that all things were
ready for his pet when she came back. And, having done all this,
he returned to the kitchen, where he found the stranger smoking a
pipe in the chimney-corner after his frugal repast, and chatting with
Mrs. Brown as if they had been old acquaintances.

" Come, Mr. Brown," said he, " I'm going to have a glass of
brandy and water, and you must take one too ; so mix them, if you
please, and come and tell me all the news."

" Polly ! come and get the hot water and sugar for the gentleman,"
said the landlord, calling to the maid, who was upstairs, as he went
towards the bar to get the two brandies. " Come, Poll ! Poll ! Polly !"
But as Polly did not come, he was obliged to bustle about himself; for
he received no help from his wife, although he called to her several
times from the bar. At length all things were placed on the little
table, and the stranger began to ask about " The Conjuror."

" The what !" exclaimed Mrs. Brown, dropping her needles, and
looking up in surprise and alarm,—while poor Mr. Brown stopped
short in the act of putting his glass to his lips.

" Hallo !" exclaimed the stranger ; " you look as if you had heard
some fellow talking treason against His Most Gracious Majesty the
King—God bless him !"—and the stranger lifted his hat, which he
had kept on out of compliment to his host and hostess. " I mean
Mr. Freeman, then," he said, correcting himself ; " I have heard such
wonderful accounts of him, that I should like to know what he can
really do."

" He would shaw you what he could do, very soon, ef he heard
you speak that word, I reckon," replied Mrs. Brown, getting up from
her seat and going to the door of the kitchen, and looking into the
passage and closing the front door.

"He doesn't like being called a 'conjuror,' then," said the stranger.

"Like it?" said Mrs. Brown, drawing her chair nearer to the chimney-corner; "iss,—just as much as you would like to be called '*no conjuror!*'"

"That's very well," said Mr. Brown, venturing on a laugh, now that his courage was being wound up by the brandy and water.

At this moment there came a clatter down the road, as of a horse at full gallop.

"Drat the boy!" exclaimed Mr. Brown, rising in great excitement; "he can't be come a'ready, can aw? To ride the mare like that es too bad! too bad! I'll kill 'n ef 'tes he. Iss fie! tes; for she's stopped at the stable-door. Dear lor'! Polly! Polly!"

When Mr. Brown went out, followed by the stranger and Mrs. Brown, there was the mare sure enough, standing at the stable-door without a rider, trembling from head to foot, and covered with foam and mud, with scarcely a dry hair on her body.

"Drat the boy!" exclaimed Mr. Brown; "he's killed—that's a sure thing—and the mare is ruined. Wo! ho! my darling; wo! ho!" And he took the mare's nose into his arms, and caressed it as if it had been a favourite daughter, while the stranger examined her all over, but could find no wound or injury whatever. She had evidently been frightened, for she was trembling still. They led her into the stable, and then began to think of the boy.

"I'd go and search for him," said the stranger, "but I don't know which way he went."

"No, nor yet I," said Mrs. Brown; "there's no knowing where that boy do go, when he's out; he's mighty fond of taking the narrow roads and bye lanes instead of the high road. There's two or three ways of going to Tol-pedn-Penwith from here; and like enough he went the way that nobody else would go ('cept 'The Maister')." This latter sentence she spoke almost in a whisper.

"While we are talking here, the boy may die," said the stranger, "if he's thrown and seriously hurt."

"The mare is all right," said Mr. Brown, coming out of the stable; "and now, if missus will get Polly to make a 'warm mash,' and give it to her at once, you and I'll go, sir, and see what can be done for the poor boy."

CHAPTER VI.

THE FAMILY PARTY.

THE two young officers had been invited to dine at Pendrea-house on that day, at two o'clock—the squire's usual dinner-hour. Lieut. Fowler had some writing work to do—rather an unusual occupation for him. However, as it was a report to be sent to head-quarters, which he had put off from day to day, he said to his friend in the morning, during breakfast, "The writing be blowed! but 'needs must when the devil drives!' so you go out, old fellow, and take a stroll, and leave me here to kick my heels under the table for a few hours. Two o'clock sharp, mind, and then we'll put our legs under the squire's mahogany, and tuck into his old port like trumps. That's an amusement which suits me a devilish deal better than quill-driving, if I must tell the honest truth for once in my life."

Two o'clock arrived, but Morley did not make his appearance. "The deuce take the fellow," soliloquised the lieutenant; "he'll lose his dinner and get out of the squire's good books. By Jove! though, perhaps he went in to have a lark with the girls in the morning, and so he did not think it worth while to come back. I'll just wash the ink off my paws, and toddle down as quick as I can; the squire won't like being kept waiting. 'Tis devilish lucky the old chap doesn't require a fellow to dress for dinner every time he tucks his legs under his mahogany;—I don't like getting into harness very often, unless duty calls—and then we must obey."

While the jovial officer is washing his hands, we will just look round his little "cabin," as he called it.

The little dwelling in which the commander of the signal-station resided, was certainly fitted up more to resemble a cabin on board ship, than the habitation of a landsman. On the ground floor there was a small room, or lobby, into which you entered at once from the front door. Opposite this door there was a door leading into the sitting-room, and beyond that another door led from the sitting-room into the kitchen. On the right, as you entered the lobby, were the stairs, leading to the two bedrooms, which led one into the other, like the rooms below. And in the ceilings were fixed iron rings, to which the hammocks were slung at night, and unshipped by day, the same as on board ship, so that these rooms might also be used as sitting-rooms, if required, in the daytime.

There were three men kept at each of these stations, besides the officer, and they had a separate cabin appropriated to them, adjoining the principal one. Their duty was to attend upon the officer; hoist signals of flags and balls, to give notice of the approach of an enemy's ship; or to signal to English ships orders from head-quarters. And these signals could be communicated to and from London in a very short time,—although not so quickly, nor so accurately, as by the telegraph of the present day.

It was not long after two when Lieut. Fowler got down to Pendrea-house, where he found the squire with his watch in his hand.

"Half-an-hour is soon lost, my boy," said the old gentleman, as the lieutenant entered the drawing-room; "but where is your friend?"

"Hasn't Morley been here, sir?" asked Fowler, in some surprise.

"No," replied the squire, "I haven't seen him,—have you, girls?"

This last question was addressed to two young ladies, whom Lieut. Fowler now approached, and greeted as old acquaintances. They had seen nothing of Mr. Morley, they said, since the day before, when they had all walked to Lamorna Cove together.

"That's queer," said the squire; "but he's a stranger, and may have missed his way,—so we'll give him a quarter-of-an-hour's grace."

And during this quarter-of-an-hour—the most awkward one in the whole twenty-four hours—we will introduce the reader more formally than we have hitherto done, to Squire Pendray and his family, the present owner and occupiers of Pendrea-house.

The squire was a purse-proud man, who had made a good deal of money, no one knew how, and purchased Pendrea estate many years before. He wished to rank among the ancient aristocracy of the county,—and his wealth enabled him to mix with them, and to be on a seeming equality; but in those days ancestral pride was very strong, and those who could boast of an ancient aristocratic pedigree, however limited their means might be, looked down with contempt on the man of a day, who had nothing but his riches to recommend him. The rich man was tolerated and patronized for the sake of his wealth, but he was still looked down upon as an inferior. Squire Pendray was one of these. But he was as proud of his riches as they were of their pedigree, and so he did not see nor care for their patronizing airs;—besides, he, in his turn, patronized those whom he considered inferior to him in wealth, and he was satisfied. Some said he was connected with the smugglers, and that they brought goods up to some of his subterranean vaults, through a secret passage which led from a cavern at Lamorna Cove up to Pendrea-house. Where the entrance from the house to these subterranean vaults was, no one could tell but the squire himself.

Mrs. Pendray was a homely, good sort of woman,—kind and hospitable, and very much beloved by the poor of the parish, to whom she distributed her bounties with a liberal hand.

Her two daughters will require a more elaborate description; for they were considered the "belles" of the west, and were toasted by all the young men of the neighbourhood at their after-dinner orgies —a custom very prevalent at that period.

The elder of the two sisters, Matilda—or Maud, as she was generally called—was a brunette, with dark hair and eyes, and a profile so regular and perfect, that, when the countenance was still and in repose, as it were, you might, without a great stretch of imagination, have fancied it a piece of tinted sculpture,—but the slightest thing would rouse it into animation, and then the dark eyes

D

would flash like a piece of polished steel when struck by the electric
fluid. She wore her hair in bands, which contrasted well with her
high intellectual forehead, and added dignity of expression to her
handsome features. Her stature was lofty, and her form elegant
and symmetrical; and when she walked across the room there was
majesty in her step, as if her foot disdained the ground it trod upon.
She delighted to wander out alone over the highest headlands, when
the wind was raging with its wildest fury, and to stand and watch
the foaming waves, as they surged and dashed against the perpendicular cliffs, until she was saturated with the spray and in danger
of being blown over into the abyss beneath.

Blanche was as unlike her elder sister as it was possible for her to
be. She was fair, and her beautiful auburn hair hung in graceful
ringlets over her soft young cheeks, as if to hide her blushes, which
the merest trifle would call forth. She was just seventeen. Her
sister was four years older; but, in person and manners, you would
think there was a greater difference of age between them. While
Maud walked out to witness the storm in all its majesty, from those
bold cliffs, Blanche would take some quiet book of poetry, and sit
alone, and read, in the little room upstairs, which their mother, years
ago, had set apart for her two daughters. And when the early spring
brought soft and balmy sunshine, Blanche would take her book and
wander out alone—not to the towering cliffs, and bold headlands,
but along the sheltered paths which led down to Lamorna Cove,
gathering wild flowers by the way. And there she would watch
the rippling waves, as they came dancing in over the beautiful
white sand, sparkling in the sunshine; and when her eyes were
weary with watching the calm unruffled sea, she would sit beneath
some sheltered rock, and read, and weep over some sad tale until
her eyes grew dim, and then would rise again and search for some
rare shell, or tiny piece of seaweed, she had read or heard of, as
being found at Lamorna Cove.

Lieut. Fowler, whose occupation caused him to wander everywhere
along the coast, in search of smugglers, or enemies' ships, would
often come suddenly on one or other of the sisters, and would then
escort them home and dine with the old squire, who liked him, and
was fond of having him there to while away an afternoon in social
chat; for the lieutenant, although not more than thirty years of age,
had seen a little service, and could tell tales that even Maud would
sit and listen to. But, for the gentle Blanche, those tales of hardship
and suffering, and deeds of daring, and hairbreadth escapes, had a
deeper charm than she dared to confess even to herself. He was not
a handsome man by any means, but he had a fine noble bearing,
and courage and daring were marked in his broad forehead. He
was sometimes the only person they saw for weeks, and, therefore,

the two sisters enjoyed his society, and were always glad when their papa asked him to dine. He admired them both, and not being in a hurry to marry, or having been knocked about too much in the world to have time to think of it, he did not see the danger he was daily and hourly incurring by being on such intimate terms of friendship with these two fascinating girls.

The old squire was very fond of his children, indulging them in most of their caprices, and he did not see any danger or impropriety in allowing them to be on intimate terms of friendship with a man whom he himself liked so well, and who was, in fact, so necessary in assisting him to pass away his time, with pleasure and comfort, in that dull out-of-the-way place. It had also been a great pleasure to the squire's family to receive the lieutenant's friend, Frederick Morley, at their house; for he, too, was a very gentlemanly man, had seen a good deal of the world, and could tell them of foreign scenes and manners, which very much delighted them all. He was more romantic and impressible than his friend. It was therefore evident that Miss Pendray preferred his society to that of the more matter-of-fact Lieut. Fowler, and would take him to her favourite wild cliffs, and point out the beauties she saw in them, to which he listened with marked attention, entering into her feelings, and admiring her pursuits, more than any other man she had been accustomed to meet; but still there was something sad in his manner, sometimes, which she could not account for. It seemed to her as if he had met with some heavy affliction in days gone by. This thought was impressed on her more than ever to-day; for he had not arrived in time for dinner,—so they sat down without him. As the day passed slowly on, and he did not appear, it made the whole family think the more of him. After dinner, Miss Pendray asked Mr. Fowler if there was anything pressing on his friend's mind, as, she said, she had often observed him sad and thoughtful, when all had been merry and cheerful around him. Now that the subject was mentioned, everyone seemed to have observed the same; and they urged the lieutenant to tell them—if he knew, and it was not a secret which he felt bound to keep—what it was that made the young soldier look so sad at times when others were gay.

"My friend, Frederick Morley, has been a romantic dreamer all his life," said the lieutenant. "He was the same at school,—sometimes as gay and reckless as the worst of us, and at other times sad and low-spirited, even when his companions were in their gayest mood. About two years ago, before he went abroad with his regiment, poor Fred had a romantic love-affair at the town in which his regiment was quartered. His sister was living in the same place, with her aunt; and Fred fell desperately in love with a boarding-school miss, and as his sister was a day-pupil at the same school, she was the messenger between them. Since his return he has searched everywhere for the girl, but cannot succeed in finding her. This much he has told me, but he will not divulge her name. So you see, ladies, my poor friend has enough on his mind to make him sad."

"Yes," replied Miss Pendray; "but this affair is of recent date, and you say he was the same at school;—it was not a love-affair then, I presume."

"Oh! no," said the lieutenant, in a grave tone; "there was another cause for his melancholy then, but that is all blown over, and therefore, perhaps, it is as well to leave it rest in oblivion. He never speaks of it now, and so, I suppose, he wishes it to be forgotten."

"Oh! do tell us, Lieut. Fowler," said Blanche. "Poor young man! it must have been some dreadful tale, I'm sure, to prey on his mind thus, for so many years;" and she looked at him so beseechingly, that he could not refuse,—indeed, why should he decline to make his friends acquainted with the history of a young man whom he had introduced to their house? The story threw no disgrace on his young friend; and if he scrupled to tell them the true story, they might suspect it was some crime or indiscretion which his friend had himself been guilty of. So, looking at the sweet girl who sat opposite him, with her fair curls thrown back from her face, the more easily to catch every word that was spoken by him whose tales she loved to hear, he said he would relate the story as well as he could. But it was a sad tale; and as it is likely to be a long one, and probably an interesting one, we will give it a chapter to itself.

CHAPTER VII.

"MURDER MOST FOUL."

"My friend's father," he began, "was an East-Indian merchant. He married a native, by whom he had three children—two sons and a daughter. The eldest son was several years older than the other two children, and he received the best education that could be got in India, and was taken into his father's factory to assist him, when he was very young. Their mother died soon after the birth of her daughter; and, when they were old enough, it was thought advisable to send the two younger children to England, under the care of their aunt (Mr. Morley's only sister), to be educated; and, as Mr. Morley was anxious to visit England once more, and thought he could make more of his merchandize, by coming himself and seeing how the markets stood, than his agents seemed to be making for him, he determined to bring the children over himself. So he freighted a vessel with a valuable cargo, and arrived in England safely with his two children, having left his eldest son behind, to manage the business in India. His sister resided at Ashley Hall, a country-seat about five or six miles from Bristol. The children enjoyed the country air exceedingly, and the scenery—so different from India— and the old gentleman enjoyed it as much as they did. He visited Bristol almost every day, and watched the markets, sometimes doing business and sometimes not. He very often walked there and back, by way of exercise, when the weather was fine. One day, about the middle of January, the weather, although cold and sharp, being dry, he determined he would walk, as he had so often done before, for he thought he should be able to keep himself warmer in walking than driving. He did a good bit of business that day, and had a considerable sum of money about him.

" It was a risk to walk home alone, but Mr. Morley had so often done it before, without meeting with any accident, that he thought he would start early, and in two hours he should be at the end of his journey. So he buttoned up his great coat, and took his big stick in his hand, and started. The stick was a very peculiar one, which he had brought with him from India. It was very heavy for its size, and had large sharp knots towards the big end,—not very handsome, but still it was peculiar, and so it had many admirers. ' A good blow from this would settle a stouter fellow than I am likely to meet with to-night, I fancy,' said Mr. Morley, as he looked with pride on the formidable weapon he held in his hand ; and he strode down the street, with the cold wind blowing in his face.

" Before he got a mile out of the town, it began to snow heavily; but still he trudged on against the wind, which was blowing strong, and beating the snow into his face, which made him hold his head down, so that he did not remark a turn in the road, about three miles out,—indeed, by this time, the road and hedges were covered with snow, and anyone who knew the road even better than he did might have taken the wrong turn. On, on he walked for several miles, when he began to think he had missed his way,—for he now observed that he passed no houses on the road, as he was accustomed to do when he walked home before. At length, after walking some distance further, he saw a light, and, thinking it might be a roadside-inn, he made towards it. On approaching cautiously, however, he found it was not an inn, but a solitary cottage, partly surrounded by a garden—the entrance to which was through a small gate at the side ; and nearly opposite this gate there was a window. The light that he had seen, came from a window in front of the house, facing the road. It was getting dark, but the white snow threw a shadow of light all round, and he opened the little gate, went round to the front, and looked in at the window, which was but partially covered by a thin blind, and there he saw a woman sitting by the fire alone. The room seemed comfortably furnished, and the table was evidently laid for supper.

"It was now getting late, and Mr. Morley was cold and tired and hungry, for he had been walking several hours; so he knocked at the door, which was quickly opened by the woman he had seen sitting by the fire. She was apparently about forty years of age, but not very prepossessing in appearance, nor very courteous at first, but any shelter was better than being out in the snow on such a night as this. He explained to her that he had missed his way in going to his sister's house from Bristol; and he begged her to let him partake of her meal, and rest a little, and warm himself—for which he said he would willingly pay handsomely; and he moreover said, incautiously, that he had more money about him than he thought it was prudent for him to travel any further with alone that night. This communication seemed to warm the woman's heart. She placed a chair by the fire, and proceeded to get him some refreshment at once.

" 'It is a dreadful night!' she said; 'and it has come on so suddenly too. Who'd have thought it this morning?'

" 'No indeed,' said Mr. Morley. 'This seems a lonely place for a habitation. You have a husband, of course. He is out on business, I suppose.'

" 'No, sir, I have no husband. My father and brother live here with me;—they are engaged in the seafaring line. My mother has been dead some years.'

" 'You are not far from the sea, then?' enquired Mr. Morley.

" 'No,' she replied; 'a very short distance. I expect my brother home soon, and was preparing supper for him. My father I don't expect home for the night, so you shall occupy his room, if you please. It is on the ground-floor, and looks into the garden. His business often keeps him out late. We are gone to bed frequently when he comes in, and then he can go into his room on the ground-floor without disturbing us. I believe that was his fancy for having his bedroom there.'"

"Why, Fowler!" exclaimed the squire, "you are making quite an interesting story of it. What it will end in, I haven't the slightest idea; but go on."

"I'm afraid I am tiring you," replied the lieutenant; "but I have heard the story repeated so often, that it is quite familiar to me."

"Oh! do go on," said Blanche, looking at him earnestly; "it is quite like a tale one reads in the old romances."

"Old romances!" said her mamma, in alarm; "why where on earth have you met with any old romances, I should like to know, child?"

"Well, if you would like to hear the end of my tale," said the lieutenant, "I will proceed; but I haven't much more to tell. Let me see. Where was I? Oh! the bedroom."

"Mr. Morley, having warmed himself and taken some refreshment, said he was feeling very tired and sleepy, and should like to lie down for a few hours, if perfectly convenient. The brother had not come in, so he followed his hostess into the little bedroom, leaving his hat and stick in the sitting-room. It was a comfortable little room enough. The bed was small, and very near the door,—so near, that immediately you opened it you faced the side of the bed, and you had to close the door again before you could pass down by the side of the bed into the room. On the other side of the bed, nearly opposite the door, stood the wash-stand, and dressing-table, and one chair. The window faced the foot of the bed.

"Mr. Morley looked out at the night. It was very dark, and still snowing a little. When he began to reflect on the acknowledged irregularity of the men in the house, he did not feel very comfortable; for their calling was evidently not a very reputable one. The woman seemed superior in her manner and address to her present situation; but there was a cunning, restless expression in her eye, which he did not at all like. They might be a gang of desperadoes connected with the smugglers that infested the coast. He did not like his position at all;—he was unarmed, and in their power, and he had left his stick in the sitting-room. If he went back for it, it would cause suspicion. He determined, therefore, to lie down on the bed without taking off his clothes, and be off in the morning as soon as he could see. There was no lock to the door, nor bolt to the window, as far as he could find. He tried the door cautiously, and found it was barred outside, and so was the window;—so far, then, he was a prisoner. He threw himself on the bed to rest, but not to sleep; and after some time he heard a man come in at the front door. Then there was a savoury smell, and a good deal of talk in whispers,—and then the brandy was asked for, and all was quiet.

"After a time he saw a man approach the window outside. He had the appearance of being intoxicated. He opened the window after a little trouble, and prepared to come in.

"'This is the father, no doubt,' thought Mr. Morley, 'come home unexpectedly, and evidently very much intoxicated.'

"The man seemed too drunk to listen to reason, even if Mr. Morley had got up and spoken to him; and a quarrel with him, in that state, would be very unpleasant, and bring the other members of the household also upon him. Besides, no doubt these men carried arms with them, wherever they went; and if this man found a stranger in his bedroom, he would not hesitate to shoot him, especially in his present state.

" What should he do? There was not a moment to be lost. The old man had by this time tumbled into the room through the window. He would be on the bed in a minute, for he was getting up from the floor. Mr. Morley thererore slid down the side opposite the door, and got under the bed, intending, as soon as the man was asleep, to get away from that house at all risks.

" The old man threw himself on the bed, and was soon fast asleep.

" The door was now gently opened, and he heard a few heavy blows struck with a heavy bludgeon on the poor old man's head, as he lay sound asleep on the bed. There was a deep moan, and then the door was closed again.

" ' Murder !' he said, as he crept from under the bed   He felt the body in his fright; it was too dark to see it. There was no motion. Blood was flowing from the wounds,—he could feel it, warm and clammy, although he could not see it. He knew not what to do. The blows were no doubt intended for himself, and if he raised an alarm he would still be victimized. He was in an agony of fright and terror. His only thought was to save his own life; for if the murderer discovered that he had not killed his intended victim, he would be back again, no doubt, to finish his work. He snatched up the hat that the old man had dropped on the floor, thinking in his frenzy that it was his own, and got out of the window, which had not been fastened again, and fled through the snow, he knew not where."

" Oh ! Mr. Fowler," exclaimed Blanche, shuddering; " this is too horrible. Oh ! don't go on ! I can't bear it ;"—and she placed her hands before her eyes, that had before been so intently gazing on the speaker.

" Nonsense !" exclaimed the squire ; " we've heard the beginning ; now let's hear the end. Go on, Fowler. Those who don't wish to hear any more can leave the room."

No one left the room ; so Mr. Fowler continued :—

" The brother and sister were horror-struck, on entering the room the next morning, to find that *their father* had been murdered instead of the stranger, and that the stranger had escaped, and was probably then giving information to the authorities. Their first thought was self-preservation. Circumstances favoured the guilty pair. The stranger had evidently touched the murdered man, and had blood about his hands—for there were stains on the window-frame—and he had worn away the murdered man's hat, and left his own behind; and it was with *his stick* that the murder had been committed. Here was circumstantial evidence enough ; so the guilty pair lost no time in rousing the nearest neighbours and constables ; and information was given to the magistrates by the brother and sister, accusing the stranger of the murder, which appeared on the face of it very plausible ; for the accused man's stick and hat were found in the bedroom, and the name 'Morley' was written inside the hat. The stick was covered with blood, and the sharp knots corresponded with the marks in the murdered man's head. The stick was easily identified. The murdered man's hat was missing too. But what motive could such a man as Mr. Morley have had for committing such a crime?" The woman said he might have been tipsy, and lost his way in the snow, and finding the window so near the gate, and so easy to enter, he had perhaps gone in, and a struggle might have taken place between him and her father, who slept in that room. There was money in that room too, she said ; but it was not believed that Mr. Morley would murder anyone for the sake of money. No one wished to believe him guilty ; but what could they do in the face of this circumstantial evidence ? There were his hat and stick, which he admitted at once were his—his name was in the hat—and the stick was covered with blood. He was easily traced in the snow, and when overtaken he was walking like a maniac. His hands were bloody and so were his clothes ; and he had the murdered man's hat on his head.

"The sister told the tale before the magistrates very plausibly. It might have been done in self-defence, she said. He might have got in at the window, perhaps, for shelter ; but why not have come round to the door, and why did he not alarm the house, instead of going off in that unaccountable way.

"He told his own tale, and concluded by saying that he had a considerable sum of money about him, which he had lost or was robbed of. No money was found, however.

"His tale did not appear plausible. The woman founded her belief that he was tipsy, she said, on the fact of his having come so much out of his way, if he was really only going from Bristol to Ashley Hall. He was a comparative stranger in England, and very few knew him except in the way of business.

"The circumstantial evidence was so strong that the magistrates could do no other than commit him to the county gaol to await his trial for murder at the next assizes.

"The assizes came, but there was no evidence against Mr. Morley, and he was acquitted.

"The brother and sister had found the bag of money, no doubt, which he had dropped in his agitation, and had absconded no one knew where. They were afraid of the close cross-examination to which they would be exposed, and under which their evidence must have broken down.

"Mr. Morley returned to India immediately, leaving his two children in their aunt's care. It was a severe shock, from which he never recovered. He felt that although he was innocent, yet the stigma of his having been committed to prison on a charge of murder would still hang over his family, until it could be properly cleared up by the conviction or confession of the real murderer. He died soon after his return to India; and on his death-bed he enjoined his children to make every search in their power after those wicked people, who had so cruelly murdered their own father and thrown the guilt upon him."

" Can you wonder, now, ladies, that my friend should feel low-spirited sometimes ? "

" It is indeed a dreadful tale," said Miss Pendray. " I wonder what became of the guilty parties ? "

" It is that which is preying on Morley's spirits," replied Mr. Fowler ; " he has searched and enquired everywhere—at home and abroad—but as yet to no purpose. They have, no doubt, taken feigned names ; but they will be found out one day, I have not the slightest doubt."

" Now let us change the subject, and speak of the living," said the squire. " What has become of young Morley, I wonder ? "

" I shall have a search for him to-morrow morning," said the lieutenant. I fancy he is gone to St. Just, for he is anxious about his brother, who was expected from India about this time, having amassed a large fortune, besides what his father left, which he was about to divide between the three children, according to his father's will. The wreck of the Indiaman, the other day, has upset him rather ; for he has an idea that his brother might have been one of the passengers."

" Poor young man !" said Mrs. Pendray ; " how many troubles he has had to bear, for one so young ! "

CHAPTER VIII.

THE LAND'S-END CONJUROR.

Mr. Brown and his companion returned, after a three-hours' search, without having found the boy or learnt any tidings of him. The mare had eaten her warm mash, and Mrs. Brown had procured the assistance of Josiah Trenow to give her a good rub-down and make her comfortable, and he was having a glass of beer after his exertions, when Mr. Brown and his companion came in.

" Thank 'ee, 'Siah," said Mr. Brown ; " I do b'lieve the mare ha'n't had such a rub-down for a month. Look here's a great strong arm, sir," he continued, taking Josiah by the arm, while he called the gentleman's attention to it.

"I shouldn't like to engage in single combat with him," replied Mr. Morley, smiling, "if he is as strong as he looks."

"No fie! no fie!" said Mr. Brown. "Peggy! Peggy! Polly! Polly! Why the women are all run away after the boy, I s'pose. Peggy, my dear!"

"Well, landlord," said Josiah; "what news have 'ee got about the boy?"

"Why no news," replied Mr. Brown, sitting down thoughtfully in his wife's chair, a liberty he seldom took, unless he was "up in the clouds," as she called it. "Sit down, sir, if you please. Why, a good many people seed the boy and the mare go up, an' a fine passle seed the mare come down again all of a rattle, without the boy, but nobody seed the boy thrawd, an' nobody have seen the boy since, so far as we can hear. Whisht, esn't et, 'Siah, boy?"

"Whisht! iss fie, 'tes whisht enough," said Mrs. Brown, coming downstairs to hear the news too.

"That boy es so sure ill-wished as ever anybody wor in this world," said Josiah; "he's in a queer por, an' ha' be'n so for a bra' bit."

"Why what are 'ee tellen', 'Siah," said Mr. Brown; "how shud 'ee think so, boy?"

"Why for many things," replied Josiah; "the boy Bill wor took out of the workhouse, worn't aw? and he ha'n't growd since—not an inch, I do b'lieve. He can hardly reach to the mare's shoulder, and yet he do keep that mare in good condition, with her summer's coat up all the year round, like the squire's hunter, and better too, I b'lieve. He's mighty fond of going out by night, too. I've seed that boy, when I've been coming home from bal, two or three o'clock in the morning, going up by Chapel-Carnbrea by hisself, whistling."

"What! our boy Billy whistling that time o' night?" said Mrs. Brown; "dear lor'! I should think he'd be afeard of the pixies. And up there, too!"

The conversation was evidently getting too dismal for Mr. Morley, and he changed the subject by ordering a glass of brandy and water for himself, and one each for Mr. Brown and Josiah.

"Come, Polly," said Mr. Brown, as he went to get the brandies. "Polly! Polly! pretty Polly!"

He got no assistance, however; for Polly was gone out on some errand for her mistress; and it really seemed as if he called the people about him more from habit than anything else, for, like him who called spirits from the vasty deep, poor Mr. Brown was not very much distressed or astonished if they didn't come. While they were drinking their brandy and water, the conversation turned again on the marvellous; and Mr. Brown said, "I wonder ef 'twould be any good to ask 'The Maister' about it."

" About what ?" asked Mrs. Brown.

" Why about the mare, to be sure," replied her husband ; " she's ill-wished as much as ever the boy es.   Something frightened her more than human, I'm sure ;—what do you think, 'Siah ?"

" Well," said Josiah, " I never seed a beast tremble like that afore. I worked my arms off, purty nigh, afore she begun for to dry, an' then she dried up all of a rattle, an' snorted brave."

" I'll go up now and ask ' The Maister,' said Mr. Brown ; " the mare es ill-wished, I do b'lieve ;"—so he drank up his brandy and water, and started at once.

It was not, even then, very late, and Mr. Freeman's house was but just outside the village.

" The Maister" was at home, the maid said.   What did Mr. Brown please to want.

" I do want to speak to him 'pon private business," replied Mr. Brown.

So Alice Ann shewed him into the best parlour, and left him there in the dark, as she had orders to do to all visitors who came to " The Maister" on private business.

Very soon he heard a rumbling noise in the room above, and then a clanking of chains ; and then he heard a voice, as if coming from the floor of the room he was sitting in, telling him to beware of what he was doing,—to keep all things secret,—and to tell " The Maister" all ; and then all would be well.   All these mysterious sounds— coming sometimes from above, and sometimes from one part of the room he was in, and sometimes from another, when everything was shrouded in darkness—were calculated to strike terror into a stronger mind than poor Mr. Brown possessed ; so that when Alice Ann came to the door and asked him to follow her upstairs, he was confirmed in his belief that " The Maister" was connected with "The Prince of Darkness," and was prepared to see hobgoblins and spirits dancing about as he entered the awful room.

Alice Ann knocked at the door three times, and at the third knock the door flew open, and Mr. Brown was pulled in by some invisible hand, and the door was closed again.   He remained standing just inside, having a screen of thick black cloth hanging before him, to prevent his seeing what was in the room.   He thought his last hour was come, and trembled until his knees knocked together, and his teeth chattered in his head. At last, a voice from the furthest corner of the room said :—

" John Brown, your business is known, without your telling it— as most things are.   Are you prepared to go through the ordeal necessary to free the mare from evil hands, and the boy from witchcraft ?"

" Oh ! ye-es, Maister," said the poor man, in a tremulous voice ;

" I'll do anything. I do know that your power is great, and your knowledge is greater."

" Then down on thy knees, trembler, and do my bidding to the letter, or woe be unto thee ! And listen to what is now to be spoken." And down flopped poor Mr. Brown on his knees, and awaited the ordeal, which he interrupted occasionally, by sundry interjections and parenthetical remarks of his own.

(*The Conjuror*) "You have a gentleman staying in your house ?"

(*Mr. Brown*) "Oh ! yes; and a very nice gentleman he is."

(*The Conjuror*) " He admires your mare ?"

(*Mr. Brown*) " He do so."

(*The Conjuror*) " He must ride her !"

(*Mr. Brown*) "He shall, Maister. (Oh lor' ! a wild harum-scarum like he to ride the mare. Oh lor' ! Peggy ! Peggy ! Oh lor' !)"

(*The Conjuror*) "Now listen. That gentleman must, within three days from this time, ride the mare to the Land's-End point, and look over the point, and the spell will be taken off which now hangs over the mare, and the boy will be restored. If not, beware of what may befal you and your household. The rider must have no friend or assistant within fifty yards of the point."

(*Mr. Brown*) "Oh lor' ! Peggy ! Peggy ! What shall I do ? No mortal man would do that. Oh lor' !"

A bell was now struck in the further end of the room, and the black curtain was drawn up suddenly, when the room appeared to be all on fire. There was a brilliant red light shed all around, and a thin vapour filled the room, through which he saw the conjuror standing, dressed in a black gown, and white wig, surrounded by ornaments composed of what seemed to be silver, and small mirrors, which reflected the furniture of the room, and multiplied them twentyfold. The conjuror then said, in a solemn voice, "Do my bidding, or beware ! your doom is fixed !"

The black curtain was then suddenly dropped again, and, after a few minutes, the door was opened as before, and Mr. Brown was pushed out by some invisible hand, and the door was locked on the inside.

Thus did this pretended necromancer work on the superstitious fears of the ignorant and weakminded, and make them believe that he knew more of their affairs than he really did ; and thus did he gain a power over them which no reasoning or persuasion could shake.

This is no exaggerated picture ; for, at that period, there were numbers, with less pretensions than Mr. Freeman, both men and women, who practised these arts and received handsome incomes— not only from the illiterate and ignorant, but from people in the higher walks of life, so rife was the feeling of superstition which prevailed at that period, not only in the county of Cornwall, but

E

throughout the whole kingdom of England. Well-to-do farmers, it was well known, paid one of these emperics annual salaries to keep the *evil eye* from their cattle. It is not to be wondered at, therefore, that poor Mr. Brown should place implicit reliance on what such a notable man as "The Maister" should tell him, and determine to have "The Maister's" commands carried out to the very letter, if it were possible that it could be done. If he had been commanded to ride the mare to the brink of the Land's-End point himself, or over it, he would have done it, without hesitation; but how was he to get a stranger to do so for his benefit? It required consideration; and, as two heads are better than one, he determined to consult his wife at once, and they could put their heads together, he thought, and the thing would be managed somehow,—for he had great faith in his wife's wisdom; so he went home to sleep upon it.

CHAPTER IX.

LOVE AND MYSTERY.

The next morning, Alrina met her lover again by appointment, on the rocks below Cape Cornwall; and here they renewed their former protestations of love and constancy, and the hours passed pleasantly away. But sunshine will not last for ever, and the brighter the sunshine the darker will the cloud seem that obscures it for a time. In the midst of their happiness a cloud passed over the countenance of Morley, and he became thoughtful.

"Tell me," said Alrina, "what has caused this sudden gloom?"

"It is nothing, dearest," said he, putting his arm round her waist; "I was just thinking how much more need we have of mutual sympathy than either of us imagined. You have your secrets which you wish to discover,—I mean as to your mother's and your father's early history, and your own, and that secret which you seem to think your father has hidden in his breast."

"Indeed, Frederick," replied Alrina, "I scarcely wish now to discover those secrets,—for I fear the knowledge of them, whenever they are discovered, may deprive me of that which I prize more than anything else on earth—your love!"

"No, never!" replied her lover; "whatever your father may have done, or whatever those secrets may be, as to the early history of your family, will not alter my love for you, dear Alrina! I have a secret too," continued he; "and mine is a terrible one—one that would terrify you, were I to tell you—and therefore it is better, perhaps, kept where it is; I can bear it better alone. But we are only dreaming—don't cry, Alrina;—all will be well in the end."

"But you have a terrible secret too, you say, Frederick?" she replied through her tears. "I have told you all I know of myself; is your's a secret to be kept from me? are you afraid to trust me, too?" —and the poor girl burst into tears, and would not be comforted. She felt herself an object of distrust to all, and her heart could not bear up against such cold suspicion.

"Be calm, dear Alrina," said Frederick, in a soothing tone; "I have nothing to conceal that you may not know. It will do you no good to know it, and it may prey on your sensitive mind too much, and therefore do more harm than good; but if you wish to know all, and you think you can bear to hear it, I will tell you the whole, —but you must be calm."

"Oh! yes," replied Alrina, drying her tears; "I would rather know all. I will be firm. I can bear anything with you, or for you." She placed her hand in his, and looked up into his face with earnest love, as he related to her the tale of his father's adventure in the snow, and his accusation and acquittal for want of evidence. He told her also of his brother, and that he was expected home from India about this time, and how he feared he might have been in that Indiaman that was wrecked on the coast but a few days before.

"Oh! Frederick, don't distress yourself about imaginary evils," said Alrina; "bad news flies fast enough. A thought struck me while you were relating that dreadful tale,—my father!"

"Your father!" exclaimed Frederick, hastily.

"Yes," she said; "why not ask him to help you in unravelling this terrible secret. He is very clever, and knows many things that other people scarcely dream of. People come here to consult him from all parts of the country, and they generally go away satisfied; so I suppose he tells them what they require to know. He is gone to some distant part to-day, I believe, to cure some poor wretch who thinks he is ill-wished. Remember, I have no confidence in that part of his scientific pretension; but I know he has a clear head to sift out a mystery, and has resources which few else have, from keeping all these 'goostrumnoodles' under his thumb, and some of the sharpest of them in his pay."

"I will think of this," said Morley, smiling; "and if I become a convert I will still consult the conjuror."

He then began to talk of his sister, Alrina's former schoolfellow. She had left school, he said, and was living with their aunt, Mrs. Courland, who had returned to her old house again near Bristol, where they were staying when that sad affair happened to their father. Alrina must go and see them.

The time passed swiftly on in such sweet converse, and they lingered on and on—rising frequently to separate, and sitting down again; and in the intensity of their love they neither of them saw that curious head, nor those curious eyes and ears, which were watching them again, and noting all their words and actions.

"Ho! ho!" said the individual, as it bore that curious head away on its shoulders; *"more secrets worth knowing!"*

CHAPTER X.

ALRINA'S TROUBLES INCREASE.

JOSIAH TRENOW resided with his father and mother in a small but neat cottage, about a hundred yards from Mr. Freeman's house; consequently, it was easy for Alrina or Alice Ann, when their elders were out of the way, to run in and have a quiet gossip with Mrs. Trenow. Her husband was underground-captain at Botallack mine, so that he was not much at home during the day.

Alrina could not settle down to anything when she returned to her father's house after her interview with Frederick Morley, related in the last chapter. She tried to work, but she could not get on. She then took a book, but could not fix her attention on the pages; and after sitting half-an-hour with the book in her hand, she found that she was holding it upside down.

Her father had returned, and had been closeted with her aunt ever since, and it was as likely as not that Alrina would not see either of them again for the night. They did not trust her with any of their secrets, of which they seemed to have a good many; and her lover had imparted a secret to her to-day, which made her feel very unhappy on his account; but he had trusted her, and confided in her, so that was some consolation; but then, if there should be any dreadful secret connected with her past history, or her mother's, of whom she knew nothing, and she were to lose his love in consequence, what should she do? She would have no one then on whom she could lean for support and consolation in her trials. All these thoughts, crowding one upon the other, made her feel very sad, and she burst into tears, as she sat down in the little parlour. Poor girl! how sad to be in the midst of relatives and friends, and yet to feel that no one cares for you! Better to be a recluse at once—far better.

Alice Ann knew that her young mistress had something on her mind that distressed her, but she did not feel herself competent to advise or console her. She peeped in at the door, however, and said,—

"What's the matter, Miss Reeney? I shud think you'd lost your sweetheart a'most!"

"No, no, Alice Ann," she replied, wiping away her tears; "if I had one, like you, and everything was going on smoothly, like your affairs, perhaps it might raise my spirits a little."

" 'Tesn't all so smooth as you may think," said Alice Ann; " I ha'n't se'n sight nor sign of 'Siah (ef that's what you do main) sence the day after the wreck, when he an' ' The Maister' had such a tussle up in the ' private room.' I looked in through the keyhole, but I couldn't see much. When 'Siah came out aw looked all flushed, but I don't think aw wor frightened, like some of them are when they do come out. Hes fe-a-thar an' mother ha'n't seed much of 'n neither since then, I b'lieve. I wish you could stay for to run down there, an' ax about 'n a bit, Miss Reeney."

That was a happy suggestion. A good long chat with Mrs. Trenow, and, probably, another secret, would relieve her mind a little from the heavy weight she felt pressing upon it—almost more than she could bear.

She found Mrs. Trenow alone, with a basketful of coarse worsted stockings before her, belonging to the men, which she was "mending a croom," she said.

" How are 'ee, Miss Reeney, my dear," said she, as Alrina entered; " the sight of you es good for sore eyes ! Why, I ha'n't seed 'ee for ever so long."

" No," replied Alrina; " I have been pretty much engaged, and my aunt has been out more than usual lately, and so I have been housekeeper, you know."

" Iss sure," said Mrs. Trenow, looking at her visitor over her spectacles. " You ha' seed an' heerd bra' things lately, I s'pose. They do say ' The Maister' es worken' the oracle purty fitty sence the wreck.'

" What do you mean?" exclaimed Alrina, in surprise.

" What do I main?" asked Mrs. Trenow, taking off her spectacles, and closing the door;—" why, this here es what I do main. The best of the things that wor picked up from that wreck es up in ' The Maister's' private room, and more wud ha' b'en there, ef et worn't for one thing more than another. There ha' b'en more people ill-wished, and more cattle an' things dead, sence that night, than wor ever knaw'd to be afore in so short a time; an' where shud they go to ef et worn't to ' The Maister?'—and what wud he do for them ef they dedn't cross his hand?"

" I don't at all understand you?" said Alrina, more surprised than ever.

" No, I s'pose you don't, my dear," replied Mrs. Trenow; " you must go abroad for to hear news about home, so they do say. An' poor Maister Brown, too, ha' b'en up there, an' came home frightened out of his life. Our 'Siah wor up to ' the public' when aw came in. He wudn't spaik a word then, so 'Siah said; but to-day Mrs. Brown told 'Siah all about et. But 'tes a secret, my dear ;—hush !"

" What is it, Mrs. Trenow? don't keep me in this suspense," said Alrina, in an excited manner; "do tell me what has happened."

" Happened!" replied Mrs. Trenow; " why, nothen' ha'n't happened yet, that I do knaw of; but how he'll git 'n to do it I don't knaw. I wudn't ef I wor he."

" What! is Josiah to do something for Mr. Brown?" asked Alrina.

" No, my dear, not 'Siah," replied Mrs. Trenow. " There's a young gentleman up there stopping, so 'Siah said, and he must ride Maister Brown's mare to the edge of the cliff 'pon the Land's-End point, an' look over, to save the man and the boy from witchcraft. Now, mind you don't tell nobody, for 'tes a secret, my dear, down sous."

" I'd see them both at the bottom of the sea first," said Alrina; " why should a stranger be mixed up with Mr. Brown's misfortunes?"

" Why! sure nuff!" replied Mrs. Trenow; " you may say Y or X, whichever you mind to, but ef ' The Maister' do give the orders to the likes of Mr. Brown, 'tes likely to be done, ef et can be any way in the world."

" What did my father know of the stranger, to give such an order as that?" said Alrina.

" That I do no more knaw than a child," replied Mrs. Trenow; " but here's fe-a-thar; mayhap he can tell."

" Your sarvant, Miss Reeney," said Captain Trenow, as he entered the room; " you're a stranger, ma'am."

" Not much of a stranger, Captain Trenow," said Alrina; "but you are so seldom at home when I can run down for a gossip with your good wife."

" Zackly like that," said the captain; " she's a bra' good hand for a gossip, I do b'lieve. I'll back har agen the parish for tongue, Miss Reeney. She don't do much else, I b'lieve in my conscience."

" Areah! then," said his wife, indignantly; " I shud like to knaw how you'd get your victuals cooked, and your clothes mended, ef I was so fond of gossipping as some people I do knaw?"

" Are 'ee going for to see the gentleman ride over the cliff tomorrow, Miss Reeney?" said Captain Trenow, by way of changing the subject. " I do hear that he's determined upon et, 'cause somebody said he cudn't. More fool he, I do say."

" Oh! Captain Trenow," said Alrina, in the greatest terror; "don't let him do it—pray, don't."

" Me! Miss Reeney," said the captain;—"why, I don't knaw the gentlemen. Nobody here have ever seed 'n, 'ceps 'Siah an' the landlord's people."

" But won't Josiah prevent him?" said Alrina.

" That I can no more tell than you can, ma'am," replied Trenow. " 'Siah es gone up there now."

" Why, Miss Reeney!" exclaimed Mrs. Trenow, who had been

looking intently on Alrina for the last few minutes: " I shud think that strange gentleman wor your sweetheart, ef I ded'nt knaw that you never clapp'd your eyes upon om in your life. 'Siah do say, f'rall, that he's a likely young chap enough."

This last expression of Mrs. Trenow's put Alrina on her guard. She did not, at present, wish the gossips of St. Just to know that Frederick Morley was either her friend or her lover: nor would he, under existing circumstances, have wished it either. There were secrets on both sides to be discovered and explained, before it would be prudent for them openly to declare their attachment to each other. Frederick had not yet even seen Alrina's father, and she was as yet entirely under her father's control. She went home, therefore, with a sad heart; and nothing that Alice Ann could say or do, could induce her to tell her what she had heard, nor why she was so sad. She hoped that it might not be true,—that was her only consolation. But it was true, nevertheless.

CHAPTER XI.

FREDERICK MORLEY OBSTINATELY DETERMINES ON RIDING THE MARE.

WHEN Frederick Morley returned to the inn, after his meeting with Alrina, he found his friend, Lieut. Fowler, there in deep conversation with Mr. and Mrs. Brown.

" Hallo! old fellow," he exclaimed, as his friend entered; " a pretty fellow you are, to keep the squire's dinner waiting, and two pair of bright eyes languishing for something more sprightly than a poor lieutenant R.N. to rest their weary lids upon. Why, where the deuce have you been? You are not *ill-wished*, too, are you?"

" It seems very like it," replied Morley; " for I seem to bring trouble wherever I go. Only last night, when I simply wanted a note taken over to you, and my bag brought back, the boy was taken off by the pixies, and the landlord's mare caught St. Vitus's dance, or something worse,—so the sooner I return to the place from whence I came, the better."

" I don't know that," replied Fowler; " for you have work cut out for you here, it seems."

" What do you mean?" replied his friend, smiling. " The French haven't landed, have they? and you want me to take the command of the volunteers?"

" No, no," said Fowler; " but our friend, Mr. Brown, has been to the conjuror about his misfortunes; and what do you think he told him?"

"I'm sure I don't know," replied Morley; "some humbug, I suppose."

"Nothing of the kind, I assure you," replied Fowler. "He merely said that it would depend on the courage and skill of the person who was the innocent cause of the misfortunes, to extricate him out of them."

"If you mean me," replied Morley, "you know I don't want for pluck; as to the skill, that's another thing,—that will depend on what there is to do."

"Well, then, Mr. Brown has confided to me the history of his visit to the conjuror," said the lieutenant, "and he told him that the gentleman (meaning you) must ride the mare to the edge of the cliff at the Land's-End, and look over,—having no friend or assistant within fifty yards of him."

"Ha! ha! ha! that's easy enough," said Morley; "I was considered the best horseman in my regiment, and I am passionately fond of riding. Why, I have jumped on the back of a colt that had never been haltered before, and broken it in, so that a child could ride it, before I got off its back again. I know the secret, and can tame a horse by whispering in his ear. So you may consider your misfortunes at an end, if that will do it, my good friend Brown?"

"No, sir," said Mrs. Brown, very decidedly; "there shall be no such risk as that run for anything belonging to me. Lev the mare alone,—she'll get round again; an' ef she don't, 'twas no fault of yours, sir."

"But, ef the gentleman esn't afeard," chimed in poor Mr. Brown, "why not ———"

"Brown!" said his wife, in a voice which made him start; "I wish to gracious 'The Maister' had told you to ride the mare yourself. I b'lieve you wud have b'en fool enough to have done et, and then I shud ha' got rid of two troubles together. Drat the mare!" And, in her anger, she took up a large bunch of furze, and threw it on the fire, which was burning on the hearth, and sent it blazing up the large chimney, while her husband shuffled away towards the door, intending to go into the stable, his usual place of refuge from the two fires, which generally blazed together within; for when his wife was in one of her tantrums, and exercised her tongue more than usual, she generally put a good blast into the chimney, and they blazed away together. Before poor Mr. Brown reached the door, however, he was brought up "*with a round turn*," as Lieut. Fowler expressed it, by the sweet voice of his wife, who said, sharply,—

"Brown! did you hear Lieut. Fowler ask for a glass of ale for self and friend?"

"No, Peggy, dear, I dedn't," said he; "but I'll draw the glasses, of course I will. Polly! Polly! Why, wherever es that maid?"

So the glasses of ale were drawn, although the order was entirely in Mrs. Brown's own imagination; for neither of the gentlemen had given one;—but it was the very thing they both wished, and, no doubt, would have ordered very soon, had not their wishes been anticipated by the landlady, who always had an eye to business.

The two gentlemen then took a stroll together, and Lieut. Fowler tried to dissuade his friend from this rash and foolish undertaking, but to no purpose. He was determined to do it, he said,—it was just the thing he liked; for English sports were so tame, after those he had been accustomed to for the last two years. Hunting tigers and lions,—that was the sport for him.

"If you are really determined," said Fowler, "I shall bring the girls up from Pendrea-house to have a look at you; but I think you will alter your mind before the morning."

Mrs. Brown had prepared a very nice dinner, and so the friends enjoyed two or three hours' social chat. Morley had heard no tidings of his brother, he said, nor had anyone found anything that was likely to have been his, as far as he could learn; and so he supposed he was not in that ship. But he should remain a day or two longer, he said, to make further search.

When his friend rose to leave, Morley said he would go out a little way with him, and he would ride the mare to try her temper and her paces.

Mrs. Brown was obliged to yield when she found that the gentleman was determined on the feat, and she trusted that the well-known good temper and tractability of the mare would carry them both through with safety,—although the fright into which the mare had been thrown two days before, without any apparent cause, as it seemed, tended to weaken Mrs. Brown's confidence in the perfect steadiness of her husband's pet.

CHAPTER XII.

THE AWFUL RIDE.

THE eventful morning arrived. But it had been kept a profound secret, fearing that, if a rumour of this dangerous feat being about to take place got generally known, there would be a concourse of people on the ground,—and the mare, however steady she was, might get frightened.

Mr. Brown walked up early to the point, and sat behind a rock, from whence he could have a good view without being seen. Lieut. Fowler and the young ladies from Pendrea were early on the ground also; and they took their stations also behind some rocks, but in a more conspicuous place than Mr. Brown. There were a few other spectators, but very few, scattered about among the rocks. They waited some time in anxious expectation, but no rider appeared.

"Morley has altered his mind, no doubt," said Lieut. Fowler to the ladies: "and I am glad of it; for it is a dangerous feat to perform, on a strange horse."

"Oh! I wish it may be so," said Blanche: "for, although I came to oblige Maud, I shall shut my eyes when he goes down to the point."

"Nonsense," said the majestic Maud; I don't think I should be afraid to perform the feat myself, if I were a man;—I should like it. But here he comes. I thought he wouldn't shew the white feather."

At that moment the object of their solicitude came towards them, mounted on the famous mare, Jessie. She had been well fed, and carefully groomed, and her master's comb had evidently gone through her tail and mane more than once that morning.

Morley took off his hat to the ladies, and chatted with them a few minutes, laughing at the idea of there being any danger in his riding quietly to the point and back. The ladies admired and patted the beautiful creature he was riding; and even Blanche thought there could be no danger on such a beautiful quiet animal as that.

Lieut. Fowler, however, even then, tried to dissuade his friend from the attempt.

"Don't be such a faint-hearted old codger," said Morley, laughing. And, taking off his hat again to the ladies, he cantered easily down towards the point.

The promontory, clothed with short grass, slopes gently down towards the extreme point of the Land's-End for about fifty yards, and then breaks off suddenly, and the cliffs go down perpendicularly some two or three hundred feet, except that, here and there, in the side of the cliff, at various distances, may be seen, by a person whose head is steady enough to look down, projecting rocks just sufficient to break the fall, but not large enough for a body to rest upon for a single moment.

At the bottom, the sea washes the base of the cliffs, coming booming in with every wave, and surging and dashing against the rocks and cliffs beneath, sending its spray sometimes in rough weather completely over those towering cliffs,—a fearful sight for a man with a steady head to look down upon, but for a horse!

On comes the bold rider,—steadily,—carefully. The mare doesn't like it at first, and turns round when she is within a few yards of the edge of the precipice. The turf is soft, and she capers a little. The rider pats her neck, and turns her head again, gently, towards the cliffs. She goes on gently! gently! he patting her neck, and sitting steadily on her back. At last they are standing on the very

edge of the precipice, and are both looking over. Hurrah!! The
deed is done!! All eyes are bent on the bold rider, and are holding
their breath. A single false step, even now, would precipitate them
into the abyss below, and both must be dashed in pieces. Awful
thought! The deed is done, however, and Mr. Brown's misfortunes
are at an end. The rider turns his horse to ride back to his friends in
triumph. He has just turned her head round towards the green turf
again, when something attracts the mare's attention. She trembles!
Her back is towards the precipice,—her hind feet close to the edge of
the cliff! Neither horse nor rider sees the extent of the danger, for
their backs are towards it. The mare refuses to proceed; the rider
urges her; she rears! Another moment and they must be dashed
in pieces,—nothing can save them. All is breathless anxiety among
the spectators. No one has the presence of mind to speak. A voice
at this moment is heard distinctly, stentorian in its anxiety,—"*Throw
yourself off the horse, and hold on!!!*" The young officer obeys
the voice instantly, as if it had been a command from his superior
officer. He flings himself off, and holds on by the turf, *like grim
death*, digging his fingers into the soft ground to hold on the firmer;
for he now hears the horse go down over the precipice,—down!
down! bumping on the projecting rocks in the fall, and *screeching*,
as horses and all animals will do in extreme danger and suffering.
The rider had fallen on the turf, it is true; but he had barely saved
himself, for *his legs dangled over the edge of the precipice!*

He could not stir. He felt as if he was holding himself up by his
fingers, which he had dug into that soft turf, and this seemed giving
way every instant; but it was not so in reality. His body was safely
lodged on the ground, although his feet were hanging over, and as
long as he could hold on he was safe; but he couldn't hold on so
very long. And then—oh! horror!—his terror and fright caused
him to fancy a thousand horrid deaths in an instant of time. Before
he had been lying on the turf two minutes, however, a tall, strong-
built, powerful-looking man, came bounding down towards him
from one of the rocks just above, and, seizing him round the waist,
lifted him up in his strong arms, and carried him to a safer resting-
place. By this time he had fainted, and was unconscious of the
attentions which were being paid him.

His providential deliverer was no other than Josiah Trenow, who
had come there to see the feat, and was standing behind a rock, at no
great distance from the point. And he it was who had the presence
of mind to shout to the rider to throw himself off, when he saw the
horse rear; and it was his strong arm that lifted the poor terror-
stricken man from his perilous position.

Had it not been for the presence of mind of this bold strong man,
the young officer might still have gone over; for he had not the

power to move a limb, and, when he fainted, and let go his hold in
the grass, he must have followed the horse,—down! down! Oh!
terrible fate!!!

CHAPTER XIII.

ITS CONSEQUENCES.

No one thought of the fate of Mr. Brown's favourite mare. All the
spectators clustered round the prostrate man. Maud Pendray looked
on him as a hero; she seemed to worship him with her eyes. Blanche
wept tears of joy that he was saved from what everyone thought
inevitable destruction. Poor Mr. Brown didn't know what to say or
do. He called upon Peggy, and said several times, as if talking to
his pet, "Wo! ho! Jessie! gently, mare! steady, now!" And then
the poor man sat down on a rock, apart from the rest, and burst
into tears.

Those of the party who alone were equal to the occasion, were
Lieut. Fowler and Josiah Trenow. They collected the few men
together who happened to be present, and, between them, they
carried the terror-stricken man to "The First and Last Inn," at
Sennen—that being the nearest public-house to the scene of the
accident.

A man on horseback was despatched to Penzance for a surgeon,
and the patient was put to bed at once.

A fortnight passed away, and the patient was fast recovering, but
he could not shake off the gloomy and depressing thoughts, which
were continually recurring, whenever he heard the sea, or saw
the cliffs.

One day, the surgeon announced that there was to be a grand ball
at Penzance, in about a fortnight,—the precise day was not fixed;
and he advised his patient to go. Change of scene, and the excitement of the music and the dancing, and the company, he thought,
would draw his mind away from those ever-present and depressing
thoughts. His friend Fowler had promised to go with the Pendray
party, and they were all delighted to learn that Morley had consented
to join them also.

Poor Alrina! it was an anxious day for her. She knew that her
lover was gone out on the mare to attempt that daring feat; and she
knew, also, the extent of the risk he was incurring,—for she had
often, in her solitary rambles, walked down to the edge of the Land's-
End cliffs, and looked over, out of curiosity, and it made her shudder
when she thought of him. Even should he be able to get the mare

down to the brink,—sitting there at the mercy of the horse, one false step, or a moment's giddiness, must be fatal to both. In the midst of her meditations, news was brought that the horse and its rider had both fallen over the cliff, and were dashed in pieces. She threw herself on her bed, and tried to believe that the report was false; but no,—she feared it must be true, for she had before worked her mind up to the belief that the feat could not be accomplished in safety.

She was overwhelmed with grief; and when Alice Ann came up, a few hours afterwards, and told her that Josiah was downstairs, and had brought a message for her from Mr. Morley, the sudden and blessed news that he was alive, affected her almost as much as the dreadful news of his death had done. She was quite overcome by her feelings. Sometimes she would laugh heartily, and then burst into a torrent of tears, until it ended in a violent fit of hysterics.

It was a long time before Alice Ann could pacify her, and she dared not call in the assistance of Miss Freeman, for she knew that her aunt did not sympathize with "young ladies' vagaries," as she called them. Besides, she was again closeted with her brother, who had been from home nearly all the day, and had but just returned.

When she was sufficiently recovered, Alrina saw Josiah, and received the kind message which her lover had sent her; and from Josiah she heard the true but sad tale. He told her all, from the beginning. Mr. Morley was as weak as a young baby, he said, and for hours after the accident he trembled all over, as he lay in bed, so that the bed shook under him. The doctor had desired that he should be kept perfectly quiet, and that a watch should be kept with him, night and day; for he feared delirium. He had left Mr. Fowler with him now, he said; but Mr. Morley had requested Josiah to return as soon as possible, and stay with him also; for he had a strange nervous feeling that he was *still falling*, and nothing relieved him but feeling Josiah's strong arm round his waist;—he felt safe then, and so Josiah had sat for hours on the poor terror-stricken young man's bed, holding him in his arms; and the sufferer would cry out like a little frightened child, if his supporter did but move, and beg him not to let him fall over,—for he could not divest himself of the idea that he was still on the brink of the precipice.

Alrina listened with profound attention to Josiah's description of the scene, and of her lover's present prostrate condition. She longed to go to him, and to be his nurse; but there were many reasons, both on his account, and her own, why she should not do so.

She wrote a short note, which Josiah promised to deliver into his hands; but he said he could not promise to bring an answer in writing, for Mr. Morley's hand trembled so that he could not hold a pen, nor even the glass in which he took his medicine.

F

Although her mind was set at rest in a measure, yet Alrina had enough to occupy her thoughts till bedtime, and so she retired to her room again, and desired Alice Ann to tell her aunt, if she enquired after her, that she had a headache, and was gone to lie down a little.

Before she had been in her room long, however, Alice Ann came to the door, and said "The Maister" wanted Miss Reeney at once.

"My father!" exclaimed Alrina; "what can he possibly want!"

"I do no more knaw than you," replied Alice Ann; "but he told me to fetch you down, f'rall I told 'n you wor gone to bed poorly."

"Well, I suppose I must obey," said Alrina, heaving a heavy sigh. "I wonder what he wants me for? it is so unusual for him to send for me. I wish I knew why he was so cruel as to order Frederick to perform that perilous feat to-day,—some hidden motive, no doubt. I'll try and find it out. I've a great mind to ask him, point blank; but then ———"

"Come, Miss Reeney," said Alice Ann, coming to the door again; "'The Maister' es axing when you're comin', so I told 'n you wor dressin'."

When Alrina came out into the front passage from her bedroom, which was in the back of the house looking into the little garden, she found her father waiting for her near the door of his "private room." He opened the door and desired her to follow him.

Her curiosity was to be gratified, then, at last, but not in the way she very much liked, for she fancied that this interview would not be a very pleasant one,—why, she didn't know. Perhaps her father was now about to reveal some of those mysteries which hung over them. At another time she might not have felt these painful forebodings, but her nerves had been unstrung by the events of the day; and she felt now as if an unkind word, or an unexpected disclosure, would upset her again. So much more terrible are imaginary misfortunes and troubles oftentimes when seen at a distance, than they are in reality, when they actually take place.

Mr. Freeman took his seat at the top of the room, near a large table, and pointed to a chair, which Alrina felt was intended as an invitation for her to be seated also. This gave her courage to look round the room. There were some large boxes about, and several cupboards and a few more chairs; but, in general appearance, the room was pretty much like other sitting-rooms, except that it required to be dusted, she thought. And, when she had finished her survey of the room, she had time to look at her father again, before he spoke. He was evidently trying to overawe her, and when she found out that, it gave her fresh courage.

Mr. Freeman, as he sat in that large, curiously-fashioned chair, seemed a fine-looking man,—much younger in appearance than he generally looked; because, as we have before stated, he affected the old man, and seemed to wish to be thought much older than he really was.

"Alrina," he said, at length, "how did you become acquainted with that young man?"

"What young man?" said she, as innocently as she could.

"Alrina!" he said again, looking at her sternly; "you know whom I mean, and therefore let's have no prevarication."

"His sister was one of my schoolfellows," she replied, "and she introduced me to her brother."

"Oh!" replied her father, smiling; "and you each became affected with that incurable malady which silly people call 'love;' and you have met him again? And where is your old schoolfellow now, pray?" asked Mr. Freeman.

"She is residing with Mrs. Courland, I believe," replied Alrina, "at Ashley Hall."

"Thank you, Alrina. That was all I wanted to know. Now, you can go to your room again, if you don't feel well, and let the servant bring you up some tea. Good night."

So, then, this terrible ordeal in the "private room," which Alrina had dreaded so much but a few minutes before, and racked her brain to imagine what her father could possibly want of her, had ended in his asking a plain simple question or two, and her giving him answers to match. And although she had intended to ask him why he had been so cruel as to order that dangerous feat to be performed by that young stranger, and many other important questions, she had been dismissed so abruptly, that she had actually said nothing.

The whole scene seemed so absurd that she burst into a hearty laugh when she reached her own little bedroom once more.

CHAPTER XIV.

MRS. BROWN TELLS THE CONJUROR A BIT OF HER MIND.

POOR Mr. Brown! he remained on the rocks long after the other spectators had left, and would have remained there much longer, had he not been roused from his reverie by a gentle tap on his shoulder.

"Billy," said he, looking up; "let's go into the stable and have a look at Jessie, boy. She must have a good rub-down and a warm mash to-night."

"Come along," said the boy. And, taking Mr. Brown by the arm, he led him home to his amiable but eccentric wife.

"What! Billy!" she exclaimed, as the pair entered the kitchen; "where, in the name of goodness ded you spring from?"

"Why, I ha'n't b'en away, have I?" replied the sly boy.

"Now, that's enough—a plenty," said Mrs. Brown, looking at the boy with her keen grey eyes. "I can see through a millstone so well as most people. I ha'n't b'en away, says aw!"

"No, have I?" said he, looking innocently at his mistress.

"Areah, thon! Now, I'll tell 'ee, Billy. He that ha' b'en your maister the last three days, may take 'ee for the next three days, for what I do care; for in my house you sha'n't stop,—there, na. My eyes ha' b'en opening wider and wider evar sence last night. A croom of chat with one, and a croom of chat with another, have opened them so wide, that I can see round a corner a'most."

"I don't knaw what you do main," said the boy.

"Iss you do," replied Mrs. Brown, shaking her head; "so you march,—and dont you come anist my door agen for a bra' spur."

The boy saw that his quondam mistress was in earnest; so he took the hint and made himself scarce.

"And now, Mr. Brown," said she, turning to her husband, who had seated himself in the chimney-corner, "what do you think of yourself, I shud like to knaw? Your Jessie mare es come to a purty pass, esn't she? Ef the young gentleman had gone over cliff too, I shud nevar ha' b'en good no more. To go for to slock the young gentleman into et like that wor a shame, an' so et wor. You an' 'The Maister' too oft to be spefflicated,—iss you ded."

"'The Maister' wor right, Peggy," said Mr. Brown;—"the boy es come back. Wo! ho! Jessie! gently, mare! steady, now! Wo! ho!"

"John Brown," said his wife, "I ha' thoft for a bra' bit that there was but one biggar fool than you in the world, an' that's me, for marryin' such a g'eat lazy, knaw-nothen' pattick. John Brown, go to bed!" And this command was given in such an authoritative tone, that Mr. Brown took it literally, and, lighting a bed-light, although it was broad daylight, he took off his shoes at the bottom of the stairs, as was his wont, and went to bed in right earnest; and in ten minutes he was fast asleep.

"Well, that's a comfort," said Mrs. Brown.

"What's a comfort?" said Mrs. Trenow, who had come in to have a croom of chat with the landlady; "you've had your drop of gin an' peppermint, I s'pose?"

"No, sure, I ha'n't," replied Mrs. Brown; "but we will now, for I do feel that there's something wantin', cheeld vean."

So the two gossips were very soon seated comfortably over their little drop of cordial, seasoned with a pinch of snuff; and they wound up their moderate carousal with a cup of tea.

"You said something wor a comfort when I came in," said Mrs. Trenow.

"Iss fie! hark!" replied Mrs. Brown, turning up her ear in a listening attitude.

"You've got a pig bad, I s'pose?" said Mrs. Trenow; "but what comfort there es in that, I caen't tell. Ill-wished again, I s'pose? Semmen to me 'The Maister' ha' got bra' work now."

"No, my dear, tesn't the pig. Hark again!" said Mrs. Brown.

"Why, 'tes up in the chamber, to be sure," replied Mrs. Trenow, listening.

"Iss fie, 'tes up in the chamber, sure nuff," said Mrs. Brown; "and there he'd sleep and snore till to-morrow dennar-time ef I dedn't rouse 'n out."

"Dear lor'! like that, es aw? Whisht too 'pon om, now that the mare es killed, I s'pose," said Mrs. Trenow. "Do 'ee think that 'The Maister' had any grudge agen that young gentleman, do 'ee?"

"What shud he knaw 'bout the young gentleman?" returned Mrs. Brown. "I'll tell 'ee, Mrs. Trenow, 'The Maister' wean't lev you nor me knaw what he do think; for thinken' es one thing and spaiken' es another, weth he, I'll assure 'ee."

"But the boy came back to the very minute, I do hear," said Mrs. Trenow, who could not be persuaded out of her belief in "The Maister's" wisdom.

"I tell 'ee, Mrs. Trenow," said Mrs. Brown, in a confidential whisper; "'tes my belief that ef they two wor to take off their shoes you wud see two cloven hoofs,—iss I do."

"Oh! lor!" shrieked both the women, as they looked up, after their little confidential whisper; for behind them stood Mr. Freeman himself.

"A glass of mild ale, if you please, Mrs. Brown," said he, in his blandest tone, as he took his usual seat in the chimney-corner.

"Yes, sir," said the landlady. And while she was drawing the ale, Mrs. Trenow took the opportunity of slipping out. Mrs. Brown was as shrewd and cunning in her way as Mr. Freeman was in his, and, while she was drawing the glass of ale, she began to reflect on the probable purport of this early visit; for "The Maister" seldom came there until much later in the evening, when he knew he should find some of those peculiarly constituted individuals there, whom Alrina generally designated "goostrumnoodles," and whom he seldom found much difficulty in frightening to his heart's content. On these occasions, Mrs. Brown never interfered; for she had an eye to business, and she knew that the more terror there was produced in the brains of these poor numskulls, the more stimulants they would consume. But, now, there was no occasion for any dissimulation; and so she determined she would tell "The Maister" a bit of her mind,—for she believed that he had some hidden and wicked motive for prompting her husband to induce that young gentleman to undertake so dangerous a feat as the one he had attempted that day.

"Your husband has met with a serious loss to-day," said Mr. Freeman.

"Iss; and I s'pose you are come down for to make et good," replied Mrs. Brown, rather tartly.

"Me!" said Mr. Freeman; "what have I to do with Mr. Brown's losses, more than having a feeling of sympathy for the misfortunes of an old friend?"

"You dedn't tell Brown that the young gentleman must ride the mare up there, I s'pose?" said Mrs. Brown, taking a cunning side glance at her visitor.

"What motive could I have had for such a suggestion as that?" asked Mr. Freeman, looking innocently at Mrs. Brown; "and who could possibly have said that I had anything to do with the matter?"

"I tell 'ee, Maister Freeman," said Mrs. Brown; "there's more of your doin's knawn than you do think. What you got out of that wreck es knawn to a bra' many, f'rall they're afeard for to spaik et out, down sous."

This made Mr. Freeman wince a little; for he had such confidence in his own cunning and ability in frightening and deceiving his neighbours, that he never for a moment supposed that they would presume to speculate on, or try to pry into, his private gains, or discuss his actions or motives.

His eyes were now opened, and Mrs. Brown perceived that he felt very uncomfortable—a most unusual and impolitic feeling for him to exhibit in the presence of so shrewd a woman as Mrs. Brown, who drew her own conclusions therefrom; and after her visitor had drank his ale, and left her alone once more, she sat down, and, putting "this against that," saw the "ins and outs of things," as she expressed it, more clearly than she had ever done before.

CHAPTER XV.

THE MYSTERIOUS STRANGER AT THE PENZANCE BALL.

FREDERICK MORLEY was getting strong again, and had met Alrina several times, and pressed her to go to the ball at Penzance; but this she could not think of doing, she said. Neither her father nor her aunt would sanction that, she was quite sure; for, although her education had been such as so fit her for ball-room society, and her beauty eminently qualified her for a ball-room belle, yet the equivocal position of her father, and the mystery which appeared to hang over them all, precluded her from enjoying at present the society of him she loved so much, in that sphere to which he of right belonged. He was unwilling to go without her, and had almost made up his mind not to go; but she knew it would do him good to mix in the society to which he had been accustomed, and she knew, also, that if he declined accompanying the Pendray party to the ball, his motives would be canvassed, and their secret love, which it was best for the present should be concealed, might become known; and so Alrina persuaded him to go.

Carriages were sent out from Penzance to take the Pendray family and the two officers to the ball, which was expected to be a very aristocratic affair. When they arrived at the hotel, they found that the best sitting-room and bedroom—which Squire Pendray wished to have secured for his party—had been engaged that morning by a strange gentleman, who came in from Hayle in a carriage-and-four, the waiter said. He was dressed like a foreigner, and had a large trunk with him, but no servant. He seemed rich, and gave orders as if he had been accustomed to be waited upon by a good many servants, and would not be satisfied with any but the best rooms. He took two tickets for the ball, the waiter said, and therefore, he supposed, he expected a friend, but no one had yet arrived.

The ball was a very brilliant one, for a country ball in those days, and everyone seemed in anxious expectation for the entrance of the stranger—especially the young ladies. Miss Pendray looked splendid. She had impressed Frederick Morley into her service, as her favoured beau; for she had taken a great interest in him since his accident, and had paid him marked attention,—indeed, she now looked upon him as a hero, whom she could almost worship. Such deeds of daring had a charm for her which few else could understand. But still, he did not come up to her standard of manly perfection. There was scarcely enough of that romantic devotion towards herself displayed, which she so much required, and demanded from those she took an interest in. This placed Morley in a very awkward position, for he could not help seeing that he had attracted Miss Pendray's attention, and that she seemed more pleased with his society than that of any other gentleman of her acquaintance. But he could not return it as she evidently would have wished him to do; for he had a secret treasure concealed within his breast, far dearer to him than all the charms of person and mind and fortune which Miss Pendray possessed. He would not exchange his Alrina's love for the fairest and brightest jewel that the world could bestow; for, without her, all the world to him would be an empty and worthless blank.

He enjoyed the ball as much as he could do in the absence of her who was uppermost in his thoughts. The excitement of the music, the company, and the dancing, brought back reminiscences of

similar scenes abroad.   His wonted spirits returned, and he entered
thoroughly into the pleasures of the moment, and forgot for a time
the scene on the cliffs, the horse's screech of terror, and the
sound of his falling from rock to rock, as he went down over that
awful precipice, while he himself was dangling on the very edge.
He danced with all alike,—one lady was the same, to him, as another,
there,—and he did not notice that Miss Pendray had withdrawn
from the dancing, and was sitting alone at one end of the room, when
the stranger entered. All eyes were directed towards the door, as the
waiter showed him in ; but his eyes were evidently attracted by the
magnificent form of Miss Pendray, as she sat alone on a seat nearly
opposite the door.

One of the stewards immediately went up to him, introducing
himself as " steward," and offering to present him to a partner.

The stranger bowed, and expressed a wish to be presented to the
lady who was sitting opposite.

He gave his name to the steward who introduced him to Miss
Pendray as " Mr. Smith." The stranger was the topic of conversation
throughout the room.   He certainly looked like a foreigner.   His
dress was that of an Indian gentleman of rank of those days. His coat
was of the finest purple satin, trimmed and ornamented with gold ;
a white satin waistcoat, tastefully embroidered with silver ; and white
kerseymere breeches of the finest texture, fastened below the knee
with a silver band ; the white silk stocking displaying to advantage a
finely-turned leg,—his shoes being fastened with small gold buckles.
He was a tall, fine-looking man, apparently between forty and fifty
years of age—nearer the former, perhaps, than the latter.   He
seemed to be making himself very agreeable to Miss Pendray ; for
she became full of animation, and her handsome countenance lit up
radiant with beauty.

The stranger would not dance, but was introduced, by turn, to
almost all the ladies of note in the room.   Miss Pendray, however,
was the principal attraction, and he returned to her side again
and again.

Frederick Morley looked at the stranger several times with earnest
attention, and, after a time, became absorbed in thought.   He
was not jealous of the attention bestowed on him by the lady whom
he had led into the room. No, it could not have been that. He did
not care enough for Miss Pendray to feel jealous of her attentions
being bestowed elsewhere. No, it was not that. He watched the
stranger narrowly, and he came to the conclusion that he was not
the person he assumed to be. "Smith" was a feigned name,
evidently. His dress and ornaments betokened him to have been a
resident in India. India was a country familiar to Morley by name,
and dear to him, as having been the residence of his father for so

many years, and the birthplace of his mother, his brother and sister, and himself. He had not seen his brother since he and his sister were brought over by their father, when they were children, and when that never-to-be-forgotten calamity befel his father, which shortened his life. That false accusation was still hanging over the family. He had been reminded of it, in almost every letter he had received from his brother since their father's death ; and, in his last letter, he said he had wound up their father's affairs, and his own, in India, and he intended to return to England by the next ship, to arrange the property according to their father's will, and to make a strict search after the wretches who had murdered their own father, on that terrible night, and caused the suspicion and accusation to rest on an innocent man. He would travel all over England, he said, and spend the whole of his fortune, to clear his father from that foul suspicion.

Frederick had but a very faint recollection of his brother ; but a strange, unaccountable idea, took possession of him during supper. He thought he observed the stranger start once or twice, when the name of "Morley" happened to be spoken by anyone at the table— as was frequently the case ; for Frederick was a stranger too, and, therefore, received great attention from the stewards, and, indeed, from the ladies, whose goodness of heart frequently prompts them to show greater attention to strange gentlemen than to those whom they are in the habit of meeting every day.

Ever since he had heard of the wreck of that East-Indiaman at Pendeen, he had been persuading himself that his brother might have been one of the passengers on board that ill-fated vessel ; and, as very few bodies had been washed on shore, it was probable that one of the boats might have withstood the storm, and, when the sea was more tranquil, they might have landed somewhere on the north coast. It was possible. There was just sufficient possibility in it to keep alive hope.

What if this stranger should turn out to be his brother ? It was scarcely probable ; but yet the idea had seized hold of him, and he could not get rid of it.

The discovery and exposure of those wretches, who had been the means of hastening their father's death, and embittering his last moments, was the constant theme in all his brother's letters, and seemed uppermost in his thoughts. Year after year he longed to be able to give up his business in India, and return to England seemingly for that one purpose. He had witnessed the effect the stain of this false accusation had produced on his father's mind and bodily health, and had seen him pine away under it ; and he had received his father's dying injunction to sift the affair to the bottom as soon as he could return to England.

He had refrained from marrying in India, that he might have no ties to keep him there after his business affairs were wound up. He would, of course, change his name in searching after the fugitives, and he might have commenced at once, Frederick thought, however remote the chance of his finding them on the narrow strip of land which terminates the kingdom of England.

In spite of its improbability, Morley could not divest himself of the idea which had taken such a deep hold of him, and he determined on speaking to the stranger after supper, and asking him if he had ever met with a merchant of the name of Morley in India. He was disappointed, however; for, almost immediately after supper, Frederick was seized with one of his nervous attacks, and it was as much as his friend Fowler could do to support him to his room; and when he came down to a late breakfast, he found that the stranger had gone out for his morning's walk.

CHAPTER XVI.

JOSIAH'S ASTONISHMENT AT THE EFFECT PRODUCED BY THE DISPLAY . OF HIS TREASURE-TROVE.

JOSIAH TRENOW had been in constant attendance on Frederick Morley, ever since the accident. It may appear strange that a young man so strong and brave as Morley, and who had seen so much service abroad, and been engaged in the most dangerous sports that can possibly be pursued, should have been so entirely prostrated by this accident; but so it was.

It was Josiah's strong arm that had lifted him up from his perilous position on the cliffs; and, for many days, he did not feel safe unless that strong arm was near, to be thrown round him when the terrible thought of his perilous situation seized him; and Josiah was beginning to like his young master—for such he seemed now to have become, without any formal agreement having been entered into between them.

While his young master was at Penzance attending the ball, Josiah went to the mine where he had been working, to put things straight, and to see the captain, and get another man put in his place; for Morley had asked him to remain with him until he was obliged to join his regiment again—which would not be for some time, as he had obtained an extension of leave, in consequence of the accident, and the strong certificate sent to head-quarters from the surgeon who attended him. He had remained at "The First and Last Inn," at Sennen, ever since,—partly to be near his friend Fowler, and partly because he fancied the removal to another place might cause a return of those dreadful feelings of nervous terror which he had now in a measure overcome.

On the morning after his return from Penzance, Josiah came into his master's room, after breakfast, carrying a small box under his arm, which appeared to be very heavy, and, placing it on the table, he said,

"I've got something here, sar, that I do want you to see. I picked 'n up in the sand after the wreck, an' I oppened om, an' wor frightened sure 'nuff."

"Frightened at opening a small box!" said Morley, smiling; "I thought your nerves were stronger, Josiah."

"You shall see for yourself," returned Josiah. And he proceeded to take out the screws with which the box was fastened, when, to Morley's utter astonishment, he saw that the box was filled to the brim with Indian gold coins, and, in one corner of the box, closely packed down, there was a piece of thick white writing-paper, neatly folded up.

"There, sar," said Josiah; "es et any wonder that I shud be frightened?"

"No, indeed!" said his master, taking up a few of the coins, and examining them; "there must be many thousands of pounds in this little box. Why, you're a lucky man, Josiah. And you consider these all your own, of course, according to the doctrine of all Cornish wreckers?"

"No, I don't sar," replied Josiah; "but I caen't tell whose they are,—I wish I cud. I b'lieve that paper wud tell, ef so be that I cud read 'n; but I caen't read writen', f'rall I can read prent, ef they're brave an' big letters. I carr'd that paper up to Maister Freeman, but I dedn't car' up the box,—no fie! Ef you had seed his face when he looked 'pon the paper fust, you'd never forgit 'n no more. 'Twor whisht sure 'nuf."

"Well, what did he say?" asked Morley, who felt more interested in hearing something about the conjuror, who had so nearly caused his death, than curiosity as to the contents of the paper.

"Say?" exclaimed Josiah; "why, nothen' for a bra' bit. He read 'n down twice, quite study, like, an' then aw looked up 'pon me, like one startled, an' folded up the paper. An' then he said, 'Josiah,' says he to me, 'I can't make this out 'less I do see the box that 'twor in; bring et to me at once,' says he. ''Tes an unlucky thing for you to keep in your house,' says he; 'your pigs will die, and, maybe, you'll all be laid down, and rise no more,' says he. 'Bring the box, and all the contents, within one hour,' says he, 'or else you are all doomed,' says he. An' weth that he wor goen' for to put the paper in his pocket; but I catched 'n by the arm, and made 'n screech ten thousand murders, an' drop the paper, an' I very soon picked 'n up

agen. An' then he tore to me, an' tried for to catch the paper agen;
but I wor too quick for 'n, an' I tripped 'n up weth my toe, an' left
'n lyin' 'pon the planchen'; and then I trapesed away down ste-ars.
I reckon the maid Alice Ann wor frightened too; for I b'lieve in my
conscience she wor harken' outside the door,—for I nearly knacked
har down, poor soul, but I cudn't stop to see."

"Let me see the paper," said Morley, who was now as anxious to
see it, as he had been indifferent before.

So Josiah took it out, and unfolded it very carefully; and if he
had been astonished to see the strange appearance of Mr. Freeman's
countenance when he perused that paper, he was perfectly astounded
now, to see the effect the perusal of it was producing on Mr. Morley;
and he began to think that the box and all it contained were
bewitched, as Mr. Freeman had said, and he entertained serious
thoughts of carrying it down to the cliffs and throwing it over. At
length, Mr. Morley, having finished the perusal of the paper for the
third time, leaned his elbows on the table, supporting his head with
his hands, in which he still clutched the paper, and sobbed aloud;
for his nerves were still too weak to bear up against any sudden
shock without giving vent to his feelings.

Josiah stood looking at his master and the box alternately, having
a confused idea of a shipwreck and a man and horse falling over
cliff, with a box of gold tied to them as a weight to pull them down.
At last Mr. Morley recovered sufficiently to see that Josiah was
looking bewildered; so he thought it right to read the paper to him,
which did not, however, enlighten him very much till further
explanation was given.

The mysterious paper contained these words :—

"*I, Alexander Morley, on my dying bed, enjoin my two sons,
William and Frederick Morley, to make the strictest search for
those two wretches, who committed the murder, of which I was
accused, and to use all possible means to bring them to justice,
or to induce them to confess their crime, that my bones may rest
in peace. The contents of this box to be used in the prosecution
thereof.   "Alexander Morley.*"

"Well," said Josiah, "I ar'n't much furder footh, I think." And
he looked at his master with a vacant stare. Mr. Morley, therefore,
thought it best to entrust this faithful and honest man with the
whole circumstances relative to the murder, which made him stare
more than ever; but it was not a vacant stare now.

"You must let me take this paper, Josiah," said Mr. Morley;
"and perhaps I had better take care of the box also, for the
present."

"By all mains, sar," said Josiah; "for, putting this and that together, 'tes surely your father's box, and sent here for a wise purpose."

"This accident has brought many sad reflections into my mind, Josiah," replied Mr. Morley. "I cannot now have any doubt of the fate of my poor brother. He was, no doubt, bringing this valued box home, that we might proceed together in the search. He is gone; but Providence has thrown this box in my way, as a powerful incentive to use my utmost exertions, single-handed, to perform the task allotted to my brother and myself by our poor father."

"You sha-ant go by yourself, sar," said Josiah; "I'll help 'ee as far as I can, ef you'll lev me to."

"You shall," replied his master. "I am indebted to you for my life, and for the discovery of this box, so that our destinies seem blended together, in an unaccountable manner. You shall not go unrewarded, I assure you. We will use this money, as it is ordered, in searching for the guilty parties."

"Zackly like that," returned Josiah; "an' ef I wor you I wud ax Maister Freeman. Whether et wor his conjuring knawledge, or what, I caen't tell; but semmen' to me I thoft he knawed somethen'."

"No, no," replied Morley; "it was the wish to get the gold into his possession that made him look so odd. He is avaricious, and he thought to frighten you into the foolish act of bringing the box to him, when he would either have kept it altogether, or have taken a large toll out of it."

"Well, sar," said Josiah, "I'll allow you for to knaw best; but ef I wor you, I'd see Maister Freeman;—he might look to his books an' tell 'ee somethen' more than you do knaw now."

This seemed very good advice; for, even if Mr. Freeman knew nothing, Frederick thought he should at least see the conjuror in his "sanctum," as he was going to him on business, and he might have a chance of seeing Alrina, whom he had not met for several days; for she did not keep her last appointment with him two days before the ball, and he feared she might be ill, or might have been prevented by some lynx-eyed Duenna, as she had been before, when he blamed her without cause. So, for all these reasons, Frederick determined he would visit the lion in his den, and make him divulge all he knew respecting the contents of that paper, if indeed he knew anything— which, however, the unhappy young man very much doubted.

CHAPTER XVII.

THE BORROWED FEATHERS OF THE PEACOCK FAIL TO CONCEAL ENTIRELY THE NATURAL PLUMAGE OF THE JACKDAW.

THE strange gentleman who had caused such a sensation at the ball, and who called himself "Mr. Smith," continued to reside at the hotel, at Penzance, in a style which evinced great wealth, and perhaps rank, as the inhabitants generally thought; so he was called on by most of the aristocracy of the neighbourhood, and invited to dine at their houses. He frequently rode out to the Logan Rock, or Lamorna cliffs, where he met Miss Pendray—sometimes by appointment, and sometimes by accident. She seemed quite fascinated with the mysterious stranger, and would meet him in the roughest weather, and wander with him over the cliffs, while he related to her tales of romance and horror, which delighted and fascinated her; and she would look into his face, and allow him to hold her hand, as they sat side by side on the rocks, while he poured into her willing ear those tales she so delighted to listen to,—and by degrees he blended, almost imperceptibly at first, his own feelings with the more romantic scenes which he depicted so well, and shadowed forth, at length, in vague but unmistakeable language, his love and admiration of the beautiful creature by his side, until the majestic Maud was subdued into a mere mortal and received his protestations and vows of love and constancy, and returned them as fully and freely and confidingly as her sister, the gentle and innocent Blanche, would have done to him she loved above all others on earth. But, although he was always so ready and anxious to meet Miss Pendray out of doors, he avoided going to her father's house. She would frequently ask him the reason of this, but he would never satisfy her. On one occasion, after an unusually tender and protracted meeting on the cluster of rocks surrounding the Logan Rock, when he thought he had gained sufficient power over her, he asked her to elope with him; at which she was at first highly indignant. She drew herself up instantly to her full dignity, and, looking down with scorn on her lover, while her eyes flashed with indignation, she said,

"Do you take me for a silly school-girl, that you presume to make such a proposition to me? No, sir! while I reside under my father's roof, it must be from his hands, and from his house, that I must be claimed and taken, if at all."

"Nay," exclaimed her companion, in the greatest alarm and humiliation; "I meant not to offend you. My life has been one of romance from my childhood, and I thought you possessed the same romantic ideas, but in a loftier, and, I perceive, more chivalrous, form. Pardon me. The anticipation of the possession of a jewel so valuable, dazzled and disordered my brain, and I feared its loss, if left to others to decide ; your father might refuse his consent, and a thousand things might happen in the delay, to deprive me of the possession of her on whom my happiness and life depend. But your wishes shall be as commands to me ;—it shall be done methodically, and in as businesslike a manner as other poor mortals perform the same ordeal: I will ask your honoured father, who will doubtless give us his blessing : we will go to the parish church and be united, as the Cornish clodhoppers are accustomed to be, and have a quiet dinner, and after tea we will jog into Penzance, and spend the honeymoon in some comfortable lodgings. Let me go now, and speak to the good squire," continued he, taking her hand, and kneeling on the grass at her feet.

"Oh ! Mr. Smith," she said, relenting a little ; "you have drawn a very rustic picture truly of the marriage ceremony. The one great event in woman's life should be a little more brilliant and exciting than that, certainly."

"Yes, yes," said he, rising and kissing her hand ; "I knew you would not be satisfied with a humdrum marriage, and so I went, perhaps, a little too far the other way."

"Oh ! Mr. Smith," she said, turning from him, and covering her eyes with one hand, while he retained the other, "I am afraid I am doing wrong, even now. I ought not to be here,—I know I ought not, and yet ———"

"Do not speak thus, dearest Maud," said he ; "you know my devoted attachment to you, and my admiration of your noble character, and the beauties of your mind and person. Your majestic and dignified form, and the brilliancy of your eyes, attracted my attention when I entered the ball-room at Penzance, and ———"

"Allow me to remind you," replied Miss Pendray, rather haughtily, "that I do not like gross flattery ; it is repugnant to my nature ; I cannot endure it."

These expressions were uttered abruptly and incautiously, and the fair lady was aware immediately that she had said too much ; but she was so much accustomed to have her own way at home, and to be treated with the greatest deference and respect by all, and was moreover so conscious of her own perfections, that any plain allusion to them was quite repulsive to her ; it was not the first time that this mysterious stranger had mixed up a little vulgarity, as she deemed it, with his more refined conversation, and interesting and romantic tales. She did not quite understand him even now. She had never before taken him up so sharply, although she had often wished to do so ; but she feared to wound his feelings. She had now, in the excitement of the moment, expressed her thoughts more fully than she intended, and she felt sorry, and would have given worlds to recall those last expressions. She was relieved, however, from her embarrassment on that account; for, just at that moment, as she turned to reassure him, a gentlemanly looking man suddenly emerged from behind one of those lofty rocks at a little distance from where the lovers were standing, and approached towards them. Miss Pendray's back was turned towards the intruder, so that she did not notice his approach; but, as she was about to speak to her companion, she saw such a terrified, horrible expression come over his countenance, as he gazed at the gentleman who was now rapidly approaching them, that she turned round instinctively to see what it was that had so absorbed his attention, when she found herself almost face to face with the stranger, as he jumped down from a rock near her. She uttered a little shriek at the suddenness of the surprise, but immediately recovered herself sufficiently to take a hasty glance at his personal appearance, before he spoke; for he was a remarkable looking man. He was considerably above the middle height, strongly built, and robust. His hair was almost white, although, from his fresh complexion and general appearance, he was evidently still a young man—perhaps scarcely forty. His face was tanned with the sun, as if he had lived long in a warm climate. He had the appearance of a gentleman, and, from his manners, he evidently was one.

"I beg your pardon, madam," he said, "for thus intruding on you. I assure you it was quite unintentional. I was searching for Lieut. Fowler. His men, at the station, told me he was out on the coast, near by, somewhere; and, as I wished to see him, I thought I would take a stroll, with the chance of falling in with him, rather than wait indoors this beautiful morning."

"Pray don't apologize," replied Miss Pendray; "I often meet Lieut. Fowler on the cliffs, and this is not at all an unlikely place to meet with him."

"Thank you," said the stranger; and, taking off his hat to the lady, he passed on in search of the lieutenant, while Miss Pendray turned round towards Mr. Smith, whom she expected to find recovered by this time from the shock, or whatever it was, that made him look so odd, and prevented him, as she thought, from speaking to the intruder, who was now out of sight. But where was Mr. Smith? He was nowhere to be seen. She looked all round, and climbed to the topmost rock, but could see no trace of him. It was very odd, she thought; and that demoniacal look haunted her. What could it mean? Did he know that stranger, and fear him for some reason? No, that could scarcely be; for he evidently saw Mr. Smith, but he showed no signs of recognition. She knew not what to think. What did she know of Mr. Smith? Who was he? Where did he come from? He was comparatively a stranger to her. These were questions which she now began to ask herself, as she walked slowly home; and she now began to think that she had acted wrong, in meeting a mere stranger so often, clandestinely, and allowing herself to be led away by his fascinating conversation, after knowing him little more than a fortnight. These reflections smoothed and softened her naturally bold and daring spirit, and, instead of feeling a wish now to soar to the top of the loftiest rocks and cliffs, and look danger in the face without shrinking, she felt subdued and melancholy, and instinctively took the path which led down towards Lamorna Cove—the spot so loved and admired by her gentle sister.

Here she met Blanche and Lieut. Fowler searching for some rare shells on the beach, to whom she recounted her adventure with the strange gentleman with the white hair, but she did not mention the other in whom she was more interested.

Lieut. Fowler knew no such person, he said, as Miss Pendray described. Perhaps it was some inspecting officer. He could not have come on duty, however, for in that case he would have been in uniform. But whoever it was, he thought he had better go and see him; so he took leave of the two sisters, and walked away in the direction of the signal-station at Tol-pedn-Penwith, wondering who his strange visitor could be.

CHAPTER XVIII.

THE BIRDS HAVE TAKEN FLIGHT.

FREDERICK MORLEY determined on going to Mr. Freeman's house, and taking a copy of that document with him, when he hoped to be able to induce the "man of cunning" to tell him what he knew relative to the contents of that paper which Josiah had found in the box; for Josiah seemed so convinced of his being able to enlighten his master, that he was beginning himself to feel that the visit might turn out more successful and satisfactory than he at first imagined.

"I'll go weth 'ee, sar," said Josiah; "an' ef we caen't, both of es, make 'n tell, why 'twill be whisht sure nuf. I'll maul 'n brave ef aw don't tell everything; for I'm sure, semmen to me, that he wudn't look like that there, ef he dedn't knaw somethen'."

"No, no, Josiah," replied his master; "we must not resort to personal violence. You shall go with me, for you know him,—I do not,—and we shall soon see by his manner what he knows, although I have my doubts, still, as to his real knowledge of anything connected with this affair. It is his object to pretend to know more than he really does, in order to mislead ignorant people; and he thereby induces them to communicate enough to enable him to guess at the rest,—and so he gets credit for a vast amount of prescience more than he really possesses."

As they walked on slowly towards St. Just, on their important

errand, Morley's mind was filled with various thoughts and conjectures, all of the greatest moment to him. He might now be on
the point of having his great secret unravelled, or at least of gaining
some intelligence respecting it, and he was about to see Alrina's
father, and perhaps herself. He should now also know the reason
why she had not kept her last appointment with him. All these
serious reflections passing through his mind, made him silent. It was
likely to be an eventful day for him. What Josiah's thoughts were
we do not know—our little bird is silent on that point. Perhaps he
was also thinking of his Alice Ann; but this thought did not seem
to disturb him. His love was not quite so ardent, perhaps, as his
master's, or his love might probably be running more smoothly; for
he disturbed the air now and then by whistling snatches of some old
song or country jig, shewing thereby to his companion, if he felt any
interest in knowing the fact, that his faithful attendant's thoughts
didn't trouble him much. At length, after a weary walk, though not
by any means a long one, they arrived at the verge of the village;
and now Josiah took the lead, as he knew every house and almost
every stone in the place. The village was very quiet, for most of the
men were out at their work—some at the mine, and others at their
little farms—while the women were busy indoors, cleaning up a bit,
and preparing the men's dinners.

They passed the "Commercial" Hotel, which seemed to be taking
its morning nap, and reposing its dignity in the sun, which was
shining brightly on its whitewashed walls, and looking in at the
windows, and stretching itself, as far as it could, in at the open door,
making the fine sand, with which the passage was strewed, sparkle
again. The stable-door was shut,—all was quiet there. Poor Mr.
Brown's occupation was gone. Morley shuddered as he thought of
the beautiful mare; but they passed on in silence until they arrived
at the further end of the village, when Josiah stopped opposite a neat
looking farm-house, and, after a few minutes' reflection, exclaimed,

"Dash my buttons! why they're gone, to be sure."

This expression, which was said in an excited tone, recalled Morley
from his reverie, and, looking up, he saw that the house they were
standing opposite, seemed to be deserted and shut up. The window-
shutters were all closed, and the garden-gate was locked.

"That's unlucky, if this is the house," said Morley; "but they
may not be gone far. Let us enquire somewhere."

"Zackly like that," replied Josiah, in a sort of bewildered manner,
while he led the way to a cottage at a little distance off, which he
entered very unceremoniously, bidding his master to follow him.

"Where's 'The Maister' gone?" said he, addressing an elderly
woman, who was up to her elbows in soapsuds, washing at a small
washtub.

"Your sarvant, sar," said Mrs. Trenow, wiping the soapsuds from her hands and arms, without noticing her son's question.

"Set down, sar, ef you plaise," said Josiah, placing a chair for his master; for he saw that he was fatigued. "Mother es like somethen' that's very good to eat when 'tes boiled sometimes," continued Josiah; "she don't always go foreright when she's wanted to."

"Areah, then," said his mother; "the world es come to a purty pass, when cheldern do begin for to taich their mothers manners."

"Hush, mother," said Josiah, laughing, and slapping the old lady on the back. "How are 'ee, thon? I ha'n't seed 'ee for a bra' bit."

"No fie, you ha'n't," replied Mrs. Trenow. "He's gone, cheeld vean, an' joy go weth 'n, says I."

"You are speaking of Mr. Freeman, I presume," said Mr. Morley. "I came here almost on purpose to see him, and we found the house shut up. Can you give us any information respecting his movements?"

"No, sar, I caen't," replied Mrs. Trenow. "About a week ago, or so—I caen't tell to a day—Miss Freeman (that's 'The Maister's' sister, sar) told Alice Ann (that's the maid, sar) that she might have a holiday in the afternoon; an' glad enough the maid wor to have her holiday, I can assure 'ee, sar. Well, she went out and stayed away till brave an' late in the evenin', an' she went home thinkin' she shud have a bra' scold for stayin' out so long; but when she came to the gate, she found it all fastened up, an' the winder-shutters up, an' the house looking quite whisht like."

"That's very strange," said Morley; "but where are they gone?"

"That's the very thing, sar," replied Mrs. Trenow. "'Where are they gone?' says you; and 'where are they gone?' says everybody, 'ceps Mrs. Brown,—she don't say nothin'. The maid's clothes wor left there for har, an' that's all she'll tell."

"Thank you, Mrs. Trenow," said Morley; "I think we must ask Mrs. Brown, Josiah."

"I b'lieve we must, sar," replied Josiah, thoughtfully. "Where's Alice Ann, thon, mother; she esn't gone after them, I s'pose?"

"No, no; she's up to har aunt's stopping a bit. Har fe-a-ther an' mother do live a bra' way off, you knaw."

"Now, I'll tell 'ee, sar," said Josiah; "you go up to Mrs. Brown's an' knaw all you can, an' I'll go down an' see what Alice Ann have got to say,—an', between es, we may find out somethen'."

"Quite right, Josiah," returned his master, "that is a very good plan." And each of them went his way on a voyage of discovery.

Mrs. Brown was laying the cloth for the midday meal when Morley entered, and her husband was sitting in the chimney-corner. The old lady was overjoyed to see her visitor, and, running towards him, she took his hand in both hers, and kissed it, saying,—

"I am glad to see you once more, Mr. Morley. It was a miraculous escape; an' I hope it will be a warnin' to you, not to risk your life agen at the biddin' of a rogue an' a fool."

"My dear Mrs. Brown," replied Morley, "it was a narrow escape; but the beautiful mare is gone! What does Mr. Brown do, without his Jessie mare?"

"The name of the mare roused Mr. Brown from his lethargy, and, coming out of his corner, he said,—

"Where's my hat, Peggy? I'm goin' to get Jessie mare out, for the gentleman to try her a bit before to-morrow. Come, sir. Wo! ho! Jessie; wo! ho. Come, Polly! Poll! Poll! Polly! Where's that maid gone, Peggy. Billy, boy, come an' saddle the mare."

His hat, which was on his head, shone as brightly as ever, but his internal brightness was gone. He never recovered the shock of seeing his mare fall over the cliff, and the narrow escape of its rider. It was very true he hadn't much to lose, poor man, intellectually. His one idea was centred in the mare, and they both went together. He wandered in and out of the house continually, and, as he didn't interfere with others, no one interfered with him.

"Poor man," said Mr. Morley, looking after him.

"It's a blessin', Mr. Morley," said Mrs. Brown, "that the mare es gone. She was no use here; and she was eatin' her head off, as the sayin' is. What is, is best, I b'lieve."

"My errand to St. Just," said Morley, "was principally to see Mr. Freeman, and I find he's gone away."

"Iss, he's gone, an' joy go weth 'n," replied Mrs. Brown.

"Where is he gone," said Morley; "do you know?"

"All I do knaw es this," replied Mrs. Brown. "He came here about ten days ago, an' said he wor goin' to take his daughter for a little trip, as she dedn't seem well,—she was so low-spirited, he said,—and he asked me to take care of the maid Alice Ann's clothes for har, untel she came back; for p'raps she wud be back before they wud. I thought they wor goin' to Scilly, p'raps, or to Truro. And away they went, and Alice Ann came for har clothes the next day. She dedn't go. Where they're gone, I can no more tell than you can."

"That's very strange; I wish I knew where they were gone," replied Morley, thoughtfully.

"You may wish agen, I b'lieve," returned Mrs. Brown; "he'll turn up again one day, like a poor penny. Come, sir, have a snack weth us; we're just going to dinner."

So poor Mr. Brown was called in, and the three sat down to a nicely seasoned beef-steak pie, which Morley enjoyed very much after his walk, notwithstanding his disappointment.

Josiah gained very little more information than his master. Alice Ann told him that, for several days before they left, her young mistress, Alrina, was confined to her room. She seemed drowsy, like, the girl said, and didn't care to move nor to speak.

"I do b'lieve, Siah," said she, speaking in a half whisper, "that she had some doctor's trade gov to har for to put har to slaip,—I do, sure nuf; and they took har away in a post-chaise while she wor slaipen'.""

Morley thought that if he could find where the post-chaise came from, he might, by bribing and questioning the postboy, gain some clue to their probable destination;—for, in addition to his anxiety to see Mr. Freeman, which was now confirmed more than ever, he was doubly anxious for the safety of Alrina, whom he was convinced her father and aunt were persecuting—perhaps on his account, but why, he could not imagine; for he was not aware that Alrina's relatives knew of his attachment to her, or that he had ever met her. He little knew the resources of the "man of cunning" for obtaining information of what took place in that neighbourhood. He left a hasty note for his friend Fowler, stating that he was unexpectedly called away on important business; and, taking Josiah with him in the combined capacity of companion, assistant, and valet, he proceeded on his travels in search of the fugitives.

CHAPTER XIX.

THE MYSTERIOUS ENCOUNTER.

WE left Lieut. Fowler on the road between Lamorna Cove and the signal-station, at Tol-pedn-Penwith. Various were the conjectures that passed through his mind during his walk, as to who the stranger could be, but to no purpose. He could not think of any of his relatives or acquaintances, who would be likely to be in that neighbourhood, without apprising him of their intended visit. If it should turn out to be a good companionable fellow, he wouldn't mind, but then, he was an old grey-headed man, as he construed Miss Pendray's description of the stranger. His friend, Frederick Morley, had gone off in rather an unceremonious manner, and had left him again to the resources of the Land's-End for amusement and companionship; and he had therefore been more frequent in his visits to Pendrea-house, and more attentive to the young ladies, than during his friend's visit.

It was not often that Miss Pendray favoured Fowler and her sister with her company; for, as the reader already knows, she had more attractions elsewhere; and so accustomed were her friends to her romantic wanderings over the bold cliffs alone, that the innocent Blanche was continually Lieut. Fowler's only companion, and the time generally passed so pleasantly that neither of them regretted the absence of a third party.

When Miss Pendray came upon them so suddenly and unexpectedly on that eventful morning, they were in the midst of a very interesting, but, to Blanche, rather an embarrassing, *teté-a-teté*. The gentleman was trying to make himself understood, without saying what he meant, in so many words; and the lady, although—sly little creature—she knew quite well what he meant to say, and wished from her heart he would say it out boldly, and not be hammering and stammering about it so—making her every moment feel more nervous and embarrassed, and himself too; yet she would not help him, even by a look, but kept turning a pebble round and round with her foot, and looking as steadily on the sand as if she was endeavouring to look underneath it, for some rich treasure supposed to be buried there.

In the midst of all this, came the majestic Maud, with the tale of her adventure with the remarkable stranger with the white hair. Wasn't it provoking to be interrupted just at that critical time? Fowler felt that it was downright ————we wont say what. He wished the white-headed stranger was at the bottom of the sea, and Maud on the top of the cliffs, or anywhere, rather than there, at that moment. However, the spell was broken; there was no help for it now; and he had nothing to do but just walk home to see who this confounded fellow was, and what he wanted.

With all these reflections passing through his mind, as he neared his little cabin, he was not prepared to receive the stranger very cordially, nor to give him a very hearty welcome. He was told by the men, as he came up, that the gentleman was inside; and, as he passed the window of his sitting-room to reach the front door, he looked in, thinking he might catch a glimpse of the fellow before he went in. He caught more than a glimpse of him; for the stranger was standing at a little distance from the window, looking out over the bold headland at the sea in the distance, apparently absorbed in thought.

Fowler started, and turned pale, as if he had seen a ghost, and was obliged to hold by the railing of the little porch for a minute, before he could recover himself sufficiently to enter.

Sailors are not easily alarmed at trifles; so he soon got over the effects of his shock, or whatever it was, and, entering the room, in his usual boisterous, sailor-like style, exclaimed, louder than there was perhaps any occasion for,—

"Mr. Morley! how are you? I'm glad to see you once more."

This stentorian reception made the stranger start, and, turning round, he said, bowing to his host,—

"Lieut. Fowler, I presume. But how you should know that my

name is Morley, I am at a loss to conceive, as I am pretty sure we have never seen one another before, and am quite sure you did not expect me."

Fowler passed his hand across his eyes, as if trying to recall something; and then he said abstractedly, as he placed a seat for his guest,—

"Not seen you before? surely, yes!—and yet, no! that cannot be." And he seemed so bewildered, that the stranger proceeded to explain; for he now began to see that the lieutenant was labouring under a mistake.

"You see the likeness to my poor father," said he.

"Ah!" exclaimed Fowler, starting up; "I see it all now. When I last saw your father, fifteen or sixteen years ago, he was the exact image of what you are now. He was older, of course, but there was the same remarkable white hair. Yours no doubt became white prematurely, causing you to look older than you really are. When I saw you standing at the window, I thought I saw your father standing before me. The likeness is most remarkable; and, almost before I had recovered myself, and without reflecting for a moment, I rushed into the room to welcome my old friend."

"I have heard my father mention the name of Fowler often," replied Mr. Morley, "with expressions of gratitude for kindnesses bestowed by your family—both on himself, and on my brother and sister, who were left here after that terrible catastrophe, of which I believe you are fully aware."

"It is true," returned Fowler, "that, in your father's younger days, he was intimate with my father, who also resided in India, but returned to England on account of his health, some time before yours came over with his two children. Your father often came to see him before that dreadful catastrophe, but never came after. He said he would never see his old friend again, until that foul stain was wiped from his name. My father did not, of course, believe that he was guilty, although the circumstantial evidence was so strong. It preyed on his mind, however, and, in his weak state, he could not bear up against the feeling that his friend was wrongfully accused; and he, like your father, pined under it, and passed away from among us in a very short time; but his death we were prepared for. Your father was a strong man then. But how did you find me out, Mr. Morley?"

"By the merest accident," replied Mr. Morley; "indeed, when I came here, I had no idea that you were at all connected with my father's old friend, although the name was familiar to me,—very familiar, I may say; for I knew your eldest brother in India intimately. He remained there long after your father left, and married a native, by whom he had one child—a daughter, I think.

I shall never forget his kindness. He was the only friend whom I could depend upon, when my poor father died. He remained with me, day and night, until the last. His wife I never saw much of: she died in giving birth to her second child which was still-born. Your brother then made up his mind to come to England. He would not do so while his wife lived; for he did not like introducing a native as his wife, to his English relatives and friends. He was in good spirits when I took leave of him, and we both looked forward to meeting in England ere long; but, alas! he never reached his native shore alive. The ship was wrecked somewhere on this dangerous coast, and he and his little daughter perished. His body was found afterwards, but the child's was never heard of again. It makes passengers, and even sailors themselves, almost dread to approach this rock-bound coast. It is to be hoped that, ere long, warning-lights or beacons will be erected all round the coast. They are beginning to do so, I see; but there are more wanted yet."

"True," replied Fowler; "there are few families residing along the Cornish coast who have not had to lament the loss of some relative or friend in the merciless waves. But I am curious to know to what lucky accident I am indebted for this visit?"

"You have had another of those dreadful disasters on the coast," said Morley. "Another East-Indiaman has lately been wrecked here. I was a passenger on board that vessel. The weather was rough for several days before, and we touched in at the Scilly Islands, where I landed, taking a trunk with some clothes and a few valuables with me; and, meeting with an old friend of my father's there, Mr. Samuel Lemon, the collector, whom you know well, he pressed me so heartily to remain at his house, that I determined to spend a few days there, and partake of his kind hospitality, and I permitted the ship to proceed to her destination without me; and a miraculous escape I have had, for I find that all on board perished."

"Not all," replied Fowler; "there was one sailor saved. It was a miraculous escape, indeed. But you must have had some property on board?"

"I had a large chest containing some valuable clothes, and silks and jewellery, and a considerable sum in hard cash," replied Mr. Morley, "and, what I valued more than anything else, a small box, which belonged to my poor father, into which he had placed, with his own hands, some thousands of gold coins, and a written injunction to his two sons, to use their utmost exertions to find out the wretches who committed that foul murder of which my poor father was accused; and he directed that those gold coins should be expended in the search. My object, therefore, in coming to the Land's-End first, instead of going on direct to my relatives, was, with the hope that this property might have been washed ashore somewhere on the coast, and my good friend Mr. Lemon told me that Mr. Fowler, the lieutenant at this station, would be the most proper person to apply to for assistance and information."

"You may rely on my doing all I can for you," replied Fowler; "but I have not heard of any boxes answering the description of yours being picked up anywhere, and I fear there is little chance of their being washed on shore now; for their weight would sink them deeper and deeper in the sand, and the calm weather we have now would not throw them up. You have not lost all your property, I hope!"

"Oh! no," said Mr. Morley; "I had sent home the bulk of my fortune, and my father's, through agents, some months ago. That, I am happy to say, is safe enough. All I regret now is the loss of that little box."

"Your brother was a true prophet, after all," said Fowler, thoughtfully.

"My brother!" exclaimed Mr. Morley; "where is he?"

"Oh! I forgot to tell you," replied the lieutenant; "I was so interested in the history of your miraculous escape. Your brother was my guest for several weeks, until he met with an accident at the Land's-End." And he proceeded to relate to his visitor the exciting tale of the fall of the horse over the cliffs, with his brother's narrow escape, and the belief that Frederick still entertained, that his brother was one of the passengers on board that ill-fated vessel.

After dinner, the two gentlemen walked up to Sennen, and enquired at "The First and Last Inn" whether anything had been heard of Frederick Morley. Nothing had been heard of him, the landlord said; but a letter had been brought there for him that day, by a boy who said he was going on to St. Just, and would call again for an answer should the gentleman return in time. The letter was addressed, in a neat female hand, to "Frederick Morley, Esq., 'First and Last Inn,' Sennen, Cornwall."

"Who was the boy?" enquired the lieutenant of the landlord.

"I don't know," replied he; "but my wife do say that she es sure 'tes the same boy she ha' seen riding the mare that went over cliff."

"I thought as much," said Fowler. "We must see that boy, and I have no doubt we shall find him in his old quarters at St. Just."

So the two gentlemen extended their walk to St. Just in search of the boy.

Neither of them had the slightest idea from whom the letter could have come, unless it was from Morley's aunt or his sister; and in that case there would most probably have been a postmark.

CHAPTER XX.

ARISTOCRATIC CONNECTIONS.

Mrs. Courland, Frederick Morley's aunt, had been a celebrated beauty in her youth. Her father, the Rev. Octavius Morley, was a scion of a high family, with a small preferment; and his wife was also of aristocratic birth. Too poor to put their only son, Alexander, into a leading branch of one of the learned professions, and too proud to allow him to work his way on as a merchant in England, they wisely sent him to India with a friend, who soon put him into the way of making a rapid fortune; for he possessed business talents of no ordinary kind, and steady and persevering habits of industry. Having thus provided for their son, their only care now was the education and marriage of their daughter, who at nineteen was one of the loveliest girls that can possibly be imagined. Rather above the middle height, elegant in form, and graceful in all her movements, she attracted admirers wherever she went—very much to the annoyance of her parents, who destined her either for one of the aristocracy or for some rich Indian merchant. High birth, or riches, were indispensable in the aspirant to Isabella Morley's hand; her heart was left out of the question entirely by her honoured and honourable parents. Not so by the young lady herself;—she had already fixed her affections on a young officer, whom she had met at a ball to which she had been taken by a lady friend with whom she had been staying in a neighbouring town. He was the younger son of a country squire in an adjoining county; but as he was neither rich nor noble, his alliance was not deemed eligible by the aristocratic parents of Miss Morley, and they therefore discouraged the intimacy, when they became aware of it, although they did not positively forbid it; for they did not really believe that a young man in his position—a lieutenant in a light infantry regiment only, and the younger son of an obscure country squire—would presume to approach the only daughter of such high-born parents, except in the way of common politeness and courtesy. And, besides, they placed implicit confidence in the lessons of ambition they had taught their daughter; and therefore, having heard the rumour of this flirtation in a casual way, and not knowing to what extent it had already gone during her visit at Middleton, the young officer was received with politeness when he called to enquire for the young lady, after her return from her visit.

These calls were repeated again and again, and *têtes-à-têtes* were observed in the garden and shrubbery, and Mrs. Morley began to open her eyes to the true state of things, when it was too late. Cupid had by this time planted his arrow too deeply to be easily eradicated. The gentleman was forbidden the house, and the young lady was kept in strict seclusion for some time; but, "Love laughs at lock-smiths,"—and the two lovers managed to meet, notwithstanding the locks and bars.

Mrs. Morley's aristocratic notions could not be properly satisfied without a lady's-maid, such as she had been accustomed to in her father's house. But she soon found that a grand, high-and-mighty lady's-maid, such as she and her sisters had been accustomed to at home, would not put up with the inconvenience of a small vicarage-house in the country, where a suitable number of servants could not be kept, and, consequently, she was continually changing. This was both annoying and expensive; so when her daughter left school, at seventeen, Mrs. Morley hired a young woman whom they met with at a watering-place where they happened to be rusticating that summer. She was the daughter of a sailor, with whom they lodged; and Mrs. Morley found her so shrewd and useful in most respects, that she pressed her mother to allow her to go back with them in the capacity of double lady's-maid—to attend on herself and daughter.

Miss Fisher was apparently bold enough, and certainly old enough, to have decided for herself,—for she was upwards of thirty years of age; but she had cunning enough to read Mrs. Morley's character, through and through, and she knew that a seeming deference to her mother's opinion would have great weight with her new mistress. The old woman did not like to part with her, but she knew it would be useless to oppose it, as she saw that her daughter had set her mind on accepting the situation, and so she consented; and Mrs. Morley returned to the vicarage with a lady's-maid to her mind, as she thought. Miss Fisher proved all she could wish, yielding to her in everything, as she supposed; instead of which, the new lady's-maid, while seeming to yield, and, indeed, yielding sometimes, in smaller things, very soon gained such an ascendancy over her mistress, that, by a little clever manœuvring, she could turn her any way she liked. Miss Morley was not so easily ruled; nor did Miss Fisher seem to wish it,—she appeared to have taken a great fancy to her young mistress, and would do almost anything to please her; and many a scold and reprimand did she prevent by her tact and cunning.

Two years rolled over their heads, and Miss Fisher still acted in the capacity of lady's-maid to both mother and daughter; and when the latter received the invitation to pay a visit to her friend at Middleton, for the express purpose of attending the ball which was about to take place there, Mrs. Morley, in order that her daughter might be properly dressed and taken care of, and also to display the aristocratic style of her establishment, dispensed with the services of Miss Fisher for a time, and allowed her to accompany Miss Morley to her friend's house. They were more like companions than mistress and maid; for Miss Morley confided all her little secrets to Miss Fisher,

and she was therefore, of course, made acquainted with the attentions
of the young officer ; and as Miss Fisher highly approved of his
person and manners, and the pretty presents he occasionally gave
her, she determined on favouring the lovers, and doing all in her
power to assist them,—so that clandestine meetings were easy,
although the young officer was forbidden the house, and the young
lady was under close confinement indoors. She was beginning to
exhibit signs of ill health, from the close confinement and anxiety
to which she was subject, and Miss Fisher suggested change of air
and scene. She was in the confidence of Mrs. Morley, who relied on
her, and believed all she told her. The young officer's regiment
was ordered abroad, she said, and therefore there could be no
danger in that quarter. This Mrs. Morley knew to be true, for
her husband had been making enquiries. Miss Fisher, however,
managed to deceive her mistress as to the time, telling her he was
to sail immediately, and begging to be allowed to take Miss Morley
home to her father's house for a short time, as she wanted to see the
old people, and she thought the sea-air would quite restore her
young mistress's health, and the change of scene might cause her to
forget this foolish love-affair. So said the designing Miss Fisher ;
and the pair went to old Mr. Fisher's house, there to reside in strict
seclusion, and luxuriate in country-walks and sea-breezes. But,
strange to say, they had not been there many hours, before the young
officer made his appearance there also, and the bloom of health soon
returned to the cheeks of the young lady, without the aid of the sea-
breezes—although they were often felt, as the two lovers took their
delightful walks over the rocks and along the cliffs. Lieut. Marshall's
time was nearly up ; but a few more days remained before he would
be obliged to leave her he loved so much. He could not bear the
thought ;—he was going to the battle-field, and might never see her
more ; or, if he lived to return, he might find her the bride of another.

"Never ! never !" replied Miss Morley ; "I will never be another's
bride. I am pledged and bound to you, dear James, by a sacred oath ;
I will die rather than break my vow. Yours, and yours only, till
death parts us."

"I fully believe and trust in your good intentions, dearest Isabella,"
said he ; "but, should a rich man offer himself, you will be compelled to break that vow, made only to me. Let us bind ourselves
before the altar, dearest ; then nothing can sever us."

Thus did he reason with the fair girl, and persuade her, when she
had no one to guide her aright ; and so ably was the young officer
supported in his arguments, by the artful Miss Fisher, that they were
married, and, within a week after, were separated—perhaps never to
meet again.

Miss Morley (now Mrs. Marshall) returned to her father's house with a heavy secret in her breast—one that she could not reveal. Letters came, through Miss Fisher, which cheered her. Months rolled on. Her husband's name was seen sometimes in the newspapers, and commented on by her parents, little thinking how near and dear he was to her whom they imagined cured of that foolish love-affair.

At last there came an account of a great battle, and, amongst the list of killed, was the name of Lieut. James Marshall. The shock was terrible. Luckily there was no one in the room at the time but Miss Fisher, who immediately rang for assistance, and took her to her room. She was confined to her bed for several days; and when she got a little better, Miss Fisher prevailed on Mrs. Morley to allow her daughter to try change of air and sea-breezes again, as they had been so beneficial before. So they went once more to old Fisher's house, by the seaside, where she stayed several months, keeping up a continual and cheerful correspondence with her parents, who were so pleased with her apparent recovery, that the visit was prolonged, week after week, and month after month. At last a letter came, peremptorily requesting her to return at once, for reasons that would be explained when she arrived.

Old Mrs. Fisher had died during her stay with them, so that Miss Fisher felt bound now, she said, to remain with her father, who did not like being left alone, although he was a strong able man yet, and did something in the seafaring line beyond fishing—but what it was Miss Morley (now Mrs. Marshall) could not make out;—they were very secret about that. About this time also Miss Fisher's only brother, of whom she had often spoken to her young mistress, returned, after a long absence. He was a handsome young man, and was much struck with the beauty of their visitor, and, not knowing at first her position, he began to pay her marked attention. This did not suit Miss Fisher's plans, nor was it at all agreeable to Mrs. Marshall. She therefore determined to leave at once, although she was not quite recovered, and would be obliged to trust to the safe keeping of Miss Fisher a secret which, if revealed, would probably cause her parents to cast her off for ever. At first, and before she was so completely in her power, she had placed the utmost confidence in the fidelity of her maid; but during her last visit to the old fisherman's cottage, her attendant's character had displayed itself in its true colours. She now saw that Miss Fisher was working entirely to suit her own wicked ends, and that her secret would only be safe, while she could supply that wicked woman with funds sufficient to satisfy her avarice. Mrs. Marshall was surprised and shocked at the sudden change which she observed in Miss Fisher's manner towards her, and could not account for it in any way, as she had always hitherto been so kind. It was not Miss Fisher's fault, however, entirely; for the idea of making money out of their too confiding visitor, was suggested by the brother. He was piqued at her indignant rejection of his attentions, and, having wormed the secret out of his sister, he suggested the plan which she was only too ready to carry out. She now saw the advantages to be derived from having this beautiful woman so completely in her power; for she was quite sure that ere long her parents would insist on her marrying some rich man;—she knew that their hearts were bent on this, and there was nothing now to prevent it, except the opposition of the young lady herself, whom Miss Fisher well knew now how to overcome.

When Mrs. Marshall returned, she found that her father had become acquainted with the captain of an East-Indiaman, who brought letters of introduction from her brother. He was about forty years of age,—not very prepossessing in appearance, nor gentlemanly in manners, but he was rich, very rich, her brother said. So here was a husband for Isabella, to whom Mr. and Mrs. Morley did not object —quite the contrary.

The captain was much struck with the beauty of Miss Morley (as she was, of course, still called at home), who looked more lovely than ever since her last illness. The rough captain paid her most devoted attention, and it was evident that he had fallen desperately in love with her.

Her parents and all her friends persuaded, and even urged, her to accept Capt. Courland's offer; and Miss Fisher urged it also most strongly, for many reasons. Having lost her first love, Miss Fisher said, she thought she ought to make a sacrifice now, to atone for her disobedience to her parents in her first marriage.

Money was a great consideration too—very great—to Mrs. Marshall now,—why, we need not enquire. Ladies are not exempt from that passion any more than men. She was a long time bringing her mind to the point, but she did consent at last. She stipulated, however, for a very handsome allowance as pin-money, to do what she liked with, and a liberal jointure in case of the death of her husband. This made him think odd things. "*A liberal jointure, in case of his death,*" was an awkward clause to be suggested by a young bride. However, this made him think she was a good woman of business, and that he should have more than beauty in his wife, after all. So they were married. And he went his voyages as usual, and returned to his lovely wife every nine or ten months, and spent a few months with her, and then off again, leaving plenty of pin-money behind, and a most liberal allowance for maintaining a large establishment.

Capt. Courland was very intimate with his wife's brother, Mr. Alexander Morley, the Indian merchant, and brought him to England when he came over with the two children, and took him back again, after that dreadful murder and false accusation.

Mrs. Courland seemed to feel it more than anyone. She had now been married to Capt. Courland, some three or four years, and he treated her with the greatest kindness and liberality; but still she seemed unhappy. She appeared not to have got over the loss of her first love,—something seemed preying on her mind always. While her husband was at home, she strove against this melancholy feeling, and exerted herself to the utmost to return his kindness; and he, knowing nothing of the former love-affair, and seeing her only at her brightest, when she did violence to her feelings to please him, during the short time he remained at home, was happy in possession and love, as he believed, of his beautiful wife.

It was a relief and a comfort to her to have her little niece, Julia Morley, with her. The superintendence of her infant education (for the little girl was then but five years old) amused her, and relieved her mind from other thoughts. And when she was old enough to go to school, she removed into a town with her, and took a house there that she might keep her still under her own eye, and sent her to a boarding-school, as a day-pupil, attended by a servant; and here Julia became acquainted with Alrina Freeman, and they became bosom friends, as schoolfellows; but Alrina was not permitted to visit or leave the school at all. These injunctions were strictly laid down by her aunt, when she placed her at school; and Mrs. Horton, who was a strict disciplinarian, carried out her orders to the very letter.

CHAPTER XXI.

THE LOVE-CHASE.

FREDERICK MORLEY and Josiah met with very little success at Penzance. No one had seen the Freemans, and no post-chaise from there had gone to St. Just, except with pic-nic parties, for a considerable time. There was not much difficulty in finding out this; for there were but few hackney carriages in the town at that time.

Determined to discover the fugitives, the travellers went on to Truro, by way of Hayle, and there they were more fortunate. A party, answering their description as to number, had passed through that town about four or five days before.

Morley bought a couple of horses at Truro, and on they went in pursuit; for he found, by dint of the strictest enquiry, that a man and woman and a young girl had gone on by Russell's waggon. These persons answered the description pretty nearly in all but the dress; but they might have changed their dresses; so Morley determined on following the waggon, which was four days at least ahead of them.

On they went, however, over the great London road, tracing the waggon, which they were rapidly gaining on, and changing their tired horses for fresh ones occasionally, for which accommodation Morley had to pay very dearly sometimes. They enquired continually at the wayside inns, where the waggon stopped to change horses, or for refreshment, and at first the answers were satisfactory. The fugitives had generally been seen by some one at the refreshment-houses, either in the house or having refreshment taken to them in the waggon. This was, so far, satisfactory; and on the two pursuers went, and came up with the waggon at Bristol.

The great lumbering vehicle was standing at the door of one of the second-class inns, to which they had been directed—the horses having been taken out, and the waggon unloaded. Morley thought it strange that it should be empty; for the same waggon generally went through to London; and while Josiah saw the horses taken care of, his master entered the inn and sought an interview with the driver, who informed him that he had brought three such persons into Bristol, and they were gone on in another waggon; for he had the misfortune to break his axle-tree as he entered the city, and was obliged to shift his load into another waggon, which was ten miles on the road by that time at least.

Fresh horses were procured, while the two travellers partook of a hasty refreshment, and on they went again with renewed hope; for the fugitives would not suspect pursuit, and would not, therefore, be prepared for escape.

That Mr. Freeman knew something of the parties connected with that document, Morley felt convinced now, having brooded over it so long, and had it constantly dinned into his ear by Josiah, who had held the belief from the first; but perhaps, after all, "the wish was father to the thought" in Morley's case. Now that he was drawing near the objects of their pursuit, a thousand reflections crowded into his mind; but, although the hope of finding some clue to "his secret" was very powerful, yet the hope of meeting Alrina once more, and rescuing her from the bondage which seemed now to enthral her, was uppermost.

In the midst of these reflections, the sight of the heavy waggon lumbering slowly up a hill, a little distance ahead of them, as they turned a corner, sent a thrill through the frames of both. There they were, and a brisk trot would bring the pursuers alongside of the waggon in a few minutes.

They spurred on their horses in great excitement, as if they thought the waggon would run away; but it still lumbered up the hill at its usual snail's pace, drawn by its eight fine horses, with the bells over the collars jingling at every step. The riders soon came up with them; and, jumping off his horse, and throwing the reins to Josiah, Morley sprang into the waggon, and was greeted by the hindmost driver, who was walking by the side of his horses, with a hearty crack of the whip, which made his back sting most unpleasantly, and brought him round to face his assailant, before he had time scarcely to look into the waggon.

"What business have you in my waggon?" cried the principal driver; for there were two.

"I came in search of the three passengers that you have here," replied Morley, who was still feeling the effects of the crack of the whip, although he thought it best not to resent it just then, as he saw at once that the driver was in the right.

"I've got no passengers here now," replied the driver. "We brought three coves along, as you say; but they left us about ten miles back, or so, and turned down a narrow lane. They're a queer lot, I reckon; and that young girl is afraid of her life of the old birds."

This was a terrible disappointment to Morley, after having his hopes raised so high at the sight of the waggon, and thinking he was about to reap the reward of all his trouble and fatigue.

"Did they say where they were going?" asked Morley.

"Not they," replied the driver; "he's as close as a box—that old chap—and the old woman is upon the next stave of the ladder, I b'lieve."

Morley gave the drivers a small piece of money for their information, and the detention he had caused them, and held a consultation with his faithful ally.

"We must follow them, my friend," said Morley, looking very much disconcerted. "Alrina is persecuted and ill-used by her father and aunt, according to that man's account. But why? There lies the mystery. She must be rescued, at all risks, and that at once."

"Zackly like that," replied Josiah, thoughtfully; "but which lane ded they go into, I wondar. I seed powers of lanes both sides."

"True," said Morley; "I forgot to ask which lane."

"'Twud ha' b'en all the same ef you had, I b'lieve," replied Josiah, "for most of the lanes wor alike, so far I could see, as we came along."

"We are losing time. Mount, man, and follow me; we must find them." And, suiting the action to the word, Morley vaulted into his saddle, and Josiah followed his example.

They turned and rode back in silence for some miles, passing numerous lanes on each side of the road; but the driver said the party left him about ten miles back. The two travellers had not retraced their steps, however, many miles, when they were accosted by a little beggar-boy, who was coming out of rather a wide lane into the turnpike-road.

Morley gave the boy something, and asked him if he had seen three travellers—a man and two females—pass up that lane.

"Yes, sir," replied the boy. "The man and the young woman turned down another lane a little way on, and the old woman went up to the house."

"What is the name of the house, boy?" said Morley.

"Ashley Hall, sir," replied the boy.

"Indeed!" exclaimed Morley; "I had forgotten the locality. I never approached it from this road before." And, setting spurs to his horse, he rode on as if Old Nick was at his heels, instead of his faithful friend and follower, Josiah. At the end of the lane, there was a neat lodge, at which the impetuous gentleman was obliged to pull up.

"You ha' found a bra' keenly lode, I s'pose," said Josiah; "'tes looken' brave an' keenly, I must say. The gozzan an' the indications do 'token somethen' good furder in.'"

"Oh! I forgot to tell you," said Morley, "that this is my aunt, Mrs. Courland's, place. I haven't seen her since my return; and this old place I haven't seen since I was a boy,—for my aunt left it for a long time, in order to be near my sister when she was at school. I meant to have seen her much sooner, but that foolish accident at the Land's-End frustrated all my plans. We will take up our abode here, Josiah, at present, and go out scouring the country every day. We will make this our head-quarters."

"Very good quarters to be had here, I'll be bound," returned Josiah. "That's a grand house, sure nuf, that es," continued he, as they rode up to the front door.

They were admitted at once, when the man saw the name on the card which Morley gave him; and, desiring another servant to take care of Josiah, he conducted Frederick into the drawing-room, where he found his sister, alone, making delicious sounds on the pianoforte —which had just superseded the harpsichord, and was then quite the rage among the affluent. She was delighted to see her brother, although she scolded him for not coming to see them before. When he told her the reason, however, and recounted the scene of the accident, which he could not, even then, look back upon without a shudder, she readily forgave him. She offered him some refreshment, which he was very glad to have; for he had ridden far, and had been harassed by anxious and exciting thoughts for several days. They had dined long ago, Julia said, and immediately after dinner her aunt was called out of the room on business, and had not yet returned. "Some more buildings, or improvements, or alterations, going on, I suppose," she continued, in a more subdued tone; "wealth has its troubles, Frederick, as well as poverty."

"True," replied her brother; "and I really think wealth brings most trouble very often. Aunt Courland has something of importance to settle to-night, I should think."

"Oh! I never mind her absence," replied Julia; "she has often engagements that occupy her a whole day, and I see nothing of her from breakfast till tea-time. But I'll go and see where she is now; she will be glad to know that you are here; and none of the servants would disturb her, I'm sure."

Julia found her aunt, alone, in a little room looking out into her private garden, from which there was a private communication with the lane which branched off from the entrance-gate and skirted the gardens of Ashley Hall. Mrs. Courland had evidently been weeping, and had gone through some agitating scene; for she trembled still, as Julia felt when she kissed her. She soon recovered, however, and accompanied her niece into the drawing-room to welcome her nephew, who was a great favourite. He, too, saw that something had agitated her, and he asked her what had happened to upset her so.

"Nothing," she said; "it will be all over in a few minutes." And she did get better; but still a cloud hung over her countenance, which she could not altogether dispel, although it was evident she made a great effort to do so.

The next morning, Morley and Josiah were on horseback before the ladies were stirring. Josiah had gained some useful information from the servants, as to the locality and the different lanes, and where they led to, and how far they were from the sea.

They rode all day without success. Every lane they saw they explored as far as they could, and enquired everywhere, but could gain no tidings of the fugitives; and they returned late, weary and out of heart.

Day after day was passed in the same way, and with the same result. Mrs. Courland requested that Frederick would use her horses to relieve his own, so that he had always fresh horses at his command. One day they rode along a narrow lane which seemed to lead to the sea. It was a lonely road, skirted on each side by deep woods of tall forest-trees. Not a house or human habitation was to be seen for miles. At length, as they approached nearer the water, the trees appeared more stunted and dwindled down to short coppice-wood. Still the road was lonely and destitute of human habitation.

Suddenly they came upon a solitary cottage, surrounded by what had once been a garden, but which was now filled with weeds and rank grass.

The entrance into the garden seemed to be at the end, through a little wicket-gate, which had fallen off its hinges; but as the low wall of the garden had fallen down in several places, Morley had no difficulty in entering; so, leaving his horses to the care of Josiah,

he made his way through one of the gaps in the wall, and approached
the front of the cottage. The door was locked and the house seemed
deserted. He looked in at the windows, and, to his surprise, the
house seemed furnished, and everything in the rooms appeared as if
they had been recently used. This was very strange, Morley thought;
so he went round the house, and, in one end, he observed a window,
rather larger than the front window; and, looking into the room, he
saw that it was a bedroom on the ground-floor, which appeared as if
it had been lately occupied. A sudden thought now flashed across
his mind, as he looked again in at that window; and, returning to
Josiah, he said,—

"We must make some enquiries about this house, Josiah; it
seems to be shut up,—and yet the interior has the appearance of
having been lately occupied."

"'Tes a whisht old house, sure nuf," replied Josiah; "a purty
place for pixies and ghostes, I reckon."

They mounted their horses again, and rode on about a mile
further, when they arrived at a farm-house. The farmer informed
them that he had not resided in that neighbourhood more than four
or five years; but he had heard that the house Morley was enquiring
about, was haunted. A horrible murder had been committed there
many years ago, the farmer said, and no one had resided there since.

"To whom does it belong?" asked Morley.

"I have heard that it belonged to the old man who was murdered
there," replied the farmer. "The son and daughter lived there with
him, I believe; but after the murder they went off, no one could
tell where, and they have never been heard of since."

"Do you know the names of these people?" enquired Morley.

"Well, I have heard," replied the man; "but I have forgotten."

Morley's conjecture was confirmed. This was, no doubt, the very
house in which that dreadful murder was committed, of which his
poor father had been accused. The murderers had gone to some
distant part of the country, no doubt, or perhaps gone abroad, and
left the house and its contents just as they were, fearing to return lest
they should be discovered; and no one else would venture near the
the house, on account of their superstitious fears of ghosts. The
premises would not be worth much, in that lonely district; indeed,
no one would purchase them after what had happened; and so the
risk of returning was not worth incurring, especially as the guilty
parties must have taken away a considerable sum with them; for the
oney which Mr. Morley had with him at the time, and which he must
have dropped in his agitation, at the time he slid down from the bed,
was, no doubt, picked up by the fugitives and carried off. This was
enough to enable them to live comfortably for a long time.

It was getting late; so Morley enquired the nearest way to Ashley

Hall, and returned by a short cut which the farmer pointed out, determined to explore the interior of the house the next morning.

Julia ran down to meet her brother when she heard he had returned, and begged him to have his dinner in the breakfast-parlour, if he didn't mind, as her aunt was engaged with a stranger in the dining-room.

"What! more mysterious visitors, Julia?" said her brother, smiling; "why, my aunt Courland must be worried out of her life."

"Yes. Now eat your dinner, like a good boy," replied Julia, leading her brother to the table, which was already laid for dinner; "and then, if you are very good, I will tell you a grand secret."

"Hallo!" exclaimed Frederick, eating at the same time—for he was very hungry; "why, this place ought to be called 'The Castle of Mystery' instead of 'Ashley Hall.' You seem to have more secrets here than were contained in 'Blue Beard's' secret chamber. But the tables are turned here, and the ladies hold the secrets, and the poor men have to guess."

"Heighho!" cried his sister, with a sigh; "I am sorry to say we haven't many men here to hide secrets from. Their visits are 'like angels' visits, few and far between.'"

"Now, one glass of wine," said Frederick, who had been going into the substantials heartily while his sister had been talking;— "one glass of wine, my little sister, and then for your secret."

"Two glasses, Frederick dear,—I must insist on your taking two glasses at least; for I want to make you able to hear my terrible secret without fainting outright." And she kissed him so kindly as she said this, that he could not refuse his little sister's request.

"Two glasses, then," said he, "if it must be so."

When he had finished his two glasses of wine, she said she had such a surprise for him in the dining-room, where perhaps he would have to take another glass of wine.

"You little mysterious puss," said he, as he drew her arm within his, and suffered her to lead him to the dining-room. "What can you have to shew me?—it isn't a lover, is it?"

"Oh! no," replied she, sighing; "animals of that genus don't acclimatize at Ashley Hall—the atmosphere here is too cold for them."

"You little satirical minx," said he, as his sister threw open the dining-room door, and introduced him to their eldest brother, William, from India.

It was a surprise indeed. The two brothers embraced most affectionately, and then they looked at each other for some minutes. At last Frederick said,—

"My recollection of our poor father is but faint—I was only ten years of age when I last saw him; but it seems to me as if I saw him standing before me now."

I

"Yes," replied his brother; "the likeness has been remarked by all our friends in India."

"I was painfully struck with it," said Mrs. Courland, "when William entered the room this morning. I felt as if my poor brother had come back again, to bring to light that awful catastrophe. My thoughts went back to that awful time, and I shuddered as he entered. I can scarcely get over it now."

"It shall be discovered, my dear aunt," said the elder brother—whom in future we will call Mr. Morley. "We will not return till the guilty parties are brought to light."

A sudden change came over the countenance of Mrs. Courland as these words were pronounced, in the solemn voice so like her poor brother's, that alarmed her nephews. Julia had seen those fits on her before; and she motioned to her two brothers to be quiet, while she held her aunt's throbbing head to her bosom.

It soon passed away; and then she rose and begged her two nephews to sit a little over their wine, as she knew they must have much to say to each other.

CHAPTER XXII.

ALRINA'S FIRST LOVE-LETTER.

THE wine and dessert had remained on the table, although all but Frederick had dined long ago. The two brothers sat over their wine, as Mrs. Courland had requested them to do; but their time was otherwise employed than in drinking wine. Mr. Morley related to his brother the history of his life, from the time of their father's death, and his miraculous escape from the shipwreck. Frederick, in return, related to his brother the incidents of his life,—his miraculous preservation on the cliffs at the Land's-End; Josiah's prompt assistance; the discovery of the box of gold; the conjuror;—indeed, all except his love-affair. That he retained as a secret still. They had much to tell, and the brothers sat late.

It was a great relief to Mr. Morley's mind to know that their father's box was safe. That Mr. Freeman knew something about the parties, he had no doubt whatever, and he was now as anxious as his brother was to find him, in order to obtain any information he might be able to give them; for Josiah, who had been sent for into the dining-room, to give them a description of the "man of cunning," and his habits and mode of life, said that "The Maister" knew "bra' things."

Alrina was mentioned by Frederick; but he did not tell all respecting her, nor did he so far confide in his brother as to tell him of the plighted troth which existed between them. Mr. Morley guessed, however, that there was something more than disinterested friendship in his brother's anxiety on her account.

The discovery of the house in which the murder had been committed was also told; and the brothers determined to go to the deserted house again the next day, and effect an entrance, when they might possibly discover some clue to the mystery.

When they were about to separate for the night, Mr. Morley gave his brother a letter which he said had been left at the "First and Last Inn" for him; but as he supposed it had come from Ashley Hall, he did not think of giving it to him before, as he had no doubt heard its contents from the lady herself. Frederick took the letter and put it into his pocket, intending to read it in his bedroom. He could not imagine who could have written it. It could not have been either his aunt or sister; for they would no doubt have mentioned it, if it had come from them.

The ladies had retired long ago; and the brothers, being tired, followed their example.

When Frederick had closed the door of his room, he took out the letter and examined the address, which appeared to be written in pencil. He did not know the handwriting. It was a neat lady-like hand. At first he thought of Miss Pendray,—but what could she have to write him about? At last he broke the seal, and was astonished as well as delighted, to find that it was a letter from Alrina—a short letter evidently written in haste. So he sat down and almost devoured its contents.

ALRINA'S LETTER.

My own dear Frederick,

May I call you so? Yes; I feel I may,—and yet I scarcely know what to say or how to begin a letter to you. But who else can I look to? Oh! Frederick, I am very, very unhappy. My father discovered our meetings. He knows our secret,—by what means I know not.

I was in a state of stupor for a long time, and when I recovered myself I was in a strange place. How I was conveyed here, or when, I do not know. I am puzzled and bewildered.

The house is surrounded by high walls on every side. My father has been absent,—I have only seen him once. I think this house must be near the sea; for the owner dresses like a sailor, and I overhear conversations which lead me to believe he is connected with smugglers. His wife is older than he is. Oh! Frederick, she is such a tyrant, and treats that poor girl shamefully. (I forgot to say they have a young girl living with them, whom they call their niece.)   Poor girl! I pity her; but I am not allowed to speak to her,—indeed, she seems to forbid it herself, by placing her finger on her lips whenever I happen to meet her.   I hear her cries, poor child!

There is some mystery about her,—I feel convinced of this. I hear whisperings.   My aunt is in the secret, whatever it is. The two women have been closeted continually.   I am closely watched and guarded—I know that; so that I amuse myself by watching too, and listening; but I cannot learn much. Yesterday the man went out, and took the girl with him; and soon after, my aunt told me she was going a short journey, and I must remain here until her return.   I am accustomed to hear of her short journeys.   She often went from home; but the journeys appeared to be long ones,—she generally stayed away a fortnight.   All is mystery.   The old woman keeps guard over me. The boy Billy, whom you may have seen in poor Mr. Brown's stable, came with my father, and he managed to get me this sheet of paper and a pencil unknown to anyone.   I am writing now as a prisoner; for the old woman locks me in when she is not with me.   I am thankful to be alone, for then I can think of you,—and oh! how pleasant the thought.   When I shall see you again I know not,—and whether I shall be able to send this letter after I have written it, God only knows; but it is a pleasure, in my solitude, to write my thoughts and my troubles, to one who will feel for me.   I shall try to send this by the boy, should he ever come here again.   Hark! I hear the bolt of the door drawn back.   She comes!   Adieu!

Your fond and loving

ALRINA.

Frederick read Alrina's letter over and over again, as he paced the floor of his bedroom in mad agitation. He had wasted his time by coming after this waggon, while his Alrina was probably still within a few miles of her former habitation. Had he received this letter before he started, he might have rescued ner; but now! it may be too late. Several days had passed,—days? yes, nearly a fortnight since that letter was written. "Fool! madman! idiot!" he exclaimed as he paced the floor. "Why did I not enquire more strictly before I took this fool's journey?"

Exhausted nature gave way at last, and, throwing himself on the bed, he slept heavily till Josiah came to call him for their usual early morning's ride. He had not taken off his clothes, so that, after a refreshing wash, he went out into the garden followed by Josiah. The fresh morning air invigorated him, and restored tranquillity to his mind; and he was enabled to tell his faithful follower the principal contents of the letter.

"Well, sar," said Josiah, "that's a whisht job sure nuf; but what's done caen't be helped. Ef har fe-a-ther es a conjuror, you arn't, I s'pose; so how cud you tell that she wor there?"

"True," said Frederick, who now began to see the folly of reflecting on himself for coming to Bristol instead of remaining in Cornwall— a mistake which it was impossible he could have seen the result of.

"We have done something by coming here, however," he continued, reflectively; "we have discovered that lonely house. Now, I think you had better remain here with my brother; for I feel convinced that by entering that house, some discovery will be made. In the meantime I will return and seek Alrina and her father. If I can find that boy, I shall succeed without a doubt in rescuing her."

"Iss; but semmen to me that two 'f's' do belong to that," said Josiah.

"What do you mean by 'two f's?'" exclaimed Frederick.

"Why, the fust es, ef you cud find the boy," replied Josiah; "and the next es, ef she's there still. You don't knaw that boy so well as I do: but 'tes no harm to try. I'll go home, or stay here, whichever you plaise; but there's one thing I ha' got to say, that I b'lieve we wor 'pon a good scent, after all."

"What do you mean?" asked Morley.

"Why, I heard somethen' spoke down in the servants' hall last night, that I ha' b'en thinken' about a bra' deal; but I cudn't, to save my life, make the two ends to 'kidgey' like; but your letter ha' opened my eyes all abroad."

"You are speaking in enigmas, Josiah," said his master.

"I don't knaw what sort of things they are, not I," said Josiah; "but putten' this agen that, I can see a bra' way this mornen', I think."

"What are you driving at?" said Morley, looking puzzled.

"Why, this here es about the size of et," replied Josiah, looking very wise,—"Miss Freeman wor in that woggen, so sure as my name es 'Siah Trenow."

"How can you possibly know that?" cried Morley, very much excited.

"Well, I don't knaw et zackly," replied Josiah; "but the porter said, last night, that there ha' b'en a woman up there two or three times spaken' to Mrs. Courland, an' he watched her in an' out o' that little gate in the garden; and by what he said, I do b'lieve 'tes she. He chalked her out zackly, semmen to me."

"Whatever could she be doing here?" asked Morley. "It is quite absurd to think of such a thing."

"Zackly like that," said Josiah; "but I do b'lieve 'twor she, an' that man an' the little maid wor the ones that Miss Reency spoke about. 'Tes some new manœuvre of ' The Maister's,' I'll be bound, an' I shall watch like a cat watching a mouse. Dedn't Miss Reeney say that he knaw'd all about you, an' everything. He wor watching you when you dedn't knaw et, down there, I'll be bound. An' now he ha' sent she for to tell your aunt somethen'."

At this point of their conversation, they were joined by Mr. Morley, to whom Frederick read the most material portions of Alrina's letter. and Josiah repeated his suspicions that Miss Freeman was lurking about the neighbourhood. If so, they had no doubt she was there on some errand from her brother respecting Frederick Morley. What it was they couldn't imagine. It was arranged therefore that Frederick should return to Cornwall again in search of Alrina and her father; while Mr. Morley and Josiah should remain at Ashley Hall, for the purpose of making what discovery they could in the deserted house, and of finding out whether Miss Freeman was really in the neighbourhood, and what she was about. So, after an early breakfast, their plans were formed, and Mr. Morley and Josiah proceeded to the deserted house, while Frederick rode on the wings of love to the rescue of his imprisoned enchantress.

CHAPTER XXIII.

THE SECRET.

MRS. COURLAND was expecting her husband's return about this time. She was anxious and nervous. He was a good, kind husband, and she endeavoured to do all in her power to make him happy. It was a great trial to her to look that kind, good man in the face, and know that she was keeping a secret from him which he ought to have known from the beginning. It made her unhappy,—miserable, —and she dreaded his return. Should he discover it now, and find that she had been deceiving him for so many years, it would be dreadful. And now he was on his last voyage;—he would now retire from the sea and live at home. How should she be able to keep the secret then ? Some trifling circumstance might occur at any time, to discover it ; and then his kind affection would be lost to her. He would not—he could not—look upon her with his wonted loving confidence, after the discovery of her deception. Oh ! why had she kept it from him ?

Julia knew that her aunt was anxious about her husband's return, and she did not disturb her therefore when she retired after breakfast to her little private room.

She retired, as usual, that morning, and sat brooding over her sorrows and anxieties, until she became quite low-spirited; for the more she thought of her difficult and unpleasant situation, the more guilty and blameable she seemed in her own estimation; and, placing her hand before her eyes, she wept in the bitterness of her heart.

Still comparatively a young woman, and still beautiful, and the admiration of all, when she chose to enter into society,—possessed, also, of considerable wealth, a noble mansion, and a splendid establishment—all, in short, which the world could bestow,—and, above all, being blessed with a kind and indulgent husband,—yet, with all these advantages, there sat that handsome and gifted lady in the midst of all this splendour, a miserable, unhappy woman.

A gentle tap is heard at the little door leading into the garden, which makes her start and turn pale. Strange that so gentle a tap should frighten her so much. Where are all the servants, that she should be obliged to open the door herself? She seems to dread the admission of the visitor; and yet she rises almost immediately, and unbolts the little door and admits the intruder on her privacy.

The visitor enters unceremoniously, and closes the door, as if she had been accustomed to visit the beautiful owner of the establishment often. She was a tall, masculine-looking woman, apparently about fifty years of age, with an eye that betokened both boldness and cunning, and a restless uneasy expression by no means pleasing. The compressed lips expressed great determination of character, and the strong and well-knit frame seemed formed more according to the model of the ruder than the softer sex.

This was the visitor who had just been admitted into Mrs. Courland's private room.

" Am I never to be at rest?" said the lady in a supplicating tone, as she took her seat again. " Say, once for all, what will satisfy you, and leave me in peace. This continual worry and anxiety is killing me."

" You know," replied the visitor, " that I am not asking for myself. It is in the cause of another that I occasionally trouble you. The poor child must be educated according to the station she may one day fill; and her maintenance must be cared for. And those who take the trouble, and keep the secret, must be rewarded—and that with liberality."

" I know all that," said Mrs. Courland, " and am willing to make a sacrifice. What will suffice? say !"

" I am acting for another, as you know; and my instructions are, five hundred pounds—not a penny less," said the woman, sternly.

" I cannot comply with your exorbitant demand," replied Mrs. Courland, in an abject tone; " I have not so much money in the house. My husband's allowance is all exhausted,—you have been a continual drain upon me. I expect him almost hourly, and then my supplies will be almost unlimited again. Pray leave me now, and let me have a little time to recover myself before his return. Then you shall be liberally rewarded."

"I cannot wait," said the visitor; "or, if I do, the money must be supplied *by himself*, and all must be known."

"Oh! no! no! not that," cried Mrs. Courland, almost in despair. "He is kind—most kind. Spare him the knowledge of that which has been kept from him so long, to my bitter, bitter cost. Oh! would that he had known all at the beginning. It would have saved me many unhappy hours." And the poor lady wept, as if her heart was breaking. Her unwelcome visitor seemed moved, and begged her not to distress herself so.

"You have not seen the child?" said she. "Let me bring her to you. Why not take her here? she might be a comfort to you. Her misfortune and dreadful calamity may induce you to pity, if you cannot love her, and will afford some occupation for your leisure hours. She is within call; I will bring her in." And before Mrs. Courland could collect herself sufficiently to decide what she would do, or to ask another question, the woman had disappeared.

The grounds of Ashley Hall, as we have before said, were skirted on one side by a narrow lane, very little frequented,—the hedges on each side being overgrown with brambles and thick thorn-bushes. In this lane, there was a door which led into Mrs. Courland's private room, through a small garden, which she called her own private property—no one being permitted to enter it, except herself, and the gardener, who at stated times was admitted to keep it in order.

Outside this little door in the lane, on the morning of this woman's visit to Mrs. Courland, stood an elderly man, dressed in the garb of a sailor, and a young girl, about fifteen or sixteen years of age—she might have been a year or two more, or she might have been less; it was difficult to determine. She was plainly dressed, and looked clean and neat; but her general appearance was not at all prepossessing. She was short and stout; and extreme vulgarity and impudent assurance, mingled with cunning, were depicted in her forbidding looking countenance, which was deeply pitted with the small-pox;—and yet, with all this, there was a look of melancholy which seemed to indicate that the girl was unhappy. Continued ill-treatment had perhaps produced this harsh and repulsive expression of countenance which she now exhibited.

"We must try what effect the girl will have," said the woman, as she merged into the lane through the little private door, after having kept her companions waiting a considerable time. "The lady says she has not much money in the house, and won't have till the captain comes home."

"She be hanged!" replied the man. "That's her game. Not money in a house like that? Tell her to pawn her jewels, or sell her carriage. I tell you, mistress, if you can't manage better than that, I shall go in myself and play Old Nick with her."

"Hush!" said the woman. "Let me take the girl in. That will be best. Leave it to me, Cooper; I know how to manage her."

"Now, mind," cried the man; "no nonsense,—money down, or else there'll be the devil to pay. I won't wait one day longer. I've got other fish to fry, and I don't like dancing attendance upon a parcel of women, like this."

Leaving the man alone in the lane, in not a very good humour, the woman took the girl with her into Mrs. Courland's private room, where she found that lady still weeping and in great agitation.

"I have brought the child," said the woman, as she entered, "and I intend leaving her here on your hands. I have a bold partner outside, who will publish it far and near, and your husband will know all immediately on his return. I have sufficient proof of all, as you have seen before."

"Oh! spare me! spare me!" cried the poor lady, as she looked at the girl through her tears. "Oh! terrible fate. Not that! *She* cannot be the child. Oh! in pity take her away, and say there is some mistake. Oh! dreadful. His child can never be like that!" And she turned her head away, as if she loathed the sight of one so hideous. Had she been a handsome girl, she might have reconciled herself to her fate; but to have a low, vulgar, hideous creature there, and to present that creature to her husband now,—she could not do it. Better die a thousand deaths than face this terrible ordeal. Her husband would despise and hate her, as much as he loved her now, when he discovered the extent of the deception that had been practised upon him. He would be at home now continually; and she would have to bear his frowns, day by day, without relief. She presented to her own mind the darkest side of the picture, and painted it in the dullest and blackest colours, like all who give way to these low desponding thoughts. While these gloomy reflections were passing in Mrs. Courland's mind, the woman disappeared through the little private door, and left the poor girl standing in the middle of the room. Here was a new difficulty. What could she do with that repulsive looking girl? She ran out through the little garden and opened the door leading into the lane. There was no one to be seen;—both the man and the woman had either gone off very quickly, or were concealing themselves behind some of the overgrown thorns and bushes. The girl was left on her hands, evidently, and she must make the best of it. Perhaps she might know where to find her friends, and might be induced to go to them if she was provided with some money. Consoling herself, as well as she could, with these reflections, Mrs. Courland returned to the room, where she found the girl standing in the same place, and looking, with stolid astonishment, at the elegant and costly ornaments which decorated the room, and exhibited the refined taste and great wealth of its owner.

Mrs. Courland seated herself once more, and tried to look at the poor half-frightened girl with less abhorrence : but it was of no use. She could not endure the sight of her : and the idea of keeping her there was quite out of the question ;—she must get rid of her, at all risks, cost what it would. The girl, seeing that she was not noticed, turned round to look at the beautiful bijouterie with which some of the tables and the mantel-piece were strewed ; and she was now standing with her back to the mistress of the apartment.

Mrs. Courland summoned up resolution enough at length to speak to the girl, but she did not seem to notice it. Again Mrs. Courland addressed her, but she neither replied nor turned towards the lady.

" You are obstinate, girl," said Mrs. Courland. " I will soon let you know who is mistress here ;"—for she felt her dignity insulted, which she was not accustomed to ; and rising from her chair impatiently, she approached the girl, and, taking her by the shoulders (for the girl's back was still turned towards her), she gave her a hearty shake, which came so unexpectedly, that the girl jumped round, and seized the lady by both her wrists, giving at the same time a hideous and unearthly scream, and looking more like a fiend than anything human. But, seeing that she had frightened her, she released her grasp, which had been so strong and powerful, that the marks of her hard, bony fingers were left on the soft and delicate flesh of the lady, who dropped into a seat, terrified and exhausted. Her situation was even worse than she had anticipated.

The girl was evidently deaf and dumb !

She could not turn such a helpless unfortunate out into the world, alone ;—even if she filled the poor creature's pockets with gold, she could not help herself nor make her wants known, and she would be robbed. What was she to do ? The woman, it was evident, meant to leave her there : and now all must be known.

The poor girl was still standing in the same place, looking at the lady with a penitent countenance ; for she saw, with natural instinct, that she had done amiss. She had been accustomed to ill-treatment, and any resentment she evinced subjected her to a more severe punishment ; and so she had become hardened and vindictive, and would take some opportunity of doing her persecutors some mischief, treacherously, for which she often got double punishment ; so that she was always conquered, and her temper became sour and morose, which gave an unpleasant expression to her countenance, that, but for the ravages made on it by that dreadful disease, the small-pox, might not have seemed so forbidding and repulsive. A mingled feeling of pity and compassion took possession of Mrs. Courland's mind, as she sat gazing at the poor creature, who now looked so penitent, and seemed to be begging for pardon, in her way. The expression of her countenance was quite altered and subdued. She now felt the pride of being the conqueror over that delicate and beautiful lady, by the strength of her sinewy hands; for there was no hand uplifted here to fell her to the ground for her temerity and rudeness. She saw, too, that the lady had been weeping, and that her delicate wrists had been hurt by her powerful grasp; for the marks of her fingers were still visible there.

She had never, perhaps, been taught to kneel in worship or in penitence to any higher being than the man and woman with whom she resided—and to them only by accident, when struggling for the mastery, or in endeavouring to evade the severity of her daily punishment. Her natural instinct now plainly indicated to her, that she was standing in the presence of a superior being, whom she had injured, and who bore the pain without resenting it. She could not express her penitence and sorrow for the pain she had inflicted, in words; so she threw herself on her knees before the lady, and, bending her head almost to the floor, burst into tears—the first she had shed, perhaps, except in pain or anger, in the whole course of her life.

Mrs. Courland's heart was touched at the natural homage and contrition of this poor afflicted girl. She raised her from the floor and placed her in her own chair, signing to her to remain there.

The lady then left the room, and returned in a short time, and placed upon the table, with her own hands, a little tray containing luncheon for two,—dainty meat and wine, such as the poor girl had scarcely ever seen before. She ate ravenously, and would have drank the whole contents of the small decanter of wine, had she not been prevented. But the kindness of those few minutes had subdued her into humble submission, more than all the beatings and harsh treatment which she had before been accustomed to receive to compel obedience.

So far, all was managed easily; but the girl must sleep somewhere —unseen and unknown. There was a small apartment within that private room, which might be used as a sleeping-room. Mrs. Courland made a sign to the girl, which she quickly understood, and in her strong arms she carried in a small couch; and with shawls and rugs, which Mrs. Courland managed to bring from other parts of the house, they made a comfortable bed and hiding-place for the stranger for the present, until Mrs. Courland could decide on the best course to be adopted.

She could scarcely make up her mind to believe it; and yet it seemed but too evident that this was the child she had grieved over so long, and so often wished and yet dreaded to see. The plainness of the girl's features she might yet get accustomed to, and art might be brought to her aid to improve her appearance;—the vulgarity in her manner might also be softened and ameliorated. But that sad calamity,—oh! that was dreadful,—no art could get rid of that.

CHAPTER XXIV.

"MAN IS BORN TO TROUBLE AND DISAPPOINTMENT, AS THE SPARKS
FLY UPWARDS."

FREDERICK MORLEY, in the meantime, was hastening on his journey. Love added speed to his horse's feet, and strength to the rider; and by dint of frequent changes on the road, he was not many days reaching Truro once more, where he halted to refresh himself and to deliberate on what course he should adopt.

It was a lone house, Alrina had told him in her letter, near the seaside, she believed, surrounded by a high wall, and not very far, she thought, from her former abode; because she must have been taken there during the night, so that the distance could not have been great. This was a very vague description. There were many lone houses, in those days, near the sea, surrounded by high walls;—indeed, the exception was, to see a lone house, without having a high wall round it, for the protection of the inmates against the lawless bands who infested the sea-coast in those troublous times. His course seemed to be, to go to the Land's-End at once, and see Lieut. Fowler, who might have heard something, or perhaps have seen the boy. He determined, however, to go by the road which would take him nearest to the sea; and, in his journey, he could look out for the house in which his Alrina was confined, and, to make sure of not passing her by this time, he determined he would effect an entrance by some pretence or other, into every house he saw surrounded by high walls in the course of his journey.

Having decided on this course, and taken some refreshment, he started on his exploring expedition; but he was obliged to ride the same tired horse, for there was not another to be had in the town. The horse, however, having been well fed and groomed, the ostler assured him that the animal was as fresh as a hunter going to the meet, and would carry him a long journey yet before sunset. So Frederick mounted once more, and, with whip and spur, got over a good bit of ground in a very short time; for the horse was one of those plucky animals that will run till they drop, under the spur of

an impatient rider. Frederick did not intend to be cruel; but he
wanted to get on, and the horse seemed willing to go, so on they went
at a good pace, and soon neared the sea-coast. The horse was
flagging a little, but whip and spur kept him up to the mark, and
on they went still. They passed several farm-houses surrounded by
walls; but none of them at all answered the description Alrina had
given of her prison. At length Frederick thinks he sees, at some
distance ahead, some high dark walls, and he fancies he discerns the
roof of a house just peeping above them. "This must be the very
house," cried he, in the greatest excitement; so he urged the horse
on, thinking of nothing but the rescue of his Alrina. The road was
rugged and the horse was tired. He stumbled over a loose stone
going down a gentle declivity towards the building; and, not having
sufficient strength left to save himself, he fell heavily. The rider
was thrown with violence against the wall; he was stunned, and
lay insensible and bleeding beneath the wall of the house he had
been so anxious to reach.

The shadows of night are closing in all round, and the man and
horse are still lying in that lonely road, no one having passed since
the accident, nor has the garden-door been opened. At last a boy
comes out; and, seeing that some accident has happened, he returns
to the house, and a man and woman come out with him and examine
the bodies. The horse is dead—the man sees that at once; but the
rider breathes and is bleeding still. The man goes back to the house,
taking the boy with him, while the woman runs for some water,
with which she bathes the face of the wounded man, and washes
away the congealed blood. The man and boy presently appear
again, carrying a board. The three, then, with their united strength,
place the wounded man on the board, and carry him in, leaving the
horse by the roadside. The wounded gentleman is placed in a
comfortable bed, and the man dresses his wounds and applies
remedies with considerable skill. Life is preserved, but delirium
comes on, caused by a slight concussion of the brain. No surgeon
is sent for;—the man says he can cure him himself; and the woman
and the boy, having apparently implicit confidence in his skill, yield
to his wishes. They watch with the sufferer throughout the night,
and the boy is despatched, in the morning, to the nearest town, for
medicines and other things necessary for the patient's use and
comfort.

Several days and nights pass, and the patient is still delirious.
The man continues most attentive and skilful. The patient gradually
gets better. He is out of danger; and, one evening, the man, after
giving the woman the most minute instructions as to her treatment
of the invalid, leaves, desiring her to keep strict watch over him,
and keep the doors locked, so that he may not get away from the

K

house until his return. The boy was left to assist the woman in attending on the invalid and keeping watch.

Frederick had now been an inmate of this lonely house about a week. He was fast recovering from the effects of the fall, but still too weak to leave his bed, although he wished most earnestly to get away, or to have his questions answered; for he didn't at all remember what took place after the horse fell, nor did he know where he was, nor who his attendants were.

The woman pretended not to know anything, and the boy generally evaded the questions, or answered very wide of them. The morning after the departure of the man, under whose skilful treatment Morley was progressing so favourably towards recovery, the boy entered the room with a cunning smile on his countenance, and said that he had a letter for the invalid.

"A letter!" said Morley, feebly, "who can possibly have written a letter to me? no one but those I have seen about me, know where I am." Taking the letter from the boy, however, he was astonished to find that it was from Alrina. He was too anxious and impatient to read it, to think of the bearer, or to ask any questions concerning the letter or its writer, until he had read its contents, which he did with such eagerness, that the boy was alarmed lest the invalid should relapse into delirium again;—not that he was easily alarmed or frightened at anything he saw or heard, but he knew that if the gentleman became delirious again, it would give him extra trouble.

In her letter, Alrina complained of her lot. She had thought, she said, that Frederick would, at least, have written her a line in reply to her first letter. She felt, now, that she was deserted by all. Everything seemed going against her. Her aunt had not returned yet; but her father came frequently, and she felt convinced there was some terrible secret, which they endeavoured to keep from her, but she was determined to find it out. The boy seemed willing to befriend her, she said, but she was almost afraid to trust him. And so she went on to the end of the letter, in the same desponding strain; winding up by asking Frederick, if he really loved her to lose no time in coming to her rescue, or, at least, to write a line, that she might know there was, at least, one person in the world who cared for her. It was a melancholy letter from begining to end, and its perusal made her lover wretched. She was evidently under restraint somewhere; but where? that was the question: even if he knew, it was impossible for him to go to her at present; he was too weak. The boy who brought her letter might know something, and he turned to ask him, but he had left the room. He tried to get up; the exertion was too much for him, and he sank back on his pillow again. His only resource was to read the letter again and again. The more he reflected on Alrina's position, however, and on the unfortunate circumstances which had prevented his receiving her first letter in time, and his consequent inability to render her that assistance and consolation which he would have given worlds to have been able to do, the more irritated and unhappy did he feel; so that when the boy returned, he was in such a high state of excitement, that his attendant was afraid, at first, to go near him.

The wish for further information, however, which he believed the boy could give him, caused Morley to subdue his feelings, and to induce him, by the promise of a reward, to be a little more communicative than he had hitherto been. By degrees, the boy approached the bed cautiously, when Morley asked him, as mildly as he could, when and where he had received the letter, and if he knew where Alrina was at that moment confined, with many other questions too numerous for the boy to answer without a little time and consideration. Before he answered any of them, therefore, he gave that cunning smile, which had so annoyed Morley before, and which now irritated him beyond measure, when he was so anxious to hear something of her to whom he felt he had unwittingly given cause for complaint; but he soon saw that he should get nothing out of the boy by threats or angry expressions, so he changed his tactics, and extracted the information he wanted by asking one question at a time. That was certainly the oddest boy he had ever met with, he thought; for, although, judging from his diminutive stature, no one would have supposed him to be above eight or nine years of age, yet, from his shrewd knowledge of the world, and aged expression of countenance, he might have been eight- or nine-and-twenty. He was the same boy whom Mr. Brown formerly employed to look after his mare; and it was said, even then, and generally believed, that he was in constant attendance on Mr. Freeman, and knew a good many of his secrets.

He was found one night, when quite an infant, lying at the door of a farm-house in the neighbourhood of St. Just, wrapped up in coarse flannel; but it was never discovered who put him there, nor who the child's parents were. He was placed in the poor-house; and when he was old enough, he was apprenticed to one of the farmers of the district; but he would never settle down under one master,—and after trying to subdue him, without success, his master gave him up to his own inclinations, and so he got his living by doing odd jobs. From his constant intercourse with Mr. Freeman, he lost the broad Cornish dialect in a measure, and only spoke in that way when he was associating with the miners. He was fond of going into Penzance and mixing with the gentlemen's servants there occasionally, from whom he picked up many a slang expression, which he would retail to the frequenters of Mr. Brown's bar, very

much to their amusement.   He was an awkward individual to
gain information from; so Morley was obliged to deal with him
accordingly, and put his questions with caution :—

(*Morley*) " I think I have seen you before, my boy ? "

(*Boy*) " I shouldn't wonder if you had, sir ; and, maybe, I've
seed you before."

(*Morley*) " You kept that mare like a picture ;—I never saw a
better groom, either at home or abroad."

(*Boy—smiling*) " It wasn't much odds, as it turned out, sir."

(*Morley*) " No, no ; but that doesn't alter the fact of your ability
as groom.   Now, tell me—there's a good fellow—who gave you
that letter."

(*Boy—still pleased*) " Why, Miss Reeney, to be sure."

(*Morley—excited*) " What ! Alrina herself ?   Where did you see
her ? "

(*Boy—putting on his cunning look again*) " Where ? why here, to
be sure."

(*Morley—more excited*) " Here ! what, in this house ? "

(*Boy*) " To be sure ; why not ?   She called to me through the
keyhole upstairs, and shoved the letter out under the door, and told
me to take it as before.   I couldn't ask her anything, for I heard
Mrs. Cooper coming upstairs."

(*Morley—rising up in bed in the greatest excitement*) " Oh ! take
me to her !—or, stay, take a message to her at once ; tell her I
am ———— "

(*Boy*) " Stop, stop, sir ; you must lend me a horse to do that."

(*Morley*) " I thought you said she was here, in this house."

(*Boy*) " So she was ; but ' The Maister' took her off with him
last night."

(*Morley*) " Then that was Mr. Freeman who attended me ; and
Alrina has been here all the time, and did not come near me ! Oh !
cruel, cruel ! she must be offended, indeed.   Didn't she ask or try
to come to see me ? "

(*Boy*) " No, she didn't, sir, 'cause she didn't know you was here."

(*Morley*) " Not know it? strange ! "

(*Boy*) " Nothing strange at all, sir, that I can see ; I have seed
stranger things than that, a bra' deal.   She was kept at the top of
the house, and you down here—under lock and key, both of 'ee ;
and last night ' The Maister' took her off with him.   Where they're
gone, I can't say,—I heard ' The Maister' tell Mrs. Cooper something
about America."

(*Morley*) " America ! do you think he intends to go there ? "

(*Boy*) " I do no more know than you do, sir. F'rall I've b'en with
The Maister' so often, an' have seed a good many of his quips and
quirks, and helped in them too, I do no more know what he do main

by what he do say, than a cheeld unborn. He ha' got something upon his mind, that's a sure thing."

The boy was beginning to throw off his reserve, as Morley thus cautiously questioned him; but he saw that if he put his questions too pointedly, the boy would "shut up" again; so he asked a few gossipping questions about Mr. and Mrs. Brown, and Mrs. Trenow, which took the boy off his guard, and he went on talking. It seemed at last as if it were a relief to him to talk of "The Maister," as he called Mr. Freeman, in common with most people of the neighbourhood,—and, in relieving his pent-up mind, he told, perhaps, more than he intended; but he seemed to feel that Mr. Morley was a gentleman who wouldn't betray him, and so he threw off his reserve and trusted him.

"You've heard of Chapel Carn Brea, I s'pose, sir?" asked the boy.

"Yes; I've been there," replied Morley; "it is one of the curiosities of the neighbourhood. No doubt it was a handsome building at one time; and those mounds near it are tombs, no doubt."

"You're right, sir," said the boy; "I've heard 'The Maister' tell stories in Mr. Brown's bar, about that place, that would make your hair stand on end, ef you b'lieved it all. The men he told it to, b'lieved every word; and they wud no more go anist Chapel Carn Brea in the night, than they wud clunk boiling lead. I've b'en there by night an' by day; for I wor curious to find out somethen'."

"You were not likely to find anything there," said Morley, carelessly—which threw the boy completely off his guard; and, being in a communicative mood, he went on,—

"I saw something there one night, that made me feel uncommon queer, sure nuf; and I b'lieve that 'The Maister' ha' got some notion that I do knaw somethen'; for he slocked me up there for to try to frighten me more than once. It was somethen' that I'm sure he must have put there inside one of the walls, that went off like a clap of thunder, and frightened the mare, that night when I was throwed; and I'm sure 'twas his doing, for, when I came to myself, I was upon a bed in 'The Maister's' house, and nobody but his sister knaw'd a word about et. He gave me some stuff, and I soon got about agen. He went out the next morning, and Miss Freeman kept me there under lock and key; and when he came home in the afternoon, he told all about the mare, and how poor Mr. Brown was sitting down 'pon a rock by hisself, fretting about it, and he sent me up to bring him home."

"So you never saw anything more than that at Chapel Carn Brea, after all?" said Morley, by way of bringing the boy back to the secret he seemed about to tell,—for he saw, by his manner, there was something more, and he was anxious to know all he could about this man, although his thoughts were, even then, dwelling, with intense

anxiety, on the probable sufferings, both in body and mind, of his
Alrina.

"Iss I have," cried the boy, eagerly; "but I never told it to a
single soul, from that time to this. Now, mind, you must promise
that you'll never tell." And, without waiting for the promise, he
went on eagerly with his tale. "When 'The Maister' came here to
live first," resumed the boy, "I was but a little chap."

"So I should suppose," said Morley, smiling, "even if you were
in existence, which I very much doubt,—for that must be fourteen
or fifteen years ago, according to the account of Mrs. Brown and
Josiah Trenow, and others of the neighbourhood; so I fancy you
are about to tell me a tale in imitation of your master."

"No, no," replied the boy; "you don't know what I'm going to
tell, and p'rhaps you won't. I'm older than I do look, I can tell 'ee.
·I'm no cheeld, f'rall I do look like one to a stranger, I dare say."

"Well, how old are you?" said Morley; "for I confess I have
been puzzled several times as to your age. In stature you are but a
very little boy; but when I look into your face, and hear your
shrewd remarks, I fancy you may be almost any age."

"Well, sir," replied the boy, looking pleased at the gentleman's
having noticed him so much as to be puzzled about his age; "I'm
above twenty, but how much I don't exactly know."

"Billy!" cried a rough voice from below,—"Billy! I say. Where
the devil is that rapscallion?"

"There!" said the boy; "Cap'n Cooper is come back, and the
old woman is gone out, I s'pose. There'll be the devil to pay if I
don't go down." And away he ran, leaving Morley in a most
unpleasant state of suspense; for he had calculated on gaining a
great deal of information from the boy, both with regard to Mr.
Freeman, and, what he was still more concerned about, the probable
movements and present abode of Alrina.

It was evident, from what the boy said, that he was a prisoner.
He wouldn't have minded the old woman and the boy so much; for
he thought he might be able to work upon their feelings, by bribes
and fair words, sufficiently to induce them to connive at his escape;
and he speculated in his mind, even while the boy was talking with
him, that he might be able to prevail on him to leave Mr. Freeman
and follow him as groom and valet, when he might be of the utmost
assistance in many ways. But now it seemed as if all his aerial
castles were dissolving into the element of which they were composed;
for here was a more formidable jailor, if he might judge by the
rough voice and the commanding tone of the fresh arrival. This
was the master of the house, he had no doubt, from the name;—
Cooper was the old woman's name, he knew. These thoughts drove
him almost mad, and he lay back on his pillow and gave himself up

to despair. "Alrina!" cried he, in his agony; "I feel that all things are working against us; but oh! Alrina, forgive your Frederick,— it was not my fault. Alrina! Alrina!" And, after raving like a madman for some minutes, he fell back exhausted.

In the meantime, the boy, locking the door behind him, as he passed out of the room in which Morley lay, hastened downstairs to meet the master of the establishment.

"Hallo!" exclaimed that gentleman, as he stood with his back to the fire; "where's all the people?"

"How should I know?" replied the boy, in the same unceremonious manner,—for he feared no one but "The Maister," and could be as impertinent as the greatest blackguard in the parish when he chose to be, for which he frequently got punished by those who didn't know him well, and these he generally took some opportunity of retaliating upon, so that no one gained much by punishing little Bill.

It was evident that the captain was out of sorts, and was inclined to vent his spleen upon anybody or anything that happened to come in his way.

"Confound your impudence," said he, advancing towards the boy, with his uplifted fist ready to make a blow at him, when he got near enough; "I'll knock you into the middle of next week, you young rascal!" And he struck at the young offender with such force, that the boy would have been seriously injured, had he not nimbly jumped on one side. The impetus of the blow not being checked by coming in contact with the boy's head, sent the man forward, and he was caught in the arms of his loving wife, who entered at that moment, and they both fell headlong on the floor together, at which the boy laughed and ran out of the room.

Nothing makes a person feel so awkward and foolish as when he measures his length on the floor by an accidental fall; and Captain Cooper and his better half felt quite ashamed of themselves, as they scrambled up from their ignominious position. Fortunately there were no spectators; for the boy had escaped, and was keeping out of sight for the present, but not out of hearing. A little corner sufficed for a hiding-place for him, and thus he frequently picked up a good many odd secrets, which he repeated to "The Maister" when he was assisting him in any of his necromancy, and obtained credit even from "The Maister" for shrewdness beyond his years.

"Where's Freeman?" asked the man, opening a cupboard and taking out a bottle of brandy and a glass to solace him after his fall.

"Gone," replied the woman, shaking herself to rights again; "he started last night, and took Alrina with him."

"The devil he did!" exclaimed the man, drinking off a full glass of the exhilarating liquor; "that's a queer game, when he promised to ———"

"Don't you know that his promises can't always be kept?" said the woman. "Circumstances alter cases. There's been a circumstance here."

"A what!" cried the man, in an angry tone; "why, you're getting so bad as the boy, Jenny Cooper."

"Hush, Cap'n! I've got something to tell 'ee," replied his wife; and seating herself on a low chair, opposite the fire, and blowing it up lustily with the bellows at the same time, she related to her husband the accident, and told him the young gentleman was still in bed upstairs.

"Whew!" whistled the captain;—"then his game is up for a spur, and t'other is out of the way and off the scent,—so no herring-pool, after all; but where is the old man gone to?"

"I don't know," replied his wife; "but I shouldn't wonder if he's gone down to the old place again, now the coast is clear. He'll be noted again in St. Just, now that the breeze is blown over, and the scent is in another quarter, as you do say it is."

"Right you are," rejoined the captain, looking more pleased than he had looked yet since his return. "And now I'll tell you our bit of spree." And he related to his wife the expedition to Ashley Hall, and how his companion had left the girl with the lady, thinking to frighten her into submission to their terms, and that, when she went back again the next day, to see how the land lay, she found the little door in the lane locked and barred on the inside, and when she applied for admission, at the front entrance, she was told that Mrs. Courland could not see her. "So she's in a fix," continued the man; "but she stayed behind, and she'll blow the gaff, if they don't come to, soon. I should have stopped too, but I thought my old friend might want to be off at once, and so I came back to get all things right and straight for the trip."

"And you'd better get things right and straight now," said his wife; "for he may be going off all the same, for what I do know."

CHAPTER XXV.

RETROSPECTION AND RECRIMINATION.

Mr. Morley wrote to Lieut. Fowler from Ashley Hall, saying that he had found his brother and Josiah Trenow there, and that they had discovered a house, which they had every reason to believe was the scene of the murder. He informed his friend also that he and Josiah would remain there a little longer, to make further search, but that Frederick had gone down into Cornwall in search of a party who had slipped through their hands, so far.

In consequence of this letter, Lieut. Fowler was in daily expectation of seeing his friend Frederick Morley at Tol-pedn-Penwith. And the ladies at Pendrea-house were in anxious expectation too; for, now that they knew more of his history, which seemed so fraught with romantic interest, he had become quite a hero in their eyes. Day after day passed, but he did not arrive. The ladies were alarmed, and feared some accident had befallen him; but Fowler ridiculed this idea, and attributed his non-arrival to the strictness of the search he was no doubt making. Who the party was that Frederick was in search of, Fowler didn't know, for the finding of the box by Josiah had been kept a secret. The search after Mr. Freeman was merely to get his help to unravel the mystery of that document, which Josiah seemed to think, from his manner, he knew something about, although it was most probable, as Frederick suggested at first, that Mr. Freeman pretended to know more than he really did, in order to induce Josiah to leave the box and its contents with him. As a drowning man will catch at a straw, so did Frederick catch at this little incident, improbable as he really thought it, in the hope that it might assist him in his search, or that the conjuror, by his skill, might be able to give him some clue to the mystery. Fowler knew nothing of all this, nor did he know of his friend's devoted, and, it may be added, romantic, attachment to the daughter of the celebrated Land's-End conjuror. Had he known it, he would, no doubt, have tried to convince his friend of the folly and absurdity of such a connection. But love is blind; and it would probably have required more eloquence than Lieut. Fowler possessed to have persuaded Frederick Morley that the lovely and fascinating girl whom he loved so passionately from the first moment he saw her, as a schoolgirl, was unworthy of his affection, because her father did not move in the first circles of society. Luckily Fowler was ignorant of this attachment; and so his friend had been spared the annoyance of a discussion with him on the subject. The old squire was as anxious as any of them to see the young soldier once more. But he didn't come.

Miss Pendray's mind was ill at ease—that was evident to all who knew her. She still wandered over the cliffs, and braved the storm; but it was not now, as it used to be, for the sake of looking at the bold scenery. Her wanderings had now a more definite object;—she hoped, every time she climbed those lofty cliffs, that she should meet with someone to share her admiration of the beautiful scenery. She had become accustomed to those pleasant meetings with one of the opposite sex; and she felt a vacuum—a loneliness—that she had never felt before. The stranger whom she met at the ball, and who

seemed so enamoured of her, had disappeared in a most unaccountable manner.   She was beginning to like his attentions, although
there was something in his manner, sometimes, which did not please
her;—she told him as much, the last time she met him.   Perhaps
he was offended: for she had never seen him since the sudden
appearance of that handsome man, who had intruded upon their
privacy at the Logan Rock.   It was a strange coincidence—those
two men, meeting in that strange way.   She was much struck with
the appearance and gentlemanly manners of the gentleman with the
white hair;—she couldn't put him out of her mind for the whole
day; and, the next evening, when Lieut. Fowler brought him to
Pendrea-house, after their return from St. Just, she thought him
the most fascinating man she had ever seen.   There was an open
frankness and ease in his manner, which were wanting in Mr. Smith.
As she reflected now on the difference between the two men, she felt
that Mr. Smith's manners seemed put on for the occasion, and that
he required to be on his guard, and to be always watching himself,
as it were, to prevent some hidden vulgarity from peeping out under
his apparently assumed garb of refinement.   It was not so with Mr.
Morley;—he was a gentleman intuitively, and, therefore, had no
occasion to watch himself lest he should say or do, inadvertently,
anything he would be ashamed of.   Mr. Morley, too, was much
struck with Miss Pendray's beauty ; but he did not tell her so, point
blank, as Mr. Smith had done on more than one occasion.   He
asked her to shew him some of her favourite scenes on the cliffs,
with which he expressed himself highly delighted, and he pointed
out beauties in the rocks and cliffs and headlands, which she had not
observed before, and described to her, in glowing colours, some of
the magnificent scenery he had himself witnessed in the East.   And
so they continued, day after day, to walk together—sometimes over
the cliffs and sometimes on the smooth sands beneath—admiring the
beauties of Nature, almost with the same eyes and the same thoughts.
They seemed to have so many ideas in unison, and each became so
fascinated with the other, that when the time arrived that Mr.
Morley thought he must in duty visit his relatives, they parted, with
sorrowing hearts, although neither of them knew what a pang the
other felt at parting.

Miss Pendray had not been accustomed, in that out-of-the-way
place, to meet with men of that stamp ;—she had never before come
into contact with a congenial spirit.   Frederick Morley was better
than most she had been in the habit of meeting ; but he would,
occasionally, appear so absorbed in his own thoughts, that he was,
at times, scarcely companionable.   Mr. Smith was bold and clever,
evidently, and as romantic in his ideas and pursuits as she could
possibly desire, and frequently fascinated her with his thrilling

stories; but there was something in his manner sometimes that did not satisfy her; and his aversion to join their domestic circle seemed most strange.

Mr. Morley was quite different, in every respect; and, now that she wandered over the cliffs alone, day after day, she could reflect on the difference between the three men. She had always looked down with pity on her younger sister's susceptibility, and often upbraided her for exhibiting, so unreservedly, her attachment to Lieut. Fowler, who was not at all suited to her, either in age or position, Miss Pendray thought.

The gentle Blanche could now turn the tables on her more prudent and high-minded sister; for she saw that the handsome Mr. Morley had made a conquest, and that the majestic Maud watched his every look and action, and was pained, beyond measure, when, even in common politeness, he paid the slightest attention to anyone else.

While Maud and Mr. Morley were thus revelling in each other's society, over the bold cliffs and headlands, Blanche and her lover were taking their quiet walks along the rocks and sands beneath, where they would, ever and anon, stop and rest themselves, and look out on the broad ocean which lay before them, talking of the future, and hoping that all might turn out smoothly in the end; for, although Blanche quite understood what her lover meant now, and returned his love with the fondest affection, and wished to her heart that all could be settled at once, yet she was still afraid for her father to be spoken to on the subject, lest he should get angry, and forbid their intercourse altogether. Poor silly child! her timid nature feared she knew not what; and the more her lover urged her to allow him to ask her father's consent, the more did she recoil from the ordeal, dreading what the answer might be. She knew her sister's thoughts and opinions on the subject, and she feared her father might hold the same opinion, for they were much alike in pride and lofty bearing; and so her timid fear overcame her prudence, and she held her lover back from doing that which he well knew and felt he ought to do, in common honesty and honour. But he loved his darling Blanche too well to thwart her; and so the two went on in tender communing, and each day brought fresh arguments on either side—the one, in manly uprightness, urging the appeal to the father for his sanction to their union; the other, in timid maidenly reserve, dreading the answer her stern parent might give, and controlling her fond lover, who felt he could not disobey her.

"Only wait a little longer," she said, one day, as she sat listening to his arguments, and looking up at him so earnestly;—"you don't know papa so well as I do. In most things he is so kind; but I fear in this he would not be so."

"Why do you think so, dearest Blanche?" he replied, taking her hand in his; "he seems to like me, and is continually asking me to come to Pendrea-house. What objection can he have? have you ever heard him say he disliked me, or ———"

"Oh! no! never," she replied; "but Maud and papa seem to hold the same opinions on many points; and she has spoken to me often of the disparity of age, and seemed so utterly against it, that I fear papa will think so too."

"It shall be exactly as you wish," said he; "but I would much rather know my fate at once, than wait in suspense;—what good end can it answer to delay it?"

"Oh! don't talk in that way," replied Blanche, bursting into tears;—"you know how much I should wish it settled, too; but then, if papa should be angry, and refuse to give his consent, I should never see you again. I cannot bear to think of that."

Poor little innocent timid Blanche! she knew not what troubles her timidity was bringing on them both. It was her first love; and, childlike, she thought only of her present pleasure. She felt like one in a pleasant dream, gliding through the air on azure clouds, wafted gently onwards by a zephyr's breeze, with her lover ever by her side to protect her from harm; and she feared lest the slightest change in their present position should cause an angry storm to rise, and overturn all their blissful happiness. She did not know, poor girl, in her ignorance, of the changes and chances that are continually going on in the world, where the greatest pleasures and the severest pains and trials last but for a season, and they are gone, and old Time keeps on the even tenor of his way, and pains and pleasures live only in the memory, and fade away as time rolls on, leaving, in the end, but a faint shadow of the past.

Blanche knew not this; and, anxious to secure present happiness, she induced her lover, in the very innocence of her young heart, by tears and entreaties, to delay his application to her father for a time, in defiance of his better judgment; for he was older, and knew the world much better than this poor innocent girl, but still he yielded, and they loved on in secret.

While Maud was so engrossed with Mr. Morley, there was no one to watch and overlook them; but when he was gone, it seemed to her as if all her occupation was gone too,—she had nothing left but to wander out alone and think of him whose image ever haunted her;—and, in her wanderings, she often surprised Blanche and her attendant lover, in one of their favourite haunts. And, wanting some better occupation, she would chide her sister when they were alone together. At first, Blanche didn't mind it much; but its frequent repetition angered her, and she spoke up sharply to her sister, contrary to her wont, which made Maud speak her mind more freely. And as they sat at work alone, one afternoon, she renewed the old subject:—

"I must tell you, Blanche," she began, "that I think it is very wrong in you to encourage Mr. Fowler to pay you such marked attention, when, perhaps, he means nothing, after all."

"I will not allow anyone, in my presence, to impeach Mr. Fowler's honour," replied Blanche, looking up from her work, her cheeks burning with indignant pride; "I have the most perfect confidence in his honourable intentions, and therefore I will not hear him traduced."

"There we differ," returned her elder sister, hastily; "and, let me tell you that, were his intentions ever so honourable, papa would never sanction the engagement of a daughter of his to Lieut. Fowler."

"And, pray, what would be the objection?" asked Blanche, indignantly.

"There are several," replied her sister; "I know papa's opinion of his position pretty well, for I have already sounded him on it."

"And what right, let me ask, had you to sound papa on a subject which you know nothing about?" asked Blanche;—"that subject has never been named by Mr. Fowler, either to you or to papa, that I am aware of."

"Then it ought to have been," replied Maud, "and that would have settled the matter at once. It is neither honourable nor manly in Mr. Fowler to ensnare your affections, and wish you to meet him clandestinely, as I fear and know you too often do. What his intentions are, I don't know; but, if I may judge from this circumstance, they cannot be honourable, and it is time papa took some measures to prevent it, before it is too late."

"I am surprised, Maud," replied her sister, coolly, "that you, above all others, should accuse me of doing the very thing that you have been doing yourself for the last two months."

"Me!" exclaimed the majestic Maud; "how dare you say such a thing?"

"Yes, you!" replied Blanche. "If I have walked occasionally with papa's old friend, Mr. Fowler, I have done so openly, and with him only,—while you have had three strings to your bow, two of whom I know you met clandestinely, often and often, my prudent sister. What has become of the stranger you met at the ball, who called himself 'Mr. Smith?' did you think your meetings with him were not known? And, having lost him, you carried on the same game with Mr. Morley. Did either of these gentlemen ask papa? If not, I say they ought to have done so, before they induced you to meet them so often, clandestinely, at the Logan Rock,—a nice secluded place for lovers to meet at, truly?"

The timid Blanche had never spoken so fearlessly and sharply to her sister before, and Maud was perfectly astonished. She felt conscious, all at once, that the tables were turned on her deservedly

—for she had an inward conviction of the truth of what her sister had said; but, like most people whose minds are filled with one great and absorbing passion, she neither saw nor knew that her actions were observed and commented on by the lookers-on in the outer world. Although she looked upon the world in general with cold indifference, and would sit for hours as inanimate as a statue, her handsome features looking, in repose, like a piece of beautifully-chiselled, tinted, marble; yet, when anyone approached in whom she took a more than ordinary interest, or any subject was introduced which it pleased her to discuss, her countenance would light up instantaneously, and you might see the fire of her soul shine out with dazzling brilliancy, in her dark flashing eyes. Nothing, then, could control the ungovernable passion that dwelt within; and the longer it had lain dormant, the stronger would it now burst forth, seeing nothing but that one object on which her mind was then intent. With such an all-absorbing passion had she, during the last few days of his sojourn among them, loved Mr. Morley. At first she was passive;—she walked with him, and pointed out the beauties of the scenery, and listened to his description of the scenes he had passed through in India, with pleasure, certainly, but not with the rapture she now felt in all he said or did. She liked him, at first, as a highly-gifted gentlemanly companion,—when, all at once, she was seized with that ungovernable love for him, which prevented her from seeing anything else; nor did she care, in her mad passion, if the whole world was looking on,—she was blind to all but him. She, like Blanche, thought but of her present happiness, but, unlike Blanche, she thought not of her father's consent nor dissent; and so she was taken quite by surprise, when she found that all her doings had been seen and commented upon. She had been like a little playful child, who covers its head, and thinks, poor little innocent, that, because it cannot see the company around, it cannot be seen by them. Maud was shocked at the discovery. It roused another passion within her—that of anger; and, rising from her seat, with a haughty frown, she swept from the room, and left her poor timid sister trembling and frightened, wondering what she had said or done to cause such a terrible commotion within her sister's breast.

CHAPTER XXVI.

SQUIRE PENDRAY GETS ON HIS STILTS, AND VIEWS LIEUT. FOWLER FROM A LOFTY EMINENCE.

WHEN Lieut. Fowler called at Pendrea-house the next morning, to take Blanche out, as he had promised, to finish a sketch she was making of a scene near the Logan Rock, he was met at the door by the old squire himself, who, bowing stiffly asked his visitor to grant him a few minutes' conversation in the library.

"This is an odd reception," thought Fowler; "the old gentleman is up on his stilts this morning." But, however, as he knew the squire was very uncertain in his temper, he followed him in silence; and, when they had entered the room, the squire requested him to be seated, and, after a moment's pause, in which he seemed to be considering how he should begin, he said, rather abruptly,—

"I have not deserved this at your hands, Lieut. Fowler."

"What, sir?" said Fowler, in the greatest surprise.

"When you came into this district," continued the squire, without noticing Fowler's remark, "I invited you to my house; and my family and myself have tried to make it as agreeable as we could to you, as you seemed lonely up there by yourself; and the return I have had for all my kindness, has been your undermining the innocent simplicity of my youngest daughter, and, in an underhand and clandestine manner, gaining the affections of an unsophisticated, simple girl, and inducing her to meet you in bye-places unknown to her family."

"My dear sir!" exclaimed Fowler, scarcely knowing what he said —he was so taken by surprise; "I protest ———"

"It is of no use your denying it," continued the squire; "for I am in possession of the fact that you have destroyed my child's peace of mind, without ascertaining whether your attentions would be agreeable to me or not."

"I acknowledge that I love your daughter, squire Pendray," replied Fowler; "but I hold her and all your family in too high respect to do anything underhand or clandestinely, to gain her affections; and I tell you, sir," he continued, rising with calm dignity, "I have not done so; and, if you had not been Blanche's father, I would not submit quietly to be taunted in this way. I should have communicated my feelings to you long ago, but ———"

"But what, sir!" exclaimed the squire, rising from his seat also.

"But for a timid feeling which Blanche possesses," replied Fowler, "that ———"

"Whatever fears Blanche might have had, sir, they ought not to have prevented you from acting as an honourable man and a gentleman. You are many years older than my daughter, Lieut. Fowler, and ought not to have led her away thus. It is well, perhaps, that the discovery has been made before it was too late. You have taken advantage of my hospitality, sir, and I desire you will not enter my doors again; and whatever there may have been between you and my daughter, it must cease. Sir, I wish you a very good morning." And, bowing to his visitor, the crusty old gentleman opened another door, which led to the upper part of the house, leaving Lieut. Fowler standing in the middle of the room, and wondering what could be the meaning of all this, and who could have informed the squire of his attachment to his daughter, and of their meetings. He was conscious of the rectitude and earnestness of his intentions, and knew, of course, that he had been prevented from making them known to her father, only by the earnest intreaty of Blanche herself. But he could not compromise her—indeed he had not an opportunity of doing so, even if he wished; for, before he had time to reply, or to defend himself, the old gentleman was gone, and there was no one to receive his explanation. At first he thought that, perhaps, Blanche might have been questioned by her father, and had been induced to confess their attachment and their frequent meetings, without having had the courage or the opportunity to explain the reason.   .

He could not remain in the house, of course, nor could he call again, after what had taken place; but he thought he should like to hear from Blanche herself how far she was implicated (unintentionally, he was quite sure) in divulging their secret, and thus causing his dismissal from a house which he had visited with so much pleasure ever since he had been in Cornwall. He determined, therefore, that he would see Blanche, if possible, before he left. So he rang the bell. The servant who answered it said, in reply to his request to see Miss Blanche for a moment, that she was confined to her room with a headache, and could not see him; so he had no alternative but to leave the house.

How little do we know what a day may bring forth! As he walked away from that house where he had been accustomed to be received almost as one of the family for a period of four or five years, Lieut. Fowler began to reflect on the changes and vicissitudes of human life, and how easily the merest trifle, light as air, will sometimes turn the scale. From his first introduction to squire Pendray, to the present time, they had been, as it were, boon companions; for the squire, although an old man, was a jolly companion over his wine, and would frequently, even then, at his advanced age, take his gun and have a day's sport with his friend, and keep up with him too, to the end of the day without flagging, and would enjoy the bachelors' dinner, and a glass of grog afterwards, at the lieutenant's little cabin, where the dinner was cooked by a jolly tar, and served up in sailor fashion, as much as if the table was spread with the daintiest dishes, and everything was done in the first style of fashion. And, only two days before, when Fowler dined at Pendrea-house, he thought, as they sat at their wine after dinner, that it was impossible his old friend could refuse him his daughter's hand, if he could only be permitted by her to ask the question; for he had been always treated more like a brother by the young ladies, than like a stranger. And now, without even allowing him an opportunity of explaining his conduct, or of exculpating himself from the insinuations thrown out against his character as a man of honour and a gentleman, he is unceremoniously expelled from the house, and forbidden all further intercourse with her for whom he would willingly lay down his life.

That some secret enemy had been at work, he had not the slightest doubt; but who it could be, he could not imagine. He was not, therefore, in a very serene state of mind, when he arrived home, as his men soon discovered. He ordered them out on night duty, and said he should himself take a long round and inspect all the outposts during the night.

Blanche had not heard of her lover's having been at the house. She was not very well, but a walk in the fresh air would have done her good, and she sat in her room expecting to be informed by her maid, as she had directed, when Lieut. Fowler called; but none of the female servants saw him come in, and they did not know he was in the house; for he had been admitted, as will be remembered, by squire Pendray himself, who, anticipating that Lieut. Fowler would probably try to see his daughter before he left the house, desired the footman to say that Miss Blanche could not be seen; and so the servant was prepared with his answer before the question was asked. Hour after hour passed away, and still Blanche waited in anxious expectation, but he did not come—as she supposed; and at length she went down into the drawing-room to join her mother and sister.

Maud had done her work cleverly and successfully, and she was satisfied with herself;—she had avenged the unpleasant insinuations and reflections cast upon her by her younger sister; and she had prevented her, she believed, from being ensnared into a connection which was not deemed eligible in any way for a daughter of the house of Pendray.

Nothing was said by either of the ladies about Lieut. Fowler; and so Blanche remained in ignorance of his visit and its termination. Day after day passed away, but Lieut. Fowler did not make his appearance, and Blanche became alarmed. She walked out occasionally with the hope of meeting him at one of their favourite haunts, but he did not come. Maud would now accompany her sister, which was very unusual, their pursuits and ideas being so widely different. Blanche could not understand it; and, after their late conversation,

she did not like to mention the name of Fowler to her sister, and so
they went on—each having a secret and reserving it in her own
breast, fearing, and yet wishing, to talk to each other with that
confidence which should have existed between two sisters, who had
scarcely ever been separated in their lives.

Blanche, at length, began to feel unhappy and uncomfortable.
She declined going out when her sister asked her, and would sit in
her own room, with her door locked, all day long, and never join
the family, except at meal-times, when she shewed evident signs of
mental distress The tears would sometimes chase each other gently
down her cheeks, as she sat pretending to eat—for it was a mere
pretence;—she had no appetite, and merely came to the table
because she was obliged to do so, to prevent being questioned.   She
feared he was ill, but she dared not ask; and thus, poor timid child,
"she let concealment, like a worm i' the bud, feed on her damask
cheek," and pined away in lonely sadness.

Squire Pendray and his eldest daughter divined the cause of
Blanche's melancholy; but, instead of commiserating and consoling
her, they privately denounced Lieut. Fowler as the cause of it all.
And, the more Blanche gave way to her secret grief, and pined for
the loss of him whose presence seemed almost necessary to her
existence, the more did they censure and reproach their former
friend.

The only comforter—if such it might be deemed—whom Blanche
had, was Mrs. Pendray, her kind indulgent mother. She, poor lady,
knew nothing of the love affair, and attributed her darling daughter's
illness to another cause, and overwhelmed the sufferer with well-
meant attentions, and loaded her with dainties of all sorts—none of
which could Blanche touch.

The old squire was concerned to see his little pet pining away,
and refusing all nourishment; but his pride would not permit him
to yield in any one particular.

Miss Pendray, too, had her moments of secret anxiety; for Mr.
Morley had not written to anyone, as far as she knew, since his first
letter to Lieut. Fowler, and he had now been gone a fortnight. Lieut.
Fowler might have heard, perhaps, but she had been the means of
precluding the possibility of knowing; for it was in consequence of
her tale-bearing to her father that he had been forbidden the house.
She did not, perhaps, calculate on the mischief she was doing, when
her pride and her ungovernable passion prompted her to betray her
sister.

CHAPTER XXVII.

THE STEP IN THE WRONG DIRECTION.

It was a curious fact that everyone who spoke of Mr. Freeman, wound up their description of him by saying that he had something on his mind;—but what that something was, or by what means they had ascertained the fact, or why they had come to that conclusion, they could not tell. There was, certainly, some mystery about him, inasmuch as he kept a good deal to himself, and generally appeared thoughtful and taciturn. He had come to St. Just from some distant part of England, many years before, and had bought the house in which he resided, and lived there alone for some time. Then Miss Freeman came. He called her his sister;—some said she was his wife; but, as neither of them cared much what was said about them, gossips got tired at last, and allowed them to be what they were— brother and sister.

Years rolled on; and Mr. and Miss Freeman continued to reside at St. Just, and to mix occasionally with the people, but no one seemed really to know them a bit better than they did at first. Their motto seemed to be, " to hear, see, and be silent."

One hot summer, an epidemic broke out in the parish. There was no doctor nearer at that time than Penzance. It was too expensive for the poor to send for him at such a distance, and many of them died for want of medical assistance.

Mr. Freeman did not, at first, take much notice of it,—he kept aloof. At length, a boy who went errands for him, and did other jobs, caught the infection. Mr. Freeman went to see him, and gave him some medicine which cured him. This got abroad, and Mr. Freeman was sought after, and he cured many others.

When the epidemic among the human beings was over, there came one among the cattle and pigs. It was rumoured that the evil eye was upon them, and that they were ill-wished. Mr. Freeman was applied to again. He had been reading the minds of the people, and getting at their secrets while he was attending them. And, storing up in his memory the petty strifes and bickerings among them, he could tell pretty nearly how they were affected towards each other; and the little boy he had cured of the fever, and who was now his factotum, assisted him; so that, by a few lucky cures of their cattle, and a very slight hint at someone with whom the ill-wished party was at variance, the ill-wisher was sufficiently indicated to procure "The Maister"—as he was now beginning to be designated —a brilliant reputation, which he profited by considerably ; and the people feared him and honoured him, for his wonderful knowledge and ability ;—but, notwithstanding all his skill, everyone thought that "The Maister" had something upon his mind. The brother and sister were an odd pair,—no one could understand them,—and so they ceased to be much talked about after a time. Their movements were very uncertain. They would lock up the house and go away, and stay away for weeks, sometimes. Some of their neighbours wished they would stay away altogether; but they would not venture to say so, even to themselves; for they believed that " The Maister" could read their very thoughts almost.

Years rolled on; and one day, Miss Freeman, having been absent longer than usual, brought home a beautiful young lady with her. Here was food for another gossip. Who was she? She was not like Miss Freeman, nor was she much like " The Maister;" but they were told she was his daughter. He had been left a widower when Alrina was very young, Miss Freeman said, and so she had been at school ever since, agreeably to her mother's dying request. Gossip wore itself out in this instance also; and Alrina was allowed to settle down as Mr. Freeman's daughter,—indeed, there was no one to dispute it; why should they?

The idle gossip of a country village may suggest and insinuate many things; but the proof is generally wanting when they come to the test. Miss Freeman went to fetch the young lady, certainly;— and why not? Gossip was at fault, and Alrina resided quietly with her father and aunt.

Whether Mr. Freeman intended to prevent his daughter from having any intercourse at all with young men of about her own age, or whether he had any objection to Frederick Morley individually, certain it is, that, as soon as he discovered their meetings, he contrived to confine his daughter to the house, by giving her some powerful narcotic. And, leaving her in the care of his sister, he went to Portagnes, to make arrangements for their removal to the house of Capt. Cooper, which was more calculated for seclusion and confinement than his own.

The two men were well suited to each other, and played a good game. Capt. Cooper was bold, rough, and daring, and was the captain of a nice little vessel in which Mr. Freeman held a large share. And in this he would go across the water for contraband goods, and Mr. Freeman assisted him in disposing of them in some of the large towns where he had friends;—and many a daring adventure had Capt. Cooper been engaged in, and many a clever run had he made, and evaded the officers of the customs, and effected landings almost under their very eyes. His house was a very large one; and underneath, there were commodious cellars, which were of great use in concealing the contraband goods.

Why Frederick Morley's appearance at the Land's-End had made these men so uneasy, it is difficult to say. He was a soldier, and was on intimate terms of friendship with Lieut. Fowler, the avowed enemy of smuggling; and, if allowed to meet Alrina as a lover, secrets might be told which she could not help knowing, they thought. This was one reason, perhaps, why they wished to get rid of him. But they hadn't succeeded yet. Mr. Freeman tried the ride on the mare to the Land's-End point, but the rider was preserved. Now he was completely in their power, but they were puzzled what to do with him. Alrina had been removed out of his way again, and the secret of his being there had been kept from her, but the boy knew it. He was the first who discovered him, when he was lying insensible under the garden wall. The boy was useful to them, but they feared him; for he knew too much, and, with all their shrewdness, they could not fathom him. He might betray them any day. He knew enough of their secrets; and, although he knew nothing criminal against them, he was a check upon them,—otherwise Cooper would not have hesitated to get rid of their troublesome visitor very quickly. Mr. Freeman, too, might have got rid of him by allowing him to perish when they found him outside the garden wall, wounded; but both the woman and the boy would have procured medical aid, if he had not used his utmost skill in restoring him,—and this would not have suited Mr. Freeman at all just at that time and in that place; so he used his utmost skill, and cured him, and there he lay a prisoner still.

That unfortunate girl, before mentioned, had been a source of profit to them all, notwithstanding her infirmity. Cooper and his wife had had her in their keeping from her infancy. The neighbours thought she was their own child; but they always called her their niece, and the poor girl was pitied for her dreadful calamity, and for the unkindness with which most people knew she was treated.

At stated periods, Miss Freeman would go to Ashley Hall, or wherever Mrs. Courland happened to be, and work upon her fears, as she best knew how; for Miss Freeman was a shrewd and cunning woman, and the best suited of the party for an expedition of this kind. And the dread of her husband's knowing her secret, generally induced Mrs. Courland to comply with the exorbitant demands made upon her. She had been applied to for a large sum, but without effect, for she candidly told them that she had not the money. This did not satisfy them. They wanted a large sum for a particular purpose, and they might not be able to come again for some time. They did not believe Mrs. Courland's statement, that she had not the money; and, in order to terrify her into compliance, the girl was brought and left on her hands, as we have seen.

A tender chord was struck in the heart of Mrs. Courland by that look of penitence and sorrow which the poor afflicted girl put on, when she found that she had injured one who bore the pain without resentment. When the poor girl dropped on her knees, and gave vent to her feelings by a gush of tears, the lady yearned towards her, and, looking at her with compassion, she said, " Yes, it may be so;"—and, from that moment, she made up her mind to keep the poor creature with her, and teach her all she was capable of learning. She would, by this, be preserving the girl from the ill-treatment which she saw by her countenance and manner whilst the woman was in the room she had evidently been subject to, and she would also, by this act, save herself from the continual annoyance of this woman's visits and importunity. She might keep this poor girl as a dependant, and account for her presence there, by saying that she came into the garden through the little private door from the lane, and fell on her knees in a supplicating attitude, which she (Mrs. Courland) understood to mean, " Take care of me,"—and she had taken care of her, out of compassion. This was, in fact, true, as far as it went; and of course the girl herself could not betray her. So, instead of concealing the girl in the little inner room, as she had intended, she sent for her niece and told her the tale.

It seemed so romantic, that Miss Morley was delighted, and amused herself by trying to talk to the girl by signs, which she soon found she understood with remarkable quickness; for, in all but the power of speech and hearing, she was shrewd and intelligent. This was a new occupation for Mrs. Courland; it opened out a new life to her; it relieved her mind from the anxieties which had almost overwhelmed her before.

Her husband might come now,—she was not afraid of the tales of her persecutors. She knew the worst, and was no longer harassed by suspense. She could tell him as much or as little as she pleased,—her silent protégé could not enlighten him further; and the people she so much dreaded before, she would not admit to her presence again.

A suitable wardrobe was procured for the delighted girl; and Julia, assisted by Mrs. Courland's own attendant, succeeded in making her look quite presentable in a short time. They were very much amused at her utter astonishment, when she looked at herself in the glass, after they had dressed her and arranged her hair, according to the "mode,"—she could not make it out at all. She looked into the glass and smiled, as if pleased with the change, and then looked round, as if trying to find her former self. They then proceeded to teach her how to conduct herself in keeping with her dress, especially in the etiquette of eating and drinking among well-bred people; and it was astonishing, how soon she learned all they wished to teach her. The next puzzle was to find a name for her; and, as she seemed remarkably fond of flowers, they called her " Flora;"—not that it made any difference to her, poor girl, whether she had a name or not; but it enabled her kind friends to designate her the better when speaking of her.

Mr. Morley and Josiah, in the meantime, had effected an entrance into the deserted house, through the window in the end, which entered into the bedroom on the ground floor.   One glance sufficed to convince Mr. Morley that this was the house,—he had heard it described so often by his father.   There were dark marks on the floor still, and the bed was blood-stained, although time had softened it down into a faint tinge only.

That bed appeared never to have been touched since that fatal night, except to remove the dead body of the murdered man from it; and the other rooms also seemed as if they had been lately occupied, except that everything was covered with dust and cobwebs, and the rats and mice had made sad inroads into the bed-curtains and everything that they could convert into food, or make an impression on with their sharp teeth.   An old rat came out of one of the bed-rooms to meet them as they mounted the stairs, and seemed astonished and indignant at the intrusion; but when he saw that the intruders were not to be daunted by looks of defiance, he turned and scampered back again to his old quarters between the blankets.   The beds had remained as they were when the fugitives left; and on turning down the covering of the bed to which the rat had directed its course, Josiah discovered a nest of young rats comfortably settled.   They soon scampered off, however, and, in their retreat, roused others; and there was a precious noise through the house, as the inmates rattled downstairs.   No wonder that the house had the name of being haunted.   These noises had been heard before, no doubt, when some daring thief had attempted to get in to rob it; and their super-stitious fears preserved the house and its contents from invasion.   It was very easy to account for the last occupiers having left all things as they were; for they were, no doubt, glad to get away as soon as possible, after they had thrown the scent off from themselves by accusing another; and Mr. Morley's money, which they must have taken with them, was amply sufficient to compensate them for the loss of the house and furniture, and to provide them with all they would require for a very long time.

The rooms were all in the same state.   Some of the drawers and cupboards were partially open, while others were locked, but the keys had been left in them.   Everything betokened a hasty flight. In some of the drawers were found a few articles of clothing, both male and female; but these were moth-eaten and discoloured.   There were no papers of any kind to serve as a clue to the discovery of the parties.

In searching one of the drawers in what appeared to have been the bedroom of a female, Josiah found a gold earring, of a peculiar pattern, with a small diamond in the drop end of it.   This he put into his pocket, with the intention of giving it to the dumb girl, to amuse her; for all the household, at Ashley Hall, had already begun to take an interest in her, and she was getting quite at home with them, and familiar with every part of the house, and she could now make herself understood, without much difficulty. Mr. Morley thought it was very strange that such a valuable ornament should be found in such a house. Those earrings, however, might have been a present from some rich lady for services performed. The other earring might have been lost; or this may have been a stray one, taken in a hurry, among other trinkets, which the owners of that house might have appropriated to themselves from time to time, when they found an opportunity; for it was evident, from the circumstances that had occurred in connection with that murder, that plunder was their principal object.

When Josiah gave Flora the ornament in the evening, she looked at it at first with pleasure, and thanked the donor in her way. She then took it into another part of the room, and examined it more minutely, and admired every part of it. At last she gave a start, and her countenance became overclouded with an expression of terror and pain. This was in the servants' hall. And, running up to Josiah, she became quite outrageous, pointing to the ornament as if in anger; and then, making a sign, as if she thought it had come from a long way off, she threw it on the floor, and would have stamped on it, had not Josiah snatched it up. They could not at all understand what she meant. Josiah was about to put the earring into his pocket again, when she snatched it out of his hand, and ran out of the room. Nothing more was heard or seen of the ornament; and so they supposed she had thrown it away or destroyed it.

Mr. Morley was now beginning to feel uneasy about his brother; for he had heard from his friend Fowler twice, and in both letters he said he had seen nothing of Frederick. So Mr. Morley determined to return to Cornwall again without delay.

CHAPTER XXVIII.

BY DOING A LITTLE WRONG, A GREAT GOOD IS ACCOMPLISHED IN THE END.

FREDERICK MORLEY'S state of mind can better be imagined than described, at finding himself a prisoner in the house which he intended to have entered as the bold deliverer of his beloved Alrina, who was, perhaps, by this time on her voyage to America. The boy continued to attend upon him, and he was beginning, Morley thought, to take an interest in him, and to pity his position; for Frederick, who was now getting strong again, had proposed taking him into his service,—at which he seemed pleased, although he did not say whether he would accept the offer or not. Cunning boy! he knew very well that he was watched closely by Cooper and his wife.

"What the devil were you and that chap whispering about?" said Cooper to the boy, one day, when the latter came down from attending on the invalid.

"If your ears had been long enough you would have heard," replied the boy, in his usual saucy way.

"Come, none of that!" said the man. "I wish 'The Maister' would come and take him off, or give the orders what to do with him; for I don't like this shill-i-shall-i game."

"Nor I," said the boy; "I'm tired too with this work. I'd rather be out than here tending 'pon the sick, like a maid. I tell 'ee what I'd do, ef I wor you, Cap'n,—I'd give'n the run of the cellars."

"What's the good of that, you fool?" replied Cooper, looking as if a bright thought had struck him all at once.

"Why, I'll tell 'ee," said the boy, coming closer to the man, and whispering in his ear,—"he'd be starved to death, or else he'd run his head agen the walls and batter his brains out."

"You young rascal!" exclaimed Cooper, looking at the same time more pleased than he intended to look; "you don't think I'd treat the young fellow like that, do 'ee? He never did any harm to me. If 'The Maister' ha' got a mind to do it, he may, but I sha'n't."

"You're turned chickenhearted all at once," said the boy. "I tell 'ee,—I don't like to be shut in here all day, when a turn of the key in the cellar-door would settle it all, and give me my liberty once more; and I tell 'ee, Cap'n, ef you don't like to do et, give me the key of the cellar, and I'll put 'n in there this very night, and nobody will be the wiser."

This was what Capt. Cooper would like to have done days ago; but he feared a betrayal on the part of the boy; but now that the young rascal, who was the acknowledged protégé of Mr. Freeman, had proposed it himself, he thought he might avail himself of the opportunity, and his friend would thank him when it was all over, and he should be very glad himself to get rid of an enemy so formidable. These were his thoughts and reflections. Why he made them, or what reason either of them had for their antipathy to this young man, did not appear. That they had this antipathy was very evident,—and that their wish to get rid of him was about to be accomplished, was now vividly apparent to the mind of Capt. Cooper without the possibility of any blame being attached to him. He had sufficient control over his feelings, however, to prevent his showing the real pleasure it gave him, to the boy; but he stipulated that, to prevent an escape, he should himself be present to unlock the door, and put the prisoner into this safe stronghold.

The boy then went back to the prisoner, and told him that Capt. Cooper had granted permission for him to take a little exercise on the beach that evening; at which Morley was much pleased, for he felt almost suffocated, shut up in a close room for so long a time. Anywhere, he thought, was better than that. So, when the boy came in the evening to let him out, he almost leaped with joy. At the bottom of the stairs they were joined by Cooper, and the three went down another flight of steps, which seemed to Morley dark and dismal. The boy whispered to him that he would soon be in the open air, but that it was necessary they should reach it by a circuitous route. The man also spoke kindly to him; and down they went, till they came to a door, which the man unlocked,—and, in his eagerness to secure his prey, he gave his prisoner a push, which sent him headlong down another flight of steps.

The sudden fall stunned Morley for a few minutes; but he soon recovered himself, and, on looking round, he found that he was in what seemed to him to be a dark dungeon. This was worse than all. The boy had betrayed him! This he was now convinced of, and he should be left there in that dark cold dungeon to perish. He groped his way round the place as well as he could, and felt that the walls were damp. He stumbled over some casks and boxes, as he went cautiously along; and by degrees, as his eyes became accustomed to the darkness, he could see that he was in an underground cellar, not very large nor very high; but in going round by the wall, he found that this small cellar communicated with a large one, which he groped his way into, through a small archway. Here he sank down on the floor from sheer exhaustion, and began to reflect on his situation.

Everything seemed going against him. It was evident, from the way in which the man had pushed him down the stairs, that he was anxious to get rid of him, and would perhaps resort to some speedy way of doing so; and he feared and believed the boy was in league with him. Why Mr. Freeman should have taken such a dislike to him he could not imagine, for he had never seen him that he was aware of. Altogether, it was a mystery which he could not understand; so he gave himself up to despair, and made up his mind that he would never be permitted to leave that place again. Whether his death would be a lingering one of starvation, or whether it would be a quick one by assassination, he could not of course tell;—he almost wished it might be the latter, for the suspense was dreadful.

Hour after hour passed away, and there he sat brooding over his unhappy fate, but no one came to end his woes. Night came on,— he could feel it although he could not see it, for all was cold and dark and dreary around him. The damp was coming out from the walls, and he felt a chill pass through his frame; for he was still weak from his late illness. Exhausted nature was giving way, and sleep was falling on him. He tried to keep awake; for he feared that if he slept in that place he should never wake again. He got up and tried to rouse himself and keep awake by walking to and fro, but it was of no use. His thoughts were terrible. It was better to suffer death than continue in that state of awful suspense. He sat down at last on an empty box, and yielded to that oblivion which soothes and invigorates the frame, while it relieves the mind from harrowing and disagreeable thoughts and feelings.

CHAPTER XXIX.

MRS. BROWN AND MRS. TRENOW INDULGE IN A CROOM O' CHAT, WHILE CAP'N TRENOW GIVES SOME SAGE ADVICE IN ANOTHER QUARTER.

THE gossips of St. Just were spared the necessity of inventing idle tales to keep conversation alive,—a practice so prevalent in small communities, where the events that happen in everyday life are generally so uninteresting and monotonous. Events had happened within the last few months which gave ample scope to the most inveterate and accomplished gossip for exercising the art of conversation to the fullest extent, and yet be most truthful; although they still had the power of embellishing the facts according to their own lively fancy and vivid imagination. They could talk of "The Maister" now with the utmost freedom; for he was no longer in the neighbourhood to pry into their secrets, and read their thoughts, and ill-wish them for talking of him and his doings. And, as a reservoir of water that has broken through the embankment, after having been pent up till it was full almost to overflowing, rushes with greater force on its first outburst,—or the pent-up steam in a mighty engine when suddenly let loose,—so did the long-restrained tongues of the gossips of St. Just now pour out, to their hearts' content, their secret spleen and antipathy to their dangerous and dreaded neighbour, Mr. Freeman. There was not a house in which some scandal was not going on continually;—and this was not confined to the women, the men being equally intent on "giving the devil his due," as they termed it.

Business was brisk at the "Commercial" Inn. The afternoons were generally devoted to a gossip over a dish of tea and a drop of "comfort," between Mrs. Brown and a few of her intimate female friends, after which the kitchen was occupied until a late hour by the men, who would drink a double quantity of beer if anyone could be found to amuse them by relating some fresh tale.

The chair in which Mr. Freeman had been accustomed to sit in the chimney-corner, was generally left unoccupied by a seeming tacit consent, the better to enable the speaker for the time being to designate the person of whom he was speaking, without mentioning any name, by simply nodding his head towards the vacant chair;—for they were, even now, afraid that "The Maister" might be listening to them in secret.

Of all her female acquaintances, Mrs. Brown preferred Mrs. Trenow for a quiet gossip, because, living very near "The Maister's" house, and having been on intimate terms of friendship with both Alrina and Alice Ann, she could impart as well as receive information.

The whole neighbourhood was teeming with news. Events of the most thrilling interest were happening every hour—and, being told and retold from house to house, they lost nothing in their transit—when, one afternoon, Mrs. Trenow paid her accustomed visit to her old friend Mrs. Brown, whom she fortunately found alone, with the exception of her husband, who was sitting in the chimney-corner, thinking of nothing, and whistling for want of thought.

As she entered, Mrs. Trenow closed the door after her, and looked round the room in a mysterious manner, much to Mrs. Brown's surprise,—for they had lately fallen into the habit of discussing their subject rather more openly, in the conscious security of the absence of the evil-eye.

"Arrah, then!" exclaimed Mrs. Brown, smiling; "the Franch are landed sure nuf now, then, I s'pose. Ef so, we'll put up a red coat to John Brown, and stick 'n out afore the door to frighten them away."

"I don't knaw nothen' 'bout the Franch, not I," replied Mrs. Trenow, drawing her chair as close to the landlady as she could, and bringing her face almost close to the ear of her friend; "but he's come back, cheeld vean!"

"Who's come back?" asked Mrs. Brown,—in a tone, however, which seemed to require no answer.

"I wor setten' up brave an' late, doen a bit of menden'," continued Mrs. Trenow,—"for, what with one body an' another comin' in chatting, I haan't done much by day lately—when I heard footsteps outside, and a woman's voice, complaining of a long walk, and how glad she was to get home once more. So, after they were gone by, I opened the door an' looked out, an' there I seed a man an' a woman. It was bright moonlight, you knaw,—an' who shud they be, but 'The Maister' and Miss Reeney. I cud see them so plain as I can see you now, as they went in through the little gate. Alice Ann was sent for again to-day, an' there they are. Where Miss Freeman es I caan't tell. They came back in a vessel, the maid said, an' wor out a bra' while. Where they've b'en to she cudn't tell, nor Miss Reeney neither, I b'lieve, for she wor kept fine an' close; but I shall knaw more another time,—Alice Ann cudn't stop more than a minute."

"Well, I'm glad they're come back, for one thing," said Mrs. Brown—"an' that's for the sake of Miss Reeney, poor young lady; I b'lieve she's dragged about more than she do like."

"Iss fie!" replied Mrs. Trenow, whispering into Mrs. Brown's ear again; "she's grieving about that young chap, so Alice Ann do say. She wor took away in the night, you knaw, an' never so much as wished 'n well; an' now she don't knaw where aw es, f'rall she ha' sent two letters to un; and she do b'lieve he's dead, for she haan't had a single line from him, ever sence he have b'en gone. An' our 'Siah' said that he wor mad after har; an' ef he's alive he wud ha' found har somehow,—that's my b'lief."

"Well, all I can say es," chimed in Mrs. Brown, "that I'm sorry for them both. I took a mighty fancy to that young man. 'Tes whisht; but I caan't think that he's dead at all. But what's become of 'Siah?"

"Here!" exclaimed that individual, in a stentorian voice, which made the two friends jump from their seats, as he stalked into the room. "Why, I might ha' walked off weth your poor dear husband, Mrs. Brown, and you wud nevar ha' know'd et; for I was standen' behind your backs a bra' bit afore I spok', an' you nevar heard or seed me."

"No, sure," said his mother; "we wor just then spaiken' about you and your young master;—why, where have 'ee b'en, Siah; we thoft you wor lost, but I'm glad you're come back, for more reasons than one. Miss Reeney will be more contenteder now,—I s'pose he'll make et up now, Siah. Ef they're so mazed about one t'other as you do say, why the sooner they're married the better."

"Married!" exclaimed Josiah; "I wish they cud be, poor souls; but where es aw, says you?"

"Where es aw!" asked both the women in a breath; "why, come home weth you, I s'pose,—where else shud aw be?"

"No fie," replied Josiah, in a more serious tone; "I wish aw wor. He started from Ashley Hall a fortnight ago, or more, an' said he wor comin' down here for to sarch for somebody, an' we thoft for to find om here. Maister Morley, hes brother, es over to Leeftenant Fowler's. Mr. Frederick not here! that's whisht, thou. What core to bâl es fe-a-ther this week, mother?"

"He'll be home from bâl about six o'clock to-night," replied Mrs. Trenow.

" I'll have a glass o' brandy toddy, ef you plaise, Mrs. Brown, an'
then go home to ax fe-a-ther's advice. He ded used to have brave
thofts about things."

Captain Trenow was very glad to see his son returned safe and
sound : for, as he had never been a great traveller himself, he could
not understand the pleasure to be derived from locomotion and
change of scene. "I can get along brave here," he would say,
" where I do knaw everybody ; but how I should get along among
strangers I caan't tell. I shud be in a whisht porr sometimes, I
reckon."

But notwithstanding his father's modest opinion of himself, Josiah
held his knowledge and shrewdness in high estimation ; so he related
to his parent the whole of his adventures, from the time he left
home until his return, and then asked his advice upon the whole—
not only as to his own course, but as to the course he would advise
his patron Mr. Morley to pursue, and especially as to the search it
seemed incumbent on them to make after his young master.

" I'll tell 'ee, boy," said Captain Trenow, after he had heard his
son's story, and had ruminated over it for some minutes,—" 'tes like
as this here, you knaw—he's kidnapped, that's what he es !"

" Hould your tongue, do," replied his son ; " that's nonsense. Why,
who wud kidnap he, I shud like to knaw. What good wud that do
to anybody ? What do anybody knaw about he, for to go for to
kidnap 'n ? No, no, ould man ; touch your pipe a bit. They'd be
glad for to bring om back agen, I reckon ; for he's brave an' heavy,
mon. No, he's no more kidnapped than you are ; he's fell in a shaft,
more likely."

" Like enough ! like enough !" replied the father, seriously ; " we
must sarch, boy,—come !" And the kind-hearted miner rose at
once, and took his hat with the intention of proceeding at once to
search and drag every open shaft in the neighbourhood. But Josiah
thought they had better see Mr. Morley first, and inform him that
no tidings of his brother could be obtained at St. Just or the
neighbourhood.

After a good supper, therefore, the two men started for Tol-pedn-
Penwith, where they arrived just as the two gentlemen were about
to retire for the night.

Mr. Morley was much concerned when he found that his brother
had not been seen or heard of at St. Just ; for he had fully made up
his mind that he would visit that place first in his search after the girl
he seemed so devotedly attached to ; and would naturally endeavour
to trace the fugitives, in their journey from thence round the sea-
coast, to the solitary house in which Alrina said, in her letter, she
was then confined.

" I am inclined to think," said he, at length, after a little consideration, " that Captain Trenow's conjecture may be true, and that my brother has been treacherously entrapped by some lawless band of ruffians, for the sake of gain. I scarcely believe he is murdered,—Cornishmen, from what I have heard of them, are not such cold-blooded villains as that,—and I am inclined to hope and believe that he has not fallen into a shaft; but wherever he is he must be found."

" With the morning's dawn," said Lieut. Fowler, " we must commence the search all along the coast, from the Land's-End to Truro. He was last seen at the latter place, you say ?"

" Yes," replied Mr. Morley; " we traced him there, but could gain no further intelligence of him."

" If Captain Trenow and Josiah can go with us," said the lieutenant, " I think they will be of greater service than my own men; for, in the first place, I shouldn't like to take so many of us off duty, and, in the next place, I think these two strong miners will be able to assist us in exploring the shafts in our way, and may tend to prevent any suspicion being attached to our search; whereas, a party of my men searching and exploring the coast, would attract suspicion at once, and put the whole neighbourhood on their guard."

Captain Trenow and Josiah readily consented to accompany the two gentlemen; and, after a few hours' sleep, and a hearty breakfast, they started on their expedition.

For two whole days they searched unceasingly, exploring every shaft they came near,—the two miners having brought ropes, by which one of them was frequently lowered down, to search for their young friend in the bowels of the earth. Houses were entered and searched thoroughly, and all manner of questions asked of the inmates, very much to the astonishment and terror of some of them, but all to no purpose. Yet on they went, searching still, and searching everywhere. At length, towards the end of the third day, they arrived at a solitary spot, which attracted the attention of Mr. Morley. It was a house surrounded by high walls on every side.

" This," he exclaimed, " appears to answer the description given in that letter, better than any place we have seen yet ! Courage, my comrades ! we have found the spot at last."

As they approached the outer door of the garden, they saw in a ditch by the side of the wall, the carcase of a dead horse, on which the crows were feeding so ravenously that they did not perceive the intruders until they were almost close upon them, when they rose in a cloud that almost darkened the sky, making a discordant noise, and flapping the air with their wings, which was heard distinctly until they settled down again in a neighbouring field to wait a favourable opportunity to return again to the feast from which they had been so suddenly dispersed.

Here was the spot, then, wherein, if not Frederick Morley, they felt pretty certain his loved Alrina was confined; and it should go hard, they said, if a clear discharge was not made of all prisoners inside, whoever or whatever they might be. Lieut. Fowler and Mr. Morley were armed with a brace of pistols each, while Capt. Trenow and his son had only their stout cudgels to depend upon.

"Never mind," said Capt. Trenow; "a stout cudgel and a strong arm ha' beat a good many men afore now, and may again;—I arn't afeard; art thee, 'Siah boy?"

"No fie," said Josiah, flourishing his cudgel round his head, and grinding his teeth with energetic determination; "I'll scat them all abroad 'pon the planchen' ef I do come nigh them." And down came the end of the cudgel on a log of wood near him, with such a crash, that the crows were frightened once more, and rose like a rushing mighty wind, and settled down again one field further off.

Whether it was the noise of the crows, or the sound of Josiah's cudgel on the log of wood, or a sudden impulse of female curiosity to see who the strangers were, the door was opened from the inside just at that moment, and a female head peeped out, and as suddenly Josiah sprang at the door, pushing it wide open, and asked as deliberately as he could under the circumstances, "ef the lady wanted to buy a hoss?"

"A hoss!" said the woman, taken quite by surprise; "no,—how ded 'ee think so?"

"Why, the crows are getten' fat upon the hoss you lost last week, and so I thoft you'd be wanten' another," replied Josiah, with the greatest coolness.

"Oh! that wasn't ours," said the woman, taken off her guard by the coolness of Josiah,—"that belonged to a young gentleman that ————"

"Hold your jaw and bar the door, and be d————d to you!" exclaimed a man, coming out of the house in a rage.

"This looks suspicious and businesslike," said Lieut. Fowler, as he rushed into the garden after Josiah, followed by their two companions. The woman had disappeared at the first rush, but they were met midway between the door of the house and the outer door of the garden, by a rough, strong-built man, who seemed half sailor and half miner by his dress.

What the devil do you want here?" said he, addressing Lieut. Fowler, who was now the foremost of the party. "I'm d————d if I don't see light through you in about two twos." And he drew a pistol from a side-pocket, and presented it at the lieutenant's breast.

"Two can play at that game," exclaimed Fowler, drawing a pistol from his breast-pocket.

"And three!" cried Mr. Morley, drawing his pistol also.

"Now, I'll tell 'ee, soas," said Capt. Trenow, putting his cudgel very coolly between the parties, and addressing the stranger on whom they had intruded,—"'tes like as this here, you knaw ; two to one es brave odds,—the one might be killed—sure to be, I s'pose. Ef you've got any more of your sort inside, comrade, bring them out and then we'll fight fe-ar ; or, ef you haan't got no backers for to fight, why lev es have a croom o' chat. Now, I've done, soas ; spaik the next who will. As for fighten, I can stand a bra' tussle ; but as for spaiken, I arn't wuth much."

No backers—as Capt. Trenow called them—came out ; and, as the occupant of the house sew that he was left so sadly in the minority, and felt, no doubt, that he had been the first aggressor, by presenting his pistol at the breast of a king's officer, as he knew Lieut. Fowler to be by his dress, he began to make apologies as best he could, very much to the amusement of Capt. Trenow, who really seemed to be the coolest of the party, and, like a good and experienced general, was equal to the occasion, and could by his coolness and shrewd common sense, persuade where he could not command. And he very soon led the way into the house, as if he had been the owner of it, and was followed by all the party.

As resistance was quite out of the question, against four armed men, and one of them a king's officer in authority, Capt. Cooper made a virtue of necessity, and became very civil and obsequious.

What the object of this visit was he was puzzled to imagine. If it was in search of contraband goods he was safe ; for they had all been disposed of long ago. He was not left long in suspense, however ; for Mr. Morley was too impatient to find his brother to delay his enquiries, and he thought the bolder he did so, the better.

"We are in search of a gentleman," said he, "whom we have traced almost to your door. If he is here you had better say so at once, and produce him. If you decline, we shall proceed in our search ; and if we find him, after a denial by you, the consequences may be serious to you and your household. If, on the other hand, you tell us honestly where he is, and produce him, if in your power, you have nothing to fear."

"If you will tell me the name of the gentleman," replied Cooper, cautiously, "I will inform you if I have seen him or not. I am accustomed to see gentlemen here on business often. But this much I will tell you, that unfortunately at present the only inmates of my house are myself and my wife ; otherwise, perhaps you would not so easily have entered."

"The name of the gentleman we are in search of is Mr. Frederick Morley," said the interrogator. "Have you seen him ?"

The mention of that name seemed to cause the smuggler to start involuntarily ; but he soon recovered his former coolness and said,

" I have no such person here ; but, to satisfy yourselves, you are at
full liberty to search my house; I will get the keys." And he left
the room in search of his wife, who was not far off; and as he left
the room, Josiah slid out after him unperceived, and saw him give
a key to his wife, instead of taking any from her, and whisper
something in her ear; so he determined to watch below while the
others went upstairs.   He had hid himself behind a door in a dark
passage, from whence he watched the momentary interview between
Captain Cooper and his wife, unperceived by them; and when
Cooper returned to the party in the front room Josiah took off his
shoes and followed Mrs. Cooper stealthily down some dark stone
steps.   It was so dark that even she was obliged to grope her way
down.   Once or twice she stopped and turned round and listened as
if she fancied she heard someone following her; but Josiah was
accustomed to grope his way in the dark underground, and could,
therefore, perhaps, see better than she could under present circumstances ; so he continued to dodge her footsteps, until she arrived at
a small secret door in the wall on the right hand, which was so
artfully concealed that a stranger, even with a lamp in his hand,
would most likely pass it, believing it a part of the wall itself. Mrs.
Cooper had evidently found the door by counting the steps as she
descended, and she now groped about with her hand to find the keyhole, which she was not long in doing, for she had evidently
performed the feat many times before.   When she had opened the
door Josiah heard her go down some more steps, into what he thought
a dungeon or vault; and he listened at the door, which she had left
ajar.   When she was at the bottom of the steps, he heard her call
to someone in a low whisper, saying, " Sir ! sir ! where are you ?
follow me and I'll save you.   Come quickly ! "
Josiah now determined at all risks to follow the woman, and see
the end of it and rescue the prisoner if possible; for he now firmly
believed that his young master was incarcerated here, and that it
was to him the woman was calling, perhaps with the intention of
murdering him, or getting rid of him in some way; so he put on his
shoes again and approached the spot from whence the woman's voice
proceeded.   She evidently took him for some other person, and,
seizing him by the hand, she dragged him along after her through
the darkness, until they heard the sea dashing against the rocks,
when she said in a hurried and agitated manner,—
" The smugglers are seeking your life ;—fly if you would be saved.
At the end of this passage you will find an outlet.   Run for your
life ! the smugglers are after you !   Fly ! fly ! "
The truth now flashed on the mind of Josiah, and he saw exactly
how matters stood.   It was evident that someone, most probably his
young master, was confined in that dungeon, and, fearing detection,

she had been sent to convey the prisoner away, and, by frightening him, and pointing out a way of escape, induce him to run into the sea over the rocks, at the entrance to the cavern, which perhaps communicated with this dungeon, or, it might be, to jump over a precipice.

She had evidently mistaken Josiah, in the dark, for the prisoner, and he was determined to turn the tables on her; so, seizing her by the wrist in his powerful grasp, he exclaimed, in a stentorian voice which struck terror into the affrighted woman, and made her sink on the ground as if she had been struck by a thunderbolt,—

"You cold-blooded old hag! tell me who you ha' got here locked up in this gashly old place, or else I'll carr' you where you wanted me to run, an' throw 'ee into the sea, and hold your head under water till you're so dead as a herren'."

"Oh! sir," said she, gasping and writhing with the pain that Josiah's strong hand was inflicting; "it wasn't my doing,—'twas that boy; he put the gentleman here."

"Come, come," said Josiah; "no nonsense! Was it Mr. Frederick Morley or who was it?"

"Oh! sir," screamed the woman, "I b'lieve that was his name."

"Then where es he gone to?" said Josiah.

"Oh! sir," cried the woman; "I'm afraid he must be dead."

"Dead!" exclaimed Josiah; "ef so, I'll break every bone in your body, and your husband's too, and burn the house over your heads. We must have a light and sarch." So saying, he dragged the woman back towards the steps which led up to the dark passage, while she continued to scream from the pain she was suffering; for he did not relax his grasp in the least.

When they had emerged on the main stairs again, Josiah flung the door wide open that there might be no difficulty in finding it again, and called out lustily for a light.

The woman's screams and Josiah's vociferous calls for a light, reached the ears of the searchers upstairs, and they all ran down in great alarm to enquire what had caused such a terrible commotion.

"He is here!" exclaimed Josiah, when his friends appeared;— "bring a light quickly."

Captain Trenow had seen a lantern in the kitchen as they passed, and, being accustomed to emergencies in his daily occupation as a miner, he went back, and, lighting the candle, appeared again with the lantern in his hand, before the others had recovered from their surprise.

Captain Cooper at first put a bold front on it, and denied all knowledge of the young gentleman, until he saw the cellar door wide open and knew there was now no escape. He then maintained a sullen silence, and preceded the party down the narrow steps into the cellar.

It was deemed advisable to send him in first, coupled with Captain Trenow, fearing treachery. Josiah still kept his hold on the woman.

On they went in double file, slowly and cautiously, searching every nook and corner, looking behind old casks, and turning up old canvass bags that lay about in corners; but no trace of their missing friend could be found.

Capt. Cooper now began to hold up his head again. It had evidently turned out better than he expected, and he called his wife a doating old fool, to tell such lies and deceive the gentlemen in that way. They had searched the whole of his house and premises, —and what more would they have? He might complain, but he wouldn't, he said. They naturally felt alarmed about the young gentleman,—who would not? He had no hesitation in telling them that Mr. Freeman and his daughter Alrina had lodged at his house for a few weeks, for change of air for the young lady, who was delicate; but they had left, and, he believed, had gone back to St. Just.

What could they do, therefore, under the circumstances, but thank Capt. Cooper for allowing them to search for their friend, and to bid him adieu? Josiah, however, still held his opinion that his young master had been confined in this dungeon, and had been got rid of somehow. He was not at all satisfied. He must have been starved to death there, he said, and the rats might have eaten him, and he believed they had. This idea, however, was not entertained by the others of the party, although they knew not what else to think.

CHAPTER XXX.

THE TWO SISTERS PIERCED THROUGH THE HEART.

OUR story now takes us back to Pendrea-house, where we left several of its inmates ill at ease both in body and mind. For, as some mighty warrior, who has borne the burden and heat of the day on the battle-field, and received bravely many a thrust from the point of a lance without flinching, when he retires to his couch after his fatigues, is worried and tormented almost beyond endurance by the bite of a small mosquito,—so were the inmates of Pendrea-house— one and all—disturbed and thrown out of their natural course, by the sharp-pointed arrows of a certain little mischievous creature, who is generally represented as a little innocent-looking, chubby-faced boy, with tiny wings and a laughing eye. He had shot many an arrow at Miss Pendray before, which merely grazed the surface of her smooth delicate skin, and the wounds disappeared almost as quickly as they had been inflicted, leaving scarcely a trace behind. But now his arrow had pierced deeper, and caused a wound which disturbed the peace of mind of this haughty beauty. Mr. Morley had paid her great attention during the short time he had been in the neighbourhood, and had given unmistakeable proofs of his admiration of her, and she had been fascinated by his handsome person and agreeable manners and conversation, and had met him more than halfway, and displayed without disguise the interest she took in him and the pleasure she felt in his society. Yet he never once spoke to her on the subject nearest her heart, and had left the neighbourhood abruptly, without seeing her or bidding her farewell; and now he had returned with Lieut. Fowler, and left again without seeking an interview with her, or even calling at Pendrea-house. She felt that she had been deceived by his attentions, and that he was perhaps after all only trifling with her. This her proud haughty spirit would not brook, and she tried to drive his image from her thoughts, but she could not succeed; for the more she tried to pluck out the little barbed arrow that had already pierced her heart so surely and sharply, the deeper did it penetrate, and the wound was now becoming almost unbearable.

She tried to soothe her troubled mind, by taking her accustomed walks along the cliffs, and sitting in solitary meditation on the bold headlands, and watching the waves as they came surging and dashing against the rocks beneath her feet. His image haunted her still, and made her very miserable. She might now have sympathized with her poor suffering sister; for she well knew the cause of her illness, although her mother and her attendants attributed it to a different cause; but her proud haughty spirit would not stoop to condole or sympathize with one who had so boldly accused her of unseemly behaviour—even although that one was her only, and till now her darling, sister. So the poor little innocent Blanche continued to suffer in secret, having no one to whom she could confide her sad tale. There was one consolation, however, which she possessed unknown to anyone in her father's house except her favourite maid, who was, as she termed it, "keeping company" with one of Lieut. Fowler's men;—this was a letter which Lieut. Fowler had contrived to send her through this medium; wherein he explained to her the circumstances of his dismissal from the house, and the cause,—reiterating his protestations of unalterable attachment, and his determination to possess the object of his fond affection at all risks and against all opposition, if Blanche was as true and devoted to him as he believed her to be.

This letter distressed while it consoled her; for she now felt in its fullest force that it was owing to her own weakness and persuasion, that Lieut. Fowler had incurred her father's displeasure, and she felt also that she ought to sacrifice everything to exonerate her generous and fondly devoted lover from the disgraceful suspicion attached by her father to his conduct. She believed that her sister, who inherited all her father's pride and aristocratic notions, had set him against Lieut. Fowler, by relating with considerable exaggeration their apparently clandestine meetings, which seemed no doubt, as she had represented them, very reprehensible, and sufficiently culpable to justify her father in acting as he had done.

Blanche, therefore, thought that, if she could find an opportunity of speaking to him alone, and explaining the nature of their meetings, which were not clandestine, as her sister very well knew,—for she generally knew when and where they met, and was frequently asked to join them,—and if she could at the same time explain to her father that it was by her own persuasion, and at her earnest request, that Lieut. Fowler had refrained from naming his intentions to him earlier, he might at least be induced to alter the harsh opinion he had formed of his former friend. This she determined she would do;—she would take all the blame on herself, to exonerate him who was all in all to her, and who would, but for her, have boldly and honourably asked her father's consent to their happiness long ago.

Squire Pendray was very fond of his children, especially of his little pet, the gentle Blanche,—indeed, no one could help liking her. She possessed the good-natured simplicity and kindness of her mother, and was beloved by the poor as well as the rich; and many a little act of charity did this gentle, loving, girl do for the poor and needy, whose cottages she often visited in the course of her rambles.

Maud was kind and charitable to the poor also, and distributed her bounties as freely and largely as her sister, and perhaps more so; but her gifts were given with haughty pride, and the recipients were made to feel their dependent inferiority, by the manner in which they were bestowed. It was not so with Blanche;—she gave as if she were receiving a favour instead of bestowing one. She conversed with the poor recipients of her bounty, and freely entered into all their little troubles, and sympathized with them as if she were one of themselves; and yet they never presumed on her condescension, but looked upon her almost as a being from another world, come down to minister to their wants; and so her gifts were doubly valuable, and she was almost worshipped in the parish.

The squire was a shrewd man of the world, and was proud in the enjoyment of his wealth and position, and happy in the possession of two such lovely daughters; and it was with feelings of the deepest regret, that he saw them both pining away under the influence of some secret malady of which he knew not the cause. The best medical advice that could be procured was called in, but to no purpose,—the doctors could do them no good whatever. At last, when all their efforts had failed, Mrs. Pendray said to her husband one night, when they were sitting alone in the dining-room, taking their solitary supper,—

"I tell you what it is, squire,—those two girls are ill-wished, as sure as you are sitting in that chair."

"Ill-wished! nonsense!" replied the squire; "who can have ill-wished them, I should like to know? What harm have those two innocent girls done to anyone, to cause them to be ill-wished. No, no, I can't believe it."

"Well, whether you believe it or not," returned his wife, "I do,—in fact I'm sure of it. What has happened to one may happen to another, any time. There was Farmer Pollard's daughter, two years ago,—she pined away, just as Blanche is doing now, and nothing seemed to do her good until her father applied to the conjuror."

"Yes, I remember that case," said the squire; "and the conjuror discovered that she was ill-wished by another young woman, through jealousy. But that can't be the case with either of our daughters."

"There are many ways of ill-wishing, and many causes and reasons for doing so," replied Mrs. Pendray. "I was talking with Mrs. Pollard about it only yesterday, and she says that it may be that someone has a grudge against you; and so they may have ill-wished our dear children out of revenge, knowing how dear they are to us."

"If I thought that," said the squire, rising passionately, and pacing the room, "I would horsewhip the fellow within an inch of his life, whoever he is;—he should have some cause for his ill-will, at any rate."

"You forget, my dear," replied his wife, "that you do not know who the party is; and I only know of one way by which you can find out your enemy."

"And that is by going to the conjuror, I suppose," said the squire, in a sarcastic tone. "I don't dispute his skill, for I have seen proofs of it among our neighbours; but I don't like the fellow,—and I believe there are many of the same opinion as myself respecting him, but they are afraid of him, and dare not speak their minds; for he has great power, and manages to know what is going on around him, and even what is said about him, in a most unaccountable manner; but I tell you I don't like the fellow, and I wouldn't go near him if all my family were dying."

"Oh! don't say that," said Mrs. Pendray, putting her handkerchief to her eyes to wipe away the tears which were trickling fast down her cheeks; "you would not see our poor children pine away, and do nothing to avert the calamity,—I'm sure you would not. Nothing seems to relieve them;—the doctors have given them up; and now, alas! we have but one sad prospect before us.   After all the love and care we have bestowed upon them from their infancy, and the many happy years we have devoted to our darling children, and the pleasant future we looked forward to, it is very hard thus to be deprived of them, and to see their strength failing them, and the hand of death stealing over them in their prime, when one word from their father would restore them,—yes, one sentence spoken by their father, would restore them to their former health, and relieve their parents from present grief, and a future of unmingled misery and woe."   And—overcome by her feelings, and the sad thoughts that arose in her mind at the melancholy picture she had drawn —the poor old lady gave way to a burst of grief, which touched the sterner heart of her proud husband, who averted his head and brushed away a tear with his hand, as he continued to pace the room in great agitation.

It may seem strange in these enlightened days, that persons in the position of Mr. and Mrs. Pendray should believe for one moment, that one person had the power to ill-wish another, or that it was in the power of any man, however skilful in the occult sciences, to counteract their evil imprecations.   Yet such was the case. Superstition was rife in those days, as we have said before, even among the best educated; and many a poor old woman had suffered seriously, for exercising the power of witchcraft which she supposed she possessed.

The district of the Land's-End was rather too remote for this crime to be visited with severity by the authorities, and so the Land's-End conjuror was left undisturbed,—indeed, he was too cautious, generally, in his dealings with those who sought his aid, to give his enemies any handle that they could take hold of against him.   Like the master of a puppet-show, he knew the mechanism of his figures, and knew what strings to pull to make them work according to his will;—the only difference was, that he exercised his skill on the minds of his figures instead of their limbs.

Squire Pendray was a man of good common sense, and a magistrate, and yet he had not escaped the common feeling of superstition which prevailed at that time—not only in Cornwall, but in every other part of the kingdom.   It was not, therefore, from any want of confidence in the skill of the conjuror, that he declined asking him to exercise it, but simply because, as he said, " he didn't like the fellow."   Probably he would have been puzzled to have given a reason for this strong dislike to a man he scarcely knew; for Mr. Freeman avoided coming in contact with the squire, as much as he possibly could, and they had scarcely ever met.   No doubt the conjuror had his reasons for this.   It would not have been convenient for him at all times to have had the squire prying into his little secret doings.

Mrs. Pendray had appealed to her husband's feelings, and revived in his breast those chords of tender affection which she so well knew he possessed, but which had, in a measure, lain dormant since his children had grown into womanhood, and were able to take care of themselves. It seemed now, however, as if his daughters had returned to their childhood again, and required the tender care of their mother as much as ever they did.

" It is very hard," said Mrs. Pendray, still sobbing, and speaking more to herself than to her husband, " that, after all our care of the dear girls for so many years, they should be allowed to die now, because their father has some foolish scruples about asking the assistance of the only man that can relieve them from the spell that has been cast around them." And the poor old lady's grief burst forth afresh, while the squire continued to pace the room more slowly and thoughtfully; for conflicting passions agitated his mind, and he was debating within himself between his hatred of the man of science and his love for his children. At length parental affection prevailed, and he determined to lay aside the hatred which he somehow entertained towards the conjuror, and be a supplicant at his door the next morning, for his aid in relieving his daughters from the spell by which he now felt convinced they were bound. It was a severe struggle; but he had made up his mind to go through with it, and no obstacle would now prevent him from carrying it out.

CHAPTER XXXI.

OUT OF SCYLLA AND INTO CHARYBDIS.

WE left our hero, Frederick Morley, fast asleep in the inner cellar at Capt. Cooper's house. He slept soundly—for he was quite exhausted—and dreamed of Alrina, whom he fancied he saw bending over him, and watching him as he slept; but it seemed as if he had lost all power over himself,—he could not speak to her. At last she glided gently away, and beckoned him to follow her, but he could not move. He seemed spellbound; and she faded away in the darkness, leaving him to lament his fate on his cold, damp couch. He continued to sleep on for some time, until he was roused by a voice which seemed to come from the innermost recess of the dungeon. He started up—for he thought his hour was come—and prepared himself to yield to the cold-blooded assassination which

he believed was now to put an end to his earthly career. He could
not defend himself, for he could not see from what point the blow
would come. It was, however, a gentle voice that called him,—a
woman's voice, he thought; he could not hear it distinctly, but still
it called to him in the distance. Could it be Alrina? Had she,
whom he had followed so long, hoping to be her deliverer, come to
rescue him? But how could she have discovered him, and how did
she get there? He knew not what to think. He answered in the
same low tone, and approached the spot from whence the sound
appeared to come, and was taken by the hand by someone—not by
Alrina, however, but by his little attendant, Bill!

"Hush!" said the boy; "follow me, and you will be saved,—
quick! before we are discovered."

The boy still held him by the hand, and drew him on; for the
place was still very dark. They entered a narrow passage, and the
boy dragged him on and on through the darkness. At last he heard
the sea, and saw a glimmer of light in the distance; and presently
a gentle breeze, which was wafted towards him, convinced him that
they were approaching the outer world once more. They were now
in a large cavern, into which the sea flowed, and he saw a small boat
moored to a rock within the cavern.

The boy told him to jump into the boat; and in a moment, the
mooring was loosened, and the boy was by his side in the boat, which
he skilfully pushed out with one of the oars, and they very soon
rode on the open sea. The boy then gave Morley the other oar, and
they pulled out with all their might; for Morley felt that he was
being rescued from the jaws of death.

When they were fairly out on the broad ocean, the boy said,
"Now, sir, you take both the oars—you are stronger than I am—
and I'll steer." So they glided swiftly over the still blue water;—for
Morley had practised the use of the oar, both at home and abroad;
and the feeling that every stroke of his oar placed a greater distance
between him and the vile wretches who had evidently sought his
life, gave additional strength to his arm, and he struggled against
nature, and for a time forgot the weakness and exhaustion which
had overcome him in the cellar and caused him to fall asleep in the
midst of the danger that surrounded him.

The subterranean passage through which they had passed, had
been excavated many years before. There was a large natural
cavern running in for some distance under the cliffs from the sea,
in the entrance to which there was water enough to float a boat at
high-tide; and beyond the flow of the tide were large rocks, which
prevented the water, except at very high tide, from encroaching on
the interior of the cavern. In this cavern the smugglers formerly
secreted their contraband goods; and many of them, being miners

as well as smugglers, and being in the employ of a former owner of the house long before Cooper occupied it, they, at his suggestion and by his order—he being a great smuggler himself, and having made a large fortune by the trade—excavated a communication between that cavern and the cellar underneath his house, by which means smuggled goods could be secreted easily and safely. Very few people knew of this passage except the parties immediately concerned. The boy, however, had been found useful on many occasions, in watching the revenue officers, and putting them on a wrong tack, and, thus knowing the secret passage, formed this plan for rescuing Morley from almost certain death.

The night was calm and serene, and everything around them was still. Several small vessels were lying in the little cove—some ready to go to sea again with the next tide, having discharged their cargoes,—and others just come in, waiting for the dawn of day to begin their work of discharging their cargoes of coal and timber into the merchants' yards; and as the little boat glided by, the watch on deck would sing out, "Boat ahoy! what ship?" or, "Good night, shipmates;" and then all was still again; for the appearance of a small fisherman's boat going out at that hour of night did not arouse the least suspicion, and on they went swiftly and steadily.

The moon was shedding her soft pale light all around; and the oars, as they were "feathered" by the skilful rower, cast showers of silvery spray back into the water again at every stroke. Some of the white granite cliffs shone brightly in the moonlight, as its rays fell full upon them; while others, hid in shadows, seemed like some huge monsters, indistinct and terrible, towering above their lighter companions until they appeared almost lost in darkness, and imagination pictured them higher by many degrees than they really were.

On, on they went, bravely and swiftly; for the fear of pursuit impelled the rower to exert his strength to the utmost. But the strength of man will not always obey his will, and ere long he fell back in the boat exhausted and faint. He had but very recently, it will be remembered, risen from a bed of sickness, and the exertion and anxiety had been too much for him. His pluck had not deserted him, but he had exerted his strength beyond its power. Nature at last gave way, and he fell back insensible. His fall was sudden, and he dropped both the oars into the water. The boy was too much frightened to think of anything but his companion at the moment; so the oars drifted away, and the boat was left to the mercy of the waves, while the boy did all he could to revive the prostrate man.

He had brought no provisions with him—not even a can of water; for he thought that a few hours' rowing would bring them to the next cove, where they would land without suspicion, and procure anything and everything they wanted. Poor boy! he could do nothing but watch the invalid, and support his head on one of the thwarts of the boat, and this he did for a considerable time,—it seemed to him an age. At last kind nature came to his rescue, and the invalid opened his eyes to the boy's infinite relief, and in a short time he had so far recovered as to be able to comprehend their perilous situation. Fortunately it was a calm night, but there they were helpless and exhausted, and drifting out to sea with no provision on board. Morley gradually regained his former vigour of mind, if not of body, but it was only to bewail their sad fate.

Out, out they went to sea, drifting further and further from the land, with no power to control the course of their frail bark. At length, as morning dawned, the current changed, and they were drifted back again; and here they exchanged the calm tranquillity of their former position for the rough encounter between the two channels—always turbulent and often dangerous, but in a little boat without oars to guide her course doubly so. The rudder was of very little use in that turbulent sea. They saw the rocks with which that part of the coast abounds, and dreaded lest an unfortunate roll of the boat or an angry wave should drive it headlong upon one of those rocks and dash her in pieces. Hour after hour passed away in dreadful uncertainty. The turn of the tide again drifted them out to sea in another direction. They heard the roar of the Wolf Rock, and knew from that circumstance that they were drifting towards the Scilly Islands. They now gave themselves up to despair; for it seemed almost next to impossible that they could pass this Wolf Rock safely without oars or any means of keeping the boat under control.

Want of food for so many hours in his already weak and exhausted state, rendered Morley entirely helpless, and listless to all that might happen to them. He lay down in the bottom of the boat without the power to move or speak. The boy bore up as bravely as he could, and tried to support his companion; but he too gave way after a time, and then they lay side by side in the bottom of the boat, expecting every minute to feel a crash against the rock, and then all would be over.

At last it came—a bump! a crash! The water seemed filling their mouths and ears. They revived for a moment, and were fully alive to their awful position. All the actions of their past lives rushed into their minds, and they seemed to live their lives over again, in that short moment of time.

Alrina's form was vividly present to Morley's mind for an instant, and then all was blank!

CHAPTER XXXII.

ALRINA'S TROUBLES ARE INCREASED BY AN UNEXPECTED DISCOVERY.

MR. FREEMAN had returned to St. Just with his daughter, but neither of them had appeared much in public since. The servant, Alice Ann, said that her young mistress was looking very whisht and palched, and "The Maister" worn't like hisself at all. He was continually locked in his private room, and she had seen him through the keyhole more than once, upon his knees before a great chest, taking things out and putting things in.

"What sort of things be they, then?" Mrs. Trenow would ask; for to her, as her nearest neighbour and the mother of her sweetheart, Alice Ann was most communicative.

"Why, powers of things," would be the reply; "silks and satins, all foreign like, and gold and silver I b'lieve—a purty passle."

Miss Freeman had not returned, so that there was no one to watch Alrina's movements, and she might have gone out and stayed out all day if she liked, but she did not care to move. She would sit in her room all day long, and scarcely touch the little dainties with which Alice Ann tried to tempt her; nor did she care to speak, unless her faithful attendant broached the subject of all others which she well knew occupied her young mistress's every thought. Days and weeks and months had passed away, and yet she had heard nothing of Frederick. She had written him, but he had not replied to her letters. Alice Ann tried to console her; but what could she, a poor ignorant country-girl, say by way of consolation to one possessing the refined and sensitive feelings of Alrina.

It was hard to believe; and yet, what could she think? He had deserted her! Perhaps he had met with another more to his taste, and more suited to him in position and fortune—one whose family history could be clearly set forth, and over whose heads no dark mystery hung. It was natural, she thought, that on reflection he should shrink from uniting himself with one whose family were so obscure and in many respects objectionable.

Many days did this poor girl sit brooding over her sad fate. She would release him from his engagement with her; it was right, she thought, considering all things, that she should do so, and she determined in her mind she would do so. She would like to see him once more, however, just to tell him this. When she had made up her mind to this step, she felt more tranquil and resigned to her fate, and she now began to walk out as usual, and wander over the rocks —perhaps with the dim hope that she might one day fall in with Frederick in the course of her rambles, as she had done before, when she could tell him her determination. Poor girl! she knew not her own weakness; for had he, whose image she had so fondly cherished from her childhood, appeared before her at that time, her fancied courage would have forsaken her, and she would have taken him back to her heart and forgiven him, even did she know beyond a doubt that he had deserted her for another.

Alas! she little knew how impossible it was for him to appear before her then, as she secretly hoped and wished he would; nor did she know, poor girl, how near he had been to her when she was under Cooper's roof. Conflicting thoughts occupied her mind for several days. It was a hard struggle; but she conquered her feelings, and the trial did not appear to her so painful, now that she had fully made up her mind that it was her duty to put an end to the engagement on account of this dark mystery which hung over her family history. She felt that in doing this she was acting honourably towards him whom she could not help loving still with all the ardour of a first love. This she thought she could bear better than the belief that he had deserted her;—she could not bear that, nor would she think so again. She felt that it was her own act now, as she had made up her mind that it should be so—not out of any angry feeling which she bore towards Frederick, but out of pure love for him, and a reluctance to place him in a position which might hereafter cause him pain, and, when the first ardour of love was over, make him ashamed of his wife's relatives.

When she had fully made up her mind to this, she felt more at ease, and would sit for hours on the rocks, in calm reflection on the past, and hopeful meditation on the future. And thus she would pass whole days without moving from the spot, watching the broad clear sea, and the vessels passing and repassing, and the graceful gambols of the sea-birds, as they flew from rock to rock, or took their flight far out to sea—never heeding the meal-time hour, nor seeming to want food or sustenance until her return, when her faithful attendant would upbraid her for staying so long without food, and force her to eat some little nice thing she had prepared during her young mistress's absence, with which to tempt her appetite.

In the meantime, her father continued to be occupied in his private room all day long, looking over papers, and examining the contents of that large chest.

One morning, while he was so engaged, there came two tall men to the outer gate of the little garden, who seemed impatient to enter; but not knowing the secret spring by which the gate was opened, they shook the gate in their impatience, and called loudly to the inmates (if there were any) to open and let them in.

Mr. Freeman's private room overlooked the little garden; and on going to the window to ascertain the cause of all this noise, he started back like a man shot, and trembled all over like an aspen leaf. Alice Ann was surprised too when she recognized one of the visitors, but hers was evidently a feeling of pleasure; for there stood her old lover Josiah, accompanied by a tall handsome gentleman, with remarkably white hair for a man of his age, as he did not look above forty.

"Dash the old gate," said Josiah, shaking it to and fro; "you're buried up brave, I think."

"Iss fie," replied Alice Ann, opening the gate; "we do knaw who to keep out and who to lev in."

"Where's 'The Maister'?" asked Josiah, as they entered the little garden.

"How shud I knaw?" returned the girl; "in his skin, I s'pose."

"Is Mr. Freeman at home, my good girl?" said Mr. Morley; "for I am very anxious to see him."

"He wor up in his room a bit a while ago, sar," replied Alice Ann, dropping a curtsey to the gentleman, "for I heard a purty caparouse up there."

"Tell'n that there's a gentleman do want to see un 'pon partic'lar business," said Josiah, "an' be quick about et."

"Not sure nuff I shaan't," replied the girl. "He said he mustn't be disturbed for nobody. Ef you'll stop till Miss Reeney do come in, she'll go up, maybe,—I shaan't, there na."

The girl was not to be persuaded; so Mr. Morley walked into the common sitting-room, as he saw the door open, while Josiah followed Alice Ann into the kitchen, to persuade her, perhaps, to go up to her master; or, probably as they hadn't met for some time, they had little secrets to communicate, into which we will not be so rude as to pry,—indeed, these little secret meetings between lovers are seldom interesting to lookers-on.

Josiah and Alice Ann would not have finished their *tête-à-tête* for some time longer, had not a thundering rap at the front door with a large stick, roused them from their pleasant conversation.

"Dear lor'! how my cap es foused, soas," said Alice Ann, as she jumped from her seat, and surveyed herself in a small looking-glass which hung in the kitchen; "whoever can be come now, I shud like to knaw. Drat thom!" And away she went to answer the knock.

"I want to see the conjuror," said Squire Pendray, in his pompous manner; for he it was who had disturbed the two lovers so cruelly.

"The what, sar?" exclaimed Alice Ann, opening her eyes to their fullest extent; for to call her master "the conjuror" was an offence for which she was sure the enquirer would suffer if her master heard it,—and what couldn't he hear?

The squire now became aware of his error; for he asked in his blandest tones if Mr. Freeman was at home.

"He wor home a bit o' while ago, sar," answered Alice Ann,

curtseying very low; for she knew the squire was a very great man, and a magistrate.

"Tell him I wish to speak to him in a case of life and death," said the squire.

"Iss sar," said the girl, curtseying again, lower than before, and leading the way into the usual waiting-room, into which persons on urgent business of this kind were generally shewn.

Mr. Morley had walked into the common sitting-room, almost without being bidden; for, although the little waiting-maid had seemed so cool in the reception of her lover, she thought too much of him at the time to pay much attention to the gentleman he brought with him. She now went up and knocked at "The Maister's" door; and receiving no answer she peeped in at the keyhole. There was the great chest still open on the floor, but she could see nothing of her master, nor hear him. She knocked again a little louder,— still no answer. She then called to him; but no notice was taken of it, and she became alarmed. She tried the door,—it was locked. She then went down to consult with Josiah, who thought they had better tell the two gentlemen; so Alice Ann went into one room, and Josiah into the other, to inform the respective occupants how matters stood,—and then there was a general consultation as to what steps should be taken. Each gentleman was surprised to see the other there; but their thoughts were too much occupied in deliberating what was to be done, to ask any questions.

It was the general opinion that Mr. Freeman had either died suddenly from natural causes, or that he had committed suicide. Mr. Morley thought they ought to break open the door; but this Alice Ann would not consent to at all. She knew her master's power, and remembered the dreadful noises she had heard in that room, and the scenes which she believed had been enacted there, from the appearance of the poor victims when they came out. The squire also had some kind of superstitious dread of interfering with the man of science, who was so much feared in the neighbourhood; and Josiah, although so powerful in bodily strength, had a touch of this same superstition too. At last it was determined to send someone in search of Alrina, and to wait her return.

After some considerable time, which appeared longer than it really was to those who were waiting, Alrina returned, and was greatly surprised to find the house occupied by two strangers;—Josiah she had known long before. They were both much struck with her beauty and quiet ladylike manner, and explained to her their position. They had come to see Mr. Freeman on business, and it appeared he had locked himself in his room, and could not be heard inside, nor would he answer to the calls of the servant. Alrina was very much alarmed; but she said her father was very peculiar, and would often refuse to answer when he did not wish to be disturbed. She went up to the door herself, with the same result; and, after hesitating for some time, she at length consented that the door should be forced. This was easily accomplished by Josiah with the aid of the kitchen poker; and the whole party entered the sacred room, expecting to see some dreadful sight,—what, they could not imagine.

There stood the chest wide open, as the girl had seen it through the keyhole; but no one thought of looking into this,—their whole thoughts were centred in the fate of the owner himself. They searched everywhere, but no trace of him could be found. Alice Ann suggested that he had probably gone up the chimney in a flash of fire, and that he might be on the housetop at that very moment, looking in upon them, or riding through the air on a broomstick. "We've heard of such things, you knaw," said she.

They were roused from their speculations on the mysterious disappearance of "The Maister" by an exclamation from Mr. Morley, who had been narrowly examining the room, and was now standing transfixed before the large chest, which was open, and from which some things had been taken out on the floor. ·

"As I live," he exclaimed, "this is my chest! How could this have got here?"

"That's the chest," replied Josiah, "that 'The Maister' found after the wreck, and told us to bring up here,—for what, we cudn't tell."

"That chest contained money and papers of great value," said Mr. Morley; "it has been overhauled evidently to some purpose, and no doubt everything valuable is gone."

"Oh! no, sir!" cried Alrina, in a pitiable tone; "don't accuse my father of robbery,—he would never do that, I am quite sure."

"My dear young lady," said the squire; "your father shall not be accused of anything that cannot be fully proved; but I am bound to say it, however painful it may be to you, that I have had my suspicions for some time, and so have my brother magistrates. He could not have lived without money, and the mystery is where he got it from. Now, pray be calm, while Mr. Morley examines his chest."

"'Morley!'" cried Alrina; "did I hear you rightly, sir? did you call that gentleman 'Morley?'"

"My name is Morley," said that gentleman, taking her hand; "I am the brother of one whom I know you have been led to believe will take you out of your present position, and raise you to his station in life."

"No, sir," replied Alrina, indignantly,—"my family shall never be a disgrace to anyone; and, let me tell you, sir, that neither you nor your brother shall ever be disgraced by me! I will never be the wife of a man who might afterwards despise me."

"That was nobly spoken," said the squire; "you're an honour to

your sex.   Gad! I wish my daughters could speak like that, and
send the jackanapes about their business that come swarming about
my house."

" Dear lor'! what a handsome coat," exclaimed Alice Ann, as she
saw Mr. Morley take a richly embroidered coat from the chest.

" Yes," said he, holding up the coat and admiring it; " that coat
cost me a great deal of money.   I had it made to wear at a grand
fancy-dress ball in Calcutta; and there are other parts of the dress
to match, somewhere.   Oh! here they are; you have never seen
anything like that in England, squire, have you?"

" Gad! but I have, though," exclaimed the squire; " if not that
same dress, there was one very like it worn by a stranger at our last
ball at Penzance.   And now I begin to think,—why, it must have
been Freeman himself disguised.   I never saw him very near that
I remember, for he always avoided me; but it struck me at the time
that I had certainly seen that face somewhere before, but he looked
much younger than he can possibly be."

" Aw! 'The Maister' esn't so old nor yet so ugly as he do make
out to be," said Josiah.

After searching still further, Mr. Morley found the bag in which
his money had been placed, but the money was all gone and the
papers also.

" Now!" exclaimed he, jumping up from the kneeling posture in
which he had been for the purpose of examining the contents of the
chest; " here's proof enough.   Now let us use all our exertions to
secure the man."   And, leaving Alrina and Alice Ann to take care
of themselves, the two gentlemen left the house more quickly than
they had entered it, followed by Josiah.   But the object of their
search had got the start of them by several hours; for his fear so
overcame him at the sight of Mr. Morley entering his house—(why,
was best known to himself)—that he opened the room door at once,
and locked it behind him, putting the key into his pocket, and
escaped through the back door, and over the back garden wall,
while Alice Ann was opening the front garden gate to let Mr. Morley
and Josiah in.   And, making his way as fast as he could to the cove,
he there got a boat which took him out to Cooper's little cutter,
which was anchored a short distance out waiting for orders.   It was
his intention to leave the country in this cutter, as soon as he had
arranged his affairs; for he found things were going against him,
and that his power was failing fast; but he did not intend to have
gone quite so soon.   He had secreted a considerable sum in gold and
jewels round his person, inside his clothes, several days before,—
so that, in this respect, he was quite prepared for whatever might
happen at any time.

The three pursuers traced him to the seaside, and were just in time to see the cutter which bore him away. But the little vessel had gone too far for any attempt to be made to follow her, with the least chance of success; so they retraced their steps with disappointed looks and feelings.

CHAPTER XXXIII.

ALRINA VISITS A KIND FRIEND AND MAKES A PROPOSAL.

ALRINA's cup of misery was now full to the brim. It had required but one drop more to fill it, and here it was. Her lover had deserted her—that was most certain; but she had forgiven him, and made up her mind that she would exonerate him from all his vows,—indeed, she would insist on breaking off the engagement for ever, on account of the dark mystery which hung over her family history.

But while the mystery was concealed, whatever it was, there was still a hope that it might turn out in the end that there was no mystery at all, and all might still be well. She secretly hoped this, although, in her magnanimity, she considered it her duty to exonerate her lover from all ties. But now the mystery was solved. It was no longer dark and concealed, yielding a hope, however slight, that it might have existed merely in her own imagination. It was no longer dark or mysterious. Her father had robbed Mr. Morley (her lover's brother) of a considerable sum of money, and had purloined his valuable papers, and had moreover gone to a public ball at Penzance, dressed in Mr. Morley's clothes. There was no getting over this;—there was no mystery here. All this could be fully proved,—and he had gone off, no one knew where.

What was she to do? She was left without a friend and penniless. There was the house, it was true; but she could not live there without a penny to buy food.

Squire Pendray told the sad story when he returned home; and good Mrs. Pendray went herself to Mr. Freeman's, and begged Alrina to go home with her, and live with them as one of her daughters. This kind offer Alrina respectfully declined. Mrs. Pendray then offered her a supply of money to purchase necessaries until her father's return.

" My father will never return, madam," said she, with dignity; " he cannot. And, although I thank you from my heart for your kindness, I cannot accept charity,—no, madam, I must gain my own livelihood, as many a poor girl has done before."

So the good lady, having failed of success in her good intentions, took an affectionate leave of the noble girl, begging her to reconsider her determination, and to come to her still if she altered her mind. "I shall watch over you, my dear," said the good lady at parting, "and shall get information brought me of your progress. Good bye! And may the Almighty Giver of all good watch over and protect you."

This disinterested kindness was almost overpowering. It was as much as Alrina could do to prevent herself from giving way to her feelings. She had borne her lover's supposed desertion, and the discovery of her father's disgrace without shedding a tear, or allowing anyone to discover how much she was affected by them. Now she could bear up no longer. Mrs. Pendray's kind offer of protection and charity made her feel the full force of her situation, and she returned to her room, and, throwing herself on her bed, wept bitter tears of distress, mingled with feelings of anger and wounded pride. She had been deserted, disgraced, and humiliated. Long did she remain in that state of desponding wretchedness. It was not in her nature to give way to her feelings, and weep for every trifling thing that went wrong; she had been brought up in a sterner school. But when she did give way, hers was not an ordinary fit of weeping and then over; no, when she wept, it was a terrible outbreak of pent-up feelings, like a large reservoir of water bursting its banks, and carrying all before it. Nothing could stop it, until it had spent itself out. And so it was now with Alrina;—she tossed and rolled on her bed in her agony of mind, and wept until she became exhausted, and then fell into a sound sleep, from which she awoke after some hours, refreshed and renovated both in mind and body. She bathed her eyes and face in cold water, and rearranged her hair, and sat in her chair by the side of the dressing-table, calm and dignified, and began to think of what she should do for the future.

The past was gone for her. She must leave the house at once, and lock it up, after allowing Mr. Morley to take what remained of his property.

She rang for Alice Ann, and told her her determination, and offered her some money—all she had in the world—in payment of her wages for the past few weeks. This the poor girl as indignantly but respectfully refused, as Alrina herself had refused but a few hours before the proposed kindness and protection of Mrs. Pendray.

"Why, she's maazed, I reckon," said Alice Ann, looking at her young mistress as if she were some dangerous animal; "do 'ee knaw what you're tellen' of, do 'ee?—*you* go out for to get your livin'—no, no,—tarry here, Miss Reeney, an' I'll tend 'ee the same as I do now, an' nevar take a penny. An' as for meat,—'where there's a will there's a way,'—we'll take in stitchen' an' sawen', I cud used to do plain work, brave an' tidy; an' you cud do the fine work. We'll get along, nevar you fear."

"It is very kind of you, Alice Ann, to offer to help me to live," replied Alrina; "but it cannot be,—I shall not remain in this house another night after what has happened, if I can possibly help it. I shall go out now for a short time, and when I return we will arrange for the future." So saying, she put on her bonnet and shawl, and went down the road, leaving Alice Ann at a loss to conjecture what she meant to do, or where she could be going in such a hurry.

"She's gone to chat it over weth somebody, I s'pose," said the girl, as she stood at the door and watched her young mistress walking quietly down the road.

Alice Ann was right in a measure. Alrina was going to chat it over with somebody, but not for the purpose of asking advice, nor by way of idle gossip. She had fully determined in her own mind what she would do; and when she had fully made up her mind to a thing it was not an easy matter to turn her from her purpose.

Mrs. Trenow's house was generally her favourite resort when she wanted a quiet chat; but, to Alice Ann's surprise, she passed that house now, and went on into the heart of the village, and she soon lost sight of her, and returned into the house to put things in order, and prepare the tea against her young mistress returned.

Alrina stopped before the door of the "Commercial" Inn as if doubtful what she should do. After a moment's hesitation, however, she walked quietly in. Mrs. Brown had been working very briskly at her needle, mending some old garment after a fashion; for she was no great hand at that sort of work,—knitting she could get on with tolerably well, because it required very little skill, and was therefore rather pleasant work. She was now sitting looking at her work with an angry brow; for, after all her trouble, she had put on the wrong piece. She had sat for several hours, stitch, stitch, at that garment, patching it up, as she thought, to look nearly as well as ever, and now all her labour was lost, for the piece must come off again;—it would never do as it was.

"Drat the old gown!" said she; "here have I be'n worken' my fingers to the bone, an' puzzlin' my brain till I'm all mizzy mazey, an' thinken' I had done a bra' job,—an' there it is."

"Send for the tailor, Peggy! send for the tailor, to be sure," said Mr. Brown from his place in the chimney-corner, from whence he seldom stirred now; for he had become feeble in body as well as in mind, since the shock he had experienced by the terrible death of his favourite mare. Mrs. Brown was very kind to him and indulged him as far as she could; but she could not help being irritated sometimes by his silly remarks; for he prematurely declined into second childhood.

"Send for a fool! and that's you, John Brown," replied his wife, testily, as she turned the garment in different directions to see if she could make it do at all, without ripping out the piece again ;—but it was of no use, out it must come.

"If that lazy maid we've got here could stitch a bit tidy she wud be some help," soliloquized the old lady; "but she's no good but to scrub the floors, and tend the pigs,—she caen't draw a pint of beer fitty. And there's Grace Bastian, the only decent maid we had in the parish for to do a bit of sewing-work, she must prink herself off to Penzance too. I don't knaw what's come to the maidens, not I. Miss Reeney! how are 'ee my dear? Come in an' sit down ;—why, you're quite a stranger," continued the good landlady, as she rose to place a chair for her visitor.

"Yes, I've been very much occupied since our return," replied Alrina ;—"but what are you about, Mrs. Brown ?—you seem to have mended your dress with a piece of a different colour. Why, here's a piece that would have matched it exactly, and, if stitched in neatly, no one would find out that it had been mended."

"That's the very thing I'm thinken' about," said Mrs. Brown. "Here have I be'n stitch, stitch, nearly all the day, putten' on that piece, an' when I had finished it I found I had put on the wrong one ; but I caen't stitch any more to-day,—my head is bad already."

"Let me see," said Alrina, taking the dress, and matching the right piece on it ;—"there, Mrs. Brown, that would do nicely, would it not ? "

"Yes, my dear; but the thing is to stitch it in."

"Lend me your scissors, and I will soon manage it," replied Alrina. "There," continued she, as she ripped off the piece that it had taken Mrs. Brown so long to put in ; "that's soon done. Now, lend me your needle and thimble,—I'll put in the piece, while we gossip a little of the latest news imported. Your thimble is too large ;—haven't you a smaller one in the house ? "

"I believe our maid Polly have got one somewhere," said Mrs. Brown ; "I'll sarch for it."

"Poll! Poll! Polly!" said Mr. Brown, catching at the familiar sound; "come out in the stable, Polly,—the mare must want her gruel by this time. Wo! ho! Jessie, my beauty—wo! ho! mare!"

"Will you be quiet, John Brown?" said his wife, as she came downstairs with the thimble.

"Here, Miss Reeney, I s'pose this is too big for your little finger."

"Never mind, Mrs. Brown," said Alrina, who had by this time pinned on the proper piece ; "I'll make this do."

The work now went on briskly—Mrs. Brown knitting, and Alrina stitching and gossiping between. While the work was going on, two miners came in, and asked for a pint of beer.

"Let me draw it, Mrs. Brown," said Alrina, putting down her work—"it will be a change of work too."

" Well, you shall if you are fancical," replied Mrs. Brown, smiling. " Take the brown jug, my dear—that's a pint exactly—and draw it out of the end cask. Blow off the froth and fill up again,—our customers don't like the jug half full of froth, I can assure you."

So Alrina drew the beer, and received the money, as if she had been accustomed to it all her life, very much to the astonishment of the two men, who seemed puzzled at being tended by Miss Reeney;— but they liked it very well, nevertheless, and ere long asked for another pint, for the sake, no doubt, of receiving it from so fair a cup-bearer.

The two men were in a little room leading out of the kitchen, so that neither party could hear distinctly the conversation of the others,—nor was there much said by either party, indeed, worth the trouble of listening to.

When the men were gone, Mrs. Brown said, " Why, I shud think you had been used to the bar all your life, to see how handy you are ; and you've nearly finished the work that I wor all the day about. Your husband will have a treasure, whoever he is."

" I shall never be married, Mrs. Brown," said Alrina, with a heavy sigh.

" Iss, Iss, you'll be married fast enough, and I think I can tell his name, though I'm no conjuror, asking your pardon."

" I have not seen the man yet that I would marry," returned Alrina, with an effort.

" Oh ! fie !" said Mrs. Brown ; " you mustn't say so to me ; I wasn't born yesterday, an' I can see a bra' way, though tes busy all, i'll allow."

" What I have told you is perfectly true," replied Alrina ; " and so far from thinking of marrying, I am going to try to get my own living,—will you take me into your service?"

" My dear young lady," replied Mrs. Brown, taking off her spectacles, and looking at Alrina steadily and seriously, " you mustn't make game of your elders, nor look down with scorn upon those you may consider inferior in station to yourself,—but that remains to be proved. Take her (a boarding-school young lady) into my service! Did you hear that, John Brown?"

John Brown did'nt hear that, or if he did he didn't understand it, for he made no reply.

" You seem as if you didn't understand me, Mrs. Brown," said Alrina.

" No, sure, I don't understand your meanin' at all," replied Mrs. Brown.

Alrina then related the circumstances of the morning to Mrs. Brown, whom she knew she could trust, and whose advice she knew she could rely on, for she was a shrewd intelligent woman. When she had finished her tale, Mrs. Brown took her hand, and said, " You must forgive me for my hasty speech just now. 'Tes an ugly business, but you shall never want a house to shelter you, nor a bit of morsel to eat while I have got it for you."

" You don't understand me now," said Alrina; "I will never accept charity, either in the shape of food, raiment, or shelter. What I ask you to do is this,—to take me into your service, to help you, as I have done this afternoon, for instance. I will take the burden of the house off your shoulders, and do the sewing, and attend to the bar. Poor Mr. Brown is not able to do anything now, and indeed requires more of your attention than you have time to give him, and I cannot but remember that it was in consequence of some advice given him by my father (for what reason I know not), that Mr. Brown lost his mare, and became in consequence almost imbecile; and it is my duty, if possible, to repair the injury that has been done. I cannot return the mare, nor give Mr. Brown renewed strength ; but I can help you, and by that means you will have more time to devote to his little comforts. I don't want money ;—I merely want a home with a respectable family, to whom I can render services sufficient to remunerate them for their kindness, without having the feeling that I am maintained merely out of charity. Now do you understand what I mean?"

" I do," replied Mrs. Brown, "and it shall be as you wish, and I shall always respect and honour you for the noble and independent way in which you have acted."

This being settled, Alrina went back to her father's house, to inform Alice Ann of what she had done; and, having arranged with Mrs. Brown that Alice Ann should sleep at her house also for a night or two, she locked up the house where so many evil deeds had been performed, and took up her residence at the "Commercial" Inn, as barmaid and general superintendent of the stitchery of the household.

CHAPTER XXXIV.

CAPTAIN COURLAND'S RETURN AND HIS WIFE'S ANXIETY.

THE man of cunning had proved himself more than a match for his pursuers. He had got the start of them, and was now out of their reach. So the squire and Mr. Morley, accompanied by Josiah, prepared to retrace their steps, angry and crestfallen at having been thus outwitted. They walked on in silence until, on rounding a rock, they met Lieutenant Fowler and one of his men, who were evidently out on duty. Fowler seemed quite taken by surprise, and

scarcely knew what to do; but he instinctively touched his cap to
the squire, and, shaking Morley by the hand, was about to pass on.
The squire, however, was too much engrossed with the matter in hand
to remember his late treatment of the lieutenant, or the cause of it,
and Morley was ignorant of the whole matter. So they both greeted
Fowler heartily, and told him the whole affair, and pointed out the
vessel which was bearing away their crafty deceiver. Fowler put
his glass to his eye, and scanned the horizon after having looked
attentively at the vessel.

"She'll be back again" said he, "before long; there's a storm
rising."

"No! no!" replied the squire; "that fellow will not return to
this coast again if he can by any possibility keep away; they'll
probably reach the Scilly Islands before the storm comes on."

"We shall see," said the lieutenant; "my men shall keep a good
watch, however, all night. Good day gentlemen." And he touched
his cap again, and was moving off.

"Where are you going in such a hurry, my dear fellow?" said
Morley, "I haven't seen you for an age. Come! I'm going up to your
station to have a serious chat with you."

"Go on, then; I shall be home soon; but I must go round to see
what the other men are about, whom I sent, some time ago, to watch
a suspicious looking craft, round the next headland. Go up to my
cabin, there's a good fellow; for I want to have a serious chat with
you too." So saying, he walked on, having seen that the squire had
got on his stilts again after the first impulse had subsided; for he had
walked on without taking any further notice of Fowler.

Mr. Morley, true to his appointment, declined the squire's pressing
invitation to dine with him at Pendrea-house, and proceeded towards
Tol-pedn-Penwith station, where he had not been very long before
his friend returned. After dinner, Fowler confided to him his
secret, and the manner in which he had been treated by the squire.
Morley at first treated it as a joke, saying, "Faint heart never won
fair lady;" but on reflection he thought there must be some mistake,
and that a mutual explanation would set all things right, which he
undertook to perform. But he was so anxious about his brother that
he could not settle his mind to anything until he had found him or
ascertained his fate. He had evidently been at Cooper's house,—that
was pretty certain, from what the old woman had said,—and it was
also certain that he was not there now, for they had searched everywhere, nor was he at the Land's-End, nor St. Just; nor had any
trace of him been seen in that neighbourhood by anyone, and the
boy had not been seen either, for some time. Mr. Morley's only
conjecture now was, that he had probably escaped from Cooper's
cellar, and had returned to Ashley Hall, thinking that, as Josiah had

seen Miss Freeman there, Alrina might be there also, concealed somewhere: and he no doubt thought that he would there also have the advice and assistance of his brother and Josiah whom he had left there; for Mr. Morley knew that neither of his letters had reached him, because he found them both lying at the Penzance post-office. He therefore determined at once to return to Ashley Hall. The more he thought of it, the more was he confirmed in this belief, and he also felt certain, that, having escaped through the underground cellar, and no trace of him having been discovered in the neighbourhood, his brother had, to avoid pursuit and suspicion, gone on board some vessel, bound to Bristol, and proceeded thither by water.

Mr. Morley wished to see Miss Pendray once more before he left; but his sense of duty prevailed over love, and he determined to start at once, that very night, and to leave nothing untried until he found his brother—dead or alive. He would have gone to Pendrea-house, just to see her for a moment, and take leave of her, but he was afraid to trust himself. She would have kept him on and on, he feared, until the chance of finding his brother might be gone. He knew her powers of fascination, and he would not trust himself to them. He would come back to love and pleasure with greater satisfaction after he had performed his duty.

He took the faithful Josiah with him; and so hasty was their departure, that poor Josiah had not time to return to St. Just, to take leave of Alice Ann, and so they did not know of the change that had taken place in the abode of the mistress and maid.

So sure did Mr. Morley feel, now, that Frederick had returned to Ashley Hall by water, that he did not make any inquiry on the road, but rode night and day, hiring fresh horses at every stage, until they reached the hall. Why he was so confident of finding his brother there he could scarcely tell; but as that was the only hope he seemed to have, and the only probable place to which he thought he could have gone, he seized it as the "forlorn hope," as it were, and brooded on it, so that it became fixed in his mind, and he would not allow any other thought to supersede it. How great was his disappointment, then, when he arrived at the hall, to find that his brother had not been seen there, nor had anything been heard of or from him, since he left it some weeks before. It was like a death stroke. He could scarcely believe it. He could not bring his mind back to the thought that his brother was lost. He searched everywhere. Mrs. Courland and Julia were alarmed also when they heard how matters stood, and even the poor dumb girl was alarmed and agitated; for she saw there was something amiss, but she didn't know what it was, and no one had the time or the inclination to tell her; so she wandered about the house, unheeded.

Captain Courland had returned, and had now given up the sea, having realized a handsome fortune, and looked forward to spending the remainder of his life in peace and happiness, with his beautiful wife, and her niece, Julia Morley, whom they had adopted as their own, and whom they were both very fond of. The first day of his arrival was a very happy one to him. He revelled in the society of his wife and niece, and nothing occurred to mar his happiness. Flora was kept out of the way in Mrs. Courland's private apartments, where she had first been introduced to the house. These rooms had been fitted up expressly for her. Here she had every amusement she could enjoy, and she liked being here alone, and would frequently spend whole days there, and in the little garden adjoining, planting, and watching, and cultivating the flowers, of which, as we have said before, she was passionately fond. A slight hint from Mrs. Courland that there was company in the house, was quite enough to keep her in her apartments the whole day; for she did not like mixing with strangers. She always seemed to have a dread, lest she should meet with someone she had seen before, and who she feared would take her away and beat her.

Mrs. Courland knew whom she meant, but to the others this was a mystery. Mrs. Courland still dreaded the introduction of this poor girl to her husband, although she knew his kind heart would compassionate a poor helpless creature thrown upon her charity, as she had represented it, as much as the other members of the family had done. But she did not feel the same repugnance at deceiving them, as she did at deceiving her husband. She had already deceived him by keeping this secret from him. And now, by the introduction of this poor girl into his house, the secret might be disclosed at some unlucky moment. She at first decided on introducing her at once on his return, and telling him the story she had framed; but her courage failed her, and she thought she would put it off until his return from London, where he was going the day after his arrival, to arrange his business with the principal shareholders of his ship. He was detained there some days, and had not returned when Mr. Morley and Josiah arrived, although he was hourly expected. All was confusion throughout the house at the intelligence brought by Mr. Morley, that his brother Frederick could nowhere be found. He was a general favourite there, and all the household turned out for this hopeless search, leaving poor Flora a wanderer through the house.

While the search was going on, Captain Courland returned from London, and, finding none of the servants in their accustomed places, he walked into the breakfast-room, where he saw a young lady standing at the window, with her back towards him as he entered, looking intently into the garden below. At first he thought it was his niece Julia, and he asked her what had occurred in the house to

make such a scarcity of servants, and where her aunt was; but, to
his great surprise, she took no notice of him,—so he went up close to
her and tapped her on the shoulder, when she turned suddenly round,
and gave a peculiar, disagreeable scream, and ran out of the room.
He thought this very extraordinary. He could not imagine who the
young lady could be, who seemed so much at home in his house,
and who treated him with such rude contempt. He sought his wife
for an explanation. On his mentioning the circumstance to her,
she seemed taken quite by surprise, and hesitated, and looked confused while she told him her tale. He thought it very strange that
she had not mentioned this circumstance to him in any of her letters,
and he asked her rather harshly why she had not mentioned it when
he was home for a day and a night, on his first arrival from sea. He
spoke more harshly to her than he had ever done before, perhaps
without intending to do so; but the consciousness that she had done
wrong, and the fear lest her secret should yet be discovered by him,
overcame her, so that, instead of explaining the reason, which she
might easily have done, she burst into tears, which pained him, and
made him think there was something more in this affair than he had
yet heard; but, in the goodness of his heart and his devoted affection
and love for his wife, he never suspected for a moment that she had
done any wrong, or was concealing anything from him of a serious
nature; while she, poor, timid, guilty creature, read his thoughts by
her own, and fancied that her husband was looking into her heart,
and reading there her guilty secret.

Had she possessed the moral courage to tell the truth in the
beginning, when they were first married, all would have been well.
But she had retained the secret in her own breast so long, and
thereby deceived her husband, that the telling of it now would
be like the confession of a twofold guilt. And if she had not the
courage to tell her secret, when it was but a little secret after all, how
could she tell it now, when years of deception had been added to it.
And so, by this little accidental discovery of nothing, as it were, her
courage deserted her, and the resolution she had formed of explaining
the way in which the poor dumb girl became an adopted inmate of
his house, was told in a way to create suspicion rather than allay it.

As his wife had adopted this poor creature, Captain Courland
tacitly consented; for, although he felt that there was something that
he could not understand in the matter, he had the heart of a true
British sailor, and would not willingly wound the feelings of a
woman if he could avoid it, especially in such a trifle as this; and
more especially as the offender, if such she could be deemed, was
his beautiful wife, to whom he was attached with the most ardent and
devoted affection. After a time he became quite attached to the poor
dumb girl: she amused him, and he would spend hours in her

private room, while she taught him to talk with his fingers; and she was interested in her task, and would laugh such a hearty, ringing laugh when he made a mistake, that the jovial captain would throw himself back in his chair, and laugh, too, till his sides shook;—and then he could burst out with a nautical phrase in her society with impunity, which, when he attempted unwittingly in the presence of his wife or niece, caused a gentle reprimand, and he was obliged to " knock under," as he expressed it.

Mr. Morley and the captain were old friends. They had met often in India; and no one was more concerned than Captain Courland at the loss of Mr. Morley's brother. Many days were spent in scouring the country in endeavouring to find some trace of him, but, alas! without effect. Nor could they gain any intelligence of the strange woman whom Josiah had seen, at a distance, and who, he verily believed, was Miss Freeman.

All their efforts having proved fruitless, Mr. Morley determined to retrace his steps back to Cornwall once more; and Captain Courland, feeling a deep interest in the discovery of his friend's brother, proposed to his wife that they should accompany their friend there, and help him in the search. This was the very thing Mrs. Courland wished—to get away from the hall and its now unpleasant associations, and, above all, to leave the object of her fear and guilt behind her. She believed that Flora would be quite happy in the undisturbed possession of her favourite rooms, and she could depend on her being taken care of by the servants, for they all liked and pitied her. This would be a great relief to her mind; and then she could give to her husband her undivided attention, without the constant dread of discovery. But when the time of departure arrived, to her great surprise and annoyance, Captain Courland made arrangements for taking Flora in the travelling carriage with them, and was quite angry at his wife's even hinting that Flora would be far happier at the hall. The captain had become so attached to her, that she seemed necessary now to his amusement and occupation. So she accompanied them.

CHAPTER XXXV.
THE DESPERATE PLUNGE.

ALRINA had been at Mrs. Brown's several days, and was beginning to like her employment, and to make herself very useful in the house, when one evening, a strange-looking man came rushing in, and asked for a glass of brandy, which he drank off in a hurried manner, and then said he had seen a ghost. He had such an odd look, and seemed

to speak in such an incoherent manner, that both Mrs. Brown and
Alrina thought he was deranged : but, knowing the suspicious treachery
of persons in that state, they feared to let him see their timidity, lest
he might do them some injury.   So Mrs. Brown pretended to believe
in his statement, and questioned him as to what the ghost was like, and
where he had seen it.   The man was well known to Mrs. Brown, as
a poor half-witted creature, who wandered about in a kind of
melancholy state, but perfectly harmless ; and the neighbours were
kind to " Mazed Dick," as he was called, and gave him meat, and
occasionally Mrs. Brown's customers would give him a glass of beer,
at the " Commercial," for the sake of having a little amusement ;
for " Mazed Dick " could perform various little feats of dexterity,
such as standing on his head, climbing a greasy pole, or dancing in
a grotesque manner, or allowing a whole pint of beer to be poured
down his throat, as through a funnel, without closing his mouth.
But Mrs. Brown had never seen him so excited before as he seemed
to be now, nor had he ever asked for brandy before ; and after he
had drank it, she wished she had not given it to him.   Without
answering Mrs. Brown's questions, he continued to talk in the same
incoherent way, sometimes laughing by way of interlude, and
sometimes screaming as if he suddenly saw some terrifying object
before him.   It was no use to ask him any more questions, so they
let him go on in his own way,—

"Down 'tween the rocks, Mrs. Brown, ma'm, a g'eat big.ship
(ha! ha! ha!), bottom up, Mrs. Brown, ma'm, bottom up, ma'm
(ha! ha! ha!), kegs of brandy, Mrs. Brown, ma'm, kegs of brandy
(ha! ha! ha!).   Little Dick creepy crawly, creepy crawly, up the
top of the bottom (oh! lor'!),—slip down agen,—see a g'eat hole,
Mrs. Brown, ma'm. Dick put in his hand to take out a keg of brandy
(oh! lor'! oh! lor'!), catch Dick's hand (oh! lor'! oh! lor'!) Dick
run away,—a ghost!—a ghost!"

From this story they gathered that a ship had been wrecked, and
thrown ashore with its bottom up. Some men who had seen " Mazed
Dick " running towards the public house, followed him, thinking he
was in a good mood for one of his performances ; but on hearing that
there was a wreck on the coast, they started at once for the spot,
taking Dick with them as a guide, who continued to repeat the same
jargon until they arrived at the cove, where they saw a small vessel,
as " Mazed Dick " had described it, jammed between two rocks, with
her bottom up. To climb up the side of the vessel as she lay thus,
bottom up, was a difficult task ; for the sides were slippery. No one
but little Dick could do it ; so he, to show his dexterity, climbed up
at once like a cat, and put his hand into the hole, which they could
see as they stood on the rock. He had no sooner done so, however,
than he began to scream and kick about his legs in a vain effort to

get clear and slide down again; but no,—there he was held, as it seemed, by some invisible power inside. What could it be? Whatever it was, however, it had not the power of holding its victim in that position long; for poor Dick was soon released, and came sliding down again among his companions, exclaiming, "A ghost! a ghost! oh! lor'! oh! lor'!"—and this was all they could get out of him. He could give no account of what he had seen or felt. So it was determined to send for a ladder and examine this mysterious affair thoroughly.

The ladder was soon procured, and with it a host of wreckers, both men and women, although it was now getting dusk, and they would not be able to see what was inside when they got to the hole; so lanterns were procured, and there was a parley as to who should go up. All had been eager to reach the spot, and would have braved any visible danger either by sea or land; but there was a mystery about this which their superstitious fears deterred them from attempting readily. In the midst of their hesitation, Captain Trenow came down to see what it was all about, and he volunteered at once to climb the ladder, and examine the interior of the vessel; for he believed it was nothing but "Mazed Dick's" timidity that made him scream, or perhaps one of his mad tricks. So up went the brave old man, carrying a lantern in his hand; and, after looking in at the hole for a few minutes, holding the lantern now on one side and now on the other, to enable him to see every part of the interior, as far as the size of the hole would admit, he came down again, and said very deliberately,—

" 'Tes a whished sight, soas ! "

" Why, what ded 'ee see, cap'n ? " cried a dozen voices.

" Why, I seed two men and a boy, so well as I cud make out," replied Captain Trenow.

" Dear lor' ! " exclaimed the women; " the crew starved to death, poor souls ! That's whisht, sure nuff."

" 'Tes whishter to be standen' here like a passle of fools," said Captain Trenow; " they mayn't be all dead, an' I don't think they are. Lev the women run up to church-town for some blankets and sails an' things, and some brandy, an' some of the men go down to bâl for some ropes an' planks, an' a hatchet or two, and a saw ; for the hole esn't big enough to hale a man through."

Here was the master mind equal to any emergency; and, so accustomed is the bâl captain to be obeyed by the miners under him at the bâl, that Captain Trenow's commands were obeyed to the letter, such discipline being as necessary in mining operations, where there is so much risk and danger, as in a military army on the field of battle. In an incredibly short time, the men returned with ropes, and planks, and more ladders, accompanied by some of the mine-carpenters, who had not left work in consequence of a breakage at the mine.

"Go up," said Captain Trenow to the carpenters, "and enlarge that hole three or four feet each way." And up they went at once and commenced their work without asking a question; and very soon an opening was made large enough to bring up any thing that might be below.

By this time the women had arrived also, with plenty of blankets and old sails, and brandy, accompanied by many more people from the village. Captain Trenow, with three or four of the strongest men of the party, now went up the ladders which were placed against the side of the vessel, taking shorter ladders with them, which they let down through the opening that the carpenters had made, taking ropes and blankets and sails with them. On descending into the vessel they found two men and a boy—the two men lying at the bottom, apparently dead, or in the last gasp, while the boy was lying on a cask near the hole. He was alive, and still retained the use of his limbs; and it must have been he who had seized poor Dick in that mysterious manner. They were soon got out of their perilous situation; and that infallible remedy—brandy—having been applied to their lips, it was ascertained that they were all alive. The boy revived considerably, but the two men, with all the remedies Captain Trenow's experience applied, only revived sufficiently to exhibit signs of life.

They were speedily conveyed to the "Commercial" Inn, and Mrs. Brown and her fair assistant prepared comfortable beds for them, while Captain Trenow and one or two strong, trusty men remained to watch them during the night. A little food was given them frequently; for Captain Trenow saw that they were suffering principally from exhaustion and want of food.

The boy did not require much attention; and, after a moderate allowance of food, he fell fast asleep. Mrs. Brown's household also went to bed, at Captain Trenow's earnest request, while he and one of the miners remained in attendance on the invalids all night. The boy slept soundly till morning, when he awoke refreshed, but hungry; so he went downstairs in search of something to eat. Mr. Brown was the only one stirring, and he was in the back kitchen giving a finishing polish to his shoes.

"What! Billy, boy!" said he, as the boy entered; "come, 'tes time to look to the mare. Come, boy! come!" And he led the way into the stables, as he used to do, and the boy followed him; for he knew that was the only way to get anything to eat. "Mare first and breakfast afterwards," was always Mr. Brown's motto.

The sad reality very soon exhibited itself to poor Mr. Brown's shattered brain; and he sat down on the pail which was standing useless against the wall with its bottom up, and bewailed his loss.

"Iss, boy," said the poor man; "I seed them both go over cliff,—

and that poor young gentleman to be killed too. 'Twas whist, Billy, boy. Semmen to me I can see them now tumblen' over. I've seed his ghost since, boy, I have."

When Mr. Brown had exhausted himself with his monotonous lamentation, on the loss of the mare and the young gentleman, the boy went up close to him, and whispered something in his ear which made him start; and, jumping up, he proceeded into the house at once, exclaiming, "Peggy! Peg! Peg! Peggy! my dear,—here's that gentleman; get breakfast quickly. What! Miss Reeney downstairs already! Good morning, ma'am. Come to see "The Maister," I s'pose. Get breakfast quickly, Peggy! Ods my life! how hungered they'll be! Out exercising the mare, es he? That's brave. Get the corn ready and a clean wisp o' straw to give her the first rub weth. Ods my life! how glad I am."

"Hoity! toity! what's all the fuss?" exclaimed Mrs. Brown, as she came slowly downstairs; "one wud think that the French were landed."

"And so they are, I b'lieve, o' my conscience," said Mr. Brown.

"Hold your tongue, John Brown!" said his wife, angrily, as she proceeded to get the breakfast. She had not seen Alrina or the boy; for the latter made a signal to Alrina to follow him out into the little garden at the back of the house, while Mr. Brown was giving his silly and futile orders about the mare, which his wife was now too much accustomed to, to notice.

Imagine Alrina's astonishment, when she heard from the boy, that her father and lover were both in that house. What should she do?— That was the first queston she asked herself; and it was as quickly answered in her own mind. She must do her duty; and her first duty was to attend to her father, however disgraceful his conduct might have been. And, under the circumstances, it was her duty also to avoid meeting her lover, both for her own peace of mind and for his;—for she had fully determined that nothing should induce her to continue an engagement, which must bring disgrace on him and misery to her;—she could never endure to marry a man whose family would despise her. She learnt the whole history of his escape from the boy, and she shuddered when he told her of the dreadful moment, when the boat bumped against the rock, as they thought, but which in reality was a vessel they could not see, as they lay in the bottom of the boat, faint and exhausted. They were picked up and taken on board, but his master was so exhausted that he was unconscious all the time. The boy soon discovered, he said, that the principal person on board was no other than his old master, Mr. Freeman, who treated them both very kindly; but a storm arose that night, and drove the little vessel back again towards the Land's-End. He and Mr. Freeman were below, he said, attending to the invalid, when the vessel struck on a rock, and her mast was blown over some-how, and they felt the vessel turn on her beam ends. The hatches had been closed down over them when they went below, for the sea was washing over the deck. The two sailors must have been washed overboard. How long they were in that awful state, beating about, the boy did not know; it seemed an age. He was the strongest of the party, he said; and, when he found that the vessel was at last stationary, he got on a cask to be as near the hole which the rocks had made in her as possible, and it was in this position that he caught the man's hand; but he was too much exhausted to speak.

Alrina consulted her good friend, Mrs. Brown, as to what she should do with her father; and it was ultimately decided that he had better be removed at once to his own house.

Who the other invalid was, Alrina did not say. Mr. Freeman seemed in a very precarious state; and if he was to be removed at all, Captain Trenow thought it should be done at once. It was early, and few people were stirring as yet in the village; and so the poor unconscious man was removed gently and quietly to that house which he had left but a short time before, knowing and feeling that his return to that place must end in public disgrace and punishment. His faithful daughter, as in duty bound, made everything as com-fortable about him as she could, and her attendant, Alice Ann, came back at once to her young mistress's assistance.

In undressing him to put him into bed, Captain Trenow discovered a belt round his waist, which, on being opened, was found to contain a considerable sum of money, principally in gold, and a quantity of diamonds and other jewels apparently of great value. The money Captain Trenow persuaded Alrina to take into her possession, and to use as much as was necessary for the maintenance of the house and for comforts for the invalid, while the jewels he placed in a drawer in Mr. Freeman's private room, under lock and key. It was evident that he had been preparing for flight for some time, and had secured enough of "the needful" to enable him to live comfortably in some distant country. Of his daughter's comfort he cared nothing; for he did not leave a single shilling behind for her, and yet she forgave him all, and came back again to the house she thought she had quitted for ever, to be his guardian and ministering angel.

A surgeon was sent for from Penzance, who said it was doubtful whether his patient would recover. By care, and attention, and good nursing, he might rally.

Frederick Morley—for he was Captain Trenow's other patient—was recovering slowly, when he learned that Mr. Freeman had been taken home, and that his daughter was there also. He immediately got up, weak as he was, and walked towards Mr. Freeman's house, determined to see Alrina, whose image had been ever present to his mind, night and day, and from whom he was now fully determined no power on earth should separate him. When he arrived at the house he was told that Alrina was in attendance on her father, who was not able to leave his bed.

He waited some time in the little parlour before the object of his adoration made her appearance, as she was obliged to school herself into the proper state of mind in which she wished to appear, before she met him to whom she must now say farewell for ever.

She had been expecting this visit, and had been preparing herself for the meeting, and thought, poor girl, that she could be firm ;— but now, when the time was actually come, she found that it was more than she could go through. She came at last, pale and trembling, but firm. And when Frederick rushed towards her with the impetuosity of a warm-hearted lover, from whom his darling had been separated so long, she recoiled calmly and coldly from his embrace, and requested him, in a dignified manner, to be seated.

"Alrina!" exclaimed he, in surprise; "what is the meaning of this coolness? After so long an absence, I expected to have been received by you in a very different manner. What have I done to deserve this? Or has some vile calumniator been poisoning your mind against me? Tell me, dearest!" And he attempted to approach her again, his eyes beaming with the fondest love and devotion.

"Mr. Morley!" said Alrina, restraining her feelings with a strong effort; "circumstances have changed since we last met; and I am compelled, more for your sake than mine, to tell you that all further intercourse must cease between us."

"Alrina!" exclaimed he, passionately; "what can you mean? — Can I believe my ears,—that she, whom I so fondly and devotedly love, can coldly and deliberately tell me that our intercourse must cease, without assigning any reason. Tell me at least this. What cause have I given you for treating me thus?"

"None!" said she; "none! you have been to me more than I deserve. It is not that, oh! no!"

"You have seen another whom you love better," said he. "Tell me,—only tell me, and relieve my racking brain,—anything is better than this suspense. I will never give you up,—I swear I will not! The villain who has supplanted me shall die!" And he paced the room in mental agony, while poor Alrina scarcely knew what to do. She had made up her mind to do her duty; and she was determined, for his sake more than her own, to go through with it. He must not think he had a rival; it would endanger some innocent person, perhaps; nor could she make up her mind to tell him of her father's disgrace. He would hear it, of course,—he must know it; but it should not come from her. What should she do?

There was only one alternative that seemed open to her. She

must take all the blame on herself, and bear all his wrath, or scorn, or hate, or whatever it might be, on her own shoulders. However painful, it must be done. And, rising with as much coolness as she could command at that awful crisis, she said, in a trembling voice,—

"Mr. Morley, we must part now and for ever; for I feel I cannot love you as I ought."

"Oh! Alrina!" he exclaimed, taking her hand, which she could not prevent; "do not say so! oh! do not say so,—you cannot mean it,—say you do not mean that. Not love me! Oh! Alrina! after all————"

"I cannot stay longer," said she, hastily withdrawing her hand; "I can only repeat that I cannot love you." And, in an agony of mind, which it would be impossible to describe, she rushed to her own room, and, locking the door, threw herself on the bed, and wept bitter tears of agony unspeakable.

Morley remained motionless for some minutes, as one thunderstruck. It seemed as if he had received his death blow. To be treated thus coldly by one who, but a short time before, had expressed the warmest affection for him, was inexplicable. He could not understand it. There was only one solution that presented itself to his disordered mind. She loved another! And that thought rendered him desperate,—it maddened him.

Revenge was his first thought. But how, and on whom? He staggered out of the house like a drunken man, and directed his steps unconsciously towards the sea. Life had become a burden to him within the last short hour. He had nothing now to live for. He looked down into the deep blue sea, as he stood on the rock. All his former hope of life and happiness had faded away like a shadow. He could have lived on with the hope that she might one day be his, knowing that she loved him still. But, now, she had told him that she could not love him, and had bade him farewell for ever! He could not endure the thought. Her coldness and the apparent cause thrilled through his frame. This feeling of jealousy maddened him; his brain reeled. One plunge into that deep blue water, and all his mental sufferings would be ended. The waters would open to receive him; and when they closed over him again, all the cares and troubles of this life would be over, and she would be free from the dread of his presence, if indeed she feared it.

His brain was on fire; he was mad; a temporary insanity had seized him; and he thought only of escaping from present troubles. One short plunge, and all would be over. Alas! he thought not of the future. What mortal, when in that state of frenzied madness, does think of that?

For if, he did,—if, in the act of making his quietus by self destruction, one sane thought remained,—"that dread of something after death—the undiscovered country from whose bourne no traveller returns—would puzzle the will; and make him rather bear the ills he has, than fly to others that he knows not of." Man's life is not in his own hands. He who gave it, and He alone, has the right to take it when it shall please Him so to do. Morley thought not of the future, but only how to escape from "the pangs of despised love," which now oppressed him. And the more he thought of this, the more did his brain seethe and boil, till he could bear it no longer; and, taking a desperate leap from the high rock on which he stood, he plunged into the deep blue water that lay so tranquil at his feet.

A splash was heard as the waters opened to receive their prey; and then they closed around and over him, and down he went,—down! down!—five fathoms deep, or more, for the water here was deep enough to swim a three-decked ship with all her thousand men on board, and guns and ammunition. 'Twas an awful plunge, not like the plunge of the agile swimmer, who jumps from off a rock and dives until he touches the bottom, only to rebound and then come up again some few yards ahead, and strike out boldly with head erect, braving the restless sea, and riding over each wave buoyant and graceful as a sea-bird, whose element it is. The plunge of the victim of self destruction has a sadder and more decided sound. Down he goes to the bottom, a dead weight, with all his sins upon his head; for in that short space of time, all the actions of his past life crowd on his mind, and he lives his life over again, as it were, in a single moment.

And so went down the body of Frederick Morley to the bottom. But as his body touched it, up it came again buoyant in that unruffled sea. Ere it rose to the surface of the water, another splash was heard, and a stout strong swimmer came breasting the waves, ready to catch the rash young man as soon as he appeared; and, seizing him in one of his strong arms, he swam with him to the shore and landed him in safety.

Frederick had not been under water long enough to receive any serious injury, although the salt water in his mouth and eyes and ears, made him feel very uncomfortable. And this might have a very serious effect, after his late sufferings and confinement; for he had risen from his bed to go to Alrina, on learning that she was at home, when he ought to have remained quiet for a little longer, in order to be fully equal to the double shock he had sustained. Perhaps had he been in robust health, he would not have taken this rash step; but his nerves were weak. The plunge into the water, however, had tended to cool his fevered brain; and, when he turned to thank his deliverer, after he had recovered a little, what was his surprise to find that he was indebted again for his life to that noble fellow, Josiah Trenow, who had thus saved him a second time from the jaws of death.

CHAPTER XXXVI.

THE BROKEN REED.

MR. MORLEY and Josiah had left Ashley Hall before the family could get ready for the journey, and had travelled with speed and arrived at Lieutenant Fowler's station on the morning of Frederick Morley's visit to Alrina; and as Josiah had been hurried away without seeing Alice Ann, he was anxious to know what had become of her; so, under pretence of going to see his mother, he hastened to St. Just at once, and made direct for Mr. Freeman's house, little thinking of the changes that had taken place there during his short absence. He learned from Alice Ann all that she knew of the history of the past few weeks, and she ended by telling him that Mr. Frederick Morley had been there that morning, and that something had happened between him and Miss Reeney, for that she was locked in her room sobbing and crying her eyes out a'most, and Mr. Frederick was gone down towards the sea, raving like a mad bull.

Josiah thought there must be something very much amiss, but what it was he could not imagine. However he deemed it prudent to follow his young master; and it was lucky he did so, for he reached the spot barely in time to see him throw himself from the rock into the sea. Josiah was an expert swimmer so he did not hesitate a moment, but throwing off his coat and hat, he plunged in after the demented youth, and saved him, as we have seen. Now that he was cool and collected once more, Morley seemed quite ashamed of the act he had attempted, and shuddered at what might have been his fate, had he not been thus fortunately rescued; nor would he satisfy his faithful follower as to whether it was accident or not. After sitting in the sun to dry themselves a little, they walked back to the inn, where they found Lieutenant Fowler and Mr. Morley waiting their return. Fowler had not heard, until the night before, of Frederick's miraculous escape from his imprisonment at Cooper's, and his preservation in the vessel which had borne away Mr. Freeman from the hands of justice;—and they came on to see Frederick, whom they expected to find in bed, and to learn the truth about the return of Mr. Freeman; for Fowler had heard only a rumour of that as yet,—the gossips being still afraid to speak out openly about him, lest evil should come upon them.

Josiah had heard every particular from Alice Ann; and Mr. Morley, being determined that he should not elude them this time, desired Josiah to watch the house lest any one should escape, while he and Fowler proceeded to Pendrea, for the assistance of the squire, whose warrant as a magistrate would be necessary for the apprehension of the guilty party. Josiah recommended Frederick to go to bed at once, for he feared serious consequences would result from his remaining in his wet clothes any longer, and he told the other gentlemen that their friend had slipped off a rock into the water. They sat by his bedside for a little time after he was in bed, and heard his adventures, and then proceeded on their more important business. They refrained from telling Frederick, however, the name of the party they were in search of, fearing the consequences, in his present weak state, and knowing the pain it would cause him, to find that it was Alrina's father whom they accused.

Fowler forgot his own wrongs in his anxiety to serve his friend; and it was not until they were within a short distance of Pendrea-house, that he remembered his position with regard to the squire and his household, and he scrupled to go on.

"Nonsense, my dear fellow," said Mr. Morley; "you are going on a very different errand now. That was pleasure, this is business; besides, we don't know what it may lead to."

Thus persuaded, but certainly not against his inclination, Fowler went on without again alluding to the subject, well knowing the old adage that "faint heart never won fair lady."

The squire was at home, and received his two visitors with politeness if not with cordiality; for his wife had got a crotchet into her head about Mr. Morley and her eldest daughter, which had been told her by one of the servants, and she had told it to the squire; and, putting this against that, as he expressed it, he thought he saw clearly that Mr. Morley had been trifling with his eldest daughter's affections, as Fowler had been doing with her sister; and so he came to the conlusion, without the aid of the conjuror, that the conduct of these two men had caused the sudden and alarming change which they had observed in the health and spirits of their two daughters, and which had baffled the skill of all the doctors. Had Mr. Morley and Lieutenant Fowler, therefore, called in the ordinary way, and claimed his friendship, they would not probably have been admitted; but they now came on business in which the squire was himself much interested; so he filled up a warrant and agreed to accompany them to see the end of it. They could take a constable from the village, as they passed, he said.

The old squire did not forget his hospitality, in his pique at the treatment he believed his daughters had received at the hands of these two gentlemen. They were both gentlemanly men, and they were now engaged in one common cause with himself, the punishment of a man whom the squire had suspected and watched for some time, and who, they now discovered, was a villain of the deepest dye. Mr. Morley had suspicions even beyond what, at present, he thought it prudent to communicate to the other two gentlemen. The squire unbent and came down from his stilts, before they had conversed five minutes, and ordered lunch, which he might in those days have termed dinner; after which the three gentlemen started on their expedition. And so eager and anxious were they in concocting their plans for the capture of the man who had so cunningly eluded them before, that, if the ladies were not forgotten by some of the party, they were certainly not alluded to. Perhaps this was avoided from policy by the two visitors;—the stilts might have been had recourse to again, if that subject had been revived just then in the mind of the crusty old squire.

The ladies knew that the two gentlemen were in the house, and expected to be summoned into the drawing-room, but they were disappointed. The three gentlemen lunched alone, and then started on their expedition. An experienced constable was procured at the next village, and on they went, a formidable party, determined not to be outwitted again by that cunning man. They found the trusty Josiah watching closely when they arrived near the house; no one had gone in or come out, he said, since he had been there. He had not even seen Alice Ann come out, and he would not venture too near the house for fear of causing suspicion. They knew the depth and cunning of the man so well, that it was necessary to use every precaution. He might feign extreme illness in order to put them off their guard, and might again escape. So it was arranged that Lieutenant Fowler and Josiah should watch the outside of the house, while the other two went in, accompanied by the constable, who was well up to his work, having been sent down from a larger place some years ago, and recommended to the office by a gentleman high in authority.

"'The Maister' es very bad in bed, sar," said Alice Ann, making a low curtsey to the squire, as she opened the door; "Miss Reeney es up in har room, very bad too, for what I can tell; for I haan't seed har for a bra' bit. I'll call har down, sar. Step inside, ef you plaise." And she ushered them into the best parlour.

As the house was well watched and guarded, the squire and Mr. Morley thought it would be but courteous to see the daughter, and smooth it over to her as well as they could. Justice must have its course, but it would have been cruel to have distressed the poor innocent girl more than was absolutely necessary. They intended to try to get her away somewhere first, and then she would not feel the disgrace so much. The constable, however, was for executing his warrant at once without showing favour or affection to anyone, man, woman, or child; and if the magistrate had not been there in person to check him, he would have made short work of it; for he was a rough, determined character, and had been in office long enough to be hardened in the stern duties he was sometimes obliged to perform. He had suffered for showing too much lenity to persons in his early career and he was determined that shouldn't happen again.

After a short time, Alrina made her appearance, pale and wretched, with swollen eyes, and a fevered brow, which her visitors, who knew not the real cause, attributed to her grief and anxiety for her father. The squire told her as gently as he could, that they had an unpleasant duty to perform, which must be done; and he advised her to leave the house, and seek the protection of some friend.

"Alas!" she replied; "what friend have I to fly to? I have no one in the world but my father and my aunt, to look to for protection. My father lies upstairs on a bed of sickness, and he has no one but myself to nurse him; and where my aunt is I know not. Oh! gentlemen, have pity on me, if not on my father;—he is my father, whatever evil he may have done. Spare him for my sake! Consider, squire Pendray, you have daughters of your own,—consider their feelings if placed in my situation. My poor father to be taken from a bed of sickness, where I have endeavoured to do all in my power to relieve his sufferings, and to ease his pain,—to be taken out by the rough hands of the executors of the law, and cast into a cold damp prison! Oh! gentlemen, on my knees I beg you to allow him to remain here with me. It may not be long." And, falling on her knees, she clasped the squire by the hand, and burst into a flood of tears.

It was an affecting sight. The squire remembered his own daughters, and their fond affection for their father, and would have relented; and Mr. Morley, although he was the one most aggrieved, turned away from the sad scene. It was heartrending to see one so young and lovely on her bended knees, praying for her father's relief from present punishment.

It was but a slight request after all.

"Why not let the constable remain here?" said Mr. Morley at last. "Two if you like."

"Yes! two!" exclaimed Alrina, rising suddenly, and approaching Mr. Morley; "only allow my father to remain here under my care and nursing, until he is able to be removed (if it must be so), and I will ask no more. Oh! squire Pendray!—Oh! Mr. Morley! continued she, appealing to each of them by turns; think what it is to have a father taken from you, and in this way! Let him remain here,—oh! pray, let him remain."

The constable was made of sterner stuff. He had been constable many years, and knew his duty when he had a warrant placed in his hands; and, seeing that Mr. Morley had given way already, and that the squire would soon follow his example, he thought it was time to speak.

"I tell 'ee what et es, squire," said he; "you have put a warrant in my hands agen John Freeman, the Land's-End conjuror, and what not, and Mr. Morley's oath es gone forth agen him; and ef you wink at et now, and the man shud escape, what do you think will

Q

be the upshot of et? Why, we shall have to take the conjuror's place
for compromising a felony,—that's about the time o' day, gentlemen.
I've suffered before for tender-heartedness, and I don't mean to do et
agen ; so ef miss will show me the room I'll follow her, or else I'll
find et out by myself."

Alrina now turned to the constable and besought him to pity her,
and, if it must be so, to remain there, and she would make him as
comfortable as possible.

"Oh ! sir !" she said, "if you have a daughter, think of her
feelings, should her father be taken from her, as you would take
away mine,—oh ! in pity think of that sir !"

"That's the very thing I'm thinking about, miss," replied the
constable ; "and I'm thinking that my daughter wud have to go
through the same trial as you are going through now, ef I wor to
lev the conjuror go.   No ! no ! miss, rather he than me, axing your
pardon.   Why lor' bless you, miss, tesn't much when you're used to
et.   We'll take care of the old gentleman, as much as ef he had be'n
the old gentleman hisself.   I've got a tidy little covered cart outside,
and we'll clap 'n in, and travel to Penzance to-night, and to-morrow
mornin' he'll be broft before the magistrates and committed, ef he's
guilty,—and he's sure to be, I s'pose,—and then on to Bodmin.
Why, 'twill be a nice little ride for 'n miss."

"Oh ! don't, please don't, paint such a terrible picture as that,"
said Alrina, looking up at the inexorable constable, with the tears
glistening in her eyes.

"Come," said he, "I'm not going to be made chicken-hearted.
Show me the way to his room,—we're wasting time." And he led the
way out of the room, followed by the others.

Alrina, now, seeing that tears and entreaties would not avail,
preceded the party upstairs ; but when she arrived at her father's
bedroom-door, she stopped and begged the constable to allow her to
go in first, to break the nature of their business to him, and prepare
him for their approach.

"No !" said the constable, sharply, placing his hand on the handle
of the door; "that dodge won't do, my pretty lady.   A cunning
man and a shrewd woman are a match for the devil, when they get
together."   So, seeing she had no alternative but to open the door
and admit them, Alrina, with a trembling hand, lifted the latch,
and, preceding the others, hastily gained the side of the bed, and,
kneeling down, begged her father not to be frightened, for he would
be treated kindly.   She said this without looking on his face ; for
she knew she could say nothing to comfort him, and she did not like
to witness the shock which this untimely intrusion must occasion,
and so she pressed her face on the bed, as she knelt, and said these
few introductory words, and waited to hear what he would say to

his unwelcome visitors. No one spoke for a few minutes. A death-like silence prevailed throughout the room. At last the constable broke the spell by saying,—

"Escaped again, by George!"

"Escaped!" cried Alrina, jumping up from her kneeling posture; "thank God for that. But how escaped? how could he————?"

She did not finish her sentence; for, looking down where she had dreaded to look before, the awful truth was but too evident. There was no mistaking it. There lay the earthly remains of her poor deluded father, it was true, but the spirit had indeed escaped, and fled to regions unknown!

The shock was too great for her. She had suffered the severest mental agony that day that it was possible for mortal to bear. She had borne up bravely while there appeared a chance of saving her father from disgrace; but now she broke down altogether, and fell on the floor insensible. Alice Ann had followed the intruders into the room; and, as all her efforts to rouse her young mistress were in vain, she asked the gentlemen to assist in carrying her into her own room.

Fowler and Josiah were called in, and a consultation was held as to where Alrina should be placed for the present. She could not remain there, under the circumstances,—that was very clear. Several plans were proposed and discussed, but nothing could be decided on for her. She might object to them all when she recovered her senses. At last Squire Pendray proposed that she should be conveyed to his house, where he was sure she would be taken care of; and he felt, moreover, although he did not express it, that the companionship of such a noble strong-minded girl might lead to the recovery of his own daughter. This was thought an excellent plan, and everyone declared that the squire was most kind and considerate. But then came another difficulty. She would not accept his offer now, he feared, any more than she would the offer that was made her by his wife, before. And in this he thought she acted foolishly,—more foolishly than he should have imagined from the good sense she had displayed in other respects.

Under these circumstances, he thought, they must get her to Pendrea-house by stratagem, and, when there, he felt sure she would like it too well to run away, and he was sure his family would approve of the plan, and would make her as comfortable as possible. So it was arranged that she should be taken carefully, in her present unconscious state, and placed gently in the covered cart, well wrapped up, and that Alice Ann should go also to take care of her, on the road. This plan Alice Ann thought capital. So the poor unconscious girl was carried out gently by Josiah in his great strong arms, and placed comfortably in the covered cart, with Alice Ann by her side, and Josiah was left in charge of the house and the dead body of its late owner.

Mr. Morley said he must go and see his brother again; for he feared that the sufferings and privations he had lately undergone, had seriously impaired his health and undermined his constitution. So he went on to "The Commercial" inn, while the squire and Lieut. Fowler proceeded towards their respective homes; and as their road lay the same way for some distance, they walked together. Fowler made himself so agreeable to the old gentleman during their walk that he was sorry to part with him when their roads turned in different directions. He did not ask him, however, to continue his companion all the way to Pendrea-house; but during his solitary walk after they had parted, he began to think that such an agreeable fellow could never really be the villain he supposed him to be with regard to his conduct towards his daughter. His opinion of him was softened a good deal; and if a satisfactory explanation of his conduct could have been given just then, and a proposal made in a straight-forward honourable way, the old gentleman would, no doubt, have consented, rather than leave his daughter pine away thus,—the cause of which he now devined so truly. But the explanation did not come, nor was the proposal made; so the old squire walked home alone to prepare his family for the reception of their visitor, who was being brought slowly round by the broad road, while he and Fowler had taken a short cut across the common.

CHAPTER XXXVII.

JOSIAH'S LONELY MIDNIGHT WATCH IN THE CONJUROR'S HOUSE.

Mr. MORLEY found his brother still in bed; not because he was too ill to get up—for the walk and the cold bath had done him good—but for the simple reason that he had no clothes to put on. Those he wore in the morning were too wet, and he had not yet received a fresh supply from the "First and Last" inn, at Sennen, where he had left his things when he started so suddenly on his journey some weeks before. So Mr. Morley sat by his bedside, and got him to relate his adventures, which he did very faithfully, until he came to the adventure of that morning; and then Mr. Morley saw there was a reluctance to tell all. But he was determined to know everything, and he pressed his brother to confide in him; and, after some little hesitation, he told all, except his attempt at self-destruction. He didn't tell that; but he dwelt long on the conduct of Alrina, and asked his brother if he could give him any clue to the discovery of Alrina's motive for treating him so coldly and cruelly.

"Yes," replied his brother; "I think I can fathom it; and although I think Miss Freeman is a noble girl, yet I think, when I have related to you my adventures of the last few weeks, you will think that she is right, and that you have luckily escaped being mixed up in a most unpleasant affair, that must have embittered your whole life, had not that noble girl been more prudent than yourself."

It will be remembered that Frederick knew nothing of his brother's search at Mr. Freeman's house, when he found his chest there, and the money gone,—nor did he know of the second attempt, that morning, to secure the man of cunning, nor of his death,—nor, indeed, had he heard of his brother's success in entering the deserted house near Bristol;—so that Mr. Morley had a long and interesting tale to relate.

Frederick was very much excited several times during the recital, and seemed to drink in every word, as it were, especially when his brother arrived at the latter part of his recital, wherein Alrina pleaded so piteously for a delay of her father's punishment.

A long silence ensued when the tale was ended. At last Mr. Morley said,—

"Now, do you see Miss Freeman's motive for her treatment of you this morning?"

"Noble girl!" exclaimed Frederick; "I see it all, she knew her father's guilt, and did violence to her feelings to save me from being involved in the sad affair. But after all, I cannot understand why she should say she couldn't love me;—why not have told me all, and have left it to me to act according to the dictates of my own feelings?"

"She knew you better than you knew yourself," replied his brother; "and I repeat that she acted nobly, and you ought to consider yourself lucky, that you have escaped a life of misery; for, however deeply you may love this girl now, in the warmth of a first and youthful love, you would find that your ardour would cool considerably, when you saw the world looking coldly on your wife, and avoiding her society, as the child of a felon, and worse, perhaps, however good and lovely she may be in herself. No! no! take my word for it, my dear brother, you will thank her for the course she has pursued, when you have calmly reflected on it."

"Never!" said Frederick, passionately; "instead of weakening my love for her, this noble conduct of hers, has endeared her to me a hundred-fold. What care I for the sneers of the world, if I have Alrina's love? I will go to her at once, and have a full explanation; and if, as you think, she declined my love for the sake of preventing my being subjected to the sneers and scorns of the world, I will compel her to marry me."

"Stay," said Mr. Morley; "you must first ascertain that my

conjecture is the right one; but I wouldn't advise you to see her yourself. Let me see her for you."

"No," said his brother; "I will see her myself." And as his clothes had arrived by this time, he dressed and accompanied his brother back to Tol-pedn-Penwith, where Lieutenant Fowler had no difficulty in accommodating them both, although his house was so small. He ordered an extra hammock to be slung up in the largest of the sleeping apartments, where the two brothers slept soundly till a late hour the next morning, as they were both very tired.

Josiah, in the meantime, kept watch and guard over "the Maister's" house and its contents. It was pleasant enough while the daylight lasted; but when night came on, and darkness covered the face of the earth, Josiah thought it was very whisht to be there in that house all alone. So he went down to his father's, and had a good supper, and something to drink. This made him feel very comfortable, and he wished them all good-night, took a lantern with him, and went back again to his solitary watch.

Josiah was a courageous man at all times when there was any real danger to be feared, and a strong man, as everybody knew. The man must be more than mortal who could make Josiah afraid, but he had a strong superstitious feeling in his composition; and who had not in those days?—and if there was an excuse for the feeling at all, it certainly might be excused in such a case as this. Here was the man who had been the dread of the neighbourhood, and who was believed to have dealings with the Evil One, lying dead in that lonely house, where so many evil deeds had been done, some of which had been discovered within the last few days. That he was a man to be feared and dreaded no one doubted; but whether he really had the power which many gave him credit for, remained to be proved yet. Josiah thought that perhaps it would be his fate to prove this; and it cannot be denied that he felt rather uncomfortable, when he found himself seated in the kitchen of that house, not only without the pleasant society of Alice Ann, but, as he well knew, without having any human habitation within some distance of him.

His mother had kindly given him a flask of brandy, that he might indulge in the prevailing amusement at that period, of "keeping his spirits up, by pouring spirits down;" and so he sat down in the chair usually occupied by Alice Ann, having first placed a glass and some water on the table, and began to reflect on the vicissitudes of human life in general, and of his life in particular; and then he began to speculate on the prospects of happiness which seemed to loom in the future, when he should have led Alice Ann to the altar, and settled down as a married man. These thoughts were all very pleasant, and so was the brandy-and-water. The candle was burning brightly and so was the fire, and he thought he was "gotten on brave."

He had got nearly to the bottom of the second glass of brandy-and-water, and was beginning to feel quite comfortable and happy. He only wanted one thing to add to his perfect happiness he thought, and that was the pleasure of Alice Ann's society. It was drawing towards midnight, and he was feeling drowsy, so he dropped off into a sound sleep as he sat in his chair, and dreamed of her he last thought of before he fell asleep. He fancied he heard her upstairs, brushing out the rooms, and knocking the furniture about, as servants frequently do, merely to show that they are doing something. She was making a tremendous noise certainly, he thought, and he called to her, in his sleep, not to make so much noise, to disturb " The Maister." But the noise continued, nevertheless; and when he awoke he found the candle burnt down in the socket, and the fire nearly gone out; so he replenished the fire first, and then looked about for another candle, but before he could find one, he heard, as he thought, a strange noise in "The Maister's" room. What could it be? No one could have got into the house; he had locked the doors,—he was sure of that, but still there was a noise—that was evident; and someone was walking up and down the room upstairs. What could it be?

The candle, which had been flickering in the socket, and wavering between life and death, as it were, for some seconds, now went out entirely, and left Josiah in perfect darkness. He searched in vain for another candle,—he couldn't find one anywhere; and then he tried to find the door of the kitchen, but he could not find it. He went round and round the room, as he thought, but no door could he find; so at length he came back to his chair again, which he found by the aid of the glimmer of light from the fire which he had nearly extinguished in his haste to replenish it, when he saw the candle flickering away.

He now fully made up his mind that he was spellbound, and that "The Maister's" spirit was walking through the house; but as the noise had ceased he became a little more reconciled, and helped himself to some more brandy, after which he fell fast asleep again, and when he awoke it was broad daylight.

He rubbed his eyes and looked about the room, forgetting for a moment where he was; and then he began to think of his absurd fancies about being spellbound and "piskey-led," and such nonsense; and he laughed aloud and went out into the fresh morning air. The doors were barred and all secure, as he had left them when he came in the night before. But still he heard those strange noises in his ears, and he could not get rid of the feeling that the "The Maister's" spirit was walking in his room last night. He locked the door behind him, and went down the road towards his father's house to breakfast.

"Why, 'Siah, boy," said Captain Trenow, laughing, as his son approached, "you're looking so whisht as ef you'd seed a ghost. "The Maister" dedn't trouble 'ee in the night, ded aw?"

"I caen't tell," replied Josiah, "what et wor, but I heerd a bra' noise in the night."

"Why, what are 'ee tellen?" exclaimed Mrs. Trenow, coming to the door; "I always thoft hes sperit wud walk, ef anybody's ever ded."

"Nonsense!" said Captain Trenow; "you're two patticks, both of 'ee."

Josiah would not be persuaded out of the belief, however, that "The Maister's" spirit was walking in his room last night.

"I'm no coward, fe-a-thar, and that you do knaw," said he; "but I arn't fitty for to stop up there another night by myself, nor I wean't nether to plaise nobody,—there, na."

His father turned the whole tale into ridicule, and laughed at the idea of noises being heard in "The Maister's" chamber, when there was no one in the house but Josiah.

"I'll tell 'ee, my son," said the old man, at length, with a wicked twinkle in his eye; "the brandy was too strong, I reckon. Ha! ha! ha!"

Josiah was about to reply indignantly to this insinuation, when they were disturbed by a knock at the door.

"Dear lor'!" said Mrs. Trenow, rising to open the door; "why, who can be come so early, I wondar?"

She soon returned, saying that the undertakers wanted to go in to do their work.

"Aw! iss, sure," said Josiah; "the door es locked, sure nuff."

"Come," said Captain Trenow; "we may as well go down too, and make sure that no more noises shall be heard. I shudn't like for 'ee to be frightened worse than you are, boy."

So they went down together; and, as Josiah unlocked the door, his father said in a sarcastic tone,—"Now, don't you be frightened, my son."

Josiah did not answer, but led the way upstairs to "The Maister's" bedroom, which adjoined the mysterious room, so often referred to in this history; and having unlocked the door, he led the way into the room where only a few hours before that affecting scene had been witnessed, which we have before recorded.

The awful escape from the hands of justice of one who seemed deserving of a severe punishment, and the consequent shock to the nervous system of a lovely and noble-minded girl, who would have braved everything to save her father from ignominy and suffering,— this scene was no novelty to the undertaker's mermidons. They were accustomed to view dead bodies continually, in their calling. They had been working all night, in order to be in time, and they had brought the fruits of their labour with them, and proceeded, without ceremony, towards the bed, when they started back in amazement! for,—the bed was empty!

"The Maister" was gone!—fled! But where?—that was the question. They searched the room, but found nothing. There was a communication, however, between the bedroom and "The Maister's" private room which no one remembered ever having seen before;—it must have been concealed by some paintings hung against the wall. It was open now—wide open. They went through, into the mysterious room, and there they found that the drawers had been opened and ransacked, and all the valuables taken away. The belt containing the diamonds and jewels, which had been put into one of the drawers in that room, was gone. Captain Trenow was the first to discover this; for he had found it in undressing "The Maister," and he it was who had suggested to Alrina the propriety of locking it up in one of those drawers.

CHAPTER XXXVIII.

THE SEARCH.

The news soon spread that the conjuror—body and soul—had vanished from the room in which he was supposed to have died; and various were the reports that got into circulation. Some said they didn't believe he had been there at all; others thought he wasn't dead when the squire and party left him; while others again believed that he was really dead, but that, by some supernatural agency, he had been resuscitated and taken away through the keyhole, or up the chimney, and that probably he was then wandering about invisible. And those who held this belief were pitiable objects; for they feared to speak a word against "The Maister," lest he should instantly appear in his bodily form, and annihilate them as they stood. The dread of "The Maister" and his evil eye was bad enough when he was alive and in the flesh, but now it was ten times worse. Little knots of gossips might be seen here and there, holding private conversations in whispers;—but that was all nonsense, the believers in the supernatural would say. If "The Maister" was walking about invisible he could come close enough to hear them, whisper so low as they would.

Josiah was rather glad than otherwise that things had turned out as they had; for his father didn't laugh at him now for fancying he heard noises in the night. Captain Trenow thought it was Josiah's duty to go and inform the gentlemen at Tol-pedn-Penwith what had happened, and Josiah was of the same opinion, but he said he wouldn't go unless his father went with him.

"What! afeard to go up there in the day-time now, art aw?" said his father; "why, we shall be forced for to have a little maid for to lead thee about soon."

"No, no," said Josiah, smiling; "I arn't afeard. Tesn't that altogether, but you knaw what 'twas this mornin' when I told the story, and it may be the same up there,—sure to be, I s'pose, weth them youngsters, that don't believe in no such thing as ghosts. No, no, I arn't going for to be made a maagum of, don't you think et."

"Well, ef that's the case," said his father, "why, I'll go too."

So away the two men started at a brisk pace; and it was well they both went, for the gentlemen could scarcely believe the tale, although it was confirmed in a most solemn manner by the old man, who did not look or speak as if he was trying to deceive them.

As the squire had taken an active interest in the affair, it was thought advisable to consult him before they took any steps to follow the fugitive, for although they did not believe that there was anything supernatural connected with it, they were at a loss to conjecture what it was, or how such a strange affair could have happened.

They appeared a formidable party as they emerged from the lieutenant's cabin, each man stooping to avoid knocking his head against the upper part of the low doorway as he came out. They were all tall and strong-built,—indeed you would not meet with five such fine-looking men again in a good distance. They were embarked in one common cause; so they kept together, and approached Pendrea-house, a strong body.

Alrina, after a good night's rest, seemed more cheerful, and was pleased at the little attentions shewn her by Mrs. Pendray and her daughters. Blanche was most attentive to her;—she would not leave her for a single moment, and seemed to be continually thinking what she could do more than she had done to make their guest comfortable. Maud received her kindly and paid her great attention, but it seemed constrained; she appeared to look upon her as an inferior, almost an infected, being, from her unfortunate connection with that man, whom everyone now spoke of with disgust and abhorrence; for all his evil doings that had yet been discovered were now pretty generally known and perhaps exaggerated.

In the course of the morning, as Alrina regained her wonted composure, her situation became more apparent and galling. She could not but appreciate the kindness of the family, and especially the delicate attention of the gentle Blanche, for whom Alrina conceived an almost intuitive love, as for a dear sister; and therefore, for the present, she thought she must accept their kindness, and when all was done that was necessary for the interment of the remains of her poor erring father, she would seek some employment by which she might maintain herself without being a burden on others.

The money and jewels which Captain Trenow had found on her father's person, she determined she would not touch; for doubtless they had belonged to others and had been unlawfully obtained. Poor girl ! notwithstanding all that the ladies at Pendrea were doing for her, and the kind attention they bestowed on her, she was ill-at-ease. She had many heavy thoughts and afflictions weighing her down, which her kind friends knew not of. Her father's death was not the greatest. Alas ! she had, in her loftiness of soul, discarded the only being in the world who could have relieved her present sufferings and made everything smooth and bearable for her at this terrible juncture. She had decided on her course, however, in that respect; and the deep love she felt for him made her now more than ever determined not to bring disgrace upon him. After the treatment he had received at her hands, however, she did not believe he would ever come near her again, or think of her but with disdain ;—indeed she did not deserve that he should,—she had taken her course, and she felt that she did not deserve his love or pity any more. This thought racked her brain, and rendered her silent and reserved. Her kind friends imputed it to her grief for her father's death, and the circumstances under which it had taken place. They knew now the strange story of the body having disappeared ; but the squire thought it best not to let Alrina know this until they had ascertained more fully concerning it, and for this purpose he cheerfully received the formidable party that now sought his aid and co-operation.

They sat long in consultation,—one suggesting one plan, and one another. Frederick Morley, however, did not feel capable of joining in their deliberations. He walked to the window, and looked out on the dreary scene which bounded that wing of the house ; but nothing that he could see without seemed so dreary, at that moment, as that which he felt within. He didn't care for the old conjuror, he said to himself, he might go to the devil if he would,—perhaps he was gone there. He wanted to see Alrina, and he knew that she was in that house, but how could he get an interview with her without betraying their secret ?

He excused himself to the squire, and went out into the garden. Here he met one of the female servants, whom he had seen before in his former visits to the house with Lieutenant Fowler. He entered into conversation with her, and asked her in what he thought a disinterested off-hand manner, about Miss Alrina Freeman. But the shrewd girl saw at once how matters stood, and she pitied them both. He tore a leaf from his pocket-book, and wrote a few hurried lines in pencil, and· asked her to convey them to Miss Freeman, which the girl undertook to do as soon as the way was clear. Cunning girl ! she knew at once, almost by instinct, that there was something between those two, which they did not wish the world to

know at present.   Even the prospect of having these few lines
conveyed to Alrina was some relief to Frederick and he returned
to his friends, who were still deep in consultation, but no plan had
as yet been decided on.   At length Captain Trenow, who had listened
to all their plans without giving an opinion, said,—

"I'll tell 'ee, gentlemen,—'The Maister' dedn't walk off by
hisself, that's a sure thing.   Now, who helped 'n?—that's the point.
Who are his friends?   Tell me that, and we may guess, purty nigh,
where he's likely to be carr'd to.

"Why I'll tell 'ee, fe-a-thar," said Josiah; "I b'lieve the friends
he ha' got are them that slocked away Maister Frederick Morley
here, and pocked 'n down in the cellar."

"Zackly like that," replied his father, looking at the gentlemen in
a knowing way; 'Birds of a feather do flock together.'"

"A good thought!" exclaimed Mr. Morley, rising.   "Don't let us
lose any time, but proceed at once."

Horses were procured from the neighbouring farmers—for there
were no gigs or dog-carts in those days at the Land's-End—and they
started on their expedition; but lest so formidable a party should
alarm the neighbourhood, they agreed to go by different routes and
to meet at Portagnes, and to go in a body to Cooper's house; for
that the body of the conjuror was taken there no one seemed to
doubt;—it was the only place they could think of at all likely.
For, although one of the party strongly believed that the noises he
heard, and the removal of the body, were caused by supernatural
agency, he did not express his thoughts on that point, but followed
the others, fully persuaded that they would find their labour in vain.

Frederick Morley lingered behind his party a little, and under
pretence of having left something behind at Pendrea, he returned
there, promising to overtake his brother and the squire shortly.
Fowler had gone another way, accompanied by Captain Trenow and
Josiah.

Frederick had indeed left something behind at Pendrea, and,
knowing that Alrina was there, he determined not to leave that place
without having an interview with her, and hearing from her own
lips an explanation of her conduct; and if it was from any feeling
of delicacy, or as he deemed it foolish fear, that by uniting herself
with him she would be bringing disgrace upon him and his family,
he would insist on her recalling her vow, if she had made one; and
if she still loved him as he believed she did, nothing on earth should
prevent him from making her his own, and claiming it as his right
to cherish and protect her against all the world. ·

This feeling had become a thousand times stronger than ever now,
since he knew that she so much wanted protection.   It strengthened
his love, if possible, and made him more determined than ever not

to leave that place without seeing her, and compelling her to give up her foolish scruples, and become his wife without delay ; and the more he thought of her present destitute position, the more did he blame himself for ever having left her.

In the meanwhile, the squire and Mr. Morley pressed on their horses towards Portagnes, thinking that Frederick would overtake them; but as he did not, they supposed he had taken the other route, and had joined Lieutenant Fowler's party. They met according to appointment; but Frederick was not there. No one had seen him since he left them to search for what he said he had left behind at Pendrea-house. However, every moment was of consequence now, and they determined on proceeding at once to Cooper's house, where they believed they should find the fugitive. No one except Josiah doubted this for a moment; so it was determined that the outside of the house should be closely watched, by two of the party, while the others effected an entrance, by force if necessary. The constable, with his warrant, had accompanied Fowler and his party ; and the lieutenant had left orders for two of his men to go round by water to the entrance of the cavern, and keep a look-out there,—so that escape was now impossible.

Lieutenant Fowler and Josiah watched outside, while the other three, accompanied by the constable, proceeded to effect an entrance into the house. They found the outer door of the garden unlocked, and they thought they should gain an easy entrance; for the fugitives had evidently either not returned there or were confident of their security. These thoughts passed through the mind of each as they passed from the outer door, through the garden, to the door of the house. Here, however, they found an obstacle, for the door was bolted. They knocked several times, and, no answer being returned, they held a consultation as to the best way to break open the door, when a head protruded from one of the upper windows, and they were asked, rather sharply, what they wanted.

" Come down, you old hag, and open the door, or we'll break it open," said Mr. Morley, in an angry tone, giving the door several knocks at the same time with his walking-stick.

" Don't be so hasty, gentlemen," said the woman; " I was fool enough to let you in last time, but you shan't come over me so easy again, I can tell 'ee. You should oft to be ashamed of yourselves,— iss you ded—for to come here with your staves and clubs to frighten a poor lone woman like me."

" Come down, you miserable specimen of humanity," said the squire, " and open the door, or it shall be broken open, and your house ransacked from top to bottom, and you will not be let off so easily this time, I can tell you."

R

" What did you please to want gentleman, when you do get in?" asked the woman, in what the squire thought a very impertinent tone.   And he was about to reply, in a manner which would have given the woman an opportunity of keeping up the conversation, and thereby keeping them out of the house for a considerable time longer, when the constable thought it was time for him to begin ; for he was a shrewd man in his way, and saw the woman's object. He believed she was keeping them in conversation outside, in order to give the other inmates time to get away or to conceal themselves in the house somewhere ; so he said in as commanding a tone as he could,—

" You know me, good woman, don't you?"

" No, I don't," she replied, " and, what's more, I don't want to."

" I'm the head constable of the district I am," said he ; " and I claim entrance, in the King's name, under a bench warrant."

" I don't care if you're the tail constable; you shan't come in here," replied the woman, shutting down the window.

" Thank you for nothing," said the constable ; for at this moment the door was opened from the inside by Captain Trenow, who had gone round the house to reconnoitre, while the others were still trying to persuade the old woman to let them in ; and, finding a window open at the back of the house, he entered that way, and now admitted the whole party.   The old woman protested there was no one in the house but herself, and so it turned out ; for they searched everywhere—upstairs and down—in the cellars and even out to the extremity of the cavern.   There was no one there ; so they beat a retreat and went back to the house they had before met at, hoping that by this time Frederick had arrived ; but in this they were also disappointed.   He was not there, nor had he been seen by anyone ; so, after partaking of a hasty refreshment, they turned their horses' heads once more in the direction of the Land's-End, crestfallen and disappointed.

CHAPTER XXXIX.

THE UNEXPECTED MEETING AND MYSTERIOUS COMMUNICATION.

While the gentlemen were holding their consulation at Pendrea-house, the ladies of the establishment were variously occupied.   Mrs. Pendrea was superintending the cooking of some nice little sweet dish for a poor sick child in the neighbourhood, and the two young ladies were seemingly playing at hide-and-seek with one another, and wandering from room to room, in hopes of hearing something, or of catching a sight of their lovers; while Alrina was left alone to meditate on her sad fate.

She had not been alone long, however, before the door was opened cautiously, and a servant entered, and closing the door after her in a very mysterious way, and, approaching the couch on which Alrina was resting, she put her finger on her lips, as much as to say, " Be silent," and gave Alrina a slip of paper on which was written, or rather scrawled, hastily in pencil—

" Dearest Alrina.—I am wretched,—miserable ! Grant me an interview for a few minutes. I have something of the greatest importance to communicate. I will be in the garden at the back of the house as soon as the other gentlemen are gone. I shall go out with them to prevent suspicion, and return on some pretence. The faithful bearer of this will assist you and let you know when.

" Adieu—my dearest love,
" Frederick."

When her attendant saw the agitation into which the young lady was thrown, on the perusal of this scrap of paper, her former conjectures were confirmed, and she determined to do her best to assist the two lovers. She had a sympathetic feeling, and she retired to the window under pretence of putting the blind straight, while Alrina perused, and reperused, these few pencilled lines, so dear to her. She thought but a few hours ago that she had overcome every feeling but that of duty and honor, and that she could look upon him whom she so dearly loved, as a a brother. It was for his good that she had decided on this course; and she believed that she should have firmness and courage to carry it out to the end; and but a short time ago she felt so strong in her mind and will, that she wished to see him once more to tell him so again. But she then feared that no opportunity would ever offer, and that she should never see him again to explain to him fully the state of her mind, and her real motives of action; for she felt that she had wronged him in what she had said, and wounded his feelings when she told him she could not love him. She knew she ought not to have said that; but what else could she say ? Her father was alive then, and might recover; she could not tell her lover of her father's faults and crimes; and what was she to do ? Now, that he was dead, all was known, and Frederick believed, she must now know all too, and she could now tell him why she could not marry him; and she wished and longed to see him once more—only once more—and now the opportunity had come; it might never come again. But her heart failed her; she could not see him and tell him calmly that they must part for ever, and explain her reasons fully, so as to make him understand clearly what she meant. No, she could not do this; and yet she felt that she must see him once more. So she decided on obeying the promptings of her heart; and calling the maid to her, she said she wished to be informed when the gentlemen left, and then she would walk in the back garden a little. It was not at all necessary to explain anything further to that shrewd girl, for she immediately saw how things stood, and managed accordingly.

The Pendrea ladies were summoned to the drawing-room, almost immediately after the departure of the gentlemen, to entertain Captain and Mrs. Courland and their niece, who had come to return the call the squire and his lady had made on them a few days before at Penzance, where they had taken lodgings. Nothing could be better for the interview between the lovers.

Grace, the go-between, as she styled herself, was delighted. She immediately went to Alrina's room, and informed her that all was ready, and that the coast was clear; which information rather astonished the young lady,—for she could not conceive how Grace should know that she wanted the coast clear ; unless Frederick had told her more than she thought was prudent. However, she had made up her mind to go through with it; and, having put on her bonnet and shawl, which the prudent Grace had brought with her, followed her conductress into the garden, when Grace shewed her prudence again by withdrawing and leaving the two lovers to themselves.

Alrina trembled at the thought of the terrible trial she was about to go through, and her heart throbbed at every step as she walked down the narrow pathway of the little garden, which was at the very back of the house, secluded from view and sheltered by high walls, with no window to overlook it, although, when you were inside, every part of it was exposed enough, for the trees were very few and stunted.

Frederick had not arrived, evidently, unless he was concealed in the little arbour at the bottom of the garden. Alrina walked down to it and looked in. No, he was not there,—something had detained him, no doubt. She waited, and waited, and walked up and down; still he did not come. She was getting cold. She climbed up so as to look over the wall, but could see nothing of him ; and now she began to think he had deceived her. He had taken this course to be revenged for the insult she had offered him, when she told him—he to whom she had so often before avowed the fondest love—that she could not love him. Yes ; he had indeed been revenged, and she felt that she deserved it all.

But hark ! she hears a footstep approaching towards the garden-door. Her ears are quick ; they have been listening intensely for some time. Yes ! it must be. She rushes towards the door, and is caught in the arms of two lovely girls.

"Alrina, you naughty girl," exclaimed Blanch, "how could you be so imprudent as to come out in this cold wind?

"Alrina!" exclaimed the young lady; "can it be possible? you, here!—and have I found you at last, my darling schoolfellow!" And the two girls, in their gushing love, embraced most lovingly and affectionately; and then there were explanations to be given and re-received, and Blanche led the way into Alrina's room, where Julia informed Blanche how they had been at school together, and how her brother Frederick had fallen in love with Alrina, when she was out walking, and how she had carried letters and messages between them, and how her brother had searched for Alrina everywhere, when he returned from abroad, and had written her to search everywhere for his lost lady-love too ; and kissing Alrina, in her girlish way, she said, "Oh! how glad Frederick will be to find you here."

Alrina could do nothing but kiss her friend, in return for all her kind expressions and caresses. What could she say? She felt glad—very glad—to see her old schoolfellow; but, under the circumstances, it was mixed up with too much pain and sorrow to give her any permanent pleasure.

Very soon Julia was summoned to attend her uncle and aunt on their return to Penzance. They had taken a very substantial lunch while the three girls had been having their *tête-à-tête.*

Captain Courland and his party had travelled by easy stages, for they had come all the way in their own carriage with post-horses. It was one of those old lumbering carriages intended to hold six inside—a regular family coach.

"Well, ladies," said the Captain, as he seated himself; "I wish you would take pattern by Mrs. Pendray; she had no hoops, nor farthingales on,—a plain homely woman. No nonsense,—everything above board."

"Yes, my dear," replied Mrs. Courland; "a very pleasant, agreeable, little woman, as I have met with for a long time; but in the country they are not always dressed for receiving visitors."

"And didn't you like Blanche, aunt?" asked Julia ; "she is such a dear girl."

"A nice little girl enough, I dare say," said the captain, answering the question for his wife; "but her elder sister seemed to snub her, I thought. 'Shiver my mizen,' thinks I, I'd haul down your top-gallant sails, miss, if I were your father."

"My dear," said Mrs. Courland, "I wish you would try to forget your sea terms when you are in the society of ladies. I observed Miss Pendray looking at you with astonishment several times, when you were giving out some of your elegant expressions."

"I wish the squire had been home," replied her husband, without noticing the remarks of his wife; for he was accustomed to these rebukes,—not that she said them or meant them ill-naturedly, but she inherited her mother's aristocratic notions, and could not endure anything approaching to vulgarity or coarseness. She had not had very much of her husband's society in former years, for he was only at home for a few months at a time, and then his time was very much occupied, being the principal owner of the ship he commanded. But, now he had nothing to do, and was at home constantly, so that his elegant and accomplished wife had more frequent opportunities of experiencing his rough sailor-like manner; not that he was at all a coarse-minded man,—it was only his manner, which he had naturally imbibed from the persons he was obliged to come into such close contact with on board ship. He was naturally kind-hearted in the extreme, and would do any good that lay in his power for a fellow creature in distress; but he couldn't overcome his habit of using nautical expressions, nor indeed did he try to now. He did try at first, years ago, to speak a little more "dandified," as he called it, to please his beautiful wife; but he found it too hard to accomplish, and so he gave up trying, and contented himself with listening to her lectures, good-humouredly, which he said came in at one ear and went out at the other: and so he had listened patiently now to her remarks, and then continued the conversation as if nothing had been said on the "vexed" subject by his sensitive wife.

"I wish the squire had been home," said he; "he's a jolly fellow. I hate to be stuck up with a parcel of palavering women, and be obliged to sit bolt upright in my chair and take out every word and look at it before I speak, or else be hauled over the coals for it."

"I'm sure you behaved very well to-day, uncle," said Julia; "I saw Miss Pendray looking at you several times, as if she admired your blunt, straightforward manners."

"Did you?" replied the captain, looking rather pleased; "I looked at her too when she got round to the starboard-tack. Brace my rigging, says I to myself; but you're as tight and well built a frigate from stem to stern as ever I clap'd my two eyes upon, save one."

"It was well you put in that saving clause, uncle," said Julia, laughing; "or you would have made Aunt Courland jealous."

"No, no," said the captain, taking his wife's hand affectionately, "I'm a rough knot; but if she never makes me jealous, I shall never make her so. Everything is upright and downright and aboveboard with me. No secrets from my wife, no, no; and I don't think she has any secrets or mysteries from me, although we do have a breeze now and then about the lingo."

"Talking of mysteries," said Julia, turning to her aunt; "who do you think I met at Pendrea? You'll never guess, so I may as well tell you. Why, no other than my old friend and schoolfellow, Alrina."

"Indeed!" exclaimed Mrs. Courland; "you quite surprise me, where did she come from?—how did she get there?"

"I don't know," replied Julia; "for just as I was about to enquire all the particulars, I was summoned to attend you."

"Has Frederick seen her, or does he know she is there," asked Mrs. Courland, with more than her usual energy.

"I know no more than I have told you," replied Julia; "I only met her a short time before we left; for Blanche and I had been wandering over the curious old house, and we were just going to have a peep at what they call their garden, when Alrina came rushing out to meet us. I was struck with her peculiar beauty at once, for I did'nt at first know her until Blanche mentioned her name. She was but a girl when I knew her at school; she has now grown a beautiful woman,—oh! so beautiful, Aunt, and so fair, with that auburn hair which you admire so much. I have seen someone very like her, but I can't remember who it is. The expression of her countenance when she met us, was so like an expression I have seen in some one before; but who it is I cannot remember,—it was so strange."

"We must ask the family to visit us at Penzance, my dear, and bring this wonderful stranger with them," said Mrs. Courland, thoughtfully; "I should like to know something more about her, and where she has been hiding so long, that no trace of her could be found."

"Oh! yes, Aunt," said Julia;" for the sake of Frederick, I'm glad she is found again; he was so passionately devoted to her."

"For his sake, perhaps, it would have been better if she had never crossed our paths again," replied Mrs. Courland, talking to herself rather than to her companions; but the destiny of all must be fulfilled. There is some mystery about this girl,—I am convinced there is."

"So am I," replied Julia;" and I shall not rest till I have found it out."

"Mystery!" exclaimed Captain Courland, in a voice which startled the two ladies; "I hate mysteries. Everything open and aboveboard, say I,–there's no occasion for mystery. I'd throw the lubber overboard, and let him sink into Davy Jones's locker, if he didn't out with it at once, whatever it was. 'Speak the truth and shame the devil,'—that's my motto. I'll have no mysteries hid from me—no matter who it is—overboard he'll go—damn me!"

This outbreak was so sudden and so unexpected, that it made the two ladies feel very uncomfortable, especially the elder lady, whose conscience smote her, and made her feel that, some day, the secret she was keeping so rigidly from her husband might be revealed to him, and then all her happiness would be gone. For she now saw, from this sudden outburst of feeling, how angry he could be, and to what lengths he could carry his vengeance, if he ever found out that terrible secret, and discovered how long he had been deceived. It was a dreadful thought and she shuddered at it, and lay trembling in the corner of the carriage, while Julia, having no such pricks of

conscience, and being, on the whole, more amused than otherwise at
the Captain's burst of passion, apparently without a cause, answered
him in his own language as far as she could; for she believed that it
was only a reminiscence of something that might have happened on
board ship, that had so roused him; and turning to him, with a
laughing eye, she said,—

"There's rough weather where you're sailing, Captain, I believe."

"Rough!" said he: "yes:—but rough or smooth, I'll have the
whole of the crew overhauled from the first mate down to the lop-
lolly-boy; I'll make a clean sweep. Mysteries, indeed, on board my
ship!"

"Why, whatever do you mean, Uncle?" said Julia, now getting
alarmed in right earnest.

"Why! this is what I mean," replied he searching his pockets;
"I'd forgotten all about it, till you began to talk about mysteries and
such nonsense. When I went out to have a look about the place there,
after lunch, a queer-looking 'son of a gun' came and gave me this
letter, and cut off again as if the devil was at his heels. Now, you
just read that, and see if I haven't enough to make me look out for
squalls! what the devil is the meaning of it? I don't know!"

Julia took the letter from her uncle, and read the contents—first
to herself and then aloud:—

"*Noble Captain.—A secret mystery, which now hangs over
you and your's, is about to be revealed; but fear nothing; be
firm, and bear it as a brave sailor ought to do, and it will add
to your happiness:—but should you be led away by passion, or
weakness, and receive it otherwise, misery and woe will be the
portion of you and your's for ever. Bide your time—you will
have further notice.*

"*A Friend,—who was formerly an Enemy.*"

Julia read this strange epistle through two or three times, and so
intent was she in endeavouring to discover what it could mean, and
who the writer could be, that she did not notice the agitation of Mrs.
Courland, and the anguish of mind she was suffering as she lay half
concealed in the corner of the carriage; and the captain was too
much engrossed with his own irritating thoughts to pay any attention
to anyone else. So the poor lady was not disturbed by anything but
her own thoughts until they arrived at their lodgings, when she
rushed upstairs and gave vent to her feelings, harrowing up the most
dreadful consequences from this revelation, which she had no doubt
was that of her own secret. But, when she became more calm, and
began to reflect a little, she saw how absurd it was of her to anticipate
evil so readily. She had forgotten, in her haste, that she was now
many, many miles away from anyone who could possibly know her

secret, and, as she became calm again, she thought how very foolish she had been,—but so it is—an evil conscience will start at a shadow. When the mind is constantly brooding over one subject, and that, the consciousness of a crime committed, the guilty perpetrator of the deed fears to look an upright, honest man in the face; for he has the feeling that his breast is transparently open to his gaze if he only gives him the opportunity to look in; and so he slinks away, fearing that, in an unguarded moment, the transparency may be penetrated. Just so did Mrs. Courland feel when she heard her husband speak in those terrible and decided tones of his horror of secrets and mysteries, well knowing that she was keeping one from him in her own bosom which she ought to have told him long ago. And then that letter! Could it be that *her secret* was about to be revealed? She would have given worlds to know: it would be a relief to know even the worst:—the suspense was dreadful.

Every moment, during the latter part of their drive home, she expected her husband would say that he knew all, and denounce her as a faithless deceitful wife. She had consented to come into Cornwall, thinking that she would be here removed from any chance of a discovery, but she found, to her sorrow, that her guilt followed her even here—at least, so she believed in her weak and self-accusing mind.

CHAPTER XL.

MISS PENDRAY'S SINGULAR ACCIDENT.

Alrina thought her cup of misery had been full long ago; but here was another drop added to it. She was now fully convinced that Frederick had taken her at her word and given her up, and, to be revenged of her treatment of him, had induced her to come out into the garden, merely to shew her that he could be as indifferent to her feelings as she had been to his; and now Blanche knew her secret love, and would of course tell it to all the family: and Julia would return, no doubt, and endeavour to renew their former friendship until she discovered who she was, and what her miserable father had been, and then she would spurn her.

Blanche returned to her after the visitors had departed, and began the usual good-humoured badinage which passes between young ladies when a secret love is discovered; she spoke in a playful manner at first: for she did not know how serious it was, and she intended, if Alrina had placed confidence in her, and told her, as a friend, of her secret love, to have imparted to Alrina, in return, her own sorrows; and she was surprised and grieved to find that, although she could see clearly there was something very much amiss which preyed on Alrina's mind, yet her friend did not seem to have sufficient confidence in her to tell her what it was: so, to gain Alrina's confidence, in some degree, she told her own secret first.   It took a long time in the telling, although there was not really much to tell; but it was the theme on which she had been dwelling for weeks, and weeks, and as it was uppermost in her own thoughts, she fancied it must be interesting in its minutest details to everyone else.   She had never spoken of it before to a single human being, and now that she had commenced, and found, as she thought, a willing and attentive listener, she dwelt on every trifling incident

Alrina's thoughts were otherwise engaged, but she sympathised with the gentle confiding creature who was pouring her thoughts and feelings into her ear, and, when she had told her tale, Alrina said:—

"My dearest Blanche, there is some misunderstanding in all this—someone has poisoned your father's mind: let some mutual friend but come between and explain, and all will be well.   But *my* love, alas! is past all healing!   It cannot be! it cannot be!" and she burst into a flood of tears, which Blanche tried in vain to assuage.

Early in the evening, Squire Pendray returned, bringing Mr. Morley with him, for the latter believed that his brother had remained behind at Pendrea-house for some private reason of his own, instead of following them to Portagnes; and, moreover, Mr. Morley was very anxious to see Miss Pendray once more, after having been absent from her so long.   He had not, it is true, pointedly asked her the question, but he had seen sufficient of her to believe that his attentions were appreciated by her, and that he had a fair chance of being accepted, should he venture on that important step: and this step would have been taken long ago, but for his anxiety to secure the vile wretches who had so stained the character of his father, and brought him to an untimely end.   He had spoken to the squire on the subject, during their ride home, and although he was rather inclined to get on his stilts again at first, believing that Mr. Morley had been trifling with his daughter's feelings, yet, when all was explained, he promised that if Mr. Morley and his daughter could make matters up, as he termed it, he would not object.   And, while the squire went to acquaint his wife with the result of the day's search, Mr. Morley went in search of the fair creature whose charms had so entirely enthralled him: and so sure did he feel that his brother Frederick had returned to Pendrea, and was there comfortably ensconced, that he did not even enquire for him when he returned.   Oh! Cupid! Cupid! thou little perverter of men's thoughts and tormentor of women's minds!

Alrina had scarcely recovered herself when Mrs. Pendray entered the room and told the two young girls the whole story of the mysterious disappearance of Alrina's father, and the fruitless search which had been made for him by the gentlemen that day : the squire thought it best that Alrina should be told the whole now, as there seemed no chance of their being able to discover the body, or the parties who were concerned in taking it away. This news came upon her so suddenly, that she could scarcely realize it. That her father possessed more shrewdness and knowledge than most other people she fully believed; but she did not believe in his being possessed of any supernatural power, as many in the neighbourhood did; and she therefore thought that the body had been removed by some of his wicked assistants, to gratify some private end of their own. Instead of giving way to tears again, she merely asked the favor of being left alone for the remainder of the night, that she might think on what course would be best for her to pursue under the circumstances; and, so earnestly did she urge this, that her friends were prevailed on to yield to her wishes, and she was left to her own meditations. The gentle Blanche was very loth to leave her thus, after the mutual understanding that had so lately sprung up between them; but, as Alrina assured her that she required repose and meditation after the excitement she had undergone, and that she should be better in the morning, her kind friends retired, begging her at the same time, to summon the domestics if she found she required anything more before they retired for the night.

Mr. Morley sought Miss Pendray every where, in doors and out, but she was no where to be found. One of the servants had seen her go out soon after Captain Courland and his party left; but no one had seen her since.—She had not returned.

This, however, was not at all unusual; she often wandered out alone, and stayed away for hours. No one took much notice of her eccentricities.

Mr. Morley enquired where she was likely to have gone. No one could tell: she might be gone to the Logan-Rock; or she might be, even then, sitting on one of the lofty rocks above Lamorna Cove, where she sometimes sat for hours watching the waves; or she might even be gone on so far as Tol-pedn-Penwith.—It was very uncertain which route she might have taken. One thing, however, the household were pretty certain about,—she was on the high cliffs somewhere, for she seldom went underneath.

Mr. Morley was determined to find her, and bring his suit to an issue at once; and he thought that, if he could have the good fortune to meet her alone on one of those distant headlands, he would have ample time to say all he had to say during the walk back; so he started in pursuit.

Miss Pendray's proud spirit could not brook the repeated slights to which she had been subjected by Mr. Morley, as she thought, and the indifference with which he had treated her: he had been at Pendrea-house again, and had not thought proper to see her or even to inquire for her. So, as soon as Captain Courland and his party were gone, she went out in no very amiable mood, and walked along the edge of the highest cliffs at a brisk pace; and so absorbed was she in thought, that she did not seem to notice the wild scenery, which generally had such attractions for her, nor did she think of the distance she was walking, until she found herself standing on one of the highest and most dangerous of the headlands to be found on that part of the coast, many miles from Pendrea-house, and no great distance from Tol-pedn-Penwith. She had, by this time, worked herself up to such a pitch of anger and disappointment, that she did not see her dangerous position. As she thought of the treatment she had received, she stamped her foot indignantly, and, in doing so, the crumbling rock on which she was standing gave way, and, with a shriek, she fell with it; but, fortunately, there happened to be a ledge of rocks a few yards down, standing out from the cliffs, which broke her fall and saved her from being engulphed in a watery grave, if she was not dashed in pieces by the fall from that great height. She was stunned by the shock, and lay insensible for some minutes on the narrow slip of rock which had so far saved her life. When she recovered her senses again she was afraid to move, lest this rock should give way too; and she shuddered as she looked down on the foaming water, which dashed against the rocks some hundred feet beneath her. And there she lay, in unspeakable terror, fearing that the next moment she might be precipitated into the abyss below.

Dreadful suspense! she had scarcely ever known what fear was until now. The shades of evening were fast gathering round her, and the fear of having to remain all night on that dread spot roused her, and something of her wonted courage returned. Looking about, she saw that the ledge of rock on which she was lying appeared to be the entrance into a cavern; but how large it was, or whether it was merely a chasm in the rock extending down to the sea, she did not know. She crept cautiously in, feeling her way, as she went. For several feet she found the rocks hard and firm; here she could rest securely. She sat and looked out on the broad ocean before her; and the more she reflected on her awful situation, the more disheartened did she feel. She saw nothing before her but a lingering death. No boat could approach the rocks underneath; indeed she could not be seen, unless she ventured out on that narrow ledge of rock again. When she had rested herself a little, she explored a little further, creeping cautiously along in the dark cavern. At last she thought she saw a light. She stopped, and looked around. The cavern was dark, except just at the entrance;

but these lights seemed to be coming from the further end. She crept on a little further, and was at last convinced that this light came from some opening in the interior; but whether it came from above or below she could not tell;—perhaps it came from below. There was probably, she thought, a deep chasm running down to the sea from the interior of the cavern, and if she ventured too near she might be in danger of falling through. She crept a little nearer, and then sat on a rock to meditate on her position, keeping her eyes steadily fixed on this faint stream of light at the extremity. She was now begining to feel cold and uncomfortable; her delicate hands and arms were lacerated by the rocks, and her fingers were sore from holding on to them so firmly: in her fear and anxiety for her safety, she did not feel these injuries before, but now her scratches and bruises were beginning to make themselves felt, and there she sat in the greatest agony, both of body and mind.

CHAPTER XLI.

MYSTERIOUS SOUNDS ARE HEARD ISSUING OUT OF THE EARTH AT MIDNIGHT. THE CURIOUS COTTAGE ON THE HEATH.

THE party who had gone in search of the body of Mr. Freeman and his guilty associates separated as they approached their respective homes: Captain Trenow and Josiah went to St. Just, Squire Pendray and Mr. Morley went to Pendrea-house as we have seen, and Lieutenant Fowler proceeded on his solitary journey towards his own cabin at Tol-pedn-Penwith signal-station. On turning a sharp corner in the road, he met one of his men, who had been ordered out on night-duty, and who ought to have been watching the coast instead of travelling along on the public road.

The man touched his cap to his commanding officer, who spoke rather sharply to him as he returned the salute.

" What brings you here, Braceley? " said he, " when your orders were to keep close to the cliffs to-night;—for there's mischief afloat, and we want the coast well watched."

" Yes, sir," replied the man; " I have obeyed orders, and have heard something that I thought best to report at once, and I came this road, thinking to fall in with your honor."

" Well! what is it?" said Fowler; " bear a hand, and out with it; for it's cold standing here in the wind."

s

"By the powers! sir," said Braceley, looking very solemn, "I believe 'The Maister' isn't far off, for I've heard queer sounds."

"Sounds," said Fowler; "nonsense, man, what do you mean?— This is one of your confounded Irish superstitions."

"No, sir! by the Holy St. Patrick, 'tis no superstition, nor anything of the kind," replied Braceley, coming nearer to the officer: "I was coming along over the cliffs, sir, and I heard voices in the air over my head,—and I spoke to them, and they answered again. Spirits, I'm sure they were, your honor! 'The Maister' is here, says I,—and I tould him to be aisy while I called the praist."

It was a queer story; but as nothing was too strange or improbable to believe, in connection with "The Maister," after what had happened within the last few days, Fowler determined he would go and see what it was himself; so he accompanied the man in silence, until they arrived at the spot where Braceley said he had heard those extraordinary sounds. It was now getting dark, and the place was very lonely; not at all the place that a nervous man would like to be in at night, if he heard anything that he could by any means imagine was caused by supernatural agency. Fowler had none of that superstitious feeling in his composition which was so prevalent everywhere at that period, and he laughed at his companion, who possessed a good deal of it, and told him that what he fancied he had heard was entirely in his own imagination. The man could not be persuaded, however, and they listened for minutes, but heard nothing, and Fowler said, in a jeering tone, "'The Maister's' ghost, no doubt, Braceley! you shall have a guard of nanny-goats when you turn out on night-duty again."

He had scarcely finished his sentence, before they heard the most piercing sounds rending the air all round them. Fowler was startled; the sounds came upon them so suddenly: he listened, but could not make out where they came from; sometimes they appeared above their heads, and then again beneath their feet: he did not believe in the supernatural, but he really didn't know what else to impute it to. His companion, however, had no doubt whatever but that it was "The Maister's" spirit hovering about, seeking rest. Neither of them spoke, but they walked on towards the edge of the cliff, and, on approaching a deep hole or opening in the rock, about fifty yards from the extreme edge of the cliff, Fowler was convinced that the sounds were coming up from underneath. This opening was partially concealed by the overhanging rocks, and might be passed unobserved by a casual visitor. He however knew the place well, for he had once, on his first coming to Tol-pedn-Penwith, made a good seizure of kegs in the cavern beneath. When they arrived at this place, he called down lustily and asked who was there, although he could scarcely believe that it could be any human being.

He was soon convinced, however, and astonished beyond measure, at hearing a well-known voice calling up to him in tones of the bitterest anguish : —

"Oh! good sir, whoever you are, assist me out of this dreadful place; I fell from the precipice several hours ago, and crept in here. I am wounded, and bitterly cold. Oh! good Christian, make haste."

"Don't distress yourself any more," replied Fowler; "you shall be extricated at once ; I know the cavern. I am Fowler of the signal-station : I will be down to protect you in a few minutes "

In her distress and fear, Miss Pendray had evidently not recognised his voice so easily as he had recognised hers. He desired Braceley to proceed at once to the station, and get ropes and lights, and all the assistance he could. Braceley had a blue-light in his pouch, which Fowler lit, and fired a pistol, which he knew would bring any of his men who were within hail to the spot at once. He then descended cautiously, by the aid of the light, to reassure the unfortunate lady, and to convince her that relief was at hand. It was a perilous adventure ; but Fowler had been down before ; and so he knew that the opening did not descend perpendicularly. He had first to slide down over a smooth rock, almost perpendicular, for several yards, and then to jump on a flat rock, and then slide on again, and so on alternately ; but in the descent the greatest caution was necessary, lest, in jumping on one of the narrow flat rocks, he should slip and be carried by the impetus headlong down to the bottom.

Miss Pendray was still sitting on the rock, afraid to move, when Fowler jumped down at her side, carrying the light in his hand. She could scarcely express her joy and gratification. She clasped his arm tightly with both her hands and seemed afraid to let go her hold. She forgot all her former animosity, and thought only of her present perilous position and his ability and willingness to save her.

Braceley soon returned with ropes and lights and more assistance, and they were not long in getting Miss Pendray up from her perilous position. She was most grateful for the attention and almost miraculous assistance of Lieutenant Fowler. She was not so much bruised but that she was able to walk, although her limbs were sore, and her arms and hands were lacerated fearfully. Fowler accompanied her as far as the door of Pendrea-house, where he was about to take his leave, but she would not suffer it : she almost compelled him to come in ; for she felt that, after all he had done for her that night, it was incumbent on her to dispel some of the clouds which had for some time hung over his happiness, and which she could not but feel she had been the means of gathering around him and her gentle sister, and which this evening's adventure had determined her to make amends for, by explaining to her father the true state of the case; for she well knew that she had exaggerated, to use a mild expression, when she told him of the clandestine meetings of her sister and the lieutenant. Anger and wounded pride had led her to commit this treacherous and ungenerous act, towards her younger sister, whom she ought rather to have advised and reproved in private if she had seen anything wrong in her behaviour. This act had been repented of often by Miss Pendray, but her proud spirit would not bend to acknowledge her fault: now she was determined on acknowledging the part she had played, and, if she could not be happy herself in the possession of the love of the only man who had ever really gained her affections, she would at least have the satisfaction of knowing she had made two others happy, by candidly confessing her own dissimulation.

Mr. Morley, in the meantime, had gone on in search of her; but, as she had considerably the start of him, he did not overtake her. He walked over the cliffs for some distance, until he felt convinced that she could not be gone in that direction; for he did not believe that any lady would walk even so far as he had gone, on those high cliffs alone at that hour; so he struck into a path which seemed to lead towards the high road, thinking that would be the safer way for him to return, as he was not familiar with the coast. He walked on for some distance, until he came to a spot where several paths met, and here he was puzzled; however, he took the one which seemed the most probable, although he had by this time almost entirely lost his bearings, for he was now on low ground, and could not see the cliffs or the sea. He walked on briskly for a considerable time, when he halted again, for he felt convinced he had missed his way. There was no house or human habitation to be seen, nor could he see anyone of whom he might enquire; so he walked on again. The twilight was now getting more decided in its character, and the shadows of night were closing in, and he began to fear that he might be kept wandering over that dreary heath all night; for he frequently came upon some other path branching off from the one he was pursuing, and he would sometimes be tempted to try a fresh one. At length he thought he perceived smoke rising at some little distance, and he made sure now that he should meet with some one to direct him; for it evidently arose from a cottage at no great distance. He thought of his father's adventures in that lonely cottage, on that dreadful night, and he braced up his nerves and walked manfully forward; when, on turning into a narrow lane which seemed to lead to the cottage, a man ran against him, and nearly knocked him off his legs. Mr. Morley was a tall, powerful man, and was armed with a stout stick which he instantly raised above his head, ready to strike if he found that foul play was intended.

The uplifted hand descended, but not to strike; for Mr. Morley, to his great surprise recognized in the ferocious and excited individual before him, his brother Frederick.

"Where on earth did you spring from?" he exclaimed; "I thought you were at this moment comfortably closeted with that unhappy girl you seemed so infatuated with."

"I left you with the intention of seeing her and having a mutual explanation," replied Frederick, "and she, no doubt, now feels that I have deserted her."

"No! no! she can't think that," said Mr. Morley; "but better she should, perhaps, than that you should unite yourself to the daughter of this man."

"But suppose she is not his daughter?" replied Frederick, looking earnestly at his brother, and speaking hurriedly and anxiously.

"That is a ridiculous speculation," said Mr. Morley, "after what we have heard and know. Of course she is his daughter; there can be no doubt about that: she has been known as such, at any rate, in this neighbourhood; and even the association with such a wretch must carry contamination with it. Give her up Frederick! let me entreat you to give her up!"

Frederick did not reply; but, taking his brother's arm, he led him back to the cottage which he seemed to have just quitted.

It was a lone cottage, and, but for the smoke which Mr. Morley saw issuing from the chimney, might have escaped his notice in the dim twilight: it consisted of several rooms, covering a considerable space, but they were all on the ground-floor. The house was commonly built, the rooms entering one into the other, without having any passages between them. There were several doors in the walls, by which a person could enter or escape, if necessary, and puzzle his pursuers. On entering the outer room, by the principal entrance-door, Mr. Morley perceived an old woman sitting at a table, on which were the remains of a substantial meal, and a good supply of liquor in a small wooden barrel or keg. The woman had just filled a jug from the barrel, and seemed about to carry it to some other part of the house; but on the entrance of the gentlemen she placed it on the table. She was a tall large-boned woman, with a commanding appearance, and looked as if she was accustomed to be obeyed; and yet there was an expression of low cunning in her countenance which was not at all pleasant, and which made strangers feel uncomfortable and suspicious. She was believed in the neighbourhood to be a witch, and people went to her to have their fortunes told, and she very often told them true, for she had her secret spies about as well as "The Maister"; but, from want of education, her prophecies were seldom so startling or so well or plausibly expressed as his were. It was generally believed that they were connected in business, and that they played into each other's hands, although no one had ever seen them together.

Sitting by the fire, on a low stool, was a grotesque looking being, somewhat between a man and a monkey ; not that he was particularly ill-formed, but the expression of his countenance as he intently watched the woman's movements, had something ludicrous in it, and but for the wild stare which occasionally lit up his countenance, he might be an idiot or an imbecile.

"Ha! ha!" cried he, jumping up and skipping about in a ludicrous manner, as the two gentlemen entered ; "'Maazed Dick' es the boy! 'Maazed Dick' es the boy!   Letter to the young maister ;—get him down here! get him down here !   Letter to the cap'n ; frightened out of his wits! frightened out of his wits! ha! ha!'"

"Richard!" said the old woman, in her most commanding tone ; "hold your tongue and sit down."

This seemed to have the same effect on "Maazed Dick" as the sharp command of a sportsman has on a well-trained spaniel dog ;— he ceased his antics and retained his seat by the fire, keeping his eyes fixed on her of whom he seemed to stand so much in fear.

The old woman then, turning to the two gentlemen, said, "What's your will, gentlemen? and what do you want here at this hour of the night ?"

"This is my brother," said Frederick, "and I want him to hear from your lips what I have heard to-night : it may tend to convince him that he has formed a hasty opinion and that all may yet be well."

"Frederick Morley," she said, rising and extending her hand in a commanding attitude, "you have heard all you will hear from me ; do my bidding and you may know more : if you neglect it, or tell what you have heard to any human being, except the one named to you, it were better you had never been born."   Saying which, she took up the jug again which she had placed on the table, and, waving her hand towards the door at which the two gentlemen had entered, disappeared into an inner room, bolting the door after her ; and, almost at the same moment, "Maazed Dick" took up the keg of brandy from the table and disappeared also, somewhere in the wall, but where, the visitors could not tell ; he could not have gone through the wall, that was very certain : there was evidently a secret cupboard somewhere in the wall ; but, if so, it was very ingeniously concealed.

As there seemed no chance of learning any more, Frederick led the way out of the house and walked on at a rapid rate, followed by his brother, until they arrived at the end of the lane leading to the cottage.   He seemed so excited that Mr. Morley became alarmed, and insisted on knowing what strange infatuation had seized him.

" You heard what that woman said," replied Frederick; " I feel that all my future happiness depends on my obeying her instructions, and I must do so."

" Nonsense ! " said his brother : " it is perfectly ridiculous to suppose that the old hag we have just seen can know anything or do anything that can possibly influence your happiness in any way."

" She has not told me much, it is true," replied Frederick; " but she has told me enough to convince me that she knows more ; but, however little I have heard, I am bound not to tell it even to you."

" Come ! this is going a little too far ! " said Mr. Morley, in a serious tone; " we are engaged in a common cause, and circumstances have prevented our pursuing our object together for several weeks : we must not separate again until these dark deeds are brought to light."

" I am convinced," replied Frederick, " that something will come out of my adventure this afternoon, which will throw a light on the whole. I wish, from my heart, I was at liberty to tell you; but it cannot be. I must work alone for a short time longer,—it may be a very short time. You are, I presume, going on to Fowler's station :—if so, we must separate, for my way lies in another direction."

" No," replied he, " I was going to Pendrea-house. I went out in search of Miss Pendray, and I believe I missed my way somewhere ; I don't exactly know where I am."

" Fortunately, then," said Frederick, " you have been walking in the right direction, although not in the most frequented road : if you take the next turning on the right you will soon be at the end of your journey."

" But you will surely come with me," said Mr. Morley, taking his brother by the arm.

" My dear brother," said Frederick, looking earnestly at Mr. Morley ; " it grieves me to be obliged to refuse to accompany you to Pendrea-house to-night, for many reasons; for I have another duty to perform which I feel convinced is of vital importance to more than one, but the nature of which, as I said before, I cannot now explain to you. Believe me, as soon as I have accomplished the task I have solemnly promised to perform, you shall know all."

As Mr. Morley saw that his brother was in earnest, and seemed determined to have his own way, he did not press him further, but bade him God-speed, and returned to Pendrea-house, which he reached soon after the arrival of Miss Pendray and Lieutenant Fowler.

CHAPTER XLII.

THE POOR DUMB GIRL'S SUDDEN RESOLVE AND ITS CONSEQUENCES.

MRS. COURLAND remained in her room, for a considerable time after their return from Pendrea-house, reflecting on the events of the day, and especially on the unaccountable and unusual conduct of her husband. What could be the meaning of that letter?—Who could have written it? While these distracting thought were racking her brain, Flora, her poor dumb protegé, entered softly, unperceived by her protrectress, and, leaning over the couch in which Mrs. Courland was reclining absorbed in thought, touched her cheek with her lips, and looked at her with a tender sympathizing expression, as if she knew that her protectress was unhappy, and was conscious that it was not in her power to comfort her, although she longed to be able to do so; but the events of the day, and the thoughts that had since passed through the mind of Mrs. Courland, had made the sight of this poor girl hateful to her. She had wished, in her heart, within the last hour, that this source and evidence of her deception could be blotted out from the face of the earth. She wished, in her agony, that she could be in any way got rid of and her existence drowned in oblivion; for, even here, in this remote place, she seemed to be followed by her dread enemies, and she believed that her secret was about to be discovered; the thoughts of those who have committed an evil deed, of however trivial a nature, being always suspicious and uneasy.

Mrs. Courland seemed suddenly to have changed her nature: from a gentle, beautiful woman, the sight of her she now so much dreaded seemed to have turned her into a demon in human form. She rose from her reclining position, and, seizing the poor dumb girl by the hair, dragged her down on the couch. What she meant to do, in her frenzy, it is difficult to say; for the action and look of the lady, together with the pain she inflicted on the poor girl, and the terror she felt, brought back the remembrance of former days, and all her old ferocity and strength returned; and, seizing Mrs. Courland by the wrists, she made her let go her hold, and pressed her back on the couch with all her might, until she screamed for help, and the servants ran in and extricated her from her perilous position.

It was more from the fear of what might happen than from what had already occurred, that Mrs. Courland gave the alarm; for she felt that she was as nothing in the hands of her protegé, when she chose to put forth her strength and her passions were roused. She had conquered again; and again did she seem to regret the part she had taken, when she saw that poor delicate lady powerless in her grasp. She released her hold at once, and the servants, having seen no violence used, believed that their mistress had been seized with giddiness, as she had told them she had, and that Flora, in attempting to support her, had, from over anxiety pressed her arms more tightly than she intended.

Flora, however, felt that Mrs. Courland had, without any apparent cause, treated her as her former associates had done: she saw and understood the look of determined hate and fury which was depicted in her countenance when she rose so suddenly from her couch and seized her by the hair. That look haunted her; she could not bear to think of it. She could not tell her thoughts to anyone, and she determined, in her own mind, that the lady, who had been so kind to her, should not have cause to look on her with hatred and scorn again. She would go away; she would die,—perhaps drown herself; she did not care what death it was; there was nothing worth living for now. All the world seemed to be possessed of the same evil passions, she thought,—they only wanted to be brought out. She put on an old bonnet and a shawl and went out: the coast was clear, for all the household were in attendance on Mrs. Courland. She walked through the town, and beyond it,—far out into the country.

It was getting late, and yet she walked on, not knowing where and without having any fixed purpose. On, on, she walked, sometimes on the broad road and sometimes through bye-lanes, she did not care where: her only object was to get away as far as she could, and to avoid being overtaken. At last she felt weary and sick at heart, and now she wished to meet with some house where she could rest herself a little; but there was no house to be seen anywhere: she had passed several at the commencement of her journey, but she did not feel so weary then, and had walked on. It was no use stopping in the lonely road, so on she walked again till her feet were sore; for she had come out in her thinnest indoor shoes. At length, when nearly exhausted, she saw a man coming towards her. She was frightened, and tried to hide herself behind a low hedge, but the man perceived her dress fluttering in the breeze, and he approached and spoke to her. She did not answer him but made signs to him, which he understood, for he had seen her before. It was Frederick Morley whom she had thus opportunely met. He had seen her before at his aunt's house, and he wondered to see her out alone at that hour, and in such a place, and made signs to go back; but she stamped the ground, and signified her intention of going on further away from her former protectress. Frederick saw that something had happened, but what it was he did not know, nor could she make him understand; she must be protected, however, for the night, until Captain Courland's family could be communicated with. He had just parted from his brother, and he at first thought of calling after him, and asking him to take her with him to Pendrea-house; but, on reflection, he thought this was a liberty that neither of them ought to take, as they were both comparative strangers to the Pendray family. He thought of the cottage he had just left, and that, perhaps, the old woman would not object to give the poor dumb girl shelter for the night; so he took her there, and the old woman received her with more warmth than Frederick expected, or than was at all necessary, he thought, under the circumstances.

Although Flora was very tired and hungry, and was glad to rest herself after her long walk, yet she did not appear at all comfortable. She seemed to look at the woman with dread and suspicion, but she was too tired to walk any further, so, after she had partaken of some refreshment, she followed the woman into an inner room, where there was a bed prepared for her. The old woman then gave Frederick some further instructions and enjoined haste and secrecy, and he again commenced his journey on the mysterious errand which had so puzzled his brother.

While her protegé was wandering through the lanes alone and trying to get further and further away, and seeking some obscure place where she should hide herself for ever, Mrs. Courland was receiving the attentions of the whole household. Her kind husband was much grieved to find his beautiful wife in this excited, and yet apparently helpless, state. She seemed to be suffering great pain too, but she kept the cause of it from them as much as she could, and covered her arms and wrists that they might not see the full extent of the bruises which the strong hands of Flora had made on her soft delicate flesh. The kind attention of her husband reassured her of his continued love and esteem, and she began to think that the mysterious letter might have been a mere hoax after all, and that she had nothing to fear: and as these thoughts occupied her mind in rapid succession, she began to feel more tranquil, until at last she came to the conclusion, that, even if her secret was discovered her husband would forgive her; and then she began to feel ashamed of her conduct towards the poor innocent cause of all this, and she sent her maid in search of Flora that she might atone for the part she had taken as the first aggressor, and make her protegé understand that she was forgiven also for the pain she had inflicted on her protectress.

The servants searched everywhere throughout the house, but Flora could nowhere be found. Her bonnet and shawl were gone, and so they supposed she had taken a stroll through the town, alone, as she was very fond of doing, and would return when her curiosity was satisfied.

Several hours passed by, but Flora did not make her appearance, and the household became alarmed; they fancied a thousand things. She might have missed her way and gone too near the sea, and have fallen in ; or she might have been entrapped by some lawless gang of sailors and taken to one of their haunts. Captain Courland and the man-servant searched the town all over; they were out nearly all night, and, as soon as it was light in the morning he and the man started for St. Michael's Mount, in the vain hope that they might find her there, for she had often expressed a wish to see the interior of the ancient castle which appeared to her to be built almost in the clouds. She had the most romantic fancies sometimes, and amused her friends very much by the manner in which she expressed her feelings by signs and pantomimic dumb-shew.

All who knew her, loved and pitied the poor dumb girl, and they all joined in the search right heartily. Julia begged to be allowed to accompany her uncle; and the women-servants, and even the landlady herself, went out into the town and explored every part they could think of, leaving Mrs. Courland in the house alone. She could not rest, so she got up very early; but she was not equal to the task of joining in the search. She was sitting alone in the drawing-room, when she heard a hasty step coming up the stairs. Her first thought was, that Flora was found, and that some one had been sent to inform her of the fact. Without further reflection, she rushed towards the door in the greatest excitement, exclaiming—" Is she found? Is she found?"

" Yes, my dear aunt," cried Frederick Morley, catching Mrs. Courland in his arms as he hastily entered the room,—" the lost is found; " and, leading her to a seat, he explained to her that her daughter was found and was now with kind friends, and that all was about to be divulged; for the parties who possessed the secret, having already prepared Captain Courland for it, he said, had determined to publish everything : but they did not wish to do it to the injury of Mrs. Courland, and were willing to give her the opportunity of informing her husband herself if she preferred doing so. The parties had other secrets to communicate also of the greatest importance, and they wished Mrs. Courland to meet them at a certain house in the neighbourhood immediately. Frederick knew the house, he said, and had been commissioned to bring his aunt there without delay, as it was of the greatest importance. She hesitated at first, but, knowing what those people were, she thought, on reflection, that it would be wise for her to meet them and hear what they had to communicate, provided Frederick would go with her, and protect and assist and counsel her, which he promised he would do. He had engaged a conveyance ; so, dressing herself in the commonest things she had, she accompanied her nephew to the outskirts of the town where the carriage was waiting, to avoid suspicion.

When they arrived within about a quarter of a mile of the cottage, they got out and walked the remainder of the distance, leaving the carriage in the road. Frederick could tell Mrs. Courland little more than he had already told her; and she was impatient to reach the place of meeting that she might know what those wicked people really intended to do, and what other secrets they had to communicate; for she felt that this suspense and uncertainty were worse than the reality, whatever that might be.

They found the old woman in the outer room of the cottage, anxiously expecting their arrival. She received Mrs. Courland with a curtsey, saying,—

"It is well, madam; you have been prompt in attending to my request. Had you delayed your coming but a few hours, you would have been too late."

"Too late!" said Mrs. Courland; "what do you mean? Has the poor afflicted girl met with an accident, or what has happened to her?"

Instead of replying, the old woman led the way into the interior of the house and beckoned her two visitors to follow her. They passed through two or three rooms, some furnished as sitting-rooms and some as sleeping-apartments; at last they came to an empty, unfurnished room, where the old woman desired them to wait while she prepared the invalid for their reception. In a few minutes she opened the door, and asked them to walk in.

CHAPTER XLIII.

THE CONFESSION.

IT was a comfortable and well-furnished bedroom; but instead of finding Flora there, as Mrs. Courland expected, the bed was occupied by an elderly woman, who appeared very ill, and was sitting up in the bed supported by pillows. She motioned her visitors to be seated, and then said in a feeble voice,—

"You do not recognise me, Mrs. Courland: illness makes great changes in the human frame. The name you first knew me by was Fisher; I then changed it more than once, for reasons you shall know presently."

"I remember you, now," said Mrs. Courland involuntarily, shrinking further from the bed, as if still afraid of the poor helpless creature before her.

"I am not long for this world," said the invalid; "and before I die I wish to make some amends for the misdeeds I have done during my life, and they have been many. I have requested Mr. Frederick Morley to attend with you, for a part of the revelations I am about to make concerns him also."

"Do you know anything," exclaimed Frederick, "of the wretches who ——— ?"

"Don't interrupt me, if you can possibly help it," she said; "for I feel my strength failing me, and I don't know if I shall be spared even long enough to finish my recital. My father was not a poor fisherman, as you supposed when you and your mother came to lodge with us. He was pursuing a lawless employment,—sometimes bringing in great earnings, and sometimes nothing. He had seen better days. In his youth he was captain of a large trading vessel, and my brother and myself received a good education. My father amassed considerable property,—more than he could possibly have done by legitimate trading; and he was suspected, and watched, and found out. He had turned his vessel into a smuggler, and, under cover of fair trading, clandestinely carried on a lucrative trade in all sorts of contraband goods. He was convicted, and fined heavily, and, in fact, ruined.

"We then retired to the small fishing-cove where your mother found us. My brother had gone to France to reside some time before, and acted as my father's agent there. He was very shrewd and intelligent, but a determined character, and one who would never forget nor forgive an injury. He was naturally cunning and crafty; and his smuggling pursuits tended to sharpen his natural gifts in this respect.

"Our fortune was at a low ebb when we first became acquainted with you; and we were glad of the assistance of an aristocratic lodger. I saw your mother's weak points, and your love of gaiety and admiration; and I thought that, by residing with you in the confidential capacity of lady's-maid, I could benefit myself in many ways. Your clandestine marriage, and the birth of your daughter, which I persuaded you to keep secret from your parents, gave me a double hold upon you.

"After the death of your husband, and while you were with us on a visit to recruit your health, my brother returned. He fell desperately in love with you;—you refused to receive his addresses, and spurned him from you with scorn. He was desperate. He begged me to intercede for him, which I promised to do, but did not; for your marriage with my brother would not have suited my purpose at all. I knew your parents wished you to marry some rich man, and, as I was now the keeper of your secret, I knew that if you married according to your parents' wishes, I could make my own terms with you. You were summoned home, and eventually married according to their wishes and mine.

"My mother died. Your little daughter was left in my care, and I was well paid. I sent her to school, but I watched her most carefully;—I could not afford to lose her, for she was my nest-

T

egg ; and she grew a lovely girl, just like you when you were her age."

"How is it possible that she can ever have been even good-looking ?" exclaimed Mrs. Courland ;—" but that dreadful spoiler of the human face—the small-pox—has done its work : it was that, no doubt, that altered her so much."

"She was a lovely girl," continued the invalid, without noticing Mrs. Courland's interruption. "My brother would gaze on her countenance for hours without speaking, and then he would leave the room in a rage. He hated the name of Morley, because it was under that name that he first knew you, and was spurned by you. He seldom took much notice of the child, except to gaze on her until he had worked his mind up to a state of maddening jealousy.

"We never lost sight of you. Wherever you moved, we followed, and lived near you under feigned names, in order to worry you by continually draining your purse, and threatening to expose your duplicity and deceit to your husband by producing the child and telling him all, of which we had ample proof, and have still. My brother would not see you himself,—he could not bear it, he said. I was always your tormentor ; and when I brought the dumb girl to you, I thought the sight of her hideous features, and her infirmity, would have so disgusted you, that you would have given us what we asked, rather than have her left on your hands as your acknowledged daughter. We were mistaken. You kept her, believing her to be your child; and you thought that, by doing this, and denying me an interview, you would be free from further worry, and there could be no danger of the girl telling anything of her former life or associates ; and if we tried to expose you to your husband, he would not believe us.

"Since that girl has been with you, we have had other things to think of ; and our anxiety for my brother's safety prevented our taking the steps we intended with regard to your secret. *That poor dumb girl is not your daughter*, Mrs. Courland."

"Oh ! thank God for that !" exclaimed Mrs. Courland, rising in the greatest excitement. "I hope you are not deceiving me again. If you can produce her, and I can be satisfied that she really is my daughter, I will acknowledge her in the face of all the world, and tell my husband all, and throw myself on his mercy. I have suffered years of torture, from having followed your advice in the beginning. Oh ! had I but acted a straightforward part, and kept no secret from my husband, my life would have been much happier. I see my error now, and am determined to keep the secret no longer. Where is she ? let me see her at once ; don't keep me in suspense."

The invalid had exhausted her strength in the recital of her tale, and this outburst of Mrs. Courland's quite upset her. She could not speak again for several minutes, until Frederick Morley handed her the glass which she seemed to wish for, and which was standing on the table more than half full of brandy. This, which she drank off at once, seemed to give her new life and energy. Then, turning to Frederick, she said, in a gayer tone than before,—

"You will be glad to hear, Frederick Morley, that the lovely girl to whom you are so devotedly attached, is not the daughter of John Freeman, the Land's-End conjuror, but *the daughter of your aunt—Mrs. Courland.*"

"Alrina, of whom I have heard so much, my daughter!" exclaimed Mrs. Courland; "impossible!"

"Oh! this is indeed too good to be true!" cried Frederick; "I cannot believe it. What proof is there of this?"

"Proof in abundance," replied the invalid; "I am ready to make an oath of the fact before a magistrate; and my brother ———"

"Your brother!" said Frederick; "where is he? is he still alive?"

"I was about to say that my brother could have confirmed my statement. Captain Cooper and his wife can also bear witness to the fact; but, even if there were no other evidence, *the likeness* would be sufficient to a person who knew Mrs. Courland as Miss Morley."

"Let me see her!" said Mrs. Courland; "where is she? It is very strange that I have never seen her, although I have heard so much about her. Why did you never let me see her?"

"That would not have suited our purpose," replied the invalid; "you would have braved all risk of your husband's displeasure, and taken her home long before, if you had seen her. I think you would have seen the likeness yourself. No, no, my brother's revenge was not complete. I led you, from the first, to believe that she was disfigured by the small-pox, and rendered very ugly and forbidding; but I never said she was dumb,—indeed, it was not our intention to have left the other girl with you entirely; it was only to frighten you into granting us the money that we required, that the poor girl was taken into your house. My brother knew that he must be found out, ere long, and he wanted all the money he could get to carry with him; for he had made all his preparations for leaving this country, and his associates and accomplices wanted their share of the hush-money also. It was the last we should get from you, and so we demanded a large sum."

"But my daughter!" said Mrs. Courland—"if in reality she is such—pray let me see her. Where is she?"

"Your daughter, madam, is now at Pendrea-house, as Frederick Morley knows. Let him go there and fetch her, while you remain here; for I have something more to tell you in connection with this

affair, which will convince you I am not deceiving you now. Tell
Alrina," continued she, turning to Frederick, "that her aunt, Miss
Freeman, is on her death-bed, and she must come at once."

CHAPTER XLIV.

MRS. BROWN ENJOYS ANOTHER CROOM O' CHAT WITH MRS. TRENOW,
AND RECEIVES AN UNEXPECTED VISITOR.

WHILE the other gossips were going from house to house, collecting
and retailing the news respecting the mysterious disappearance of
"The Maister," Mrs. Brown and Mrs. Trenow were having a serious
chat over their "drop of comfort," according to custom.

"So, you don't think he's carr'd away by the pixies, then," said
Mrs. Trenow.

"No, I don't," replied Mrs. Brown? "'tes some of his hocus pocus
work, you may depend. I'm glad the old cap'n es gone weth Siah
to see the gentlemen. They'll find 'The Maister' somewhere, I'll be
bound, afore come back."

"No, no more than you will, cheeld vean," said Mrs. Trenow.
"The Pixies have got 'n, or something wuss, so sure as my name es
Mally Trenow. They'll be home soon, I shudn't wonder, and then
we shall knaw. They've be'n gone evar since the mornin', an' now
'tes come brave an' late. Aw! here they are, sure nuff,—'spaik o'
the Devil and his horns will appear.' Well, where's 'The Maister,'
soas," continued she, addressing her husband and son as they entered.

"We do no more knaw than you do, old woman," replied her
husband; "we've sarched everywhere we cud think upon, and now
we've returned, like a bad penny. Two glasses o' brandy toddy,
Mrs. Brown, ef you plaise, for we've had a bra' tramp."

"Iss sure," said the landlady, proceeding to execute the order;
"you must want somethin' to drink after your hard day's work; but
you haven't be'n to the right place, I reckon."

"No fie, we ha'n't be'n to the right place, sure nuff," said Josiah.

"You shud oft to ha' kept a sharper look-out, Siah," said Mrs.
Brown, taking a side glance at Josiah, as if she meant something
more than she said.

"Zackly like that," said he, looking very serious, as he sipped his
brandy and water; "Needs must when the devil drives" es an old
sayin' and a very true one; and I tell 'ee, Mrs. Brown, you may
laugh so much as you will, and squinny up your eyes till they're so
small as the button-holes of my jacket; but 'tes my belief that the
Devil es at the bottom of et all. He put me to sleep, and fastened

the door, so that I cudn't get out; and he took away 'The Maister' to have his desarts,—that's my belief, down sous; and now you've got it all."

Mrs. Trenow looked very serious at her son's earnestness; for she herself held the same opinions, although she didn't express them;— but Mrs. Brown continued to look at Josiah in her sarcastic way, without uttering a word.

"Where's Alice Ann, mother?" asked Josiah, at length breaking the silence.

"She's gone up to her aunt's again for a bit," replied Mrs. Trenow; "the ladies wanted her to stop over to Pendrea-house too, I b'lieve; but she thoft that one stranger wor enough for them to take in; and they wor very kind to take in the one that wanted it most. Poor Miss Reeney! she's worth her weight in gold. Talk about Cornish diamonds, soas! why, she's a Cornish diamond, every inch of her, and a bright one too. But where ded 'ee lev the young gentleman, 'Siah, boy?"

"Aw! he's right enough, I reckon," replied Josiah; "I thoft how 'twould be. When we went to sarch for 'The Maister,' he went to sarch for somebody else, I reckon; and I s'pose he found her, for we nevar seed he no more for the day."

"That's very well!" chimed in poor Mr. Brown, from his seat in the chimney-corner. "We sarched for the boy everywhere; but the mare came home safe. Wo! ho! my beauty; she shall be rubbed down, she shall! The boy came back at last, f'rall, zackly to the time,—dedn't aw, Peggy, my dear?"

"John Brown!" cried his wife; "hould your tongue!"—which had the desired effect of stopping that unruly member, and bringing John Brown back to the contemplation of the fire on the hearth— and nothing more.

Early the next morning—very early indeed—almost before the sun had taken down his shutters, Mrs. Brown was awoke from a sound sleep by someone, as she thought, knocking gently at the front door. She listened, and heard the same sound again, rather louder than before. At first, she thought it might be some sailor or fisherman who had been out fishing all night, and wanted his morning's dram to warm him.

"You must wait, whoever you are," said she to herself, as she turned round to have a second nap. Still the knocking continued at intervals, and prevented her from indulging in her morning's nap. "Whoever can it be?" said she, as she sat up in the bed and listened; "I don't think it can be any of the sailors; for they'd have rapp'd the door down by this time, or else have gone away. I'll see who it es, at any rate." So she went to the window, and, drawing back the blind a little, saw a figure standing under the window which very

much astonished her. It was not a sailor, certainly. She put on
some of her clothes, and went down as quietly as she could, and
opened the door to——Alrina!

"Why, wherever ded you come from?" exclaimed Mrs. Brown;
"why, you're mazed, to be sure, Come in, do, and sit down, while
I do light the fire and fit a cup o' tea for 'ee. Dear lor'! wonders will
nevar cease. Miss Reeney here this time in the mornin'!"

It was indeed Alrina, exhausted and hungry. She had walked all
the way from Pendrea-house to St. Just through the night. Her
father's death she had borne bravely, after the first shock, and she
intended to have remained at Pendrea-house until after the funeral,
and then to have gone into some respectable service to gain her own
livelihood, as companion to some invalid lady, or nursery governess.
She was very grateful to her kind friends, but she could not impose
on their good nature. Then came that cruel treatment which she
supposed Frederick had planned, in order to be revenged for the
coolness she had shown towards him. She deserved it,—she knew
she deserved it; but it was hard to bear. Then came Blanche's
discovery of her secret love, and, to crown all, the news of the
mysterious disappearance of her father's body. Her friends would
still be kind to her—she knew that—and would pity her, and
alleviate her painful position as much as lay in their power. Of
this she was quite sure; but this was repugnant to her feelings;—
she would rather die, than live to be pitied,—she could not bear to
think of it. She requested to be left alone for the night, as she was
tired and wanted rest.

What should she do? If she remained there till the morning, and
named her intention of leaving, the family would not hear of it;
they would compel her to remain, and would probably watch her, in
their kindness. After thinking over her position for some time, she
made up her mind that she would leave at once, or at least as soon
as the house was quiet. She would find her way to the road as well
as she could; and then she would go direct to St. Just, where she
would be able to learn the full particulars of this mysterious affair.

The house was not quiet until late. Miss Pendray's adventure
caused great commotion, and kept the servants up late: but the
interest they took in their young mistress's adventure, and their
concern for her, and joy at her narrow escape, drove all thoughts of
their visitor out of their heads, and she was left quite undisturbed.
She wrote a letter to Mrs. Pendray, thanking her for all her kindness,
and saying that circumstances compelled her to leave; and when the
house was perfectly quiet, she put on some of the warmest clothing
she had with her, and went out into the cold night. She missed her
way several times, but at length got into the broad road, which she
knew pretty well, and arrived at Mrs. Brown's house, where she knew

she would meet with a hearty welcome, before any of the inhabitants of St. Just were astir.

It was early, too, when Frederick Morley arrived at Pendrea-house that morning in search of Alrina. In his haste and excitement to communicate the delightful intelligence he had just learned to the one nearest and dearest to his heart, he quite forgot the carriage which was waiting in the lane, so that he was some time in reaching the house ; and when he arrived at the door, he was exhausted and out of breath, and totally unfit for the duty which he had come there to perform. So he thought his best plan would be to have a private interview with his brother, and ask him to be the bearer of the message to Alrina from her supposed aunt.

Mr. Morley was very much surprised at the tale his brother told him. He could hardly believe it could be true; but as Frederick said that Mrs. Courland seemed satisfied that Alrina was her daughter, and was at that moment receiving more proofs of it, he felt bound to adopt the belief too, and promised to see Alrina at once, and induce her to go to the cottage to see her aunt.

Frederick thought that, after what had occurred, it would be better for his brother to see Alrina alone ; for, although he had started with the full determination of seeing her himself, and bringing her with him to the cottage to hear the welcome and delightful news, yet, when he considered the manner in which she had treated him in their former interviews, and remembered also that he had solicited an interview with her the day before, and had not kept his appointment, his heart failed him, and he proposed that his brother should see her alone, and he would wait his return.

After some little time, Mr. Morley returned, saying that he had sought an interview with Alrina through her friend Blanche, who immediately went to her room, and found no one there. On the table she found a letter, expressing her deep gratitude to Mrs. Pendray and all the family for the great kindness they had shewn her in her distress, but stating, at the same time, she could not, after all that had occurred in connection with her and her's, trespass on their kindness any longer. She knew that their goodness and kind hospitality would not permit her to leave them, she went on to say, if she remained to take leave of them ; and, therefore, to avoid pain to all parties, she had taken this step, which she felt seemed like in-gratitude,—but it was not so. From her heart she thanked them all ; and should she succeed in getting into some situation, whereby she could gain her own livelihood honourably, they should hear from her. If not,—God only knew what might become of her.

Mr. Morley read this much from the letter which he held in his hand, and then handed it to his brother.

"Gone !" cried Frederick, at length ; "gone ! just as the dark

cloud was being lifted, which had obscured her so long! Can it be
possible? Gone! But where can she have gone to? She had no
friends—she has often told me this—no friends but her father and
aunt."

She is most probably gone to her father's house, to enquire for
herself into this mysterious affair," said Mr. Morley.

"Yes," exclaimed Frederick; "she is gone back to the old house,
no doubt. I will go there immediately, and seek her."

"Stay," replied his brother; "let us first consider what is best to
be done. I think I had better go to St. Just in search of Alrina,
while you return to the cottage to inform our aunt of her sudden
disappearance."

"That, perhaps, will be the best arrangement," said Frederick;
"I will be guided by you, for I know not what to do or say,—I am
quite beside myself. My brain seems bewildered; I cannot think
steadily on any subject. Let us go at once; I shall not rest till she
is found. She is, perhaps, even now, out on the cold bleak common.
The whole country shall be roused to search for her. Oh! why did
I permit myself to be led away by that wretched scarecrow;—but
he said she was there,—yes, he told me Alrina was at that cottage
awaiting my arrival, and the letter he brought confirmed his
statement. Oh! cruel, cruel fate!"

"It will doubtless turn out all for the best," said Mr. Morley.
"Had you neglected the message of that unfortunate woman, she
might have died, and then her secret would never have been told,
and Alrina would have lived on, believing herself still the daughter
of that guilty wretch."

"True," replied his brother; "I will believe in the wisdom of
Divine Providence. We see His hand in all things. I will trust,
and all things may yet be well."

The brothers did not think it advisable to tell Squire Pendray's
family anything respecting their aunt in connection with Alrina;—
they merely expressed their great concern at her abrupt departure.

Mr. Morley had not an opportunity the night before of seeing Miss
Pendray alone,—indeed, she was too much excited and overcome by
her late adventure, to receive his addresses with composure, and he
was too much rejoiced at her safety, and anxious that she should
seek repose after the terrible shock she had undergone, to think of
himself. She saw how anxious and concerned he was, and she was
pleased at it. Her object was gained; for she saw that he was feeling
more than he could express on her account.

Lieut. Fowler was prevailed upon to stay and partake of their
evening's meal; for, although the squire had not forgotten his former
opinion of the lieutenant, which he in a measure still entertained,
yet he had been the means of preserving the life of his favourite

daughter; and ingratitude was not one of the squire's failings. Fowler would not, however, intrude on the squire's hospitality longer than politeness compelled him, but took his leave of them as soon as he possibly could after supper.

Mr. Morley had arrived some time before; and nothing was talked of but Miss Pendray's accident. Almost immediately after Fowler left, Miss Pendray rose from the table also, and, pleading fatigue, retired for the night, leaving the others to entertain their visitor. Soon after she left the room, a message was brought, that the squire was wanted on business.

"Dear me," said he, "who can want me at this time of night : it can't be to tell me that the conjuror is found, I suppose."

It was no stranger that wanted him. Miss Pendray had sent for him to explain and atone for the injury she had done her sister and Lieut. Fowler by her mischievous tale-bearing: she felt that she could not rest until she had made that atonement which was due to them both.

The squire was astonished to hear the confession of the proud and haughty Maud, and, had it been at any other time, he would have been very angry; but the recollection of her late sufferings and miraculous escape, and the preservation of her life by Lieut. Fowler, subdued him, and he promised to forget and forgive, provided he found that all was straight and above board. But he was determined that he would not be the first to invite him back to his house; for he still believed that Maud had exaggerated a little in her estimation of Fowler's conduct, out of gratitude for her own preservation. However he returned to the supper-table a happier man then he had been for many a day, and paid more than usual attention to Blanche, who could not understand the change.

Mr Morley determined that he would not leave that house again without knowing his fate; and, when breakfast was over, he told Frederick that he had something of importance to settle there before he could leave, but that if he would go back to the cottage, and relieve their aunt's anxiety and send her back to Penzance in the carriage, he would meet him at the cottage as soon as he had finished his business, and they would then go on to St. Just together.

This pleased Frederick very much, for he wished to go with his brother, but did not press it before, as Mr. Morley seemed to think he had better go alone: Frederick, therefore, returned at once to the cottage, where he found his aunt and Miss Freeman anxiously waiting his arrival with Alrina, and they were very much distressed when they heard that she had left Pendrea-house unknown to the family. Mrs. Courland had received sufficient proofs to satisfy her, she said, that Alrina was her daughter, and she was most anxious to see her, that she might have the further test of the likeness. As

that was impossible, at present, Frederick persuaded her to return
to Penzance at once, fearing Captain Courland might return before
her and might be angry at her absence, which she could not at
present explain to him.

Mr. Morley did not keep his brother waiting very long, for his
business was soon over. Miss Pendray knew quite well what he
wanted, when he requested an interview with her; for she saw by
his manner the night before, and from the tender concern he
appeared to take in her miraculous escape, and the expression of his
fine handsome countenance when he looked at her, that he felt a
deeper interest in her than she had before supposed from his seeming-
indifference to her during the past few months. Perhaps she mea-
sured his feelings by her own, and when they met, each being
anxious for the other's love, and well-knowing their own feelings,
and each being ready and willing to meet the other more than half-
way, the betrothal was soon settled, and Mr. Morley left the house a
happy man.

Horses were procured, and the two brothers were not long in
reaching St. Just. They put their horses in Mr. Brown's stable, and
went in to consult Mrs. Brown. She had heard Alrina's account of
her having left Pendrea-house without taking leave of the family,
and her reasons for doing so, and she also knew her determination
as to the future, and her wish to avoid being seen by any of her
former acquaintances at present. Mrs. Brown listened attentively
to the tale the two gentlemen told:—that Miss Freeman, Alrina's
supposed aunt, was lying at a cottage near Pendrea-house on her
death-bed, and wished to see her niece before she died.

This was very "whisht" Mrs. Brown thought, and Alrina ought
to go and see her aunt; for, however wicked "The Maister" had
been, she never heard that Miss Freeman had been concerned in his
wicked doings, so she determined that she would persuade Alrina to
go. After thinking therefore for some minutes she said,—"I was
tould not to let anybody knaw where Miss Reeney es, but in a caase
like this, when a relation es upon her death-bed, I think she oft
to go.—Stay here, gentlemen, for a few minutes, and I'll go and
fetch her."

"I think we had better accompany you," said Mr. Morley, "for
I fear she will take alarm and be off again."

"As you plaise, gentlemen," she replied, "you may go by yourselves if you like; she es now in the ould house trying to find out
the mystery: you are gentlemen and men of understanding, and
your judgment, perhaps, es better than mine."

So they went to the old house, where so many scenes of different
kinds had been enacted within the last few months. Here they found
Alrina, wandering through the rooms alone. She was perfectly calm,

and talked to them both in a quiet and dignified manner. She looked pale and care-worn, and bowed down with grief and suffering. The beautiful roseate hue which formerly gave such a charm to her delicate complexion was gone, and her bright laughing eye was now cold and stern. Frederick could scarcely trust himself to speak,— the change which had come over Alrina within the last few days quite shocked him. Mr. Morley took her hand gently and led her to a seat, while he told her of the illness of her whom she had been taught to call aunt: he then imparted to her the tale he had heard his brother relate. She seemed like one in a dream while he went on unfolding the dark cloud, and displaying, by degrees, the silver lining ; and when he had finished his tale, she looked from one to the other of the visitors, without uttering a word ; she seemed to be trying to realize it all. At last she burst into tears, exclaiming,— " Oh, Mr. Morley, can this be true ?—Can it be really true ?"—and, giving way again to a burst of hysterical tears, which she seemed to have no power to control, she rose and hurried out of the room.

The brothers heard her go upstairs ; and there they sat in silence : neither of them spoke for several minutes ; at length Mr. Morley said,—" Poor girl ! how sensitive she is !—the prospect of a happy future has affected her more than the misfortunes to which she had almost become reconciled before. I hope it will not have any serious effect on her : but what can we do ? "

" I'll go for Mrs. Brown," said Frederick, whose feelings were ready to burst forth also ; and, had he not thus escaped into the open air, he felt that he should have been unmanned, and have made a fool of himself before his sterner brother.

Mrs. Brown readily accompanied Frederick, and by the time they arrived at the deserted house he had recovered something of his former spirits. Mr. Morley told Mrs. Brown that Alrina was over-come at hearing the news they had communicated, and had gone upstairs in hysterics. They did not tell her the extent of the news, so she naturally concluded it was hearing of the serious illness of her aunt that had so affected her.

Mrs. Brown went upstairs, and remained there so long with her charge, that the gentlemen began to think it was a more serious matter than it really was : at length they came down together. Alrina was still very pale, and her eyes were swollen with weeping ; but she was tranquil and more composed,—almost cheerful. She was leaning for support on Mrs. Brown, who looked on her sweet face and smoothed it with her hand caressingly, as ladies will some-times smooth and caress a favourite lap-dog, playing with it as it were, and fondling it, while she expressed her love by kissing the smooth white forehead. It was a touching scene,—that kind, good, old woman leading in her whom she loved and respected so much, and caressing her as if she were a little child, while she looked up so lovingly in return, thanking by that look her kind friend who had been to her a second mother, and feeling that to express her gratitude in any other way would be more than she could do.

Mr. Morley, at that moment, thought he had never seen so lovely a creature before; and Frederick,—we will not tell his thoughts,—we cannot.

Alrina had told her kind friend all, and now Mrs. Brown wished to hear it all over again from Mr. Morley, who told his tale once more; and, with Frederick's assistance, a little more was added which he had not before remembered.

Alrina had not yet begun to realize her position:—her thoughts seemed to be wandering; her brain was bewildered, and she knew not what to say; her future had seemed before obscured by a dark cloud,—she could see nothing but gloom before her; now the cloud seemed brighter, but it was not quite dispelled. She had met with so many disappointments in her short life, that she feared there might be a greater one than she had hitherto felt still in store for her. What, if this tale should turn out to be a fabrication of her aunt's,—and after she had buoyed herself up with the hope of future happiness, it should be discovered that she was not Mrs. Courland's daughter after all? This overthrow of all her hopes, after having tasted of their pleasures, would be worse than remaining as she was. All these thoughts, and a thousand others, passed through her mind in rapid succession as she sat listening to the tale for the second time, and hearing questions asked by Mrs. Brown which the two young men could not answer; for Frederick knew nothing more than what he had heard Miss Freeman relate to his aunt: he had seen no proof; all he could say was, that his aunt seemed perfectly satisfied when he returned to take her to the carriage, and was most anxious to see Alrina, that she might judge of the likeness, as far as a person can judge of her own likeness.

Mrs. Brown thought that, at all events, it was Alrina's duty to go and see her aunt at once: but she could not go alone, nor could she go with the gentlemen without some female companion. Mrs. Brown could not leave her husband so long, nor the business; she suggested, therefore, that Alice Ann should be sought,—she was in the neighbourhood she knew. "Josiah will find her," said she, "if one of the gentlemen will run down to Captain Trenow's house and ask him.

Frederick volunteered to go; for although he was happy at having Alrina to gaze upon, yet he was not comfortable, nor was she, evidently; for neither knew how the other felt. They had both done violence to their feelings,—the one intentionally, the other unwittingly, and a mutual explanation was necessary before they could be certain how they now stood towards each other. Frederick could scarcely bring himself to believe that Alrina really meant that she had ceased to love him;—he could not think that, after what had passed between them. But she had told him so, and was he not bound to believe her? If so,—if that was really true, he must try and win her love back again. He could not give her up,—he would not. These were his reflections as he hastened on his errand.

Josiah was gone to Tol-pedn-Penwith signal-station, Mrs. Trenow said, in search of his young master. He must have gone the other road, and so he had missed him.

Frederick told Mrs. Trenow his errand, saying that Miss Alrina had come back to see the old house once more, and she wanted Alice Ann.

"I'll run up for her myself, sar," said she, "tesn't very far. I'll just clap up my 'tother cap fust. Where shall I tell her she'll find her missus?"

"I think you had better tell her to come to Mrs. Brown's," replied Frederick.

CHAPTER XLV.

AN AWFUL CATASTROPHE.

MRS. TRENOW was not long in executing her errand, and Alice Ann was quite delighted at the thoughts of being once more in attendance on Alrina.

There were no conveyances to be had, so that the gentlemen were puzzled how they should convey Alrina and her attendant across the country to the place of rendezvous. Alrina had already walked from thence to St. Just, that morning, or rather in the course of the night; so that, although the distance was not more than six or seven miles, her walking back there again was quite out of the question. It was decided that Frederick should ride straight to Penzance, as fast as he could, to inform his aunt that Alrina had been found, and to send a carriage for her if his aunt wished it; and Alice Ann proposed that Alrina should ride on the other horse to the cottage, while Mr. Morley and herself walked by her side. As no better plan could be thought of, Alice Ann's suggestion was adopted, and the party set out at a slow pace, which gave them time for reflection and conversation on the road. Alice Ann could tell them many a legend connected with the different places they passed, and especially about Chapel Carn-Brea, where many a terrible deed had been done, she said, in times past, and where ghosts might be seen walking now, if

U

anyone had the courage to go there at the midnight hour. "That boy, Bill could tell a sight of stories about this and that," said she, "I b'lieve he and 'The Maister' ha' be'n there brave an' often together."

"I wonder what has become of that boy?" said Alrina, joining for the first time in the conversation, "I am sure he knows a great deal about many things that are mysteries to other people."

"He do so," replied Alice Ann, "he wor the cutest chap for his size that evar I seed; and as for tongue, why, he would turn 'ee inside out in a minute, ef you dedn't keep your eyes abroad. What's become of he I caen't tell; but I can give a purty near guess, and so can Mrs. Trenow too, so she do say."

"Who was this boy?" asked Mr. Morley, "where did he come from?"

"I can no more tell than you can, sar," replied Alice Ann, "he wor found one night when he wor a cheeld, outside the workhouse door, an' wor broft up by the parish, so I've heard; for tes a bra' many years ago,—f'rall he's so small."

"Do you think he knew anything of my fa——, of Mr. Freeman's mysterious doings?" asked Alrina, who seemed now to take more interest in the conversation than she had done during the first part of the journey.

"Do I think?" replied Alice Ann, "I do knaw that he ded." 'Siah have seed that boy up to Chapel Carn-Brea in the middle of the night, when he ha' ben coming home from Bâl, and 'The Maister' havn't ben very far off, an' he whistling like a black-bird, that time o' night. I tell 'ee Miss Reeney, that boy Bill wor no good. What's become of the boy? says you.—What's become of 'The Maister?' says I.   Find the one, and you'll find the t'other; that's my b'lief."

Thus they wiled away the time during the journey, until they arrived at the brow of the hill which overlooked the cottage to which they were directing their steps. Mr. Morley had turned round when they arrived on this eminence in the morning, to view the surrounding neighbourhood, and to mark the spot, that he might be able to find it again easily, for it was situated in rather a secluded valley, the approach to which was by a narrow path branching off from the main road.   Everything looked serene and calm then, and, but for a thin jet of smoke rising from one of the chimneys and curling up against the clear blue sky, the cottage and its locality would have passed unobserved by a casual traveller; for it stood very low, as we have said before, all the rooms being built on the ground-floor: the walls were rudely built of clay—earth and straw wetted and well mixed together,—called in Cornwall, "Cob;" the roof was thatched with straw; and the partitions, inside, were made of thick wood, collected, from time to time, from the wrecks of vessels, with which that part of the coast of Cornwall abounds in the winter season.

As the party halted now on the top of this eminence, to enable Mr. Morley to reconnoitre and take his bearings, to guide him in the selection of the right path leading directly to the cottage, he saw, instead of a thin curl of smoke, such as he had seen in the morning, a large volume of black smoke rising from the spot, almost darkening the sky ; and, at short intervals, a long tongue of fire would rise into the air above the smoke, and disappear again, as a darker and more dense volume of smoke issued forth.

"The cottage is on fire!" exclaimed Mr. Morley. "Follow me, as well as you can; take the second turning to your right:" and away he ran, leaving the two females to take care of themselves and the horse, and to find their way to the cottage as well as they could.

When Mr. Morley arrived at the spot, an awful sight presented itself to his view. The cottage was in flames, which the straw roof and wooden partitions were feeding most bountifully ; and, as they consumed the dry combustible on which they were feeding so greedily, their long tongues would issue, in fantastic spurts, from the doors and windows on the leeward side of the building. It was a fearful sight; a good number of men and women were already there, attracted by the smoke, which could now be seen far and wide. Josiah had been there some little time : he had received intelligence of the fire, as he was returning from the signal-station, and he hastened down to the spot at once, having sent a messenger on to Lieut. Fowler with all speed. Josiah, and the few persons who were there when he arrived, did all they could in carrying buckets of water from a well at a short distance off ; but their efforts seemed at first to be increasing the fire rather than abating it. They continued however to pour water into the rooms on one side of the building which seemed the most likely to be inhabited, and, by opening the doors and windows on the other side, they, in a measure, diverted the fire to that side ; but whether they were doing right or wrong they could not tell ; they could only conjecture on which side the inmates, if any, were located.

Lieut. Fowler and his men, followed by a number of people from the surrounding neighbourhood, had just arrived, and the lieutenant was in the act of marshalling his men, when Mr. Morley rushed down among them, in the greatest excitement, asking all sorts of questions, as to how the fire had originated, and if there were buckets enough, and if the inmates had been got out ; but instead of replying, Fowler took him by the arm, saying. "Take half a dozen men to the well, Morley, with buckets and ropes, and keep them there. Let them fill the buckets as fast as they can, and I will organize a double row of men and women from thence to the cottage to pass the full buckets

up and the empty ones down; and my men and Josiah will then pour
the water where it will be most available for extinguishing the
flames." And to Squire Pendray, who also arrived about the same
time, he allotted the task of keeping the double row of men and
women steady at their work.

The commanding voice of the officer, and the example of his men,
accustomed to obey, very soon restored order, where there was
nothing but confusion before; and, by his judicious management,
and the courage and bravery of his men, assisted by the strong arm
of Josiah, the flames were soon got under sufficiently to enable some
of them to enter the house. Fowler set a guard outside each door
to prevent the mob from entering, and then, taking Mr. Morley and
the squire with him, they entered the house followed by Josiah, and
opened some of the inner-doors to let out the smoke, when something
flitted by them and rushed into the interior of the house; but
whether it was a man or a woman they could not make out.
Josiah however, seemed to know what it was, for he followed
immediately in full chase, leaving the others behind, who thought
their most prudent plan was to emerge into the air to refresh themselves, and be prepared for anything that might turn up; for, in a
very short time, the smoke would have evaporated sufficiently to
enable them to go through the house with ease and impunity.
Josiah did not return ; so after a few minutes, the three gentlemen
entered the house again. The entrance-rooms were not very much
damaged; but as they proceeded, the ravages of the fire were fearful.
The straw roof was entirely destroyed, from one end to the other.
They passed into one room, if a room it could be called now, where
the fire seemed to have raged in its greatest fury, and, looking into
what was once another room, divided from the place where they
stood by a thick wooden partition, they beheld a sight which made
them shudder. The door, which was not so thick as the partition, was
burnt to ashes, and a portion of the thick partition was also burnt:
it was evident that the interior of the room had been partially
preserved by the water which Josiah and the first comers had thrown
in when they first arrived; but it had been the scene of a great
conflagration, and the smoke had hardly cleared away yet : the walls
were blackened, and the ornaments and pictures which hung against
them had dropped off with the heat. It had evidently been a well-
furnished room, the remains of which were still to be seen. The
bed was reduced to ashes, and it seemed as if the flames from the
bed had communicated to some inflammable substance in the room,
and thence to the straw roof which was not protected or covered on
the inside, and was at no great distance above the head of the bed. But
their attention was not long confined to the destruction of the bed
and the other furniture of the room ; for a more awful spectacle

presented itself to their view. On the floor, in a corner of the room, lay two females, the elder one having her hand entwined in the long hair of the younger, who grasped the elder woman's arms in a strong determined grip. That it had been a death-struggle there could be no doubt; but how they got there, or what the struggle was about, neither of the three gentlemen could divine. But there they lay, behind the door, dead!—They had been suffocated, no doubt by the smoke: their clothes were burnt and their flesh had been scarred by the fire.

The younger of the two, seemed well dressed, as far as they could judge by the little that was left of it, and she must have been a well-formed comely figure, in the hey-day of youth: the elder was an emaciated figure, evidently the occupant of the bed which had once stood in the middle of the room. It was a dreadful sight, and the three gentlemen left the room in search of information as to their identity, when they met Josiah, holding a boy by the arm. Mr. Morley pointed to the room from which they had just retreated, and looked enquiringly at Josiah. "Iss, sure I've seed them!" said he," and 'tes a whisht sight, sure 'nuff; but there's a whisheder sight for 'ee to see yet. This way ef you plaise, gen'lemen:" and he led the way, still holding the boy by the arm, till they came to a room at the other end of the house, which seemed to have suffered more from the fire then any they had yet seen; for this end had been neglected ,by them all, supposing that nothing of any consequence would be found there.

This part seemed more securely built, and to have been better furnished than any of the other rooms. The partitions were of thicker wood, and the doors and windows were better finished with bolts and locks: the door had not been burnt through, as the other doors and partitions had been. Josiah said he had burst open the door from the outside, and it now stood wide open. On the floor lay the body of a man, whose lower extremities were literally burnt to a cinder; but his features, although blackened by the action of the fire, were still discernible. One look was enough! The whole party hurried from the scene with horror depicted in their countenances, and it was not until they got out into the open air, that either of them could find words to express their horror and dismay at what they had just witnessed.

Josiah still held the boy by the arm, who seemed very much distressed. Outside the door they encountered Alrina and Alice Ann, who were most anxious to hear all particulars.

"You shall know all, after we have made the necessary enquiries," said Lieut. Fowler.

At this moment a carriage drove up to the scene, and the post-boy handed a letter to Mr. Morley: it was from his aunt, begging him to bring Alrina to Penzance at once; he therefore told the squire and Lieut. Fowler that he was obliged to go to Penzance, but would be back again immediately; so the squire requested all the others of the party to go on to Pendrea-house and wait until Mr. Morley's return; for he said they must need some refreshment after the fatigues of the morning. Josiah took charge of the boy; for they all believed he could enlighten them on all that had happened. Alice Ann accompanied her mistress and Mr. Morley in the carriage to Penzance.

CHAPTER XLVI.

THE DREADED INTERVIEW.

HER husband had not returned when Mrs. Courland reached their lodgings after her early journey to that ill-fated cottage.

This was fortunate, in many respects: it gave her a little time to reflect on the events of the morning, and to prepare herself for the ordeal she had yet to go through. Had Captain Courland returned before her, she must have accounted, in some way, for her absence, and that might have led to a premature confession, which she thought had better not be made until she had seen Alrina, and been fully convinced that the likeness could not be mistaken. She had received quite sufficient proof from Miss Freeman of the identity of the child, and she had, moreover, received from her a sealed packet, which she said would reveal all more clearly, and other mysteries besides; but she made her promise, most solemnly, that the packet should not be opened until after her death, which she knew could not be far distant, she said.

While Mrs. Courland was deliberating on these important matters, her nephew, Frederick Morley entered the room in great haste, telling her that he had found Alrina, and that she was gone on with his brother to see Miss Freeman, and he was to send a carriage for her if his aunt wished it.

"That is my first wish, at present," replied Mrs. Courland; "I must see Alrina before I confess my life of deception to my husband. Oh, how can I tell him that I have been keeping this secret from him and deceiving him for so many years! How could I have deceived him, who has been so kind and good to me! It was his goodness that made me keep it from him: I didn't like to wound his feelings: he will never forgive me—he cannot! Oh, Frederick, how can I look into his honest face, and confess my guilty secret!" and burying her face in the soft cushions of the couch on which she had been reclining, she burst into tears.

"My dear aunt," said Morley, "you are wrong to meet trouble half-way: my uncle's goodness of heart will forgive all; and, when he sees Alrina, he will take her to his heart as if she had been his own child:—I know he will!"

"No!" replied Mrs. Courland"—you don't know him: he has the most utter abhorrence of deception—he hates secrets and mysteries: he expressed his opinion, in the severest manner, on this subject, only a few days ago. Oh, I cannot—I cannot go through with it! Should he even, in kindness, forgive the deception, he would look upon me with scorn and suspicion during the remainder of my life: oh, that would be terrible!—I could not bear it!—I could not live in such a state!—I should be wretched and miserable!"

"But consider, aunt," urged Frederick, "if you believe Alrina to be really your daughter, what injustice you will be doing her by withholding this confession.—What is to become of her? Would you send your daughter out into the world a houseless wanderer? Think of this, my dear aunt; oh, let me beg of you to think of this poor girl! Will you spurn her from your door, after permitting her to know what has been told her to day?—It would be cruel—most cruel! Uncle Courland must know it then; although Alrina would rather die than tell it herself; this I am sure of; but others would not be so scrupulous. Consider, aunt,—consider, before you send your daughter out unprotected into the wide world; those she once looked to for protection are gone,—scattered abroad on the face of the earth. Consider, Aunt Courland, her position and yours."

Frederick spoke with energy and warmth; for, in pleading the cause of Alrina, he was pleading his own cause too.

For some minutes after he had finished Mrs. Courland remained with her face buried in the cushions; at length she rose and wiped her eyes, which bore evidence of the tears she had shed, and the hard struggle that had been going on for [the last few minutes in her breast, to subdue her haughty, proud, spirit to the task of making this humble confession of guilt, which she now felt she must and would make, whatever the consequences might be. Frederick had touched a tender chord in the mother's breast, and, rising with calm dignity, she approached the table and wrote a brief note, which she desired Frederick to send to his brother at once, with a carriage to bring him and Alrina to the hotel to wait the result of her dread interview with her husband: but whatever that result might be, she said her daughter should be cared for as her daughter.

Frederick lost no time in despatching the carriage, and waited impatiently its return to the hotel, where Alrina would remain until after Mrs. Courland's interview with her husband, the result of which

Frederick still seriously feared and doubted. For although he could scarcely believe that the captain would refuse to take in this poor wanderer as one of his household, yet he knew his temper was sometimes hasty and impetuous, and he might say things in the first burst of passion, which he might be sorry for after, but which would decide his aunt in her course ; for she posessed the haughty pride of her aristocratic ancestors, and would never bend to ask, as a favour, that which, in a hasty moment, might be denied,—even though the denial were made madly, in the heat of passion. Frederick, therefore, although he had urged the confession, and painted its reception by his uncle in as mild colours as he could, still dreaded the meeting of two such spirits, for such a purpose. But it must be done : and he thought "If it were done, when 'tis done, then 'twere well it were done quickly."

Captain Courland returned soon after Frederick left, disappointed and out of spirits : they had not succeeded in discovering the slighest trace of the fugitive.

Julia was not satisfied with the search that had been made the night before, and she was gone to some houses a little way out of the town, which she knew Flora was fond of visiting sometimes; so the captain returned alone. He observed that his wife's spirits were unusually depressed. She had been weeping, evidently ; but he imputed it to her anxiety for their poor afflicted protegè. She was sitting on the couch, resting her arm on a table, and supporting her throbbing brow with her hand.

Her husband seated himself by her side, and, taking her other hand in his, affectionately, tried to comfort her by saying that he had no doubt Flora had wandered out into the country and missed her way, and, from her infirmity, she could not, perhaps, make any-one understand who she was nor where she came from. " So cheer up my dear," said he, " all will turn up well in the end, no doubt."

" My dear husband," said she, withdrawing her hand, " I am not worthy that you should treat me so kindly : I have a dreadful secret to unfold to you, which I feel I have kept from you too long."

" A secret !" exclaimed her husband, rising hastily, " I tell you I don't like secrets : everything right and straight and above-board—that's my plan ! I don't want to hear any secrets ! Who says that my wife has been keeping a secret from me ? I don't believe a word of it ! Who says it, I should like to know ? I'll have him strung up to the yard-arm !"

He seemed in such agitation, as he hurriedly paced the room, that his poor wife trembled for the result. She saw that a crisis was close at hand, and probably her happiness was gone for ever : but she had made up her mind to tell her secret, and she was determined to go through with it, let the consequences be what they would. So she asked her husband, in as calm a tone as she could command, to sit and listen for a few minutes to what she had to say, and then she should throw herself on his mercy, and would submit to any punishment he might think she deserved; but she begged him to hear her tale to the end before he judged her.

This serious appeal took the captain quite by surprise. He didn't know what to do or say, so he took a chair, and prepared for the worst.

With averted eyes, his guilty, trembling wife commenced her tale and told all: her former marriage, the birth of her daughter, and the concealment of the child by Miss Fisher: her treachery and heartless importunities for money, and threats: and, above all, her own weakness and guilt in keeping the secret from her good, kind husband.

When she had finished, she leaned her head on her hands, and burst into a torrent of tears. She had been keeping her feelings under control during the recital, that she might not interrupt the narrative which she had to relate. She could not restrain them any longer; and now she expected a terrible outburst of passion from her husband. The crisis was at hand. She waited the awful doom which she felt she deserved; but it did not come. She dared not look at her husband.

He had sat perfectly still and silent all the time she had been speaking, and after she had finished he was silent still. At length he rose, and approaching the couch seated himself by the side of his poor weeping, trembling wife; and, taking her hand as he had done before, he said,—" I knew my darling wife had no secrets that her husband was not cognizant of."

"No secrets!" she exclaimed, looking up in astonishment,—"I have been confessing the knowledge of a secret that I have been keeping from you for years and years, to my sorrow and shame!"

"I heard what you have been telling me," replied her husband, "but you have told me nothing that I didn't know before. Why I have known all that for years."

"You have known it!" exclaimed Mrs. Courland, in amazement. "How is it possible! Who can have told you!"

"Well, now 'tis my turn to spin a yarn, as we sailors say," replied the captain. "Your first husband's name was Marshall. He had a brother in the Indian army. After your poor husband was killed, his brother came to England. He had been informed of the secret marriage; and he had been enjoined by his brother, in his last letter, after he received the wound of which he died, that when he came to England, he would see his wife, and do all he could for her. He came to England in my ship, and he saw you."

"He did," replied Mrs. Courland.—"It was soon after the birth

of my little girl. He came to Fisher's cottage. Miss Fisher told
him a plausible tale, saying his brother wished that the marriage
should never be known until he came home to claim me as his wife.
As the marriage had been kept secret so long, it was thought best to
keep it so entirely. I was sent for to come home to my father's
house, where I found you waiting my arrival. You paid the most
devoted attention to me.—You were rich.—My parents and all my
friends urged it, and we were married. I was persuaded by Miss
Fisher not to tell my secret, and so it was kept; and it has been a
burden on my mind from that time to this."

"My beautiful wife," said the captain, kissing her affectionately,
"Marshall returned with me to India, after our marriage, and he told
me the secret, so that you see I have known it almost as long as you
have known it yourself; but I never mentioned it, fearing to distress
you, well-knowing that you had been imposed upon by a designing
avaricious woman."

"My good, kind indulgent husband!" exclaimed his wife, caressing
the bluff old sailor, as if he had been a little spoiled child.

"And now that we have had all these explanations," said the
captain, "and might be happy with our daughter, she is lost!"

"She is found!" exclaimed Mrs. Courland: "our nephews have
found her, and by this time she is in Penzance; we will send for
them."

A servant was despatched to the hotel, which was very near, and
in a few minutes, Mr. Morley appeared with a beautiul girl leaning
on his arm.

Both the captain and Mrs. Courland were struck with her extreme
beauty, and the captain at once exclaimed,—"Isabella Morley the
second, by all that's beautiful!"

"No, sir!" replied Mr. Morley,—"not Isabella Morley, but
Alrina Marshall!"

"My long lost child!" exclaimed Mrs. Courland, rushing towards
Alrina, and embracing her tenderly, "I see the likeness myself!"

"Good heavens!" cried the captain, "is this our daughter?
Then what has become of the other?"

"What other?" exclaimed Mr. Morley and Mrs. Courland in a
breath.

"Why, the poor girl we have been in search of all night," replied
the captain: "I concluded she was the lost child!"

"Alas!" said Mr. Morley,—"she is indeed lost!" And he briefly
related the dreadful catastrophe which he had witnessed so recently,
which threw a gloom over the whole party. They soon recovered
their spirits, however, and, leaving the newly-formed family group
to enjoy their unexpected happiness in quietude, Mr. Morley accompanied by Frederick, who had remained at the hotel while his brother

took Alrina to her newly found parents, hastened, as fast as possible, back to Pendrea-house, to assist in unravelling the mysteries connected with that ill-fated cottage and its unfortunate inmates.

CHAPTER XLVII.

MYSTERIES EXPLAINED.

Josiah did not let go his hold of the boy until they were safely seated in a room at Pedrea-house. And, even then, he would not let him go until the door was bolted, and he had seen that all the windows were fastened, and had even looked up the chimney.

"He ha' ben in queer places in his time I reckon," said he, "and seed a bra' many things : he ha' gov'd us the slip oftener then he will again."

Refreshments were ordered in and done justice to by all; and, when Mr. Morley and his brother arrived, the squire requested all the party to attend him in his library or Justice-room, as the domestics persisted in calling it.

Josiah still kept the boy in custody, and when all were assembled, Squire Pendray said, addressing the boy,—"It appears that you can enlighten us on all we want to know respecting the inmates of this house, and we wish you to relate all particulars respecting them. You can gain nothing, now, by keeping anything back ; but may benefit yourself a good deal by confessing everything, and informing us who were there, and how they got there, and the origin of the fire, if you know. Fear nothing : I tell you, in the presence of these gentlemen, that you shall not suffer, in any way, for what you may reveal to us. If you do not tell us the truth, and we think you are concealing anything that you ought to reveal, you must suffer the consequences."

The boy looked from one to the other, and seemed to hesitate for several minutes before he spoke. His eyes were directed more than once towards the door, as if he expected to see someone enter to relieve him of his perplexity; no one came, however, and he seemed to feel that he was standing alone in the world. His old friends (if friends they were) could help him no longer, and his shrewdness told him he had better make a virtue of necessity ; so after a short pause, as if collecting his scattered thoughts, he began his confession. He had been too much mixed up with the conjuror to have imbibed very much of the Cornish dialect, although he sometimes used it. Thus he began in very intelligible English,—" 'The Maister' saved my life, gentlemen, by his knowledge in medicine, and I was grateful for it. He took a liking to me, and I helped him in his business : call it what you will,—conjuring if you like. I never grew after he took me into his service at eight years old : perhaps I don't look more than that now, but I am eight-and-twenty. I was useful to 'The Maister' on account of my size : I could worm out a little secret by hiding in odd corners, and I never forgot what I heard ; I liked the post, and gloried in seeing the astonishment of some of the people to whom 'The Maister' told some secrets he had heard through me, which they thought no one else knew but themselves. Our adventures were varied and frequent ; the last was an awful one, when we came on shore under St. Just in a vessel bottom uppermost. 'The Maister' persuaded me, when I went to see him at his house afterwards, that he had been the means of saving my life again, in return for which he wanted my services. He expected the officers of justice. He was not so ill as he pretended ; but it would not have been safe for him to be taken away by his friends then, nor to be supposed to have escaped in the ordinary way ; he would have been traced at once. I had the means of getting into his room at anytime from the back premises, through a passage that no one knew but ourselves. He had some drug by him which would cause the party taking it to appear dead for a short time. I was in the room when the constable and some of you gentlemen were below entreating Miss Reeney to take you up into his room. We heard you coming : I gave the mixture to the 'The Maister,' and crept under the bed, and when you entered you pronounced him dead, and left almost immediately.   Another mixture, which he had previously prepared, and which I had ready to give him, restored him at once ; and that night, with the assistance of our friends, whose names I need not now mention, whom I had communicated with by means of the poor fellow commonly called 'Mazed Dick,' whose swiftness of foot is well known, we got 'The Maister' away, and the report that he had been taken away by the spirits favoured us.   We brought him to the cottage that was burned down to day, where we knew Miss Freeman had been for some weeks confined through illness, brought on by exposure to the cold ; she fell and fractured a limb, in walking from Penzance to Lieut. Fowler's station, where she was going on some errand in connexion with that dumb girl—what it was I don't know. She slipped her foot and fell and broke her leg, and there she lay, on the cold ground, all night, until she was discovered by 'Mazed Dick' in one of his rambles, and was taken to his brother's cottage. I could not desert my master ; I believed in his power, and do still. He was recovering fast : he could get up and walk about his room, and intended being off in a few days ; I was to have gone with him. This morning, to my surprise, I saw the dumb girl come out of a room at the further end of the house ; the mistress of the house, and her son, 'Mazed Dick,' were gone away, and the outer door was locked : I watched her,

but was not seen by her. She peeped into several rooms, and tried
the door of the one in which 'The Maister' was; but that was always
kept locked and bolted on the inside. She then went on to the room
in which Miss Freeman lay in bed. She seemed to know her at once;
for she darted into the room, and drew something from her bosom;
it seemed like an ear-ring, as well as I could see it; and she
pointed and made signs, which Miss Freeman seemed to understand,
and which seemed to irritate her very much. Miss Freeman had a
lighted candle, on a small table, by her bedside, for the purpose of
reading some papers. The room was very dark, although it was
early in the morning, but the windows were small, and half-hid by
the thatch of the roof, which hung down over them. She tried to
snatch at what the girl held in her hand; and, in doing so, she
overturned the candle on the bed, when a bottle of something inflammable fell with it, and the bed in an instant, was in a blaze. She seized
the girl by her hair, and dragged her on to the bed, when they both
caught fire, and the poor girl seized the woman by the arms to make
her let go her hair, and so she pulled her out of bed, and they both
fell together on the floor, a mass of flames. I could not assist them,
so I ran out through a side-door which I knew how to open, in order
to call assistance, when I met Josiah, and he sent me on to Lieut.
Fowler, but I believe Josiah didn't know who I was, he seemed so
frightened at what I told him. When I met him again, it was at the
door of 'The Maister's' room. He had followed me when I ran
through on my return from Lieut. Fowler's. The door was locked
and bolted on the inside. I told Josiah whose room it was, and he
forced the door open; for the wood in which the bolts were fixed
was still burning, and easily gave way: the fire had reached this
room and blazed in all its fury; and I suppose, from the burning of
the roof and the wood all round, the bolts of the door soon became
too hot for 'The Maister' to touch them, and so he was burnt to
death. That is my tale, gentlemen, and all I have spoken is the
truth."

So saying, the boy or man which ever he might be called, placed his
hands before his eyes and awaited the result of his communication:
whether the thought of the awful death of "The Maister," whom he
seemed to have looked up to with fear and gratitude, drew a tear
from his eyes or not, was not known. His tale was believed; and,
after a consultation among the gentlemen present, it was agreed that
something should be done for the poor fellow, on his promising to
lead a new life and give up all evil practices in future. This he
very readily and sincerely promised,—and the party separated for
the present, as Mr. Morley said he must return to Penzance to see
his uncle and aunt previous to his commencing, in company with his

brother, the search after the wretches at whose hands his poor father
had suffered such grievous wrong, and which had been retarded by
the occurrence of recent events. Now they would have nothing to
retard their search, he said,—and he would not rest until he had
found them and brought them to justice or confession.

CHAPTER XLVIII.

A BRILLIANT CORNISH DIAMOND DISCOVERED AND PLACED IN A
GOLDEN CASKET.

JULIA was very glad, when she returned, to find her old schoolfellow
Alrina with her uncle and aunt; and astonished beyond measure,
when she learned that she was also her cousin. The story, altogether,
was so romantic, she said, that it reminded her of something she had
read a long time ago in one of the old Romances at Ashley Hall;
and she was so interested in it, that, when her aunt had finished her
recital, she begged her to repeat it over again; but this she was
prevented from doing, even had she intended it, by the arrival of
Mr. Morley and Frederick.

Julia had not seen much of her brothers lately; she received
them, therefore, with warmth, especially Frederick, whom, being
nearer her own age, and better known to her from their having been
thrown together in their childhood, she loved with the tenderest
affection. She saw that the meeting between him and Alrina was
not what it ought to have been,—nor did the coolness wear off: so
she took Alrina out of the room, on some pretence, and asked her
the reason; for she knew that two fonder hearts never pledged their
troth to one another than those two. Alrina hesitated, at first, and
seemed at a loss what answer to give, until Julia reminded her that
they were now not only old friends and schoolfellows, but were near
relatives, and, unless there was some secret that could not be revealed,
she should feel very grieved if her newly-found cousin could not place
sufficient confidence in her as a friend, to tell her what had caused
the coolness between two, who, but a short time ago, seemed so
devoted to each other. "If Frederick has said or done anything to
annoy or displease you," she said, "I am sure it was unintentional
on his part; and, if you will tell me, in confidence, I will do my
best to set all things right."

Still Alrina hesitated, and Julia began to suspect that the coolness
she had observed was caused by something more serious than she had
at first imagined; but, whatever it was, she thought it had better be

explained, and, as Alrina did not seem inclined to speak, she went on
with her persuasive arguments. " Consider, Alrina dear, what years
of pain and mental suffering my poor aunt endured on account of
her reticence. Had she revealed her secret in the beginning, she
would have been much happier, and your life would not have been
subject to so many changes and vicissitudes as you have experienced.
If your secret is not one that you cannot reveal, pray unburden your
mind to me, as your near relative and dearest friend."

Thus importuned, Alrina felt that she could not any longer refuse
her confidence to her friend, and, putting her arm round Julia's
waist, she led her into her own little room, which had already been
prepared for her, and there she told her all, as they sat folding one
another in a fond sisterly embrace.

" You noble girl ! " exclaimed Julia, when her cousin had finished
the recital of her troubles, and had told with what bitter pain and
anguish she had done violence to her feelings, by telling Frederick
that she could not love him, in order to save him and his family from
marrying one whose father's evil deeds must throw disgrace and
shame upon all connected with him.

" I would rather have died than brought this disgrace on Frederick
and his family," cried Alrina ; " and, having thus discarded him who
is dearer to me than my life, how can I think that he will ever look
upon me again in any other light than as a fickle wayward girl : he
can have no further confidence in me ;—indeed, I will not ask it; I do
not deserve his love or confidence after my cruel treatment of him."

" We shall see,"—replied Julia, smiling and kissing her friend
fondly,—" We shall see, my sweet cousin."

While the two cousins were having their confidential chat, Captain
and Mrs. Courland and their two nephews were talking over the
events of the past few days, and Mr. Morley related to his uncle and
aunt the boy's confession.

" Before you leave us to prosecute the search you are so anxious
about," said Mrs. Courland, addressing the two young men, "I should
like to open the packet entrusted to me by Miss Freeman (or Miss
Fisher as I always called her): she is dead now, poor woman ; so
that my promise is at an end."

" Yes ! " said the the captain, " let it be opened, now,—we wont
keep any more secrets or mysteries here."

The packet was therefore produced and opened. It contained a
long manuscript, written in a neat hand, and was headed,—

" *The Confession of Maria Fisher, alias Freeman*" :—
and Mr. Morley, being requested to read it, read as follows :—

" I, Maria Fisher, alias Freeman, being on my death-bed, make
this confession as the only atonement and reparation I can make for

the evil deeds I have done during my life: I have injured almost
beyond reparation, the whole of the Morley family.

"First Isabella Morley was the victim of my avarice. I kept her
little daughter, to serve my own ends, and palmed off the poor dumb
girl (of whom more anon) on her as her child. Alrina, whom I called
my niece, is Isabella Morley's daughter. Proofs sufficient can be
found.—The Coopers know all; and my sinful brother knows all.—
Sift it out. That poor dumb girl was found by Cooper, washed on
shore from a wreck: he picked her up and carried her to his house.
She had a peculiar pair of ear-rings in her ears, very handsome and
costly: I have one in my possession now—the other I have missed.
Her linen was marked 'Fowler.' We have since learned that
Lieut. Fowler's brother and his little daughter were wrecked on
this coast on their voyage from India. He was drowned; the child
was saved. The Coopers know more;—my brother knows all. This
child's infirmity was useful to us: she was kept at the Coopers'.
Sift this out to the bottom too: here is the clue:"—

"Oh, miserable woman!" exclaimed Mrs. Courland,—" what a
life of sin and wickedness she must have led!"

"Yes!" replied Mr. Morley,—" but that is not all: let me go on.
The remainder of the manuscript is not quite so legible: it seems to
have been written under the influence of stimulants: it is blotted,
and some words are erased with the pen and written over again:
I will read it as well as I can, but you must give me time." And,
having smoothed out the manuscript, and turned his chair, so as to
let the light fall full on the paper, he resumed his task. There were
many stoppages in the course of the reading, and many exclamations
of surprise and horror, which we will not notice here, but let the
confession go on smoothly, to avoid confusion and tediousness.

"If the first part of my confession has startled the reader (whoever
he may be)" it went on, "let him close the MS.—What has been
told, is as nothing to what remains. How to approach this part of
my confession I know not. Brandy will assist me. Brandy! Brandy!
That will drown my better thoughts, and bring me back to that
dread night, and help me to tell my tale as fearlessly and heartlessly
as the deed was committed.

"Now I can go on again. Mrs. Courland, the once beautiful
Isabella Morley, had returned to Ashley Hall. My brother and
myself followed, and took a lone cottage near the sea-coast.—Our
father lived with us. He was a rover, though an old man; unsteady
and intemperate in his habits: he was useful to the smugglers, and
they paid him well for his assistance. My brother took a higher
walk in the smuggling line. He got connected with some of the
Cornish smugglers,—Cooper among the rest; and they bought a

little vessel of which Cooper was the captain; and my brother, living at a distance, and being connected with merchants, sold the goods. One night! I shall never forget that night!—a gentleman was driven to seek shelter in our cottage from the snow: he had missed his way.—My father and brother were both out. My father's bedroom on the ground-floor, was vacant: I did not expect him home that night, so I put the gentleman there to sleep.—To sleep! Yes!—It might indeed have been a long sleep!

"My brother returned. I told him Mr. Morley had entrusted me with his name;—he had money, too, he told me,—a large sum. My brother hated the name of Morley: he had been spurned by a Morley:—his love had been rejected with scorn:—he was a man of strong passions. The brother of her whom he now hated as much as he had loved before,—the man who had introduced the rich captain to Isabella, and so overturned his hopes of marriage with the lovely creature he had so passionately loved, was in his power. Revenge seized hold of him. He called for brandy: he drank deeply, and raved like a madman; then he became more calm. He took Mr. Morley's stick and examined it: it was a curious stick. I left him still drinking, and retired to my bedroom.

"I knew not the extent of that night's work until the morning; when, oh, horror!—my brother had murdered our father instead of ———! What was to be done? My brother's ready wit hit on a plan. The intended victim was gone; perhaps to inform the authorities. He had worn away the murdered man's hat. His hat with his name in it, was left: it was with his stick the murder had been committed: he was accused and committed. My brother found the bag of money; we fled into Cornwall, changed our names to Freeman, and took up our abode at St. Just: that money enabled us to live comfortably. My brother was clever, and earned money in other ways easily. My confession is finished. My conscience is satisfied. The minds of the Morleys are relieved. When this is read I shall be no more, and my brother and the Coopers will be out of your reach. Search,—sift as you will, you can know no more!—We have outwitted you!—Ha! ha! ha!"

The latter part of the manuscript was blotted and stained, as if brandy had been spilt over it, and the writing was almost illegible, indicating the unsteadiness of the hand that wrote it.

When Mr. Morley had finished he threw the MS. on the table and exclaimed,—"I had my suspicions of that fellow from the first. Our minds are now set at rest, and we can publish this document to satisfy the public of the perfect innocence of our father, and the double guilt of those wicked, lawless people."

"I think," said Captain Courland, "that it is sufficient that you are satisfied, yourselves, and that the guilty parties have confessed:— the public have forgotten all the circumstances long ago, and the stirring it up again, now, can answer no good end."

"Perhaps you are right sir," replied Mr. Morley, "the guilty wretches have had their reward in this life!"

"What a shocking death it must have been," said Mrs. Courland, with a shudder: "torture and pain the most acute and agonizing. How rarely the guilty escape punishment, even in this life."

"I should like our good friends, the squire and Fowler, to hear this confession," said Frederick, "for they knew the story of the murder, and all the circumstances connected with it, and felt, I am quite sure, a deep interest in our search after the guilty parties."

"Of course," said the captain;—"they ought to be informed at once; and I have been thinking of inviting them all here. What do you think of it, my dear?" he continued, addressing his wife. "We cannot have so large a party to dinner at our lodgings, of course; but there is no reason why we shouldn't ask them all to dine with us at the hotel."

"I should like it above all things," replied Mrs. Courland, "and, if Frederick will undertake to deliver the invitations, I will write them at once, and invite the whole party for tomorrow. The ladies must come also, or I shall have nothing to do with the party."

"The ladies, by all means," said the captain, as his wife opened her writing-desk.

"I really think I must petition for Josiah to be invited, to be entertained by Alice Ann," said Mr. Morley, smiling.

"Of course," said the captain, in high glee; "and that poor boy mustn't be left out. Shiver my topsails!—young sirs—we'll have a jovial party! I'll go down to the hotel myself in the morning and superintend the selection of the wine: we'll have the very best the landlord has in his cellar,—and plenty of it too.—The squire is a two-bottle man—I'll take my Solomon Davey to that!"

While Mrs. Courland was writing the notes, Mr. Morley took up the MS. again, and, on turning over another sheet, he exclaimed,— "here's something more!"

All ears were instantly attentive, and he read on:—

"I, Maria Fisher, alias Freeman, as an atonement, in some degree, for my sinful conduct towards her, give and bequeath to Alrina Marshall, formerly known as Alrina Freeman, the daughter of Mrs. Courland of Ashley Hall, all my worldly goods and moneys now in my possession or in the possession of my brother, John Fisher, alias Freeman, belonging to me, and all property of any kind which I may possess at my death; and I hope I shall be pardoned for my sins."

This document was written in a legible hand, as if after due deliberation, and properly signed and executed. It, however, gave very little pleasure to the parties concerned, except that it shewed a shadow of proper feeling on the part of Miss Freeman to make amends for past misconduct.

The notes were at length written, and Frederick was despatched with them. The captain thought they might have been sent by a servant, but Frederick would not hear of it. He wished to be the bearer of the welcome news to Fowler, he said, with whom he should remain for the night, as he had had riding and excitement enough that day already.

When Alrina and Julia returned to the drawing-room after their tête-à-tête, Frederick was gone: it was evident, therefore, Alrina thought, that he didn't care for her now: she had offended him beyond forgiveness, and he had given her up; she felt that she deserved it, and that feeling made her more wretched than ever; she had treated him shamefully, and had, she thought, wounded his feelings unnecessarily. Had he treated her cruelly, she could, and would, have forgiven him; but she could not seek him out, and ask him to forgive her. No, she could not do that—besides, he seemed to avoid her. What could she do? She must endeavour to bear it. She slept very little that night;—her thoughts were too much occupied. The pleasure and happiness she felt at the course events had taken in her worldly career, were quite absorbed and overbalanced by the painful reflections she experienced with regard to the hidden secrets of her heart. In the midst of all the newly acquired pleasures of birth and fortune, and a happy home, her heart was crushed and sad.

Mrs. Courland could not make it out. She thought her daughter would have been to her a delightful companion, and she had looked forward to years of happiness; but she found Alrina silent and reserved. She asked Julia if she knew the cause, and she told her aunt all. They both honoured and respected Alrina for her noble conduct:—they both knew, very well, that it only required a kind friend to explain to Frederick the state of affairs, and all would be well.

Mrs. Courland took the first opportunity of telling her husband how nobly their daughter had acted (for she kept nothing from him now), at which the old gentleman expressed the highest gratification. "We have found a treasure, my dear;" said he, "many have searched among the Cornish mines, and spent their all in the search, without finding such a precious jewel as we have discovered here :—we will preserve her as the most valued diamond that ever was discovered in Cornwall."

"Don't be so absurd," replied Mrs. Courland, smiling, "I'm really afraid our long-lost child will be spoiled if she remains with us."

The captain's dinner-party was a right jolly one: and, soon after the desert was set on the table, and the servants had withdrawn, he said,—"I am not in the habit of throwing a wet blanket over any company, especially when I have invited the party to my own table; but I am sure you will all like to hear what these wretches say for themselves; so, before we begin to enjoy ourselves, I will ask Morley to read the confession which was placed in Mrs. Courland's hands a few days ago."

Mr. Morley, accordingly, read Miss Freeman's confession, at which all the party were horror-struck, although several of them had heard it before.

Lieut. Fowler was perfectly astounded to learn that the dumb girl was his niece, and was grieved at her sad end.

"Now," cried the captain, when Mr. Morley had finished, and all had made their remarks on the sad fate of the inmates of the cottage, "splinter my topmast! but we'll have no more of this! pass the bottle, squire, and we'll drink to the health of my newly-found daughter;—she's a noble girl! we have found her among the Cornish mines, and so we'll christen her *The Cornish Diamond*!—ha! ha! ha! and the old gentleman leaned back in his chair and laughed right merrily. It was one of his old, hearty laughs, such as he used to indulge in when he was in Flora's room, and thought no one heard him;—a sort of exhilirating laugh, which no one could help joining in, without great difficulty: and all, except two of the party, did join in it,—even the glasses on the sideboard echoed their sympathy. There were only two who did not join in the laugh, and they were Alrina and Mrs. Courland. The former felt that it tended to make her more conspicuous than she wished just at this time, and she blushed up to the very roots of her hair, as we have seen her blush before; while the latter was shocked at the vulgarity (as she deemed it) of her husband, and dreaded lest he should expose his free and easy manner still further to the Pendray ladies; so, in order to check it, as she thought, she said, with quiet dignity, when the merriment had a little subsided, "My dear, you really must remember that you are not on board ship.—What will the ladies think?"

"I tell you what it is, Mrs. Courland;" he replied, in perfect good humour, "you've had it your own way a long time, and have put a stopper on my lingo often enough; I mean to steer the ship my own way for once, and to-morrow you shall take the helm again if you like. So, drink my toast, ladies and gentlemen:—'The Cornish Diamond!' and a brighter one was never discovered in the best of our mines. No heeltaps, mind! Fill what you like; but drink what you fill!—that's my rule."

Many other toasts were drank, and everyone except the party most concerned and one other, spent a right merry evening. These two melancholy ones were Alrina Marshall and Frederick Morley.

Julia saw how unhappy they were, and, in the course of the evening, she took Frederick aside, and told him (in confidence) the state of Alrina's mind, and explained to him her reasons for saying that she could not love him. He fully believed it, he said; for there was nothing too noble and disinterested to believe of Alrina; and he only wanted an opportunity to throw himself at her feet, and beg her to recall the rash declaration she had made.

"Come with me, then," said Julia; and she conducted him into a small room, in which Alrina was sitting waiting for her cousin, who had excused herself for a moment, having this object in view; and the mischievous creature, having brought the two glumpy ones together, as she called them, left them to fight it out in their own way. There was no fighting, however; for, when they appeared again, they were the merriest of the party.

CHAPTER XLIX.

THE WEDDING BELLS.

THE next morning gossip was rife in Penzance: nothing was talked of but the captain's dinner-party, and the circumstances connected with it.

Three pairs of lovers walked out from the hotel in different directions, while Julia took a quiet walk with her uncle and aunt, who pretended to pity her, because she was not so fortunate as the other three young ladies of the party. They little knew what was going on behind the scenes; for, if the truth must be told, Julia had received a letter, that very morning, from the most devoted love-sick swain that ever wrote sonnets to the moon, or vowed eternal constancy to the most lovely of her sex. So Julia was perfectly happy, whatever her good uncle and aunt might think.

It was very hard, Captain Courland said, to be obliged to give up his daughter again, as soon as he had found her, but Frederick was a good fellow, and he should have her; and to enable him to procure a suitable casket to keep the precious *diamond* in, the captain gave him a handsome sum as a wedding present.

Maud was so happy in the consciousness of having gained the affections of the only man she had ever known who possessed a congenial spirit with her own, that she used all her persuasion with her father, in favour of Lieut. Fowler's hopes with regard to her sister. The squire was taken by surprise he said: to lose one daughter was bad enough, but to lose both at the same time, was more than he could consent to. However, he promised to talk it over with the captain over a bottle of wine after dinner: and, either the wine had a peculiarly persuasive flavour, or the captain was more than usually eloquent; for the consent was given the next day, and it was agreed that the three weddings should take place at Penzance on the same day; as soon as the necessary preliminary preparations could be made.

Josiah and Alice Ann had not been idle. Perhaps love-making is infectious; if so, they caught the infection from their betters; for Josiah popped the question, and was accepted, about the same time that their master and mistress (Mr. Frederick and Miss Alrina) were making up their little imaginary differences at the hotel.

While the ladies were making their preparations for their weddings, the gentlemen, finding time hang heavily on their hands, proposed going to the conjuror's house, at St. Just, and having a regular overhaul, as Lieut. Fowler expressed it.

Alrina's consent was asked, and granted, as a matter of course; for what had she to do with the conjuror's house now? So they went, and in their search, they found money and jewels of great value; for, in his haste to get away, the conjuror had not taken very much with him;—the belt was gone, and this had, no doubt, been refilled. There was no one to claim the property, nor to hinder them in their search, so they made a minute investigation; and that nothing might escape them, where they supposed or imagined there was a secret drawer, they did not hesitate to break the piece of furniture in which they suspected it into a thousand pieces. There could be no doubt, now, as to the disposition and ownership of the property. The conjuror's nearest relative and representative was his sister, and she had disposed of all her property to Alrina. But Alrina, fortunately didn't want it now; so, after consulting her good friends on the matter, it was decided that Squire Pendray should lay out a portion of it for the benefit of the boy Bill, and Mazed Dick and his mother, according to his judgment; and that the remainder should be given to the poor and for charitable purposes

There was nothing wanting that money could procure to render the wedding everything that could be desired by the most fastidious of gossips.

Mr. Morley and Frederick presented Josiah and his wife with a handsome sum of money on their marriage, which took place soon after their own, to enable them to purchase a farm, to which the happy couple retired after their wedding.

Mr. and Mrs. Brown continued to keep the "Commercial" hotel for several years, and were visited, frequently, by Mr. Morley and his brother and their wives. But, of all her friends and customers, Mrs. Brown often declared that she never loved anyone half so much as she loved Miss Reeney, who was worthy, she said, of the name Mrs. Trenow had given her,—"THE CORNISH DIAMOND!"

PRINTED BY W. CORNISH, THE LIBRARY, PENZANCE.

www.ingramcontent.com/pod-product-compliance
Lightning Source LLC
Chambersburg PA
CBHW030812020726
47499CB00006B/1879